ALSO BY ROBERT HICKS

The Widow of the South

A SEPARATE COUNTRY

ROBERT HICKS

F
HICK

GRAND CENTRAL
PUBLISHING

New York   Boston

LARGE PRINT

Copyright © 2009 by Labor in Vain, LLC

Grand Central Publishing
Hachette Book Group
237 Park Avenue
New York, NY 10017

Visit our Web site at www.HachetteBookGroup.com.

Printed in the United States of America

First Large Print Edition: September 2009
10 9 8 7 6 5 4 3 2 1

Grand Central Publishing is a division of Hachette Book Group, Inc. The Grand Central Publishing name and logo is a trademark of Hachette Book Group, Inc.

Library of Congress Cataloging-in-Publication Data
Hicks, Robert
   A separate country / Robert Hicks.
       p. cm.
   ISBN 978-0-446-58164-6 (regular edition)—ISBN 978-0-446-54715-4 (large print edition) 1. Hood, John Bell, 1831–1879—Fiction. 2. New Orleans (La.)—History—19th century—Fiction. I. Title.
   PS3608.I287S47 2009
   813'.6—dc22   2009006085

The Large Print edition published in accord with the standards of the N.A.V.H.

For New Orleans

full of sorrow,
full of grace

CHAPTER 1

Notes of Eli Griffin, August 1879

I woke sick to the sound of an envelope slid under my door. Outside the cotton presses clunked and smoked, the roustabouts shouted oaths at the screwmen, the river slipped past silent and heavy with mud and men and their craft. I listened for the footsteps of the messenger but heard none. They'd begun to burn the sugar down by the molasses sheds, where the Creoles I'd bested at faro the night before would now be standing overseeing the sugar niggers, nursing their own illnesses of indulgence, and finding themselves unable to do anything but mutter *oui, oui* and call for more coffee. San Domingue rum is a hell of a thing, I should say. Oh Lord, my head. I wondered if M., lying next to me, could hear the bones in my head creaking when I breathed. The sound in my head was loud, like the sound of two ships scraping by each other at the quay. It must have made sound. Or maybe that squeaking was me. Quite possible.

Though I lived near the docks, I was not myself a dock man. I was an iceman. I worked in the ice factory and therefore I was suspect, an outsider, someone very odd. I spent my days in the cold, in rooms with no smells and little light. The little factory was an alien thing to New Orleans, the opposite of hot. We icemen were very possibly magicians or devils and I liked the reputation, and I very much enjoyed my job. Good for early morning pains too. I considered going to work and taking an extra shift just to lean against the frozen condenser coils and think of snow angels.

I shook my head to clear it, and immediately regretted moving at all. I became nauseous. I sat down at the small table under the window and inhaled the air pouring through the cracks. When I'd got my bearings, I took stock of the situation.

Had I won at faro last night? Really and truly? That's what I remembered, but that didn't mean nothing. I remembered being an innocent boy once, but that wasn't possible. Couldn't have been. In my bed slept M., my twiggy Irish girl, my sole companion for many months standing. If she was still selling time to grunting cigar chompers in the plush house on Royal Street, it was only because I couldn't keep money very long. We didn't talk about her work, though she still called me her caller. *The one who never pays and who owes me,* she'd say. Not never pay, I guess, but there's no use arguing with M. For instance, this particular morning. If I had won at faro the night before, there was no longer any sign of the victory. M. had my cash now, and most of my little bed, and still when she woke she would call me her caller. She sucked at her bony freckled knuckle while she slept. I tried not to wake her when I went to get the envelope under the door, but the floor creaked and she stirred, cursing me sweetly in a language I'd never heard. I cursed her right back and crossed the bare, dust-mortared floorboards to the envelope, which was brown and sealed with black wax.

"What is it, hon?" M. called from her

pillow, suddenly friendly, probably thinking it was money. She prayed every evening that she would be saved from that fancy house on Royal Street, and so every unexpected thing came to her first as a possible sign of deliverance. Always disappointment, always expectation. I opened the envelope at the wax, using the long middle fingernail I cultivated for desperate fights in saloons. I sharpened it like a knife twice a week.

"It's a letter."

"Oh Christ."

"What do you care? You can't read."

"Such a nice boy, you are. The girl swoons, boyo."

"Not in the bed, there's a bucket in the corner."

She swung her feet to the floor. Her feet were tiny, perfect, and her ankles had freckles. Everything had freckles.

"I'm leaving."

"Kiss me for luck."

"You don't got no more coin for that."

"Don't ever work anyway."

A striking, pretty, bony little thing was my M. She stood up to my chin and could look at me so that I would be afraid. She was delicate, nearly no flesh on her except for the sweet turn of her bare ass and the muscles in her shoulders. I looked on her, naked and smirking, and I felt real fondness. Love? Heavens. Great fondness? Sure. She covered up quick, stomped around picking up pieces of her ensemble here and there until she was dressed and ready to march on. She could dress instantly when it suited her. I assumed this was a professional, cultivated skill. She stopped beside me before walking through the door. Her eyes, flecked and hazel, turned down sadly, either from the paint or the wear or both. She carried a small black purse in her hand, which she pointed at me like a pistol.

"What do I care?" she said quietly. "I care for lots of things, things I ain't ever told you these months I been to your bed. But someday, if you're very good and God sees fit to save me, I will tell you, we'll talk a long time, you'll be sick of my talk. Now I'll only say this." She reached up and stroked my jaw, rubbing at the stubble before pinching my ear.

"I'll say this. What do *you* care about, boyo?"

I didn't answer quick enough and she gave a little whoop.

"Nothing! That's it? You care for nothing?

Ah, the world is so black, how do you ever stand it?"

She laughed and tippietoed down the back stairway, chuckling to the ground. I walked back to the table to consider the thing that was not money but had been slipped under my door. I also, and I will admit this here now that I know how things turn out, I also prayed real quick that she would get back to her fancy house safely, and that she would be protected. See, there were things I weren't going to tell her either. Ha. As if I didn't care for nothing.

I recognized the letter immediately. In the cold wax lay the seal of General John Bell Hood, formerly U.S. Army and Confederate Army, currently a ghost haunting the uptown provinces, New Orleans. Not truly a ghost, I don't believe in that mess, don't believe in the spirits and goblins that I'm told parade through this city in their nightclothes and masks and all manner of costume. What I mean is, the man now lived at the edge of everything, cast out from his old habitats, which included the ice factory where he had once liked to nap and harass me in the cold dark. Before his wife's funeral the month before when I had seen Anna Marie laid in the ground at Lafayette Cemetery, I hadn't seen Hood in almost a year. Since the epidemic. I had assumed he'd died or fled, but later I was corrected by one of the high collars down at the cotton exchange where I wagered money on the afternoon's Shell Road races. "Not dead, young ice wrangler, just mad," he'd said, slipping my money into his vest pocket.

Since insanity was about as remarkable as water in the city, I had given up hope for Hood and the rest of the family. It was sad but inevitable. Hell, *I* was half crazy and well on my way to full-bore lunacy. That is an overstatement. I was eccentric, and becoming more so. I didn't know what I could do for Hood. And I suppose I was afraid. I am a sinner, I am the man who walks right round the wounded man on the road to the Temple. I never went out to the house on Third Street to see for myself, see. Went right round it, so to speak, until I heard of Anna Marie's death from a nun who had been teaching me the catechism.

I was becoming a Catholic—there's something I care about, M.! Pasture and horseshit and all that waiting for rain, all the country in my blood had been bled from me, and the poor-ass country boy I'd been had begun to disappear with it. And I had learned, as the sister had taught me, that death had power, that death must be witnessed. Unlike insanity, which is best left to itself in my opinion. Don't know what the Church has to say about that though. Ought to check.

Eli Griffin
Top Floor
Levi Fabrics and Rooming
August 17, 1879

Forgive me my neglect, Eli. It has been a very strange year and now we are dying.

I quietly folded the letter and replaced it in its envelope before going on. I put it in the dead center of my eating table, out of the sun that spattered the room through my wood blinds. I got dressed. It seemed disrespectful to be reading such a thing without clothes. Black homespun trousers, blue cotton shirt, longshoreman's boots. Simple.

I saw you at Anna Marie's funeral, so first please accept my gratitude. There were very few of our friends there, and I appreciated

your gesture. I may call you a
friend?

I read the rest of the letter and when I
had finished, I folded it into my shirt pocket.
I rooted around for my adventuring bag before finding it under some muddy clothes. I
checked the contents: a fork, a pigsticker, a
Bowie knife, rope, an extra shirt, dried salted
beef, bandages, the key to the ice factory, a
pencil, a small sack of field peas, a crucifix I'd
found in a garbage pile on the levee. Then I
walked out the door for the journey uptown.

I do not tell you this, that Lydia
and I are stricken also, to elicit
sympathy, only to make clear the
urgency of matters at hand. I have
no time for Creole time, so to speak.
You are a Tennessean, despite ap-
pearances. (I have heard of your
visits to the cathedral.) You are
not yet so much a Creole that you
can't occasionally move quickly. I
ask that you move quickly.

You hated sympathy, old man, but I still had
some for you. I stepped out of the way of a

dray splashing colored and oily water up and over the cypress-paneled banks of the street-side ditch. I walked fast, knocking shoulders and not looking back. Decatur Street was full up with carts and drays carrying rice and cane back and forth. Sometimes a hearse, too, sometimes a wagon full of Sicilians settled in among their tomatoes and okra and turnips. Too many people in my way, so I turned down toward the river and the more open spaces of the wharf and the sugar sheds.

Even there I had to push my way upriver toward Hood. Here were the pale German street boys sliding through the crowd of sugarmen outside the Broker's Charm, handing out samples of sugar in tiny brown envelopes, drumming up business for the men at the top of the Bonded Warehouse, who owned the thousands of hogsheads piled up on the quay. The nervous men with money. I took some sugar and continued through the crowd and into the straight rows of molasses sheds, where the negroes boiled cane and sucked on pickled, salted onions. I ran down those straight alleys until I was beyond the black smoke and bittersweet air of the sugar district and could breathe proper again.

I passed the statue of Henry Clay, where the

mumbling old soldiers lived their days upon the great circular pedestal. At Canal I turned up toward St. Charles, past Touro Row where the man at the piano shop ragged a tune without much interest, and past Cluver's Drugs where I stopped for a bottle of headache spirit. Women dressed in billowing curtains of black from bonnet to hem drifted up the boulevard like loose puffs of coal smoke from the great clacking double-stacked riverboats that crowded at the foot of the street.

Smells washed up on my nose and drew back like waves: shrimp shells, old sweet potatoes, new-cut stone, wet cotton. Water ran down the cypress street gutters though the sun was high. A crop of lightning rods reached up across the city from nearly every building, black against the blue sky. I navigated by the church steeples, and steered toward St. Patrick's.

Before I am utterly out of my mind, I must make a request of you, I must ask you to settle a very delicate matter for me. I am certain you long ago thought me mad, and that was insolent. Now I forgive your insolence, and admit that though I wasn't mad, I must have seemed so. I forgive everything, and only hope you will forgive me also.

At St. Patrick's the Irish were seeing off another of their dead, a full-time occupation for the city's tunnelers, diggers, chippers, carvers, and trenchers.

"Drowned, crushed, or fevered?" I asked as I passed.

"Crushed, *then* fevered," said a little man in a big black suit, inhaling his pipe and mumbling an Our Father through the smoke.

The old General wanted forgiveness? My forgiveness? His army had come to my town, and afterward I was orphaned and raised by saloonkeepers, gamblers, and madams in every brokeass river city down the river from Memphis to Natchez. Not once had he said, *My, Eli Griffin, you have made something of yourself despite all!* I had, of course. My girl M. might have suspected there was nothing I cared about, but there was in fact something I cared about right much: I cared about Eli Griffin, marooned boy, hustler, grifter, now a maker of ice. I vowed years before while hauling piss buckets down brothel stairs that Eli

Griffin would get his share and hold on to it and not give a damn, and I had done it. I was not playing the jug for pennies down on Jackson Square.

The General might have had his own grudges, I ain't saying he didn't have reason.

> *I call on you because you tried to kill me once, and now that I am in fact dying, I believe it is time to settle accounts in that matter. Which means, of course, you owe me for sparing you the pain of revenge and the shackles of the Calaboose.*

I crossed the Place du Tivoli, a circle traced by a ring of old live oaks. I looked over toward the new canal straight north and saw the cotton boll clouds twisting and piling atop each other. A storm was coming. I watched a pack of dogs shy and snarl at each other. I walked faster, out across the circle where, soon, they would cut down the trees to raise a statue of General Lee atop an ugly tower sunk in a mound of cut granite. Even now I could see the cypress coming down in the swamp beyond the houses, to make room for more houses, and occasionally I heard the shouts of the men on the felling crews.

I slipped through back alleys behind the new houses, hopped black iron fences, stepped through sharp old quince bushes, dodged the horses pulling families and lovers in carriages across Coliseum Square, and finally turned left down Third Street.

I suppose he had decent enough reason to bear a grudge even to his deathbed, if he was going to put it that way. *Because you tried to kill me once.* Yeah, I had done that and I owed him, for that and other reasons besides. He had been kind to me since that first meeting when I'd put the knife to his neck. That had been unexpected.

I walked under drooping banana trees and between two dwarf date palms bristling with spikes, and then I was in the Hoods' yard, a green wrestle of vines and swamp grasses twisted up together in an awful tough fight. Up against the back stoop, overhung by a small porch roof, I saw a wide and deep pile of pork bones, carrot tops, rotted squash, broken furniture, soiled sheets, black-haired rag dolls, broken liquor bottles, one mirror, three busted clocks, a rusted frying pan, and a mess of white paper covered in nonsense scribbling. Such things should have been carted off to be burned or buried, but that pile had obviously just kept growing outside the door. The vines had wrapped over part of it and beneath them I could see movement, leaves shaking and crunching. I threw a rock and out popped a black ship rat that took stock of me and then walked calm under the porch to wait me out.

I should prepare you for the situation here at the house. Most of the children are gone off with some nuns and safe away from the city. Only Lydia is still here. I can hear her down the hall, in her bed, moaning and singing children's rhymes. I shall go look in on her soon, but I am terrorized by the sight of her, my girl. I still have hope, but that is all. The truth is that she will join her mother soon and, when that happens, I hope that this fever, this yellow jack, which I can already feel creeping up in my bones and polluting my blood, will take me

*soon after. It is inevitable, and I
don't want to be alone very long. I
want to see them again and soon.
And so you can understand the
urgency of this letter, I hope. The
mission I am to assign you is the
most important thing now. The
other children? Yes, of course important, but I ask you to do this, in
part, for them. They should hear
the truth from me. The truth!*

I went around to the front door. It was unlocked and I pushed in.

At least some part of the truth.

The windows in the house had been locked
shut and the air was dead. There was sweat in
it, and something sharp like vinegar. The General's clothes had been thrown over chairs
and piled in doorways, like he'd been pacing
the hall while dressing and undressing himself. Dust fairies blew around the sunbeams
that slipped past the drawn curtains, and I
thought of the times I'd seen little Lydia jumping to catch the dustlight in her hand.

Lydia. I stopped at her door and listened for

a rasp of breath or the sound of sheets twisting. There was nothing, and when I pushed open the door it was dead black.

Then Lydia's face lit up in the gray light from the doorway. Her eyes had stuck open just a little. She looked like she was waking up, but nothing moved. She looked strapped down. They say the dead let go of earthly burdens and become lighter, but I have never seen that. I had only seen them get real heavy. Lydia was dead and she was weighed down by it. Her face had gone white like a fairy's.

If Mrs. Hood had been alive the house would have been under control. There would have been light and air. The other ten children would have been home, sitting quietly, praying for their sister and their father. Lydia would not have grown cold in her bed, alone. But the yellow jack had got Anna Marie, and the nine healthy children had been sent off. Hood and Lydia were all that remained, too sick to leave. They were the ruins of what Hood said was his own separate country. There had been enough Hoods for a country, or at least a small town, but that wasn't what he'd meant and I ain't figured it out.

I closed the door quietly, like I might wake Lydia up, and walked toward Hood's room. I opened each door as I passed, and each window inside. By the time I reached Hood's room, the air had shifted. I smelled jasmine, hot dirt, and boiled fish. The outdoors. Hood had fallen asleep with a smile on his face and his sheets gathered up tight in his big right fist. I opened the window in his room. The breeze woke him up.

"Where have you been, Mr. Griffin? I await your report."

"My post is secure." This was our standard greeting.

He said nothing, only stared up at the ceiling, where a lizard stalked a crazed mayfly. I searched around the room for a rag to wet, and finally tore off the bottom of his sheet. In the next room a washbasin still held some clear, cool water and I soaked it up. When I returned he had rolled on his side to face the window where a mockingbird shuddered and strutted and cocked its eye at him. I put the rag on his forehead and let the water drip down his face. I looked outside for someone to carry a message, but the street was empty. The neighborhood was empty, I knew: it was summer in New Orleans, and no one with any money stayed behind to face the yellow jack and floods and heat.

"Do you think I am humorous?" The General looked at me out the side of his eye. I wished he'd stayed asleep. I decided I wouldn't tell him Lydia was dead. He was too close himself, he'd see his girl soon enough.

Humorous was not the first word I would have suggested, but there was some truth in it: Hood didn't tell jokes, and he didn't make silly faces, but he *did* enjoy talking foolishness behind that beard, and he knew the joke was that grave-damned face of his. Here was a dying man, a man who had lived his life as if cast in a Great Tragedy, the first man I had ever seen a mockingbird actually *mock*, and what he wanted to know was if he was funny. His face was soft and mournful. It was a serious question.

"Yes sir, I think you're humorous."

"I don't think people know this about me. I should have told them."

"Some people do. And you can't tell people you're funny, anyway. Otherwise they think you're not funny for sure."

"I have no time for paradox, but I will accept your judgment. Still, I want them to know this. Not that I'm funny. I am not funny. Dwarves and monkeys are funny."

Not all dwarves are funny, I thought, and I

believe he was thinking the same thing about the same person, our friend. It made him smile.

"Anna Marie knew it. She always did. She did not marry me for my countenance, my money, or my gentle good grace."

I'd not thought much about why she had married him, some things being better not considered too hard. She had been a beautiful and educated woman who had studied in Paris with Frenchmen. She could ride a horse like a country-ass Acadian, paint like a man, and pray like a saint. If there were proper rules, I reckon that marriage would have been barred.

"Anna Marie thinks I am humorous."

"Yes, she does." Wherever she's gone.

"She was the only one who wasn't surprised to discover it."

He turned back over and stared at me, as if sizing me up. His beard had twisted and matted into three thick strands.

"You received the letter. I had begun to think you hadn't, or that you had ignored it."

"Hard to ignore such a thing."

"Staying away is easy. Staying out of strange business is what we do."

"Maybe. Got no thought on it."

"I thank you for coming."

I didn't say anything more. He blinked hard, fast. I could see his eyes spin up, like they were moving on their own, and I knew he was pushing back against the fire in his head, burning off the layers of his mind, twisting it, disordering it. I'd seen it too many times since getting to the city. Madness in those eyes. He fought it. He looked at me, straight and hard.

"I take it that, because you're here, you accept the idea that you owe me?"

"I'm here because you asked me to be here."

He shook his head. Sweaty hair stuck to the side of his face.

"No, no, it's important that you realize you owe me. You are obliged to me. You cannot have honor until you have discharged your obligation."

Fancy words, words you were supposed to obey. Words that could snuff a man's life. I wanted to tell him I cared nothing about honor, and whether I had it or not. I'd meant to say it for years, but now a dying man lay before me. All things were sucked in by that man's body and his voice, there was nothing else outside the walls of that room, the magnolia drooping in the sun outside the window was not real and was fading away. I could only nod my head at him.

He sucked in air and I heard the dry flapping rattle in his throat.

"You tried to kill me once, and now that I am dying and you are receiving your wish, you are obliged to make amends. This is truth, you can't escape it, son."

"It's not my wish for you to die, General."

He puffed up his yellowing cheeks and blew out. His mustache flapped slightly.

"Don't try to confuse me with your paradoxes and feints, your false charges," he said.

"I'm not."

"I know you don't want to kill me now."

"That's right."

"But you must answer for your sin, like the rest of us."

"Yes. I will, someday."

"No, now. And you must see it that way, and not merely as a favor for an old man who may be abandoned once he's in the grave."

How he could talk, even on his deathbed.

"I see it, yessir," I said.

He asked me to help him sit up, and so I grabbed him underneath the arms and pulled until his back leaned against the headboard.

He was very light and too tall for the bed. He smiled at me.

"This is not only about *your* sin. It is mostly about my own. I must make sure it is destroyed, it and all the shoots and tendrils that have grown from my sin are withered. I've run out of time, you'll have to finish. I have written a book, or at least part of one."

He had been writing a book since I'd known him, but it weren't about sin. It had been about war, *the* war, and it had been his one great task, his obsession. "The war memoirs."

"No, not that book. I care nothing for that book anymore. It is a lie. Or, no, it was a true story built of lies I didn't understand were lies until very late. Too late, really."

He had spent years writing that war book. Ten years of his life working on it, writing his letters and analyzing his reports, putting together his great defense—that he had been right, and a great general. Most people who knew Hood knew of this book. There had been years in which it was all he had talked about, and there were hundreds of men in nearly every state and territory who could paper their houses with his letters: requests for information, for maps, for papers, for recollections, for assessments, for apologies.

Sometimes he'd tell me about the book while we sat in the dripping dark of the ice factory. The old warmonger. He told me how perfectly true it was, how it would vindicate him, how it would make him a hero once again when all the world thought him a bloody-minded fool who had thrown his men upon certain death with as much concern as kindling upon a fire.

General John Bell Hood could go to Hell. But this man in the bed, I hadn't thought of him as the General in a long time. He was just Hood now, called Papa by his children and John by his wife. I felt sorry for the man Hood, who had carried the deadweight of the General, part of his soul, all this time since the war.

The pieces of soul can't be cut out without filling them up again, that's a real law right there. God's law. Can't cut out the pieces any more than you can go around with a big hole in your gut. Got to be plugged up, replaced somehow. Hood wrote another book.

I stood watching the brown thrashers pecking and rattling in the weeds beyond the window, but all of that faded to nothing as he told me about his other book. *The truth,* he called it. *The important story.* He wouldn't say what was in it, only that it was the thing he wanted to say to his children, and that it was not about the war.

"This book, the pages of this book, are in my library, Eli, though I've hidden some of it and forgotten where," he said. "The other book, the war book, is in the possession of General P. G. T. Beauregard. You know of him?"

"Yes, of course." He lived in one of the biggest houses of the old city and liked his drinks and his dancing girls. He was a hard man to miss.

"It has been suggested to me by an associate that you would be the proper person to take charge of this book, that you would do a fine job of seeing to its publication. There are problems with it, and you must overcome them. Grave problems. Beginning with this: I want you to get that other book from Beauregard, and then I want you to destroy it."

Like a priest making his prayers, repeating the words, Hood had repeated for years, *I was right*. It was a shock to realize he didn't believe it.

"Are you sure, Hood?"

He had closed his eyes and I could see the crust in his eyelashes, which now opened slowly.

"I *was* an arrogant man, Eli. I *did* send men off to die without good reason. I *was* a murderer. Don't you think I understand why you tried to kill me? I always understood. If not for me, you'd be a young farmer up in Middle Tennessee raising corn and beef cattle, and you'd have a beautiful country wife and some country children. Instead you're a gambling and fornicating ice maker in the Devil's city."

I began to protest his description of me, but he was right enough and so I stayed quiet. I looked down and saw the edge of his bedsheet twisted up in my fist. My family had disappeared like water into the soil, but I had no earthly idea what would have become of me otherwise. It weren't worth thinking about.

He went silent for a few minutes. His whole body seized up. I thought his eyes would pop. A small trickle of blood ran from his nose before his body relaxed. He was as exhausted a creature as I'd ever seen, as if he'd been awake since they crucified Christ. He had only a few more minutes of words in him. He knew it too.

"I have tried to make amends, anyway. I believe I have acquired some wisdom, I think I understand now. That's the story in the other book. I believe I've done my penance, and I want the children to know this. I want my countrymen to know it. This is an important task. My associate said you would treat it that way."

The eyes rolled. He wrenched them back again.

"Get the book from Beauregard. Destroy it."

I nodded.

He coughed. "I cannot be the judge of whether I have fought my sin successfully and done my penance. Neither can you, you are too young. If I have succeeded or failed, the evidence is in the other book, the true book."

The light was going out in him. The blood drained out of his face.

"You want it published," I said. "That can be done."

He reached a hot, dry hand for my own. He held it and tried to squeeze it like he might have when he was powerful and wanted strict attention. Now, I could barely feel the hand move against mine.

"No. Or perhaps later. If you think it's good. But first, you will take it to a man who can judge my humility, whether I have made amends. You will ask him to read it. He will refuse you, but you must insist. Then you ask him a question."

I waited while he coughed, and then I wiped his mouth with my handkerchief. He nodded in thanks.

"You are to ask him if the mark of the Devil has been removed from me. If he says yes, publish it as you see fit."

"This ain't right. No sir."

"And if he says no, you are to destroy that book also."

I dropped his hand. He closed his eyes. Yes, I would do what he told me to do. I would make him this gift, though it was craziness.

"What is his name, Hood?"

"His name is Sebastien Lemerle. You will read about him in the book. It's all in the book."

"Where does he live? How do I find him?" I had a hundred questions, but he'd begun to babble. He managed to say only one more thing that made any sense.

"Take care with him, he's a killer."

I grabbed his hand, hoping to yank him back to my world for one last moment. "If I burn everything, what will I tell your children? What am I supposed to tell them? What do you want them to know?"

But he was out of his mind and tore at the bedclothes I tried to draw over him. He grabbed me by the back of the neck and pulled my face down to his so that those hard, blue, stone eyes were all I could see. They looked into me as if I'd stolen something and hidden it in my skull.

I knew not to deny a man at his death. I would have done his bidding merely because he asked. I wish he'd known that. I was a better man than he knew. He fell asleep, and I'd never see him awake again. I began the job he'd set me to. Get it over with quick, that was my thought. I went down the hallway again.

I knew that in his library I'd find piles of paper, hundreds of piles on chairs, tables, his desk, the windowsill, each of them a different height as if they had grown independently like children of his mind. How was I to know which was the preferred child, the all-important book?

The library had always been an unlikely place for a general. It was pink. Light pink, almost the color of a young conch. There were no shelves and no books. The white curtains twisted and ballooned in the slightest breeze like steam, and through them the yard and the street seemed soft and temporary, always about to fly off or change as the shadows shifted. Hood had worked at a trestle table, surrounded by his piles of paper and a few rag rugs. Light played off the tall walls and the desk. It was a room for sewing, or practicing music, not for generals.

I looked for a new pile of paper in a place of honor, a pile neatly arranged with a cover or a title. I saw nothing like that. His inkwell was uncapped and the ink had dried hard to the bottom. I saw no pens, no sign of any book he might have written. The only things out of place were the papers scattered on the floor around the waste can, some of them crumpled. I stopped to pick them up and throw them away properly.

I picked up the first piece of paper and the large and glistening wood roach that had been hiding underneath ran over my hand and into a dark corner. I suppose it's possible that but for that critter I would never have found the manuscript. A roach scuttled across my hand, I looked down in surprise, and on the paper in my hand I found these words:

When I met him, Eli was a silly boy.

I began poking through his trash, looking for more. I have a sinful man's appetite for the secret thoughts of others, especially when they concern me.

There wasn't much more about me, but every one of the discarded pages contained something I'd never heard the General say. I found pages on regret, pages on love, pages on sadness, and yes, pages on humor. The war was on those pages, too, but not the war as a general would remember it. A humble man, no general, had written those pages. This was the new manuscript, it couldn't be anything else. The pages were moments of a man's life, and so they were rough here, fine cut there, lollygagging, wandering, quick. He was thirsty, like a man cutting corn in August, but not exactly like that. Got no words of my own for it. They were the confessions of John Bell Hood. I could see that.

The book had been scratched out in fading ink, sometimes only a sentence on a page, sometimes crowded so full of letters and words it looked as if the page had cracked into a thousand pieces. He had not numbered any of them. I began to order them while kneeling there by the rubbish can. I found the rest of the manuscript shoved between the bookcase and the wall.

For that pile of paper I traveled the city a dozen times, tracking people down. I went into the wilderness, too, into the swamps.

I knew very little about the Hoods until
I found those crumpled pages, and after
I found them I couldn't do much else but
read them and obey. They worked magic
on me, made me dumb for everything but
puzzling out those pages and obeying their
commands.

An hour passed. The last of the pages were
stuck in a strange book by a fellow named William Blake, and I was reading that crazy book
when I heard a knock.

"General Hood?" A voice from outside.

I got up and looked out the window sideways. Down toward the front door I saw a
little man with no chin and a black, drooping
mustache standing at the front door.

"Are you there?" He rapped at the door
with his first knuckles, dainty but insistent. I
knew him.

"It's Doctor Ardoin. Is anyone home?"

The little doctor should have stopped in
days before. I snatched up the papers and, having no coat or bag, began to stuff them in my
pants. *The doctor shouldn't see them.* I was
just walking down the hall, trying not to jostle
them or make much noise, when Dr. Ardoin
let himself in.

"Mr. Griffin! How nice to see you! Have you been to see our patient?"

What else would I be doing here? I held my tongue and stood stock-still, stuffed like a scarecrow.

"Yes, Monsieur Ardoin, I have. He is off his head and Lydia is dead."

"Oh dear. Poor girl."

"That she was. Now she's just dead in her bed. Don't know if anyone knows when she died. Do you?"

"Mmmm, well, it's hard to say."

"Don't matter. Reckon General Hood is not long behind her. I've tried to cool him off, but there's not much else I can do."

The little man shook his head sadly and fiddled with the brim of his homburg.

"No, nothing to do now. A great tragedy."

"Don't know what's so great about it."

He picked up his bag and brushed past me on the way to the bedrooms. I made only a very slight papery sound, which he didn't seem to hear. I waited until he was a good piece away before waddling stiff-legged toward the front door. I thought if I could get outside into the garden, I could stash Hood's pages somewhere safe before going back inside. But then the doctor called.

"Mr. Griffin, are you there?"

"I'll be right there."

"I need your assistance."

I waddled for the door.

"Mr. Griffin, please. Now." I couldn't refuse him again or he'd think I was hiding something, and men like Ardoin don't know how to leave alone the things being hid from them, got to root 'em out.

And so I returned to Hood's bedside. The pages made me sweat, and I worried about the ink. (Later M. discovered that some of the words got themselves tattooed on my back.) Hood had sunk deeper into the bed. Ardoin held his wrist with two fingers like it was live crab ready to snap, and he held a wet handkerchief to his own mouth. I leaned over to mop the cold sweat from Hood's brow, and while I did that Ardoin went and sat in a chair pushed into the corner. He watched and stayed away. *Tsk, tsk, so sad.* When I left Hood was still alive, though silent and unseeing. I walked slowly home, looking behind me for the pages that slipped out and lay on the ground in my path.

When I returned to the house the next day, Dr. Ardoin and a small crew of Irish laundresses were busy cleaning up, balling the sheets and clothes that needed burning, opening up the whole house to the air outside, and scrubbing the floors. I should say the *women* were busy. Dr. Ardoin only sat in that same corner of Hood's bedroom, out of the sun and half in the shadow of the plain cypress wardrobe. He puffed at a straight pipe fashioned in the shape of a growling gargoyle and scribbled some notes. Hood and Lydia had both been removed. The doctor rubbed his eyes with his free hand while bent over his notes, which I guessed were an account of Hood's death and the doctor's own heroic efforts to save him. Newspapers loved that kind of horseshit when someone famous died. The death of the General would get their attention.

"Morning, Doctor Ardoin."

He looked up with big hound eyes, as if the only thing he had wanted in the world was for me to appear in the doorway. He smiled, I crossed my arms and nodded. He smoothly slipped his notebook into the pocket of his coat.

"A terrible night, friend. He did not go quietly. Much yelling, carrying on. Visions! A horror!"

"Surprised he lasted into the night."

"Ah, the will of the man! The bullheaded-ness, the strength. He fought like a wounded lion."

He raised his eyes to the ceiling, and I reckoned he was remembering to remember that description.

"He was tough, sure enough," I said. "Did he say anything?"

"Oh, so much. A rather patriotic defense of the late Confederacy, a poem—"

"And what did he really say?"

Dr. Ardoin looked at me close, frowned, but didn't say anything. I reckon he thought I wouldn't rat on him, even if I disliked him.

"Have they cleaned Lydia's room?" *Better get my business done and get out,* I thought.

"I believe they have."

"I'll go make sure they do a fine job rifling through her things."

"Mmmhmmm."

He had returned to his notes. I turned to leave.

"Mr. Griffin."

"Yes."

"If he *had* recited a poem, what do you think it would have been? Something heroic, no? But short?"

Good Christ. I walked away.

"Probably a psalm," he said to no one.

If the charwomen had indeed been poking through Lydia's things, they had probably found nothing to interest them. Nothing obviously valuable, that is. What would a woman want with a child's things, especially those of a child whose family was well known to be poor. The silver lockets, the ivory-handled brushes, the place settings, all that had once been part of their rich lives, they'd been sold off. I was sure of that.

But I knew there *was* something to be had in that room, and I aimed to get it. I'd remembered it the night before, unable to sleep and spending the time counting M.'s breaths. I lay flat out in the moonlight, staring up at the shining white face of it. When I got tired of M.'s hisses and whistles, I turned to counting the moon's flaws. Then I got up and tried to keep reading Hood's book in the dark, but it hurt my eyes. And then I remembered. I nearly jumped up and ran across the city just then, but thought better of it. Too many knives and garrotes in the dark. Wait to morning.

A month before, at Anna Marie's funeral, I had stood at the far edge of the mourners, who were mostly Anna Marie's cousins. I didn't listen to the priest, I'd heard the service too many times before. *Requiem aeternam dona eis, Domine, et lux perpetua luceat eis,* I heard it in my dreams, I knew it all, though I still got no idea what it means. I watched Lydia instead. She had her father's long, straight nose, his high brow, his small ears. She had his same quiet and tired face. The face that made her daddy look sad and mysterious had made her look beautiful and fragile, even at ten. She wore a blue dress, no trimmings, and dark blue shoes with new paint on the heels. She did not move while her mother was committed to the tomb.

At the end of the service, I watched a cousin, maybe a great-aunt, approach the girl and pull her behind a tree to yap in her ear. This woman could have been the resurrection of Anna Marie Hood: she was dark, slim, simply dressed, and she waved her hands and made faces just as Anna Marie had done it. That day she was a woman who wanted to be heard and obeyed, no mistake. Lydia kept saying, "But Aunt Henriette, please!" Over and over.

In her arm Aunt Henriette carried a small bundle of ledger books. She held them dangling from her fingers. I tried to get closer, but there were mourners standing between us. The woman appeared to be pushing the ledgers on the girl. Lydia shook her head and gnawed at her knuckle, eyes big. The other mourners finally trooped out of Lafayette Cemetery, leaving only the four of us—the lady and Lydia, me and Hood. Hood kneeled before Anna Marie's tomb and prayed. I stepped behind a tree so he wouldn't notice me, and so that I could watch Lydia, see if she needed help. Hood hadn't said anything to me, and I reckoned he'd want to keep it that way. I tried to listen to what the woman said to Lydia. Then I thought, *What the hell is Lydia doing here, anyway? She should be gone, out of the city.* Later, when she was dead, I heard that Lydia refused to leave her mother behind.

Lydia kept shaking her head and sliding toward her father, until finally Hood got to his feet and walked over to take her hand. The woman hid the bundle in the folds of her umbrella before Hood could see.

At the house, the family of Anna Marie gaggled on the front lawn. There were no drinks, no food, and no one went into the house. It had been contaminated by disease, and in the custom of some New Orleanians, it was thought that it was courting death to enter a yellow-jack house so soon. Hood and Lydia received the mourners under the oaks, shin-deep in the dark, green ripples of their uncut lawn. When they moved, tiny beetles, leaf-hoppers, and spittlebugs flew off like spray in their wake. I stayed back, leaning against the edge of the porch. My head got hot and tight, but I didn't cry.

Not all of the mourners stayed outside. I watched that Aunt Henriette from the cemetery edge toward the sidepath until she had disappeared around the house, heading toward the back door. I followed slow and careful, and then hid behind a mulberry bush to watch her as she wrapped her face with a fine and embroidered white handkerchief, pulled the ledgers from her umbrella, crossed herself, and went into the house through the kitchen. I stayed put. If she was so on fire to give the girl those useless ledgers, and that's what I figured her for doing, I saw no reason to stop her. When she came back out and removed the handkerchief, the ledgers were gone. Tears shined her cheeks and made her nose red. She kneeled right there on the step and prayed. Grief is a kind of craziness, and I knew better than to interrupt.

*   *   *

Now, a month later, I stood in Lydia's room, which had been stripped and mopped and emptied. I had to find that bundle. I had come to think that it weren't just numbers in those books. If I was going to do Hood's bidding, I wanted to know it all, every secret, whether Hood knew them or not. Especially if Hood didn't know them. I wouldn't mind knowing more than him for once.

The ledgers were easy enough to find, hidden under a small pile of scarves in the bottom of Lydia's wardrobe. There was a note tucked into the top ledger:

Cousin,

Please be sure Lydia receives these. She will want to read them someday. John must not know about them, for obvious reasons.

A.M.

That night I finished reading Hood's book and I began on Anna Marie's notebooks. Two nights without sleep. When I had finished, there was nothing left to do but begin the job Hood had set out for me, or be a coward. A traitor, to Hood, to Anna Marie, and to any hope that this life isn't just a crazy pile of accidents. I slept all the next day.

CHAPTER 2

From the Secret Memoir of John Bell Hood, Written Between September 1878 and August 1879

I came to New Orleans with $10,000 in my pocket. In a small valise, to be absolutely truthful. This was money borrowed from my family's acquaintances back in Kentucky. I had once dismissed Kentuckians as ditherers and cowards unwilling to sacrifice even a drop of blood or a pound of coin to protect the homeland. I had fought for Texas, instead. *Texas, where the Comanche maimed me.* After the war, I went to Kentucky as a pariah Confederate and I begged from those same men I had once insulted and abandoned. They had the grace to forgive me. I had been another man when the war started, they said. I was now a humiliated man, a worm, albeit a worm with $10,000 in United States currency packed in a leather bag at my feet.

I remember rolling toward the train station by the lake that first time. The lake mirrored the sun, fracturing it into an infinitude of tiny fires, flaring and extinguishing while I held my breath. Not having been to New Orleans, and a little travel weary besides, I mistook it for the river. An old, hairless man in black slept on the seat across from me. When I said to myself, *The river is worth the trip,* the man snorted and wiped his eyes with the heels of his hands as a child might.

"Ain't the river, General Hood. You'll know the river when you smell it."

"How do you know my name?"

"Your name? Everyone knows your name. I think what you mean is, How do I know your *face*?"

He unwound and stretched before sitting up straight. He was old, but his arms were tight coils of tendons, a workingman's arms. He was brown, sun-brown, from the crown of his freckled head to the ankles that emerged sockless when he stretched his legs. He was tall, and I had to look up at him.

"Yes, my face. How do you know it? Who are you?"

"I am merely an old fisherman, *un pescador*. But I hear things, and I see things, and they tell me you are you."

Ungodly bastard. I had heard about the mystical blasphemies popular among the Louisiana negroes, but had not known that white men indulged in them as well. He was Spanish, I assumed, and I decided that this explained his foolishness.

"Please spare me your superstitions."

"Of course, General. But are you sure you would not like me to read your hand? Not the lame one, of course. Perhaps I might examine the hairs of your beard and tell your future?"

He winked at me and settled contentedly into his seat, and I knew he had been joking. I tested this by smiling, and he smiled back. Let it be said now: John Bell Hood knows a joke and he can laugh too.

"How do you know my name, then?"

"The conductor is my friend. He sat me with you because he knew I wouldn't bother you with talk. He likes you, I assume. Once he told me your name, I knew it was true. Your face has been in the papers many times, General, and it's not a face to forget. You've got that wood leg too."

I had removed my leg and tucked it under my seat beside the satchel.

"I understand," I said. "Thank you for correcting me about the river."

A small cloud of smoke from the engine floated through our window and he waved it from his face.

"Well, it wouldn't be right to let a general loose in the city without giving him a bearing. Even Orpheus knew his way around. A little guidance is the last I can give you."

At first I thought he'd said *least*, but I realized soon that he'd said *last*. I felt that familiar dread again. He looked out and spit a mouthful of soot through the window. He checked his tongue for specks, wiped his hand over his shiny brown head, and looked down at his shoes. For a moment he didn't look at me, or anything in particular. He watched the void in front of his face, where I suppose he could see time moving past. Years into moments into eternity and back.

"We should have all had some guidance," he said to whatever it was he watched.

"You had a son," I said. It was obvious. I was embarrassed as soon as I said it. He'd had a son, and that son had marched under my flag. He had eaten whatever food I decided to give him, he had slept when I told him he could sleep. He had made friends, he had written letters and those letters had been carried back to the rear when I thought I could spare a messenger. Without knowing, and I would have never dared to ask, I decided he had died at Franklin, on the cold slope littered with shoes, hats, canteens, rifles, fallen osage orange trees, the bodies of other men. He was nearly to the entrenchments, nearly to a breakthrough and some kind of safety. He might have hidden in a corncrib or a smokehouse had he made it that far, but instead he fell just in front of the Union line. Perhaps he'd been close enough to be bayoneted. What had he thought of the cold in Middle Tennessee, that son of a Spaniard from south Louisiana? I hoped that he had died quick, and hadn't shivered his life away there. At the time I wouldn't have cared, but now I did. It shouldn't have happened that way. I shouldn't have ordered that charge. But I knew better, I was the Gallant Hood, and the Gallant Hood ordered a charge into near certain death for most of his army because I saw no other choice and it was good for their sense of Southern invincibility and pluck. I sent them up and laid them down before the Union's fire like so many sheaves of wheat. All in rows. I had killed thousands of my own people because I, the Gallant Hood, had led as if battle was a bracing bit of exercise, a game. I knew this, and yet I could not admit it then.

He smiled. "Now who is the voudou witch?" He nodded his head.

"And he died."

"Yes."

"Under my command."

"*Sí.*"

I had no children, and at that moment I could not know what pain he might have felt. I know it now, but *then* all I could think to imagine was his anger. His pain was merely an abstraction.

"Your son did not die in vain." Such a stupid thing to say, such an arrogant, ignorant, brutal thing to say. The man took a minute to answer me.

"He died. That's all."

I thank God I had the sense not to say anything then.

We sat silent during the last few minutes of

the ride, each of us swaying together as the train turned and wobbled and banked. I had some trouble staying upright without the leg, so I bent over to strap it on. I could feel him watching me.

"You've made your sacrifice, General."

I didn't say anything.

"May I tell you something?"

I nodded my head while crouched over my leg. I stayed like that, listening for him.

"I won't be the only one who will recognize you. You are not easy to miss. You would be better off looking us all in the eye. If you are ashamed, you will not last."

I sat up. "I am not ashamed."

"Ah, my mistake. I assumed."

He had no bags. I watched him stand at the end of the platform, watching the red sun bleed into the horizon. Meanwhile porters scurried to load my great, varnished, ironbound trunks onto the back of a four-in-hand. When he walked over to the stairs and stepped down from the platform, he looked over at me and scanned me from head to toe, as if looking for something. Or judging me. I watched him walk, on fisherman's legs bowlegged and steady, moving fast down the Shell Road toward the city. He was soon lost in the

dust clouds that kicked up in the wind that
now rushed in off the lake as the sun disappeared. I never thought to offer him a ride.
When my coach passed him on the way into
town from the station, he had stepped off the
Shell Road to piss. He grinned up at me.

"Don't look back, General!" he shouted
over the clatter of the horses. He was laughing when we turned out of sight.

New Orleans was, very simply, the only
Southern city that still worked, where a man
might still make a dime in those years just
after the war. Briefly my mind turned to the
subject of money: its acquisition, cultivation,
its transformative properties, its promise of
freedom. I had never cared much for money
before, but war had changed that. Forgive the
young general, forgive me.

I can remember what I thought standing
for the first time in the St. Louis Hotel, watching the traders and fixers mingling in the red
and alabaster of the lobby, sharing their whiskey and passing around bills of sale. They
were smooth-faced and tailored. Their shoes
glowed. They moved lightly between couch
and chair and bar. I stood on the precipice,
a scarecrow, a lump of earth, a pile of broken things, and watched them flow and slip

around each other like dancers. They were full of grace, the earthly kind, and I was full of heaviness. No one acknowledged me. *The old man was wrong about that,* I thought then, but now I knew he had been right: I was seen, recognized, and ignored. Negro waiters, wrapped in bright white coats and bearing trays of glasses and tobacco, drifted between knots of men who honked and brayed at each other in pleasure. The waiters bowed and shuffled just as they would have before the war. What had changed? Men laughed, they shook hands. The mirrors were polished, the landscapes framed in bright gold and hung straight. The whole place was *easy,* unperturbed, secure. In that one spot, in that one city in that singular state far from my enemies, this was how things had been, how they were, and how they always would be. I realized for the first time that the war had not been all-consuming. It had consumed me, but not these men whose suits were not pulling apart at the seams and whose legs did not thump and scrape across the gleaming tile. There had been men who had flourished while Chickamauga raged, men who had gone home to their wives and concubines while other men dragged their squadmates off the field at Little

Round Top and laid them in bloody piles. I was not angry to realize this, though it was a shock even so. I became confident and certain in this knowledge. I became gleeful at the thought: *These men owe me.* My cause was right, and my cause was not just money but compensation. *Look at my leg,* I thought, pushing through a boisterous group of Creole cotton men and planters in gold cravats. *Who will bid on my leg?*

The city embarrassed me, or I was embarrassed for the city, one or the other. Blacklegs walked the streets like kings, arms thrown over the shoulders of the innocent, hands on the asses of whores. The whores dressed better and spoke more eloquently than the dark-haired and pious wives who spent their days fumbling with beads, their heads wreathed in cloying smoke. Stray cotton bolls, lifted across the quay on light wind, drifted against walls and collected in doorways like old, peppery snow that no one bothered to remove. The Italians lived like dogs in their secret courtyards redolent of the old vegetables and shrimp shells that brewed in their stews. In came the innocent and hopeful, and out went the dead. It was an indecent town.

Nothing mattered but the money. Oh Lord! How could there be so much money? It floated down the river, funneled from the mountaintops to the valleys to the fields to the docks, and on to the hive of cotton offices, insurers, bankers, and saloonkeepers. The money bought sculpture and flesh, tombs and exquisite gardens laden with lemons and bananas. It bought leisure, the most important thing.

Any man with even a little wit could open an office, buy a desk, hang a sign, and accept the money as if by right. It was possible to look out the window of the office and see each person as a chit to be banked, every crowd a living body of future accrued interest, every new friend a mark to be plundered for treasure. It was not so much different from imagining men as lines on a map, every small line merging into a larger one aimed at the enemy's lines, each man merely a walking rifle.

I found partners in the city eager to open a cotton factor's office with a famous, or infamous, Confederate general who had no experience of commerce. They told me I was a respected man with a well-known name, and that this would draw customers. They flattered, but what they meant was that I was a curiosity. I had friends upriver with cotton, brothers in arms who would surely prefer to sell to me rather than to the dissolute and lazy-tongued traders of the Creole classes. It took two years, nearly all of my own investment, and the disappearance of my partners to relieve me of those fantasies.

This is how I begin my memoir. I am older, I am wiser, I've got nearly no money. We have embarked on a new life that looks mightily like the old one, only with no servants, fewer changes of clothes, and no more days settled into the soft red chairs of the St. Louis's lobby. Recently I have spent hours instead sitting in the parlor on a three-legged stool ("Two more than you have, Papa!" the boy John Junior says), carved from old river-strewn cypress. Right now I am in my library sitting on my unforgiving four-slat chair missing several inches of its cane bottom, bent over this piece of paper, this is what I do now.

These last ten years. Ten children, and in the spring our eleventh. I am married to a flower of the Creole world who had the bad sense to be dragged down with me. Yet she still looks at me and flirts during supper. She sits with me on the front porch overlooking Third Street, drinking the very last of our cognac. I have $173, which we keep in a can in the pantry next to the dried field peas. The children know of that money, but they do not steal it. Their friends parade the street in shiny calfskin boots aboard sweet, well-broken ponies. My children dig after bugs and capture butterflies in what Anna Marie diplomatically calls our wildflower garden. They are barefoot most of the time. The older children once had ponies. Lydia's pony, Joan, was perfect black except for the white blaze and her four white stockings, and Lydia rode her through every yard and into every swampy and secluded stand of cottonwood and cypress she could find. The two of them often returned covered in sharp thorns and burrs. I am told by old friends that she resembled her mother most at those moments. Joan was the last of the ponies we sold. Lydia has never once asked me about her, nor does she look covetously at the neighborhood children who still have ponies. She is the leader of the butter-fly snatchers now. She calls every butterfly Joan, but I think this is out of fondness and not out of resentment. She likes the name, she likes the things in her life that have been named Joan.

This sounds nothing at all like the memoir of a famous, or infamous, Confederate general. I pray that it is unlike such writings in every way. This is the record of a man finished with war. I spend my days in our house, or walking the fragrant wet streets, louche with jasmine and camellias and gardenias and unnameable strange rambling vines winking their purple and red and yellow blossoms at the sun. I spend my nights reading to children and holding my wife to my broken and amputated body. Ten years ago I would have thought such behavior foolish. What joys does a poor man have? These days there is love, to begin with, and also the possibility of salvation. I am the rich man who discarded (or, more accurately, *lost*) his riches. Perhaps I will know a savior now. Perhaps it is Anna Marie. Perhaps it is my own conscience.

Does this seem small, this new world I describe? It is not, but judge for yourself.

I write this on October 3, 1878. Anna Marie is pregnant. Again. That itself is something of a miracle. Last spring I thought I would never touch her again, never be allowed into that bed, never see her smile at me. I didn't care. But much has changed, even in just a few months.

I should begin by telling you how I met the woman with whom I now live in blessed penury.

I was not such a chastened man ten years ago, no sir. I lived in red upholstered rooms high above the Vieux Carré, and in the mornings I received admirers in the lobby of the St. Louis. I did not drink on those mornings, sitting by the tall windows and talking the history of the late war with twiggy-limbed and swarthy Frenchmen whose closest encounters with the rage of battle happened right there, during the occupation, when their women were insulted by the Union occupiers and they plotted their imagined duels and sword thrusts over boiled shrimps and morning brandy in the clubs. *It was outrageous,* they told me. *It was intolerable.*

"And yet you are here, you must have tolerated," I jested.

"We are a resourceful and proud race," they said, very seriously.

I entertained offers of business partnerships on those days. I could have been a railroad investor, a restaurateur, an importer of West Indian cloth, a brothel owner, an investor in Mrs. Pontalba's apartment houses around Jackson Square, a maker of fine rum, and a partner in a firm that pumped water out of the city and into the river. I turned them all down, although I could picture myself ruling my own restaurant, tasting the soups, watching the butchering of the tender and giant green turtles, listening to the woody ping of fine knives chopped down on hard blocks. I could imagine inspecting the cleanliness of my plates.

But it was cotton I chose. I cared nothing for the crop, there is no romance in cotton, only the seas of white monotony. But I reckoned myself a clever man, cleverer than everyone else, and I knew cotton was the clever man's bet. Cotton factoring—the brokering of cotton between farmer, shipper, and manufacturer—would be my business, though I knew nothing of it or, truthfully, about any business at all.

What did it matter? Men respected and admired me for being the General. Few could have named a single battle I'd engaged, a single victory, but no matter. I was a man to whom attention must be paid, and I felt capable of all things.

I hired men who knew cotton and installed our offices in the Vieux Carré, close by the wharf with a view over the river to Algiers. Not once in the three years of my proprietorship did I set eyes on a cotton boll. Cotton never came through the door except on the backs of men and in their handkerchiefs. I let the others concern themselves with the product.

I spent my time writing letters on fine letterhead to my West Point classmates requesting their help as I began the composition of my war memoir. I thought I would call it *Advance and Retreat*, which was both simple and complete, as was my life. I had been a titan of battle, now a respected man of business, and soon a writer of memoirs. I could not have lived according to the laws of civilized man with any more faith, except for the matter of finding a wife.

I wore my wounds proudly, but privately they revolted me, even after several years with them. In my rooms, which were spare and glowing and polished, crouched a monster who draped the mirrors in black as if in mourning. He didn't like to see himself. He avoided the floor-to-ceiling windows that opened to the gallery that looked out over a street loud with the perambulations of the happy and the whole and the ignorant. The monster, withered and chopped, paced his rooms muttering of calumnies and, when moved, he flung himself at his desk to write down every slight he'd suffered at the hands of the graceless warrior victors and, even worse, from men of his own tribe, his Confederates. My war memoirs were composed in a rage and intended to offend and to destroy: reputations, lives, complacency.

I *had* deserved command, and I had commanded in victory and in defeat. There's not a general who did not suffer defeat. I suffered defeat. I did. I suffered. Lee also suffered defeat. He stood at the edge of that battlefield at Gettysburg as what was left of his army filed back past him in retreat. I saw him that day. We had been defeated, but I had given a good fight. I expected to hear his congratulations as we passed, but instead he looked down from that great white horse, Traveller, and bent his head toward my men as if in supplication. "I am sorry," he said. I thought his apology unbecoming, which shows how little I understood about General Lee, war, and the minds of men.

I felt at home in the city. Me, a Kaintuck country cracker. I had spent most of my life sleeping out on cold jabbing ground, and so I came to cherish my feather bed and thick blankets, the soft sound of my footfall on thick carpets, meals prepared in kitchens, meats diced and filleted rather than ripped off the bone and skewered on hot red bayonets in the starless dark. On the street I learned the mongrel language of English, French, German, and Spanish, not a language so much as a mercantile code spoken by shopmen in single bursts and grunts. One word, such as *déjeuner*, contained a weight of agreed directives and responses that, ultimately, brought poached eggs and ham and a chickory-laced milk coffee to my table. I admired the efficiency of our shared dumbness.

The most I ever saw of the Irish were the hearse carts piled with dead Irishmen newly fallen in the pits of the latest canal, all of them covered in dried yellow mud like totems of a lost civilization. I had known Irishmen in the war and knew them to be valiant if also sentimental and incautious. General Claiborne died at Franklin like a private. Well-loved, but dead, and what good is that? I listened to the banshee call from their lairs in dark pubs and from the backs of blue-dark sanctuaries. I pitied them.

*   *   *

The negroes controlled the market, they ran the wharf gangs without which none of us would have made any money. They built things, they spoke their beautiful, strange French and, all in all, seemed a closed society well in possession of itself. Then it came time to root them out like plague, and the Irish—and the Spanish, the Germans, the Americans, and even the white Creoles—burned and stabbed their way over the negro, establishing forever the hierarchy of piteousness.

I was invited to participate in the parade of the Krewe of Comus that first year in the city, my first Mardi Gras. The men of Comus, a secret society of white men, had imported from England a barge full of costumes, monstrous blasphemies all. A grasshopper with a bear's head, a singing fish with a beaver's tail. This was Mr. Darwin's vision, or so they said. My eagle with a frog's legs also had a negro's lips. I took the costume to the Pickwick Club, home of Comus, and asked about that particular detail of my costume.

"Eagles don't have lips," I said.

"That one's got nigger lips," said the old, sun-blackened man who would be the King that year.

"Precisely my question," I said.

"It isn't a question," he said.

"Pardon me?"

"I was just observing that your eagle has nigger lips, which is as it was designed. But, General, if you'd prefer a different costume we can arrange it."

"I might like that . . ."

"We've got a mouse-giraffe with a Hottentot ass, and a pelican-snake in blackface."

I kept my costume, thinking it most appropriate that I mask as an eagle because of my service in the war, especially in light of the other options. I marched in a parade of menacing hybrids, a fantasia of men obsessed by purity and breeding, horrified at the notion of their daughters' future half-negro children. Which is to say, their daughters' *negro* children, as there are no half negroes. To transform their grandchildren into negroes as men from fish and apes seemed, to the maskers on my left and right marching down Canal Street, the worst kind of alchemy.

About the time I understood the full meaning of the parade I had joined, the stump of my leg began to ache, and so I pulled out and sat down on the banquette and removed my eagle head and, when I had gathered my breath, my wooden leg.

"That is an awfully scary costume, mister," said a short, raven-haired boy in a harlequin's stockings and mask. His parents, dressed as the Pope and His Lover, watched us closely and I smiled. They did not smile back.

"I reckon it must be hard pretending your leg been et off, mister. That's what makes the scariness."

Later that day the men of Comus attacked some negroes and some Republicans, and possibly one Italian potter hawking his beer mugs along the parade route. The police, many of them colored, beat them all, severely splitting the costumed heads down the middle with their clubs and gouging out eyes when they could find them in the riot of feathers and garland papier-mâché. I, luckily, had given my eagle head to the little harlequin and so I could watch the disaster unmolested.

This was what had become of our war. We had once fought with honor on the field and now we fought dressed like idiots in the streets. I vowed to avoid politics but I still needed a wife.

* * *

I began to attend balls, I trimmed my beard a little, I practiced French and Spanish. I bought new clothes. I learned to dance again, and to seduce. I was almost the man I had once been when I was a colonel, when I was strong and fiery and courted the finest women in Richmond, back when I didn't limp.

And so it was that I found myself again in a mask, in May of 1867, at a ball in the old part of town. I masked, as they say it here, but I was easily recognizable. After a little while of turning about the edges of the ballroom and greeting the grave chaperones and their flowery charges, I sat down in the foyer and began massaging the stump of my leg until it tingled again, and watched a small, erect, audacious, and insolent young woman march across the foyer to confront me from behind her peacock mask.

"The Gallant Hood!" she said.

"I believe it is the protocol of these disguised gatherings to refuse such identifications, ma'am, and so please excuse me if I say, Who?"

I was tired and bored and could think of nothing wittier to say. I tried to get to my feet in proper greeting, but I forgot my leg on the seat next to me, and so it was easy for the young woman to catch me off balance and ease me back onto the seat. She did not sit, though I made a space, and so I was forced to look up at her. She let her chest heave in a great sigh, she watched me watch her in fascination. Then she chuckled.

"If you are not Hood, then I must go."

It had been years, since before I had been wounded and separated from myself. I had been the tall Kentuckian by way of Texas, spinning round the parlors and dance floors of Richmond with the best young ladies, the proper young ladies, the kinds of women General Lee had meant when, back in Texas years before, he'd told me to marry well. During the war I had been a man in demand. I had shared many glasses of bourbon with nervous fathers. But then I was butchered and I took myself away, ashamed and weak. In four years I had not been seduced by any woman who wasn't paid to do it.

"I'm Hood," I said too loudly, half rising to my foot again. I surprised myself with my desire to keep her near. *I'm tired,* I thought. But what was true was that I was lonely.

What had I known of beauty? I had known nothing, that was instantly obvious the moment she removed her peacock feathers from her face. I had known prettiness, the prettiness of the shiny and extravagant, but not the beauty of singularity. What I mean is, there stood a young woman by a broken man unable to keep track of his leg. There was a horde of prettiness gliding in island silks behind her, but she had chosen to stand by the broken thing in the room. She chose to be alone with me, and by that gesture, she became alone in the world. Alone, but not lonely, for God's sake. While we talked young men drifted by across the parquet, heels clicking and chests billowing before them like sails. They watched us out the corner of their eyes, or looked over each other's shoulder at the cripple wooing the girl with the long white neck, the cascading dark hair, the thin waist. They admired her as they might have admired a horse at the track. I saw only her eyes.

And what do I mean by beauty? The other men might have looked at us and seen only a rough man and a pretty girl. But I saw that if I had gone through my life intent on the ugly and difficult (as I had!), shedding every delicate and perfect part of my soul like so many raindrops, Anna Marie must have followed behind me gathering what I sloughed off so that one day I might sit in a ballroom in New Orleans and see for myself what I had lost. No other man could have seen what I saw, which was the light that went with my darkness.

I don't know how else to say this: I was confirmed at that moment in all that I didn't know that I knew, simultaneously aware of the beautiful pieces and assured of their truth. I wanted to kiss her and more, and had I not been hobbled, I might have jumped up and done just that. Instead, I could only look up at her and hope I wouldn't foam at the mouth.

She sat down next to me, so close I could hear her breathe and watch the fine hairs on her arm rise up in goose bumps.

"You are a famous man," she said. "I care very little for fame, it makes a person so tedious and unnatural."

She could have told me she was a goat with a preference for clover and I still would have loved her. "Infamous might be the better word," I said.

"Not among my people, they think you're a hero! The great Confederate! The misunderstood American Achilles!"

"I would like to meet these people of yours to thank them properly."

"Oh, I don't know that they would actually

want to *meet* you, my parents and my cousins. They just like to know you exist."

She blushed and held her hand to her mouth.

"I'm sorry, that was terribly rude of me. I sometimes forget that there are real people at these things, and not only masked boys in borrowed frippery."

I bowed my head and noted how her hands lay enfolded on each other in the caress of her lap. Extraordinary.

"I am pleased to meet you, ma'am, whoever you are."

"Anna Marie Hennen. I have somehow lost my chaperone."

By *somehow* I came to understand that she meant *through great effort and ingenuity.*

"And where is *your* chaperone, General Hood?"

"I did not know I required one. I am remiss."

"You have your reputation to consider."

"I am at risk?"

"Well, perhaps not *you.* But one should be careful."

"Are you careful?"

"I have nothing to fear."

Her words spooled out relaxed and precise,

the cadence of an educated person. Sure and bemused. Her face was white but her arms, where I could see them above her gloves, were brown and freckled. She sat erect and I had the impression she sat this way because she was strong and had a good back, that she was unafraid of work even if she had no need of it. She had not been cinched up and trussed into the posture of a superior and mysterious being. She naturally sat that way. I took solace from the gap in her front teeth and the freckle on the edge of her earlobe, but even these imperfections could only be exceptions to the rule.

I have nothing to fear. She couldn't know how these words jabbed at me, and how much I wished she *did* fear for her reputation while in my company. I wished that I seemed the kind of man who *could*, for instance, bend her over my arm and trace the ligaments of her neck with my lips. *My God, what am I thinking?* I took control of myself.

"I shall be your chaperone, then, while you're without one. I am the Gallant Hood, after all, and I assume gallant means the same here in the humid latitudes as it does elsewhere?"

"I'm certain 'gallant' means the same. But what of 'Hood'?"

"I don't understand."

She rolled her eyes and reached over me to pick up my wood leg. The straps and buckles jingled softly against the wood. She rubbed it along its shin, feeling the fine finish. She seemed to be daydreaming.

"What I thought to say was, What does Hood mean? And more specifically, What does he mean for me?"

"I mean nothing for you at the—"

"Does he mean, for instance, to escort me into the courtyard through that door?" She pointed at a small door at one end of the foyer. Through the fanlight above I could see Mars. "Does he mean to escort me into the garden and down by the gardenias, where there is a secluded bench perfect if I were to swoon at the effect of the flowers and the excitement of the evening and at the scent of the stranger next to me?"

"I—"

"I wonder, because that is how it is done here in the humid latitudes when a lady has abandoned her chaperone in order to make the acquaintance of an unsuitable man. We

are all about to die, there is not time for pro-
crastination, General, so get to your feet."

As I said before, under her brief influence
I was already better known to myself. I did
not know what *Hood* meant until we walked
through that little door and into the sweet,
swaying garden, but I soon understood and
would never forget.

The bay leaves and sweet olives reflected
silver in the open night sky, but the slick
leaves of the gardenias that surrounded us
on that wrought-iron bench seemed blacker
and deeper in the light, as if they could draw
around us and keep us perfectly hidden. Anna
Marie, as she'd promised, leaned her head
against my chest. Without thinking, I stroked
her hair with my good hand. We talked about
our lives as children. She had been a wild girl,
hauling fish in from the river under the guidance of her family's negro gardener, who ate
nothing but what he could find in the river
and what she could sneak out of the larder.
I told her that the dirt of our Kentucky farm
was fine and cool on early April mornings. Between our retreat and the tall, glowing windows of the ballroom stood a statue of St.
Joseph—husband of Mary and patron of loyalty and peaceful death—atop the lilies of a

tittering fountain. She asked me if I went to
church, and I said that I was a believer who
had not yet found a church as fine as the field
on which a friend baptized me before battle.
She asked me if I was always so laughably dramatic and sentimental, and I said yes.

"You don't have a chaperone, do you?" I
asked.

"Oh, of course I do," she said, sitting up and
tucking her hair behind one ear. "She just happens to also be a widow just out of her black.
She has her own interests, shall we say."

"Very convenient."

"She is a very popular chaperone this
season."

In the light from the ballroom, St. Joseph
cast an open, beckoning hand across Anna
Marie's cheek, and I kissed it. My beard tick-
led her face, and she said so. She reached up
and smoothed the whiskers from my mouth.

"There."

I kissed her again, hard. Unwilling to trust
my instincts—*Did she not know I was an
animal, a predator, a killer?*—I sat back
again to watch the night sky and listen to the
night. Anna Marie relaxed against my shoulder. Mars had almost set beneath the treetops.
For the first time, I heard other people around

us: whispering over in the corner of the garden beneath the magnolia, rustling crinoline behind the old, spindly lilac. *This was how it was done in the humid latitudes? Fine then.*

I did not deserve such happiness, of course, but I would accept it before its inevitable disappearance. I had learned that much about happiness, at least—it was best to take it and consume it before it flitted away, incontinent and fickle. Love it now, hate it later. This was the miserly wisdom I had taught myself.

For the moment, the happiness could only last until the music stopped and the shadows in the tall windows quit moving past.

"May I call on you?"

I couldn't hear her answer. She had dozed off with her head buried against the lapel of my coat.

"I suppose that's a no?"

"No, no. I mean, yes," she said, straightening up. "I'm sorry, I know you're not a pillow, but you are so comfortable. But yes, you must call on me. Bring your best leg."

"I only have one."

"Then polish, polish, polish, my boy. First impressions and so on."

She laughed. I told her I would set my leg on fire and wave it about her like a torch if she kept mentioning it, and she recoiled in mock horror. We giggled—*I giggled.*

A stillness. That's the only way I can describe what became of me in the months following that night. I was still. There was a man who lived next door to my solitary bachelor's apartment on Decatur overlooking the docks. He was an old yellow-toothed man who limped worse than I did and whose family were all dead or gone for good. He had been in the habit of telling me that what I needed was a woman, that a woman would smooth me out and scare the gray out of my beard and polish my *baton* and so on, and though I didn't disagree with him, I always declined his offer of introduction to women of his acquaintance.

"You got more gray than I do, General, and you know why of course! Of course!" He'd smack his lips and say it nearly every morning. He was old enough to be my father.

A week after I began courting Anna Marie, he stopped talking to me. I would see him out in the courtyard eating oranges, always avoiding my eye. I wanted to tell him that there had been no baton polishing, but I decided to let it lie. I supposed I was too smoothed out to be trusted on that score.

I squired Anna Marie here and there, and we ventured into the harder and dirtier districts on something of an exploratory mission. I kept her under my protection, and the street people made way for us. I shielded her from the coarser sights, I didn't want to upset her or corrupt her. She was a lady.

I never felt in danger of losing her, and I nearly never felt I needed to apologize for my deformities while in her presence. She didn't seem to care. I began to trim my beard. I bought cigars for her father, the judge. Her mother introduced me to a cobbler who made very fine shoes for my wooden leg, and I always wore those shoes to their house, whatever the weather. I was grateful to the Hennens.

Her father was impressed with me, I think, though he took pains to conceal it. Later he would tell me that I had always enjoyed his support in the courtship, that a commander of men could command his daughter. No, that's not how he put it: *It requires a commander of men to command my daughter.* What he did not know, what few besides Anna Marie knew, is that I, General Hood, had no interest in commanding anything anymore. Command had coarsened me, and separated me from God and His mercy. I had lost my way. I tried to learn to ask for forgiveness, and Anna Marie taught me some of the words. I was the General only when I was angry, when I was at my end, and then I became a frightening and foolish man, a man at war with himself. I suppose that, at last, I married Anna Marie because she had no desire to know the General, and didn't care one bit for him. A fresh start.

We were married the next year, 1868, and less than a year after that Lydia was born. Now we have a house full of children and very little money. I'm afraid I have not provided, nor have I always made Anna Marie happy. There have been months that we've hardly talked at all. I have kept myself busy with work, true, but that is not the whole story. There are times when I do not feel that there, on Third Street, rests my house and family, times when I'm sure that they are strangers. Or I am the stranger, a guest in the house. During those times I have stayed away, keeping myself busy. Busy, busy, busy. I also have my hiding places, and I admit now that I have hidden like a coward in them.

But this last year, this last year since the great epidemic, has been a revelation. I have had little else to do but chase after the children and take walks with my wife. Anna Marie and I have spent hours talking in the dark, and I feel like I did once before: still. I feel stillness.

That is, until she makes her jokes about my leg and starts saluting me, and then I grab her and carry her off to our rooms.

CHAPTER 3

From the Diary of Anna Marie Hennen Hood, Written in Ledger Books Between April 1879 and August 1879

Something has happened that I must explain, Lydia. I do not know whether I have been brought to ruin by this marriage, or whether I have been saved by it. They do not tell you when you are veiled and kneeling before the altar, your man at your side, that you will ask this question and that there will be no answer. Or that the answer is both ruin and salvation. The pen will sort this for me. Before it answers, before I set this down, I wish to stipulate (as your grandfather the attorney would have put it) that there was never any question of love. I have loved, and I do still.

When I named you, my oldest daughter, I thought I would never have another child, and so I gave you the longest possible name. Lydia Marie Hennen Hood. I wanted to be sure that there was a child who would carry all of the important names: my sister, Lydia's; my father's, Duncan Hennen; my husband's, John Bell Hood; and me, your mother, who always loved the Marie more than the Anna in her name.

You will find this explanation amusing for two reasons, and they are contained here in the little swaddled lovely asleep in the bassinet next to me as I write this. You will find it funny because the baby, your sister, is my eleventh child. There was never a shortage of children to bear names, I should not have feared that, of all things. We ran out of names. She is the second daughter I've named Anna. Your little sister Anna Bell had eight years alone with her name, perhaps she won't mind sharing it with this one, Anna Gertrude. Or, perhaps, only Gertrude. Is that a prettier name? Marie is still prettier, but we have three Maries already: you and the twins Marion Marie and Lilian Marie.

It's too much to expect much more sharing of *that* name.

Anna Gertrude has a cold. I hear her breathing, a rasping and rattling. She coughs so quietly it's a rough whisper. Her eyes are pale blue like her father's, but her black hair is mine. (You have my eyes, Lydia, nearly black. They're pretty on you.) Anna Gertrude is as beautiful and mysterious as every one of our babies. I am grateful. She sleeps in a wicker bassinet that has sprung most of its weave. Sharp, broken pieces poke out on every side. The paint has mostly flaked off, and in certain spots it's still possible to see some of the seven other shades of color your father added to the contraption. Now it is falling apart. The bassinet will not last much longer, and most of my old friends would have burned it years ago. It wobbles on its legs, it sags in the center where ten other babies once lay. It is the vessel, though, that has borne each of my children along into the world, and I will not give up on it so easily.

I begin this way because I am nervous, Lydia. I imagine that you are reading this when you are old, and that you hate me and your father for the life we led. You are poor now, and perhaps you are still. Most of the children don't remember the servants and the fine flatware and the bolts of paisleyed French cloth propped up in the corners, from which we had men sew us our dresses and curtains and bed coverings. You, at least, would remember the prestige of being the family of John Bell Hood, you would remember the men who paid court to him and laughed at his half-remembered jokes. You would remember when the stray dogs were afraid to sneak through our fence, and when the roses still produced flowers and didn't just ramble across the yard. Because you would remember all that, I wonder if you hate us for abandoning it all.

There are many reasons for me to write to you now, and the bassinet is one of them: I should explain why the bassinet fell into such a state, and why I still keep it and love it.

There are many things like it in this house now. The floors are scratched and rutted, the stove is broken and will not fire anymore, John Junior has outgrown his short pants but has nothing else to wear. What furniture is left has been tied together at the joints, and the old trap is missing some of the red spokes from its right wheel. It sits in the sideyard gathering to it vines and some chipped pots in which I've planted lilies. We walk nearly everywhere now. The horse is long gone, and there is no oil for the lamps. We still have candles, though I've noticed that you children have no more interest in them. Or, rather, that you have no more interest in doing the things that require candlelight. You and your brothers and sisters sleep when the sun sets and rise when it warms the counterpane. I think this is healthy, though our neighbors must think us eccentric.

Only John still insists on mastering the night. I hear him thumping around the parlor now, I hear him cursing, and then I hear the snick of a match. He moves too fast, even with his wood leg. I try to tell him that the wind he makes walking so quickly will always snuff a candle, but he will not slow himself. He worries about me, and this makes him want to move, to grab up things and put them back down. I have heard him arranging and rearranging his books. I have heard him shaping the hollies outside into perfect round balls of green, using only his old bayonet which he keeps paper-thin sharp. God help us, he has even cooked our food, which as you know always comes out of a big pot. He cooks us camp food in the fireplace. It is garrison food, the food that soldiers make for themselves when all they have is the overripe turnips and sprouted potatoes and bacon ends they scrounge from trash heaps and on old harvested fields. He makes for us the food of desperate men grateful for small things, and I suppose that is what we are now, though I wouldn't mind if he would discover salt, pepper, maybe some thyme. Perhaps you will help him with that. My little helper Lydia.

Surely you have noticed how empty this grand house has become. You've seen how we rattle around inside, hidden beneath its soaring roof and filigreed gables, loose inside its solidity like seeds inside an old, dry, and still perfect gourd. The life we live now is not the life this house was supposed to contain. It is a house of great ambition, built for entertaining and leisure amid beauty and grace. It is a house that was built by much younger people who had every reason to think that they would have everything they ever desired and that they would need a place to put it all before they ran out of room and found a larger house to fill. I have all I desire now in this rickety bassinet and the sound of you children crawling into your beds, but I'm afraid this is too little for such a house. There is grief in it, as if the house itself could see and feel and harbor wishes that could be dashed. It must know now that it will never again be so grand as the two who built it, just as we ourselves will never be so grand. I hope it does not resent me.

Like Gertrude, I am also sick, though I fear I am much worse. This is the last reason for writing to you. I might not live to tell you these things in their own good time. I was old to be having any more children. I was old the *last* time, with Oswald, who was born precisely nine months ago when the city itself was sick. Thousands dying around him of all manner of contagion, and yet Oswald remained considerate. He waited until we were safely removed from the city and out of the reach of the miasma bearing yellow fever and cholera and scarlet fever and measles, until we were safely settled on the other side of the lake, until it had become clear that we would never return to a city exactly as it was, until it was clear that we, the Hoods, had been changed, and only then did Oswald choose to come into the world. Such an awful time, and yet such a perfect birth. I was forty years old, I had no business having a baby. Even so, I was walking around the little fish camp the next day and, a week later, I admitted the General back into my bed.

Now, when we are poor but happy, after the best year of my life, I give birth to a little girl who takes most of me with her. I will not be coy about the blood. It ran from me as if I were a fount, a headwater. Everything was red and hot and humid in that room. It smelled like metal, I could taste it in the air. If not for the negress sent by my old friend Rintrah, I would have died I'm sure. But she made poultices and mumbled words in a broken tongue I could not understand, I suppose it was Houdou language though it might have been Latin. Or both. When the bleeding stopped they burned the sheets in the back courtyard. I remember hearing myself beg them not to burn so many sheets, that we had none to spare. I sounded tired, I think.

It's been three weeks and I am still very cold. I am shivering, though it is April and the sweet olives are sending off their scent, which drifts in on the river breeze. I have a fever, the negress says, but I will not die from it. How does she know? She stands at the foot of my bed, freckles dashed across her cheeks and hair up in a green tignon, eyes constantly blinking and round like a doll's. She rocks from side to side, saying her blasphemous Mass, and I am comforted. She says I will not die yet. *Good*. But I will take no chances.

There are things I must explain to you. You should know how we have become who we are. You should be *proud* to be a Hood, to be one of these Hoods. There wasn't always a good reason to be proud, but now there is. You will understand. Let me begin.

I remember taking the coupé out and over to Esplanade, through the faubourgs and between the saplings, the day before you were born, Lydia. It was John's idea. His first child, and I suppose all he could remember were the cows of his Kentucky boyhood, and so he went out to exercise his woman and encourage you along. Perhaps he thought I would drop you in a nice, soft pile of hay miraculously deposited on the wayside? I asked him this, and he blushed. (Have you seen him blush? He can, you know.) I laughed and he laughed and it was grand. Scandalous. The delicate and properly appointed Creole ladies gawked at me, bouncing along swollen and sweating. John smiled as if he'd won a great prize. The ladies yapped like terriers and shied away from us in a spray of skirts, as if they could catch whatever had so obviously addled our brains. I was a Creole gone mad. I was a white Creole, a new distinction that hadn't been nearly so important before the war. A *white* Creole expecting her child would lie on lounges in dark corners berating the service, the consommé, the pharmacist, and her husband. Birth, that consuming pain measured in brief moments of sweetness, was an evil visited upon the white Creole lady. Such ladies did not ride about, and certainly not alone with their husbands. The *colored* Creole women either didn't complain, or we just never heard about it. Our city, Lydia, is full of silliness.

John was scared. Hard to tell behind the tattered curtain of beard, but it was true. Of death? It is strange that while a life gathers we think of death, but it was inescapable. I'm sure it crossed his mind. I thought of it very little.

I believe he thought that you and any other child would appear into the world broken, ashamed of him, and implacable. That you would bear his mark and never forgive him for it. The truth of John Bell Hood, and what made it possible to love him, was that he cared what you thought of him. You, little you, Lydia. He would fight others over what they thought of him, but he did not love them. And Lord, do not think he *spoke* of love! To name it would turn it against him, or cause it to fall apart. *Better not to say* is the twin of *Better not to know.*

A man pulled his carriage out of a porte cochere just as John gave the horses their head, urging them on so that I would laugh at the way his whiskers blew over his shoulder. The horses stumbled in the dirt and nipped each other. I fell forward against the console before John could yank me back.

The man in the carriage looked at us, stared briefly at me, and told John he was a drooling fool with no business on his street. *En français,* of course.

"What did he say, Anna?"

"He apologized."

"Did not sound like an apology."

The other man stepped down, erect, gray, girded in black like a smokestack. *Unblemished.* I am sorry to write that word, but it is what I remember. It is what I always thought when I saw John next to another man. John stepped down from our coupé. Heavily. He leaned toward his left leg, away from the wooden one, and in that position his left arm, half useless, hung down, straight and unmoving. While John composed himself, he could sometimes look as if he might fall apart, especially when he was angry and his face glowed red as if from the effort to hold his pieces together. But he moved very quickly. The tall man stepped back and soiled his heel in a puddle.

"Did you wish to speak to me, sir?" John's blue eyes disappeared into a squint.

"No, no. *Non*."

"I believe you do."

"It is over. Please go back to your wife."

"I do not take . . ."

John was near to telling the old man that he would not be ordered, that *he* would give orders and that the man had angered him and would not be allowed to retreat unscathed. Then, at that very moment, the creases in his face sloughed off and he stood placid and silent before the Creole. I watched. I knew what he was thinking, what he was willing himself to think: *Perhaps he is right. Return to Anna Marie. I foreswear the fight. I refuse.* It was a litany, words he forced upon himself as others might force the *Bona Mors* upon themselves at their own deathbeds.

Something in him had died, and something

better had grown in its place, right there where John now stood. He bowed his head and limped back to the coupé without speaking. He looked at me. I saw blue, pure blue. He sat up on the driver's box and quietly waved the old Creole on. The other, puzzled, took the reins and drove off. John put his good hand lightly on my leg and in a whisper asked if I had been hurt. I said no. We drove off slowly, this time quietly admiring the sweet, drifting scent of orange trees in bloom.

That was the General, not as I'd met him, but as he came to be. He could do nothing but fight. It was his character. But he had learned to find different sorts of fights. He fought for love, for instance. Believe me when I say he didn't understand the first thing about love when we met. But with love, the struggle replenishes, the combatant rarely fails to rise. You were born the next day, our first child.

I hope that you never leave this city. I hope you will love it as I have, imperfectly, inconstantly, but passionately. I am captured by this town of my ancestors, by the heat and milky bright light, by the smell of sweet olives. There has been little for me but this city. I wonder if I could breathe the air outside New Orleans, whether I would drown. Has any person ever been so perfectly formed by such a small place? It can't be left behind: the streets I walked on, the doors I entered, the steeples I navigated by, the bright and ringing crystal I raised to my lips, the river, the carriages, the gliding crowds of nuns. I could see myself laid out in every direction, street for blood and building for bone. I am glad of this place only because I could not survive anywhere else.

I remember days in my peignoir, reclining below the window, the breeze lying on me and gliding over me, the men on the banquette stealing glances and hurrying off, eyes cast down. This was New Orleans, too, the city I had made. A funny city arrayed between the flesh and the cross. Paris had been that way, though older and weighed down by centuries. *Its* flesh sagged, *its* crosses gathered dust, but my home was young and avid for both cross and flesh. None of those men passing by my window and stealing glimpses of the girl draped in lace would have guessed I had a volume of Livy open in my lap, and a slender copy of *Songs of Innocence and of Experience* under my pillow. I was a young woman and all around me things ripened when I passed, or they were made new again.

This was the woman who married your father, who met him at another senseless ball, another night of light across dark gardens, sweet dough frying, the hollow thump of my shoes on thick carpet, violins glistening on the shoulders of black-suited young men. The geometry of the parquet stretched out in every direction, uninterrupted by the twirl and slide of bodies orbiting each other like planets, their gravities stronger every minute. The servants laughed and made jokes at the top of the stairs, performing their own dance and coming together by their own physical laws. They spoke French.

No, this is not precisely the woman who met your father. I must try again. Why do I write this? It is this pen. It is smooth and black, edged in gold with a gold nib. It fits my hand perfectly, as if it isn't there. I've never noticed it before, but how many inanities have I forced through it onto paper? Thousands. Letters and notes crossing the city year after year. Have I written anything to remember me by? This pen questions me. Will I write something of use? It is a beautiful pen.

You could not understand the girl who met the General without meeting the girl who flung her clothes off for the thrill of being watched, who remained chaste even so, and who slippered about the streets like a Helen without a war and no idea how to start one. Silly girl, I still love her. But do not let me catch you posing nude for old men, Lydia. I have friends at a convent that would take you, *chère*.

I was a young woman but still a child, stepping along the banquettes with my dress caught up in my hand to avoid the mud and the sharp corners of the boxes piled everywhere. Young and beautiful. What has happened to that skin, that shiny hair? Who was that girl? I hardly recognize her now. She was buoyed by desire, it carried her down toward the opera house: her desire and the desire of the men who lingered in the dissipating fog of her lavender scent. I remember that she wanted to be touched, and yet on every block down Royal and over toward the Opera she was not even brushed in passing. Crowds parted, children ceased their jump roping, delivery boys gave wide. I was the blushing, buxom figurehead of a cutter parting the sea of mortals. I trembled. So much power.

This is what I remember. The truth is lost, and unimportant anyway. This is what I remember: I was walking to meet a man who had promised that no one would ever know my name, that he would be discreet. I looked classical and Greek, he said, and I felt it. I had power bestowed on me in curves and color and angles. I had little idea of what to do with it, what I was expected to do with it, what others did with it. The only idea I had, a dream really, was of soft, dark tapestries encircling me and a man, some man powerful and deep-eyed. We fell and fell without end in sweet air. I knew nothing of such things, of course, and so I found myself skipping along the banquette to a rendezvous with a failed painter. Posing for him seemed obvious.

The little man was pocked and the corners of his mouth were wet. He wore black, his legs were bowed and thin. Bent and charred twigs. I lay on his chaise while he fiddled with the stove, cursing it until it warmed. He made tea. I heard the cups nervously twittering on their plates when he came back into the room. I took pleasure in saying I was not thirsty. I was cruel. I had draped my clothes over his washbasin, as there were no chairs. The yellow satin drape fit me perfectly, and I arranged it as I'd seen in sculpture. Modestly at first. He stood behind his easel and unknotted his cravat. There were no other paintings in his room, a third-floor garret around the corner from the Opera with a view of the muddy river. I smelled fish and burning sugar, wonderful scents to me now. He scratched at the canvas with a brush he held like a pen. He asked me to pull the drape down and I pulled it down to my waist. I gathered my hair behind my head and leaned on one hand. The other traced my hip. He came over to adjust the drape, and when I felt his hand sliding across me, I bit him. He yelled and I screamed theatrically. He begged me to silence. I put on my clothes while he stood in the corner, staring. There was no paint on the canvas. He asked me to have mercy on a forgotten man.

I am not cruel, but I was very cruel that day. How could I know what I possessed without seeing it reflected in someone else's face, in the way they walked toward me, in the way they cowered? I was rapt during my walk home. It had been a joy, a secret had been revealed. I was mindless of anything but the fast-expanding boundary of my world, so much so that I neglected the mud and the nails in the boxes piled along my way. When I arrived home, disheveled and dirty, trailing threads of my dress like a ruined train, my mother thought I'd been attacked. *I fell,* I told her, and giggled.

Silly little girl. Had I been an ape with a bosom the old man might have still invited me up to his studio. The intoxicated mind sees what it desires everywhere. And how long did I think I could play the coquette? Not forever. I write this now while listening to one of my ten, soon to be eleven, children pulling another's hair. Perhaps that child is you, Lydia.

My city: Fat men in vests trading cotton and rice straight from the quay. The horses in their stalls at the fairgrounds. Smoke on the streetcar, watermelon cast into the water of the St. John by playful boatmen. Drunk men, men with monkeys, men without shoes, men without sense, men in tall hats and thick beards. Mandolins on the galleries. Beautiful boys, deformed boys, strong boys. Christ in every possible pose and dress, in every church, on every street, above every rambling of headstones. *Corpus. Iesus nazarenus rex iudaeorum.* King of the Creoles. King of the Spanish. King of the Irish, the Germans, the English, the *américain.* King of the Negroes. Christ everywhere. Christ above me, Christ below me, Christ at my right hand, Christ at my left hand. The Creoles had their cathedral, and then the Irish. Even the Germans built their own big church down by the tracks near the wharf. We prayed. Flowers sprouted in walls, through walls, around walls. All things grew. We picked sprigs of jasmine and set them behind our ears. We gaped at the dirty girls with bright white teeth hawking Creole tomatoes down along the market. In the faubourgs, we knew a place where the old quadroon slept beneath her awning and served good coffee and cold milk. Palms rattled and scraped, dry and green, in the air above her. We craved her chicken, baked in rosemary and served with cress.

I smoked cigars and rode horses. I rode them fast so that the gaudy new houses lately raised by Americans in our neighborhood— Creoles called it *the country*—would streak together until they were indistinguishable and mere sloppings of color. Mud in my hair and on my nose, hooves clattering over canal bridges. Riding away from town, the wilderness stretched to my right. There were trails, and at night, campfires ringed by men in foreign clothes cackling nonsense. Italians and Germans. Sometimes there were families of negroes, but they had no campfires and tried to hide from me. They were like

Indians. I smiled at them. I was not the law, I thought.

I now know that I was naïve, and that the law always follows certain of us whatever our intentions. It was good that I was also a private girl and hated telling anyone anything about my adventures. The negresses often had children at their breast and others sitting by or climbing the old knotty cypresses. During the day they were alone. I brought them what I could sneak out of the house, usually bonbons. Sometimes it was pralines made by the colored women down at the market. They were little things, luxuries, ridiculous things of no value in the deep woods of their exile.

Do not think too much of your mother, do not think she was a particularly charitable or kind girl. Those people in the woods were my playthings, my amusements. My father never caught me carrying off supplies into the woods, though I'm sure he suspected.

This was the way we maintained civility amid cruelty: we'd rather not know, and we wished there was nothing to know in the first place.

I cast myself out from my family, although they never ceased their efforts to bring me back. I roamed, I ate ices straight from the

Italians making them on the street, I studied dirt. I loved my family, but I would not be their possession. I hope they understand that now.

I fell in with other outcasts and they became my family. Michel Martin, who you know as Father Mike, Rintrah King the clown, and the lovely fine-fingered and light-footed boy who had named himself Paschal Girard because no one had bothered to gift him a name. He was a boy of other worlds, a hunter of fairies and fleeting beauty.

The most important thing that ever happened to me, the thing that changed my life and eventually your father's, long before we were married, happened the night the four of us—Michel, Rintrah, Paschal, and I—first came together as mere children. Nothing about my life was the same afterward. I sometimes wish it had never happened, but now I cannot imagine who I would have become without them.

I went to the backswamp as I've told you I liked to do. I was older then, older than you, old enough to have become a woman and still young enough to trust in the protection of my horse and in my mastery of the close dark of the backwoods paths I knew by heart.

Michel, one of the altar boys in our parish, followed me that night on foot. We had been at Mass, and as I was dipping my fingers in the holy water on my way out, Michel drew me into an alcove guarded by a blue Virgin.

"Why do you run?"

"I don't live here at the church, Michel. My bed is at home, and that's where I will be soon."

"I long to be in that bed."

"You would not be in it long. Father would toss you out quick enough."

"So you would have me to bed except for your father?"

"Except for my father and the fact that I have no earthly idea why I would want you in my bed."

"Do you not? Really?"

"No."

"I love you."

"You are a silly boy. I'll go now."

"Come outside with me."

"No."

"To the woods."

Always so brazen, he was.

"Hmmm. What do you think, blessed Mother of God who looks over Michel's shoulder? You look so sweet this evening. Guide me, Holy Mary. Is this the boy, and do you approve of love in the dark wood with a drunk boy, rolling around on the sticks and vines?"

"Who's drunk?" He smiled and sniffed at his robes. He was still an altar boy. Years before he had discovered where Father Achille kept his liquor, and now Mass was always great fun for Michel. But I knew that he would not like the idea of the Virgin overhearing his rather clumsy seduction. He was a boy who thought it was possible to hide from God so long as he wasn't in sight of His monuments, His churches, steeples, tombs, and priests. He was a boy who thought enough of the Lord to hide.

How old was I, perhaps fifteen? I knew Michel had enjoyed the favors of girls and women. He was bigger than most men. I had seen him swimming in the Bayou St. John, and I knew his body. He was broad and thick, his arms were brown and violent and tense. Webs of veins lay upon his forearms when he turned them up to the sky and called upon God to bless his swimming hole. He joked that he was John the Baptist, but I believe now that it was not much of a joke. He had a beard before he was sixteen.

He was an outcast in his own home, among

his family. He had grown up outside, very rarely and briefly allowed inside, never walked on their worn rugs or sipped from their glass. He took his meals on their back stoop and studied his letters and Scripture by lamp while battling the mosquitoes and moths and beetles drawn to him. His father, the sweet and jolly clerk, believed in sin and the personification of sin, and he saw sin in his son. He saw sin in a son who had been four years old when he was first exiled to the yard. The father had been afraid of the son, afraid of contamination. His wife believed it, too, though she always took great care with the food she set out on the back step, and found the best tent available once Michel outgrew the lean-to. Now the son was bigger than the father and could force himself upon the household if he liked, but he chose to stay outside. When it rained, there was always the church.

I should have known not to trifle with him in that alcove, or to call on the Holy Mother in his presence. I knew better, but I was also a young woman who wanted to feel her own force, to see it move about in the world. Michel wanted to join me in my bed, and I wanted to make him suffer for it. My mistake was thinking that my bed, or more likely the little clearing in back of the church property, was the only destination he had in mind.

"You'll have to catch me." I said this knowing that he had no horse and wouldn't know how to ride one if he had managed to steal one. He had very little, Michel did.

"I will."

I rode off expecting that the next time I saw Michel would be at Sunday Mass.

It was October, I remember that because the oaks were beginning to turn and the air was clean and light and sharp. The mosquitoes and june bugs were gone, and I could ride as hard as I wanted and not feel them against my face, only the cool, moist air. I clattered past Creole families lounging on broad porches, and American families sitting down to suppers of cold chicken and biscuits steaming and covered in lace. In the twilight so much was clear, I thought I could see through walls.

I was agitated. I was not used to thinking of a boy's body on mine, I was not accustomed to my curves or the hot, nervous sweetness of imagining a man fitted to those curves—the hard and violent desires. I suppose I rode longer because I was thrilled by the knowledge of desire, if not by the particular boy doing the desiring. I had no interest in Michel Martin.

He was my childhood friend, the image of him thrashing about upon me only made me laugh. But the idea of such thrashing, in general, would not leave me be.

I rode into the backswamp, taking my paths, spying the stars through the branches. Venus hung just over the treetops, Jupiter seemed to be running away, off to the south. I could smell the sweet rot, the heaviness of the forest air, as if the trees were breathing out the fine dust of bark and dirt and leaves and dark swamp tea. I went deeper along the paths, deeper than usual. I let the branches reach out to me and stroke my cheeks and batter my arms. One caught my blouse and pulled it open at the neck. The wind cooled me and my blouse billowed behind me. I untucked it. Squirrels raced me through the understory, shouting at me to go back, go back. I came across the campfire.

A dwarf and a thin, tall boy sat on rotted logs. I skittered into their camp, which had been pitched without much thought across a well-traveled path and not off the trail far into the underbrush. They looked up at me over their spitting, smoking, wet fire. At their feet lay old canvas laundry bags filled with what little they had chosen to take with them, each bearing a rough cross in blue paint. It was a dream, I thought. The tall boy smiled sweetly when he rose to his feet. His head was perfectly round and poorly clipped. He had bald spots, as if he'd tried to cut his own hair. The dwarf's hair was blond and similarly haphazard. I dismounted and saw that he was tall as my waist and possessed of great and powerful hands. He scowled at me and balled those hands as if to strike.

"Pardon me," I said. "Do you know you are camped on the path?"

"Why are you here?" said the dwarf. "Leave us alone. Who sent you?"

"I ride this path often. You're in *my* way."

He had huge blue eyes and a stub nose. He'd lost one bottom tooth, which made him seem even more feral. Every bit of him was belligerent and tense and ready to spring.

"Rintrah, stand down," the taller one said. "She's just a girl."

"She looks like a novice to me. Sent by the nuns."

The tall boy picked up a dented old coffeepot that had been sitting in the fire. Inside it they had been boiling roots and onions. He offered me some, as if I'd come calling. He looked dumb, like a man who couldn't imagine harm coming to him, but I watched him inspecting the woods behind me, his eyes calmly moving side to side, and I knew he could take care of himself.

"Please, eat."

"I'm not hungry, but thank you."

The dwarf called Rintrah circled me.

"Yeah, she's rich. You can smell it."

"No you can't," the taller boy said.

"Yes I can."

It had been nearly a year since I'd run across travelers in the backswamp. And these two were unusual, even for travelers. They looked well fed, though I wasn't sure how far they'd get on roots and onions. They carried identical bags. I'd seen those bags before, or bags like them.

"You come from an orphanage," I said.

"We come from the loving embrace of our mothers, first," said the tall boy.

"You don't even know who your mother is, or which one of your parents was colored. How would you know?" The dwarf spoke quickly, and then realized he'd given away the truth to me. He glared in my direction again.

Paschal ignored Rintrah.

"My name is Paschal Girard, and it is a pleasure to make your acquaintance, ma'am."

I knew the trouble they were in, at least out there in the darkening swamp. They needed to get off the path, they needed to hide, they needed to know that the next person to run across them would not be a curious rich girl with a fondness for runaways and a fast horse. The swamp was where the men and women who could not live among humans lived, the murderers and pimps and houdou soul snatchers and slave stealers and highwaymen and the insane. The swamp protected all sorts, not just orphans.

"I will go for some more food, Paschal Girard. You should put out this fire and scatter it. Hide over there"—I pointed to the left, near an old cypress—"and wait for me. I will be back. But get off the path."

Rintrah had snuck around behind me and the horse and now leaped up out of the darkness to take the reins. He was quick and strong, and soon he was atop the horse. His legs stuck out and he had a devil of a time maintaining control of the horse.

"She was going to run for the constables, Paschal!" Rintrah shouted. "I knew it, we can't let her leave."

Paschal, who now looked obviously and instantly colored to me, poked around at the coals of the fire, spreading them out with an elaborately carved stick I hadn't seen before. A snake, in relief, wound its way up the cane and bared its fangs from the handle. It was painted red and black like the stuffed coral snakes wound up on our mantel at home, souvenirs of my father's youthful escape to Mexico. The boy watched the sparks float up into the trees. Some of them, by some miracle conspiracy of breezes, rose up through the canopy and into the air above the trees, yellow among cold white stars. He watched them, and I thought I saw him speak to them.

"She wasn't going to tell anyone, Rintrah," he said.

"How do you know? She got no use for men like us, people like her would rather people like us stay in our cells."

"It's not true," I said.

"I know," Paschal said. "Get off the horse, Rintrah. Give it to the lady."

My horse didn't much like the odd little man fidgeting on her back, and so she began walking sideways around the fire pit, running him through a gauntlet of old cypress branches. Rintrah spit out the fine cypress leaves that lodged in his teeth, but he refused to give up his mount. Finally my horse gave up and stood at the diminishing fire like one of the rest of us, fascinated by the glowing coals and the dancing sparks.

"I'll bring you food, candy, whatever you want," I said. "I've done this before."

"Oh ho! She's done this before!" shouted Rintrah, dutifully dismounting from the horse, which meant hanging on to the saddle, like a man clinging to the side of a ship, until he'd summoned the courage to fall to the ground. He dusted himself off. "I wonder how many poor fellas are in chains right now because of this girl. She's a hunter, don't make no mistake. I know the white people, Paschal, and she's a killer. She'll send us to the prison!"

Paschal just nodded, and then slapped Rintrah playfully across the back of his head. "We would be grateful for such a gift, but we would never expect such a thing. Perhaps it's best just to let you go on home and out of these woods. Lord, I didn't know they were so dark."

I walked toward the horse.

"We will meet you at the old, bent cypress you picked out. Please don't tell anyone else, and don't bring anyone with you."

I mounted.

"And hurry," Paschal said. "I'm scared of this place."

"Not me," said Rintrah, burning me with his eyes.

"Yes you are," Paschal said.

I rode off fast, urging the horse on and wiping the sweat from her beautiful neck. I bent over to avoid the branches. They were two boys running away from the nuns. They were well fed, they didn't seem terrified of what was behind them in the city like so many others I'd discovered in the woods. Perhaps they weren't running from anything in particular, but running *to* something. They were orphans. Some days I thought there wasn't a soul in the entire city who wasn't a cousin of mine, or married to a cousin, or in love with a cousin. I had no earthly idea what it would be like to be alone, no faces floating past to remind you of yourself. Of course I had wished I was an orphan on those days when every single thing I did or said registered with a member of the family who, *pardonnez*, thought my parents should know what their darling had done, *for her own sake, no?* But those two looked tired and resigned. As much as Rintrah had pretended he didn't need me, I had seen his eyes widen at the idea of real food.

I left the horse up the block, tied to a rigid plane tree, and snuck into the house. Thank God for thick rugs. Father had a cigar and a visitor in the library, and I could see him through a crack in the door as I glided past. *The negroes are human, friend, no mistake. That doesn't make me a nigger lover. There's nothing about being human that inherently recommends itself to me. I dislike most humans. Dirty grunting animals. I see no reason to burn them in their homes, though. Yes, yes, I know you had nothing to do with that. But it's not good for business, you must agree with that.*

Chocolates and a bit of dried pork shoulder, into the bag. Day-old bread. Blankets from the stable. I packed them tight in a tack bag. In the darkness every cricket and moth screamed at me, begged me to stop. *Go on upstairs, comb your hair, read something, fall asleep atop the lace coverlet, so cool.* Mother flipped the pages of her prayer book upstairs, always looking for the perfect prayer, never too long or too specific. I watched her through the window.

Back on the horse, I rode calmly back to the woods, not wanting to draw attention. I avoided the puddles that pushed up against the banquettes, afraid of the sound of the splash and the telltale wet trail behind. No one could follow me, they must not. *They could be killed, or taken prisoner.* I suppose I always thought that the negro families knew what they were doing, those who had made the swamp their rabbit hole, into which they would disappear and emerge free on the other side. I thought of them as born for escape, bred for escape, raised in the art of escape. I imagined that all negroes knew the way out, and all of them were marking time for their chance. But two orphans? They would never make it.

I heard the sound behind me but ignored it. Could have been a possum or coon. Leaves scraped against leaves, twigs cracked. The boys waited for me at the bent cypress. There was no time to indulge fear of the dark woods and its unfathomable sounds. Twigs cracked, the forest breathed, there was nothing to fear. A sweet lie.

I left the horse just off the path and walked the last stretch through the tripping underbrush. The bag became heavy, I could smell the pork swaddled in canvas. I would die of hunger, I thought.

Something scraped a branch and I hurried

the last few feet. Paschal and Rintrah sat with their backs to the trunk of the tree, on opposite sides as if they'd been fighting. Rintrah was the first to his feet, his nose in the air, a smile cracking his face.

"Ham, pig, pork. Yes, yes, yes."

Paschal told him to hush and grabbed the bag. I was surprised by this. He snatched it and twisted my arm a little. His face was stone, he didn't look at me. Rintrah praised me as a princess, a goddess, a seraphim of the highest order. He would write me songs, he said, and he began to make up words on the spot. His voice was low and resonant. Paschal grabbed him by the arm and shook him.

"We must leave, brother."

"But the chocolates?"

Paschal was already walking into the dark.

"This is rude, brother. Are you a gentleman or are you not? Because you blather on about the ways of gentlemen, and I have to tell you that you bore me with that talk, but I *tolerate* it, because I love you, brother, but now I know you have been wasting your breath and my time. Bring those chocolates!"

Now I heard it. I heard it clearly. Or rather, now I recognized it. Paschal had heard it and had disappeared. Rintrah had not heard it, or could not hear it over the sound of his delight. *The colored boy will make it, but not the dwarf,* I thought. The twigs snapped in rhythm, the leaves whispered across something broad and fast. Footsteps, a body shoving the forest out of its way.

"Hide, Rintrah. Hide! Now!"

"What?"

I had been followed. The beast crashed through the small clearing and on into the underbrush that had closed behind Paschal. Rintrah tried to climb the tree but fell. He whirled angrily, looking for something. There was Paschal's stick, and he took it up like a snake handler. I thought he would run the other way, but no: he marched after the beast. I was alone in the clearing.

There were shouts and thuds, curses and the wet slaps of fists. The beast roared and the others whimpered. I felt the trees shake, but it was only my own shoulders. I hugged them until they were still. My horse wandered off slowly, easily. I didn't go after her and I didn't go after Rintrah and Paschal, the lost boys. I stood waiting.

It was Michel, feral and massive, bent on murder. He dragged the two back to our tree, deposited them on the ground, and began to speak quietly.

"Which one of these things is yours, Anna Marie?"

He had followed me from the church, on foot. He would never have found me had I not gone home. Stupid. I was contagious, I had brought pain.

"Michel, stop this."

"It's the tall one, isn't it?"

Michel struck out with his boot, sharp at the toe, and buried it between Paschal's ribs. The boy couldn't breathe, but he would not look away from Michel, either. He stared at him, passively, and this enraged Michel. He kicked him again, and then lifted him up by his throat. It was like watching a cat maul a piece of string.

Rintrah had lost the snake stick. Tears of blood ran down from below his eyes where he had been cut. I tried to go to him but Michel held me back. Rintrah watched him paw me and got to his feet.

"I'll kill you," he said.

He ran at Michel and ducked a flying foot. He hit Michel in his privates and Michel howled before dropping Paschal and knocking Rintrah to the ground. Rintrah stayed down. I tried to go to him again, and Michel pushed me back.

"What is it about this one, Anna Marie?" he said, pushing Paschal back against the tree.

I made my great mistake then.

"He is a gentleman, that's why. He's graceful and you're a monster."

Michel turned to me, puzzled and surprised. I knew then that he hadn't expected an answer, or that I would make his path clear.

"Graceful? We'll see, mademoiselle."

He gently pushed Paschal to the ground, keeping his big mutton hand pressed against the poor boy's chest. He stared into Paschal, a curious frown on his face, as if he weren't sure what would happen next.

"Why, you're a colored boy."

Rintrah groaned and was motionless. I slapped Michel once, twice, three times, but I was alone, and when he told me to sit I obeyed. He turned back to Paschal, who watched him closely and without apprehension, as if he knew what was to happen but would be damned if he would enlighten Michel. He didn't struggle. Michel took his right foot and twisted it around as if winding a clock. Slowly, as if unwilling. Paschal tried to flip onto his stomach, to relieve the pressure,

but Michel stopped him with his boot. Paschal
watched, not saying a word. Michel put that
boot to the twisted knee and stepped down.
The knee popped and the leg went loose, detached. Paschal screamed silently and endlessly. The great *O* of his mouth might have
swallowed us all.

I screamed, too, only my scream sounded
out, deafening, piercing the rotted air and
coursing through branch and leaf. Michel laid
Paschal's leg down and sat heavily on the log
beside me. I spit on him and he didn't wipe it
off. He watched Paschal, who could not move.
The pain pinned him there, I guessed, between the cypress knees and below the dark.
His breath was quick and exploded from him,
but he did not scream. He cried, silently.

Rintrah gathered himself and crawled
over to Paschal. Paschal closed his eyes and
fainted. I got up to run and Michel held me.
He watched Rintrah, who ran his hand over
his friend's leg, his forehead, his arm. He
went into one of their bags and pulled out
a bladder of water, which he poured over
Pascal's head and into his mouth. He moved
the ruined leg and Paschal's hand shot out
and throttled him until he let go. Rintrah
turned to us and stared, crouched on his

haunches, running his hands through his thin hair.

They were hog-tied to each other from that moment on. Michel knew it, he knew it as he sat holding me roughly by the arm and returning Rintrah's stare. They spoke silently to each other, in the language of orphans. Who did they have to come rescue them, to fix them, to set them on the right path? Who would tell them what to do, who gave a damn? Michel was an orphan of sorts. The great bear, the tumescent beast, drunk and pawing, had grown up in a lean-to outside his parents' house.

"You didn't come out to see him, did you?" Michel said, not looking at me.

"No. Not at first."

"You came to help him. Them."

"Yes." He scared me. I thought we would all be killed, perhaps. We had to be killed now, he'd committed a crime, we were witnesses. Michel and I had been children together, but that had no meaning anymore. Not children now. He had seen something in Paschal at the last moment, even before maiming him. He had recognized something, but it wasn't enough to stop him. Now he laid his great head in his hands and wept.

I watched Rintrah pick up the rock and

didn't stop him. I didn't watch, either. I heard the dull thud, the swallowed cry, and the slow crackle of the bush behind us collapsing under Michel's weight.

Now we were two. Rintrah told me to sit still, not to move, and that he would get the horse. He stumbled off, cursing all of us. I found a long, straight piece of an oak branch, and I began to bind Paschal's leg with strips of cloth torn from the clothes in his bag. He woke three times to shout at me, each time passing out from the effort. I felt his strong, long leg beneath his trousers, another perfection, and this only made me sadder. Michel had ruined something beautiful.

"Don't tie the bindings so tight on him."

Michel was on his hands and knees, shaking his head as if to fling something from it. Mud and rotted leaves clung to the back of his head, his hands.

"I think you shouldn't tell me what to do anymore, Michel. You're mad. You're evil."

"Perhaps, but I know that if you tie it too tight he'll lose the leg."

"And wasn't that your intention? Why should I trust you now?" I loosened the bindings even so.

"Don't know what my intention was. I was

angry. Natural." He paused and dropped his head so it kissed the ground. "Natural, Lord."

Rintrah came back, stomping through the clearing. No horse. He jumped upon seeing Michel and raised his fists. Michel nodded his head.

"Hit me, yes. I deserve it."

"You deserve worse."

Off to our right, in a clearing surrounding some open water, I saw the flash of two white egrets lifting off from the edge of their domain and flying bent-necked into branches high above. They were only flashes of white in starlight, bright and then gray and then gone. They were imperfections of the dark, denying it while absorbed in it. The woods opened, every shadow possessed a light, in every direction there was a way out. Then the light went down and closed each way in turn, until I was back again with the three boys, Michel apologizing to Rintrah and Rintrah circling him, spitting insults.

"Will you all please, *s'il vous plait,* quit gabbling and carry me out of here?" Paschal's voice came through gasps. "I can't stay here. I shall die."

Rintrah walked over and tried to help him up, but it was impossible.

"We're not going to get away, are we, Paschal?"

"No, I don't think so, brother, not now."

Without a word Michel got to his feet, picked the boy up tenderly, and laid him across his shoulders. He was gentle and spared Paschal every bump and stumble, always supporting the leg he had just snapped. I didn't know why he cared so suddenly about the other boy's pain. He mumbled to himself, and occasionally the breeze carried back bits of prayer, the familiar Latin lilt of the dimly lit altar, the comfort of the priest's dark and murmuring box. He had so much to confess, it was true, but I'm still not certain why that confession began at that moment in those woods. He had done worse in his short life. He had beaten and stabbed men twice his age, he had waded into bars swinging his fists in every direction, if the rumors were true. He was all instinct and fire and power and sinew, a rage. He had always lashed out, though, at those he thought mocked him or took advantage of him. Perhaps now he'd seen how close he had come to the murder of an innocent, the mortal sin. I never found out, and he never volunteered the story of his epiphany. Paschal and Rintrah never talked about it either.

He said to Paschal, over and over again, "I'll get you there. I'll get you there. . . ."

I carried their orphanage bags, and Rintrah got the pork and the sweets. We followed behind and talked shyly. They had run away from the orphanage because they, the oldest boys, were to be signed over by the end of the week to merchant ships as apprentice seamen. They had grown up together, the two oddities: one dwarf, one nameless colored boy. They called each other brother and meant it. They'd thought they could run someplace else, far out of New Orleans, and live a different life. They had planned their escape for weeks, afraid that if they weren't smart they'd be found and dragooned by the merchant captains. Rintrah was particularly afraid of what he would become on board a ship. *What they gonna do with me? I ain't no toy, ain't gonna be a toy of any kind.* They'd picked that day as their one chance, and but for meeting me, they would have spent the next day slipping through the swamp and up the bayou until they were far from the city, and then they would have gone north. Maybe Chicago, Rintrah said, where the cattle lined the streets and a man could hide and make something of himself without always being gawked at.

That was over. We marched them back into the city.

Michel carried Paschal to the church and handed him over to the priests and nuns, who kept him out of the orphanage and tended him. Michel said he'd found him fallen out of a tree, and Paschal never said otherwise.

A week later Michel walked into St. Louis Cathedral, barged into the bishop's office, got on his knees, and prayed loudly for the blessing of the vocation. The bishop, no small man himself, slapped Michel across the face and Michel smiled. This is what he told me years later. What I know for sure is he didn't throw the bishop through the narrow, gray window of his office chamber, that the bishop took him on as his special project, that after some years Michel became Father Mike, and that Father Mike never quit paying for the sin he committed that night in the swamp.

I didn't, either, now that I think about it. Always paying for that now. I'm glad of it. Yes, I am.

Neither Paschal nor Rintrah left the city again. Michel left it only briefly, to attend Assumption Seminary down in Bayou Lafourche, but he quickly returned. I went to France to study, and there I was finished, as they say of girls like me. When I returned I returned for good, and before meeting your father, the only three people I cared for in this city were the boys who had fought in the swamp that day.

I tell you this because I want you to know that your dear *maman* was not always surrounded by children, not always *bien souffrante*, not always waddling about bearing her belly before her like a great round shield. I was not always this way, the boundaries of the world were not always the gates of the General's house. I saw and remembered everything. I did not know then how to fix a cough or calm a fever, but I could dance.

The General. John. I shall call him that here. He's John whenever we are out of your hearing. *John*. The General John Bell Hood, leader of men, stung and maimed by men, abandoned by men. That was the General when I met him.

He makes much of that first ball. He tried to dance with my cousin's friend, but he slipped just as they were to turn and pass. He caught himself with the cane he had hung over his arm, paused, and escorted the girl, a flitting little bird, back to her seat with my cousin. He bowed low to her and said nothing. He carried the war with him like a ratty coat that invokes both pity and silence. The silence, I think, drove him crazy. I suppose he thought that after all that he had done, all that he had suffered, that he would be thanked, at least forgiven his strangeness and his deformities. It took him some time to understand that he would never be thanked in the way he hoped, with genuine love, and that deformity would be pitied but not forgiven. No one thanks the executioner, they wish he would stay out of sight. The cripples too.

He knew this, but who can resist a dance? A ball is a great pretending, an imagined thing. All ladies are beautiful, all men are gracious and handsome, all flowers are fresh and all music is perfect. It is a beastly lie. A ball is a fantasy dreamed up and populated by humans, and humans are hard even when they pretend they aren't. They spin and glide and tell themselves wonderful stories, but their feet don't ever leave the ground. I've looked.

Mother would have said that the man was lost, meaning lost to *us,* not to himself, what he thought of himself was of little importance.

He was not dead, he had merely never been born, and anyway, I was not raised to cavort (that would have been her word for it) with men so rough and so awkward. I was to concern myself only with men of possibility, who understood the subtle ways of the Creole world and who knew how to dress themselves and pick out flowers and avoid death at duel. I'm sure such men bored her as much as they bored me, and certainly my father was no such man. *But your father was the exception, he was a different sort of* américain. *He was too large and grand for the Creoles, but he was a man of consequence. He was grand! And yes he was rough, but he could be trained! Remember that. The training he took!* She and I were very much alike, though she would not admit it.

I think I haven't described John as I saw him, only as the others saw him, and as Mother would have seen him. But I saw him, too, and I watched closely. I saw a man who went off to sit by himself and watch us dance, shunned from the conversation, and who seemed to accept that fate. He was used to it, he accepted it, and yet there was more to it than that. He watched the bodies twirling by, the flying blooms of purple and yellow brushing the floor, and he seemed to take pleasure in our happiness and in our beauty, even if he seemed to possess none of his own. He smiled slightly and drew his shoulders in humbly and looked up at us. I stopped dancing and stood near my cousin, whose billowing dress hid me while I spied on him. He tapped his cane to the music, a fiddled quadrille, and made himself small. He moved to the dark corner of the settee in the foyer where few could see him. He watched and he watched. Later he told me that a reviled man could not take for granted the moments of otherwise forbidden beauties, and so he didn't think of himself as ill-treated, but mostly blessed. Sad and blessed. Someday you will know people like that, the sad and the blessed, and they will be saints or they will be thieves. Possibly some of both.

That night I left my cousin to her talk of chivalry and rare blue African fabrics and walked over to John. It was a dream, I didn't know I was walking until I was halfway there. I heard my cousin call out to me but I knew that if I turned or stopped I would never make it, I would turn back and end my life old and draped in black lace, nattering on with my cousin as always, probably about our disappointing grandchildren. I wondered if my mother had felt the same way when she took the big paw of Duncan Hennen. *Get me away,* that's what I thought.

He watched me walk toward him, and when I came close he struggled to his feet, pressing hard on his cane. I didn't know then that he had lost a leg.

"Thank you," he said. Those were the first words between us.

"For what?"

"For being kind. It's not common, you know."

"How do you know I'm being kind?" I sat down at the other end of the settee and swept the gathered folds of my pink dress close to me. We sat pressed against our ends of the settee, as if each thought the other contagious.

"Because the woman over there, the one staring with her mouth dropped open, she looks like you. The one you were standing behind. She watched you come over here, and I don't think you saw this, but she took a couple steps. To stop you. If you're here to make a joke of me, then she's not in on the joke, and if I'm not missing my mark, she appears to be exactly the type of person who would love a joke on a cripple. So you're not here to amuse your friends. Also, you're looking me in the eye, and kind people do that."

I was. But God, his eyes! They were not the blue you see in the eyes of men. They were wet and deep and clear, the blue of the sky reflected in a clear creek. There were clouds in them too. I should be forgiven for looking him in the eye, though it was not demure or proper.

"I am not making a joke of you, you're right. I'm not sure why I would, what is there to have fun about with you? Are you famous?"

He could only move one of his arms properly. The other hung at his side, bent permanently. He draped his good arm over the back of the settee and leaned toward me. Now the eyes were darker blue. They changed shade, I swear it!

"Not famous enough, obviously."

That arm was powerful, his chest was broad, his face was long. And that beard, that silly old beard. I thought it made him look old, like an old billy goat. I could not see his mouth, only the mustache moving. He was a man, not like the fops. He was a foreign creature and mesmerizing. I forgot about my cousin.

"But you should not assume I'm being kind, either."

"I choose to assume it anyway."

"I am not kind."

"I assume it because otherwise there would be no hope for this party, and because I want you to be kind. To me, if that's not too forward."

I heard a shout from the entrance to the ballroom, the scrape and clang of men with canes and swords, but it was soon washed away in the ocean roar of the blood rushing to the tips of my ears and, I assumed, the tops of my cheeks. I could feel the heat there. *Good Lord,* I thought, *who is this man?*

"And your name, sir? I require the names of the men to whom I extend that sort of charity." I was trying to parry, but my wit had fled me. It was good that he did not appear to hear me. He had stood again, looking toward the door.

"Please excuse me, Miss Hennen, I shall return in a moment."

He knew my name. Of course he did. He was not a creature of this world. I watched him limp quickly to the door, where a man in a uniform, a Federal officer, was trying to gain entrance. His way had been barred by two young men, one of whom I knew had fought in the late war. Swords were half unsheathed when John got there.

I didn't hear what he said. But I could see that when he spoke all three of them listened intently. His face flushed and looked angry, but he kept his voice too low for anyone else to hear. Some of the dancers stopped to watch, or to join in, but when he looked up at them stone-eyed they beat a retreat and spun around the dance floor again, looking glad to be out of his way. The three who had been on the point of a fight straightened while he talked, and sheathed their swords. They looked down like little boys caught fooling with Papa's guns. He dismissed the two Creoles and took the uniformed man aside. Always talking, never allowing an interruption. Finally the man nodded his head, saluted, and stepped out into the night. By now the news of the near battle had spread and the music had quieted for a moment. People watched as John walked back. Back to me, I realized of a sudden. Then they watched me, too, and my cousin let her mouth drop open and tried to mouth something to me I couldn't make out. He sat down at his end of the settee again, in the dark. He spoke.

"You asked me something before, Miss Hennen."

"Who are you?"

"John Hood."

"That's all, John Hood?"

He looked back toward the doorway and sighed.

"General John Bell Hood, of the late Confederate States of America."

I slid closer to him so I could hear properly, and I didn't care what my nattering cousin thought.

"They knew you."

"Yes they did."

"So you *are* famous enough."

"Famous isn't quite the right word."

"Respected."

"Feared is another way of putting it."

Could a man be so arrogant as to think that men feared him, and also be gentle and grateful that someone had walked across the floor to sit with him? He was either two men or one man of two worlds. I could see this in the way he hid his mangled arm from me and snuck glances at the door, on watch for the other, the harder thing, the one that had maimed him and plunked him down in a dark corner of a bright and perfumed ballroom. He looked at me and his face sagged and relaxed, as if he had just shifted a great weight. I knew that one of the men in John Bell Hood, or one of his worlds, would not hold on much longer.

May it be the other one that dies, I thought, and not the soft and funny man I imagined he contained within, the kind man, the man of nearly childlike enthusiasms and hopes I believed was sitting on the settee with me. I had prayed to meet such a person, but I hadn't thought he would be so strange.

After the ball he came to court me. Father, a big man with perfect olive skin who wore ties with perfect knots, was nonplussed by the man. He had been *trained* to be skeptical of the *américains,* you see, though they were not such different men. Here, on his doorstep, was a general, a commander of men, large and wire-haired and thick and wounded, asking after his daughter. Father always gave John a good cigar, but left him to snip the ends himself, which was difficult because of John's ruined left arm. Father noticed, but let him struggle anyway. I'm not sure if this was cruel or respectful.

My parents had known since I was a girl that I'd do what I wanted to do whether I had their blessing or not, so they gave John and me permission to be seen together in public. In public, where their army of aunts and servants and cousins and friends moved about and made their notes. Had John and I been forced to meet on the sly, in the dark, in the underworld of the city where there was music and drink and places to kiss under great spreading figs in secret courtyards, my parents' army of spies would have been lost, blind. In the daylight I wore my finest day dresses and maintained a respectable distance from John when we walked, down by the riverside and up Esplanade Avenue, then back down toward the market for tomatoes and oranges. I would not be denied the pleasure of a kiss under the fig tree, though, nor the thrill of disappearing into the dark with my man to see the riverboat men play for extra cash in the saloons where the colored girls sang. I would sneak out, tell lies, dress plain and dark like the servants who walked across the city to clean the houses of my people, all those coloreds and Irish and Germans. My parents wouldn't have to know everything.

When we'd been courting for a few weeks, I began to show him our streets. He had been a country child, and then a man who lived on horses and slept on the ground. I don't know that he'd ever walked the streets of a city. Perhaps Richmond, but what was there to see there? He was embarrassed by his limp, but soon, after many months and miles along streets he could not pronounce, his leg became strong and he hardly wobbled on that wooden pin once he had a little speed.

We met boys recruiting clients for the opium houses and others recruiting souls for the Church. They spoke French like Creoles and English like Irishmen.

There was a dwarf, a fruit seller who also sold tips on the horse races, and this man became his friend. On the Rue Chartres we'd find him, wide-legged upon a fruit crate, pulling at his great mustache, greased and black, shouting about his pomegranates.

A typical Saturday morning:

"General! I've got oranges and I need the money."

"You dress better than I do, Rintrah."

"Yes, but who don't, mate? Got nothing to do with wanting to be buried proper. Expenses gone up."

"Surely they would give you a discount, friend? A volume discount?"

"I want a damned full-size coffin and a real grave marker. No one got to know my affliction when I'm dead. The marker don't got to say, 'Here is Rintrah, Who Could Walk Under Horses.' I'll be a man like any other. Now buy some oranges."

John enjoyed the moments with my little man, my friend. Rintrah looked every bit the gentleman down to his thin, delicate shoes. He wore black like a Creole and cocked his flat-top hat like an Irishman. Rintrah amazed and humbled John. He owned a house and carried a cane sword. He was not afraid, not to be seen nor to be threatened. He was strong. I know that John came to think of Rintrah as a superior, an example, a mentor. It was a measure of John's foolishness and sadness that he, at least at first, thought his afflictions matched Rintrah's.

I had known Rintrah for many years. We are the closest of friends, though we hardly see each other, not as we did long ago. Our friendship was nearly impossible to explain, at least to someone so new and innocent like John. Yes, innocent! Perhaps the most innocent man I ever knew, about nearly everything but killing and war. I worked hard to shatter that innocence, but he was hard to conquer.

At first I didn't tell John about my past, and neither did Rintrah. There was no point to it. The little man had not always been such an upstanding merchant, an example to crippled generals, but how to explain this? Goodness, Rintrah was not upstanding *then,* when John met him, and he never would be. Rintrah had his reasons for this, of course. So, John was missing a leg, yes, and most of the use of an arm. But what had Rintrah missed? He was always the little man, unable to hide. He had been given the part of the world no one cared about, the life below the gaze, the space that was dirty and untended, scuffed by boots and clad in an unceasing course of stucco and mortar. Above, out of sight, hid the delicate filigree of gable carvings, iron twisted into flowers, the reaching and grasping hands of saints lifted up to the Lord on tapestries and high into colored windows. Rintrah had seen these things, of course: propped up on a chair, lifted onto someone's shoulder, in a painting. The problem had not been that they were unattainable, but that they had not been meant for him. Nothing had, not out of spite but out of forgetfulness. The world of men forgot Rintrah. No one forgot the General, and it was the General's world even if he limped and clunked down the banquette. John thought Rintrah's hopes for death were jokes, the little man's way of banter. I knew Rintrah longed for death, and also that he would never hasten it. The idea that he would miss something, not see something he might have seen had he been more patient, had sickened him his whole life. He would not willfully cut short the chance he would see something new. So he waited for death to come to him, and then there could be no regret. In the meantime, he ruled his bright corner of the demimonde, a far more powerful man than most people knew. Boys twice his size spent their days running his messages through the Vieux Carré, spitting tobacco all the way.

I'm glad John came to enjoy his company. He was funny and interesting and watchful with Rintrah. John did not treat Rintrah as a curiosity. He silently bargained with the man that, if extended the same courtesy, he would treat Rintrah as a whole man unremarkable but for his wit. They would poke fun at each other, trade gossip, and part as men and not fellow cripples.

"You might want to get your own self measured for a box, General. You never know when the demon coming. Never."

"As long as he doesn't look like you, all is well."

"Can I have your leg when you go? I need to fix my banister."

Rintrah was but one of the landmarks of the street. I dragged John around to show him the city I had known. I told him I was merely offering the grand tour. The truth was that I wanted to be the one standing alongside him when he discovered the secret courtyards, the ecstatic rituals of death at Congo Square, the cabals of old warhorses endlessly plotting a French restoration while sipping liquor from small bottles at Maspero's. I wanted to explain the beauty and refinement of the brothels, the domains of the exquisite octoroons. I wanted to bring him to the Ursulines so that he would know the nuns and not fear them. I wanted to explain the plagues and the floods so that he would know we were only tested, not punished. I wanted him to sit in the wet courtyards below the palms and among the iron plants, hidden from sight and watching the sun carve its track across the unmarked sky. I wanted him to see and smell the swamp, to sense the miasma drifting out and among the town houses and cottages and American mansions, carrying threat and making us humble. I wanted him to see these things first, so I could explain. I *wanted* to explain. I wanted him to love it, filth and wonder and all, as I'd come to love it. I wanted him to stay so that I could stay beside him. I taught him a little French so that it would make sense when the old men cursed him on principle, for being American.

Whether he fell in love with the city or me, you'll have to ask him yourself. He stayed, whatever the reason, and we were married.

Does the reason matter? It does not when I wake and the light through the tall windows draws little dark shadows in the crevasses of John's muscular, broad shoulder and back. He stirs, the bed trembles, and I can hear the rough sheets of cotton drawing across his bare skin. It does not matter when I flush, listen to him breathe, and loosen the ties of my peignoir. He has not cured me of everything. I am a woman and he is a man. I have ten children, and that is the fact of me that shocks the society ladies most of all: not being pregnant, but their imagination of all those moments just before. I am now older, and I touch my husband. He stirs. The linen curtains push out the window in the breeze as if displaced by our breathing. His leg, where it was divided, is smooth as if polished. He is power and blue eyes. He absorbs me, releases me, annihilates me. When I was young I devoured him, he was a powerful man, your father, made more powerful and primal by his wounds, the absences in his body. I found myself thinking of his wounds when we were tangled up together and moving swiftly. I wondered who had fired the round that had severed his leg, and what he had thought lying on the field without it, and how it had felt once the pain had subsided. Did he feel lighter, did he feel any pleasure in the relief of that great pain? I felt pleasure, I certainly did, feeling him hot upon me. It was all so mysterious. Whatever had battered his shell, he was still ravenous. I blush to think of it. I was constantly with child. The strange heat of pregnancy smelted contentment, anger, misery, joy, and the nearly overwhelming desire to run away, and I gave in to urge after urge, mood after mood, desire after desire.

May you be so absorbed someday, Lydia. And my Lord, may you be old when you read this! I would not mind if you made a religious vocation for yourself, but I do not want to drive you to it in horror.

Cover your eyes, but I cannot censor this small tract. This pen will not allow it. I shall write one thing of use with it, and that thing shall be entirely mine and truthful. I refuse to leave behind only the whisper of my modest skirts in quiet salons, the fast-fading sound of my polite laughter at table, my string of worn rosary beads. I will leave one more thing, a thing that is only mine. Why do I write as if I am dying? We are all dying, but I shall live many more years to pester you, *ma petite.*

I suppose it is the child I bear, the eleventh. Bearing a child is a little death. A part of me revolts and then abandons me. Or perhaps it is just very hot today.

As I said before, you were born the day after our outing in the coupé, the day after that pinched old Creole nearly got beaten by John.

I remember that it was still and gray, though it did not rain. Dr. Ardoin and two nurses stood by. John circled the house on foot, endlessly inspecting the plantings, always pausing beneath my window to listen before moving on. I watched for him while you slowly made your way into our world. Once, he carried a spray of asters, the next time round they were gone. You pierced me, Lydia, and filled my body with an ache that tightened and loosened until I felt no longer human. Only a vessel. I shouted out at last as your body slipped from me. I had been staring fixedly at a cobweb in the mullion of the window. John stopped and turned as if to crash through that window and save me. Then you began to scream, and the nurses began moving about urgently, and I could see that John was in a state. I prayed he would look at me, and he did. I smiled at him before leaning back to take the last of the clenching pain. When I looked back up, he had gone from the window.

Later I heard him thumping around the hallway, and I asked Dr. Ardoin to let him in.

I thought he would come to me then, but he didn't. He went to you, Lydia, swaddled in your bassinet at the other end of the room. He unwrapped you and you cried out. He studied you, pink and blue and white, and he touched your toes. Then he wrapped you up and brought you to me. The nurses tried to stop him. He growled and they stepped back. I held you to my chest.

"She's all there," he said.

"You took an inventory?"

"It seemed wise."

"And if she had been incomplete? Missing something?"

He didn't say anything. He looked down at us and stroked your tiny foot. It kept slipping out from the swaddling. The nurses were shocked by his behavior, his interest in an *infant.* Dr. Ardoin had already helped himself to the brandy and did not care about anything, certainly not propriety. The little drunk.

John sat down.

"I had not considered that a child of mine could be whole."

He didn't hate himself, or what he had been, Lydia. He did not think that you would inherit his wounds, certainly not the physical ones. No, your father only thought, and always thought, he didn't deserve what he had been given. He didn't deserve you, he told me. He didn't deserve *me*. This did not make him sad, he said, it was just a fact. But it was *not* a fact. There is no deserving, there is no explanation for the good that happens, any more than there is a good explanation for the bad. There is no logic. I reminded him of one of the first things that he had said to me: *a reviled man could not take for granted the moments of otherwise forbidden beauties.*

"You don't deserve it, John," I said, suckling you. "You don't deserve it, and none of the rest of us do either." We are all like the reviled man, I said, blessed by beauty every once in a while for no good reason. "Don't be a fool, and don't ruin it with explanations. Come lie with us." He laid that great, powerful body next to us, Lydia, and promptly fell asleep. He loved us, you know, and that's enough for loving someone back. You don't need more reason than that.

When you were older, he loved to carry you on his shoulders so you could watch the ants in the magnolia blossoms and listen to the baby finches call out from the nest in the porch eaves.

CHAPTER 4

Eli Griffin

I let a couple days pass by my window before deciding what I would do next. I lay in bed, or slumped in my bowed cane-back chair, and watched the clouds push in, roiling over each other like dogs at the hunt before disappearing past my window. I listened to the sound of Levi's factory thumping and screeching below, and I listened for the yodeling of the fruit cart arabs who pulled their bananas and oranges and mangos through the streets below on the chase for the noontime trade. I listened for the ghost of Hood, the sound of hooves clattering and the scrape of a sword come swift out of its scabbard. That would be the sound of Hood's spectre, if I believed in spectres, which I don't.

In my rooms there were now two new objects, each wrapped neatly in hemp twine: a stack of green ledgers, and a pile of thin writing paper, each page so thin that the black scrawl upon them seemed written on the sky when I held them up to the window. Two piles of paper, nearly equal in size, alone atop my thin-legged eating table, which I cleaned and oiled once a week. I'd made it myself out of barge wood, I was proud of it. I'd made most everything, and if I couldn't make it, I usually didn't want it. So there were no curtains on the windows and no rugs on the floor. No pictures on the walls, no trinkets on the windowsills, no mirrors. I had my books. The catechism and a worn-out Bible. A book of courtly love poetry that I detested but read anyway so I could understand the fops at the clubs, always on their airs and talking nonsense. *Paradise Lost,* which I read obsessively but only the parts I could understand, mostly the parts what talked about the agony of Satan the traitor. I read grammar books and dictionaries when I could find them. I read

City of God. I read what I thought would help me to burn away the Tennessee in me, the bumpkin in me, and make me into a lettered man, or at least one who sounded like he was lettered. I tried to talk different, and I tried to write things, though I was only half successful most of the time, I reckon, but I kept trying as I'd been trying since I'd arrived in New Orleans four years before, where no one knew or cared who Eli Griffin had been. I'd have killed the bastard who touched one of my books, which I kept neatly stacked on a shelf above the doorway.

I cleaned the windows of my rooms with old cider vinegar and waxed the floors with candles I stole from saloons after everyone had gone down the liquor hole and become too stupid or blind to see me. I'd built a bed and stuffed feed bags full of stolen and scrounged cotton. I'd bought two pairs of blue denim work trousers, two thick white double-sided shirts that could be worn inside out, and two pairs of leather boots, of what animal I don't know. I wore black suspenders always, and a black hat that sat low over my head, wide brim. I wore those clothes everywhere, I didn't give a damn. The beautiful ladies in their fine silks, and the tailored men who paid for them, they could poke and titter at me all they wanted. My coin was still good and, you might imagine, I had saved a lot of it by living as something of a niggard. I kept the money behind a loose wallboard, stowed in an old wooden arm I'd bought off an old soldier, which I'd hollowed out. Pretty safe, I thought. I lived as if I had no intention of staying, and I had lived this way for years now.

A lot of that money had come through the good graces of the one other object in the room, the deck of cards worn soft by use and stowed in their own zinc cigarette tin, whose hinges I oiled once a month.

Now, though, those two piles of paper ruined everything. They tipped everything wrong, nothing seemed in its right place anymore.

I knew what I'd been told to do, which was to go gallivanting around the city and countryside bearing loads of paper here, removing them there, searching out a man known to be a killer, and another man known to be a notorious Confederate general and leading citizen.

I knew what I *wanted* to do, which was to burn the damned pages, the ledgers and Hood's scribblings both. I'd even gone so far as to take them out back to Levi's burn pile, where I stood for a time trying to imagine my hands reaching out and letting the papers through my fingers into the pungent green-orange flames. Levi came out from the back of the building right then, with an armful of cotton cloth I assumed had been accidentally dyed the color of the river, dull and red and muddy. He tossed his armload on the glowing fire, and the green flames danced up and over it all. He turned to me. He was a small man, and I could look down on him and see the perfect circle of red, slick skin at the back of his head. He'd rolled his sleeves up to his shoulders against the heat of the factory, but he still had his tie knotted up neatly and hung down to the middle of his little round belly. He smiled often, and I liked him.

"On the horns of a dilemma, I see," he said, rubbing the singed hair of his thick arms.

"What?"

"Can't decide. What you're going to do, that is."

"How did you know that?" I was alarmed. Maybe the whole city knew of my task, shoved on me by a dying man. Now I could see it, every urchin and vendor and priest and waiter watching me pass by and whispering about my chances. I shook my head, it was ridiculous. Levi spoke.

"When a man is standing by a fire with an armload of paper and hasn't yet thrown it in, it's usually safe to assume that he is having a problem deciding whether to burn it. The horns of a dilemma, you see."

A smarter man than I'd thought. A beautiful, dark-eyed woman, head covered with a blue scarf, stepped through the back door and called for Levi. He held up his hand as if to deflect the sound of her voice. His young wife.

"My advice, and this is after years of considering the question, is that if you can't burn the thing straightaway you shouldn't burn it. Take it back with you, think on it some more. There'll always be the fire, but it ain't a place to be making decisions, and you can't do a thing with ashes."

Guidance. I lay on the bed thinking about that word, and looked over to the two piles topped with neat bows. *Have to do something with them,* I thought. The whole room seemed to tilt toward them. *I can't live with them, I can't be the only one.* So I gathered them up, placed them gently in my adventure sack, slipped into my boots, and marched out the door toward Rintrah's house.

I knew Rintrah, knew him because I'd known Hood. There was a time when one went with the other. Bread and molasses, dace fish and water. They weren't that way in the end, but there'd been a time when to know one was to know the other. Rintrah had got me my job at the ice factory, and on occasion I'd been useful to him as a cardplayer when he wanted to get money off someone or, better yet, put them in his debt. Rintrah used debts as an enlistment into his army of thieves and politicians and drunks and artists and longshoremen and society boys: once enlisted, you got to serve your time however Rintrah saw fit for you to serve it, and only then was that debt discharged. His debts rarely paid off in cash and that's how he liked it.

"This way I can buy things off men they wouldn't normally think to sell," Rintrah said. "Like convenient blindness, or stupidity, or incompetence. Convenient to *me*. A man don't think to sell such things, but I *depend* on them. Seems right I should be able to buy them things, a body can buy any other damned thing. I need a man to be sick a certain day, I already bought that sickness when he came

into my debt. I need a man not to hear something, I already bought that. I need a man to
forget something, I got that in the bank. Nothing would get done if I couldn't buy a little
of the devil off a man from time to time. And
believe me, my friend, this city would be a
damned lousy place without me."

I never tired of that speech, though on the
riverboats and in the saloons of my childhood
and education, I'd learned the golden rule of
the underground: pay your own damn way. I
always had.

I went to Rintrah as an equal and not on my
knees. He could tell me what to do and how
to do it. He could tell me how to get in with
General Beauregard and maybe he could even
tell me where to find a killer with some kind
of special relation to Hood. I prayed he might
help me, he and his army.

Rintrah lived and worked out of a big and
very old Spanish house on Chartres Street,
just downriver of Jackson Square. Most people knew him as the eccentric fruit seller on
Royal Street, but that was just his way of keeping track of the street and his affairs. From
atop his fruit crate he could see opportunity,
he once said to me. From atop his fruit crate

he ruled all that he saw, or so he said. And when he was done surveying his kingdom, he'd pack up his fruit and push it on back to the mansion where he'd have his servants peel what was left and serve it up to him on stolen silver trays.

A large wrought-iron gallery poked out onto Chartres from the second floor, looming over a broad, arched carriageway that led back to the courtyard far in the distance. The iron railing twisted its grapevines in its center to form the initials *RK*. I paused before walking under the great arch and across the clammy, waterslick cobbles of the carriageway and back into the courtyard. I'd learned that it was prudent to take a look around first. Didn't want to walk right into the middle of something, and there was nearly always something going on at Rintrah's that I didn't want to know about.

But that day there was nothing to see except for the lookouts stationed permanently at Dumaine and Chartres, and farther down at Ursulines Street. They were chameleons, the lookouts, never dressed or acting the same way twice. Today the French boy at Dumaine was wearing a sandwich board advertising a potent cure for sale at the Circle Pharmacy on St. Charles, which just so happened to be made out of ingredients Rintrah himself supplied. The other lookout, a colored boy, was shining shoes down on Ursulines, eyes everywhere but on the shoes propped up on his box. Both boys watched me steady. I turned down Chartres toward Rintrah's house and disappeared down the carriageway into a courtyard conquered long ago by banana trees and date palms and giant yucca and vining things blaring their little yellow trumpets wherever the sun slipped past the fields of chimneys above. I had nearly pulled out my own knife to hack a path to the table I knew I would find in the middle of the jungle, a place where I could collect myself and decide what the hell I would say to Rintrah, when I heard the little man's voice calling to me from among the fig leaves, a voice out of the wilderness.

"Come around the other side, Eli, it ain't grown back that far yet. Got a path on in here."

I walked around to the back of the courtyard where the wood balcony of the servants' quarters hung miraculously from the adobe wall, and on it two colored girls leaned and smoked, ignoring me. I found the path and followed it until I had emerged into a small clearing containing one cypress-slabbed table and two similar chairs.

When the garden had been well tended, every tree in its place, every orchid blooming heartily, all the potted fruit trees trimmed into globes, Rintrah had hardly ever come out into the courtyard. The courtyard had been for appearance, the courtyard had been for women and swells who preferred to do their business outside, under the illusion that they were dealing with a landed aristocrat with an unfortunate height affliction, a wealthy jungle exotic, a pasha of Chartres Street. In fact, they were doing business with a brilliant thief who would have preferred to meet in a dark cellar, drunk, and with the sound of a fiddle ribboning out devil's tunes. But lately he'd banned anyone from touching the plants, which had responded by overrunning their sawed-off cistern tubs and their rocked-in borders, going rangy and twisted and wrapping upon every rail, pole, chair, and downspout within reach. It was an insouciant garden now, uncontrolled. I immediately understood it to be Rintrah's sanctuary.

He was a thick man, as most people like him are, but he had a fine nose and delicate eyes, white teeth. Dark red, nearly brown hair. His hands were powerful and crushing, and he'd spread them out on the table in front of him as if he were making an inventory. His brow slumped inward in a nearly perpetual frown, topped by thick red eyebrows. He was wearing nothing at that moment. I chose not to notice anything unusual.

"Don't think I need to dress in my own damn house if I don't want to and when I'm not expecting guests, which," he said, rubbing his eyes, "I'm not."

"If I had your physique, Rintrah, I might walk around as God intended also," I said, making light of the situation with an utter lie.

"If you had a physique like mine, young Eli Griffin, you'd have been dead years ago. You don't got the stomach for it."

Which I didn't. I sat. Rintrah shouted for some tea and sherry, and I heard one of the girls on the balcony flick her cigarette off and down onto the cobbles, where it sizzled and popped.

"As you can tell, I'm busy, Eli, and I'm not in a visiting mood. So why are you here?"

"Hood's dead."

It was quiet then. Rintrah leaned back in his chair and rubbed his brow thoughtfully. His lips moved, he was talking to himself, having an argument. The girl brought the tray of cold tea and sherry and biscuits, and Rintrah didn't look up at her. When she was gone on silent slippered feet, Rintrah looked back at me.

"How?"

"Yellow jack."

"Were you there?"

"I saw him dead, yeah."

He plucked a fig from the limb above him and nearly swallowed it whole. He spit the stem across the table.

"Excuse my manners."

He rubbed his mouth with his hand, and then rubbed his hand on his hairy chest to get the fig juice off, I suppose. He looked at me out one eye, looked away, and then squinted at me with the other eye.

"And now is the time for you to tell me why it happened that you were there. Was there anyone else?"

"Doctor Ardoin came later, right before he passed."

"That sounds about right, useless git. Who else? Nurses? Maids? Footmen? Sergeants of the guard? The governor?"

He was snorting and frowning. He knew better than that and I told him so.

Rintrah stood up and came around the table. He stood square before me, daring me to look, and so I did. Dark bushy hair down there, sagging old balls and an unexpectedly normal cock that looked big on him.

"Had to look, didn't you? Had to see what the little man's got, hmm? Pikers like you always got to know who's biggest, right? Who's the big cock, right, lad?

"*I* know better than that? I know a lot of things you'd pray to forget, on your knees before the Holy Mother begging forgiveness for thinking them, even. Yet you reckon you'll come on up in here and tell me what I should and should not know. Well, *I* got the big cock, you follow? So be a good boy."

He walked back to the other side of the table and sat down, picking at a biscuit.

"You were there with Hood and no one else?" he said.

"For a little while."

"You just decided to go out and pay the General a visit? Wash his face, sing him lullabies, right?"

"No, that's not it."

"What'd you steal? And believe me, whatever it was, you're giving it back."

"I didn't steal anything! God no."

Rintrah fumbled around above his head, looking for another fig, all the while keeping his eyes locked on mine. His hand came away without a fig, but his smile made me think he'd found something anyway.

"You took something, though, hmmm?"

"He gave me something. It's why I was there, he sent for me."

"To give you what? His empty purse? His official portrait? What would he have to give you?"

"No, nothing like that. It was a book."

"You read?"

"Yes."

"Surprising. Whose book? Have I read it?"

He turned his head up toward the balcony and called for his clothes. A few minutes later down they came, shirt, trouser, vest, stockings, braces, tumbling through the blue sky and into the opening between the ficus and banana trees. His shirt, tailored and monogrammed, hung up on an orange branch and I handed it to him. I thought he'd be angry and shout and curse the colored girls to Hell, his natural response to things unexpected, but he only smiled and dressed. The same colored girl who had brought us our drinks, green-eyed, tall, and freckled, now came into his sanctum with his shoes in her hand.

"Don't want to trow dese, *non,* might hit de young friend, no?"

"You just don't pay no attention to the young friend here. He's just leaving."

Rintrah turned back to me, sitting back down in his chair to slip on his oxfords, somehow smaller with his clothes on. "I want to know what it is. And you're still taking it back unless you convince me otherwise. You get *nothing* out of that house. That was Hood's house, but it was Anna Marie's also, and I speak for her."

I doubt he could have spoken for her, knowing what I know now, but I kept that to myself. I blew the air out my cheeks and finally threw down a cup of sherry for strength. What I was about to say might help me greatly or go very badly.

"It was his book. He wrote it."

"The war book."

"That's what I thought, but no. Something different."

"How?"

Now he was interested. He shoved the tray aside so he could see me better.

"It's about the time after the war. About New Orleans. About him and Anna Marie. And Father Mike. And disease and killing and penance and salvation and love and every other damned thing you wouldn't think he'd ever thought, let alone write down."

"And me?"

I had been dreading this also.

"You're mentioned, yes."

"Give it to me."

"Now, hold on, there's more I got to say."

Rintrah must keep a pistol stuck up under every godforsaken table in the Quarter, because now he had one pointed at my head.

"Give. Now. In that bag, I know it's there because you don't always think things through, like what would happen if I just decided to take the thing off you. It's a weakness, young Eli, and one of your charms."

Thank God he hadn't asked for the whole bag. I went into it and pulled out Hood's manuscript without disturbing Anna Marie's ledgers. He didn't need to know everything. I handed him the Hood manuscript, which he opened delicately while tossing me his pistol. Hammer rusted open, cylinder empty.

"Truly, son, I don't know how you avoid being robbed every single day, what with your street sense," Rintrah said. He began to page through the book. I sat quietly there for an hour while Rintrah read. He flipped through, pausing here and there, and spent a lot of time on the last few pages of the book before looking up.

"And you expect me to believe he gave this to *you*? Of all people?"

"Why would I steal it? What the hell would I want with it?"

"You? Big-ass hay-haired cracker idjit? Maybe you'd sell it, get you some shirts to fit them ape arms of yours, buy you a horse or two, or a lifetime of fatback. Who cares? Maybe you seen a way to embarrass a good family while you're at it. Jealous bastard."

"Now hold on."

"And, anyway, I don't believe for a second that Lydia would just up and let you waltz on out of there with her daddy's things. She's a smart girl, she'd have sent for me to sort things out. No, you snuck them out of there."

I wanted to hurt him, really put the screw in him, but I knew if I beat him down a half-dozen men would be there to stick their knives in me before Rintrah even hit the ground. So.

"Lydia's dead too."

Silence.

"I had Doctor Ardoin arrange to have them

both buried in Lafayette Cemetery yesterday. Next to Anna Marie. It's done."

At this he slumped in his chair and stared at me without blinking.

"Why didn't . . ."

"She was dead when I got there."

"Where?"

"In her bed. She looked peaceful."

"You know damned well it was anything but, nothing peaceful about the fever."

"I know. Even so, maybe she's at peace now."

"Oh, to hell with that."

Lydia had been his special love, the first of Anna Marie's children, his goddaughter. She laughed and screeched at his jokes and called him Mister King, respect nearly no one else bothered to extend. His thick shoulders flinched with every wave of tears.

I knew everything, I knew what had happened to them all, I knew what was in the hearts of Anna Marie and Hood up to their very last moments. I could guess what was running through Rintrah's head at that moment: he was completely alone now.

What I couldn't know, and couldn't possibly begin to guess, is what would happen to *me*, carrier of the secrets.

"Rintrah."

He flapped his hand at me as if he could bat me away.

"Rintrah, I need help."

More silence.

"Hood gave me very specific instructions about that manuscript. I don't know that I can follow them. I don't think I can. I'm not *streetwise,* like you say."

Now he looked up, wiped his face on his sleeve, and folded his hands on the table in front of him, one upon the other. There ain't nothing better for grieving than to think there might could be something only you can do to help, and being streetwise was Rintrah's whole life, his purpose. He could do that.

"What instructions?"

I told him everything: getting the war book from Beauregard, destroying it, finding the killer Sebastien Lemerle, and, at his direction, either publishing the other book or burning it too.

When I got to the bit about the man Sebastien Lemerle, he stopped me with a shout and a fist brought down hard on the table.

"You must have heard him wrong, Eli."

"He said it a few times, Rintrah. He told me to watch out for him, that he was dangerous, but he was right clear about giving him the manuscript."

"It can't be." He got up and chased the sparrows out, grabbing at them as if to crush them, as if to devour them. He shuddered.

"Sebastien Lemerle cannot have this book. He cannot touch it, breathe on it, look in it, and he certainly can't decide its bloody fate, for chrissakes." He shouted each word.

"I can't abandon my word, I gave it in good faith."

He stopped pacing. Again he looked at me queerly, first out of the side of one eye, and then out the other.

"First he picks you, the iceman, the man who, by the by, tried to *kill* him, he picks you to be the bearer of his great treasure. Then he decides that the fate of the thing will rest in the paws of the man I hate most on this earth, who Hood should have hated just as much. That is, if he weren't lying to us all this time."

He pondered that idea, that Hood was a liar. I *knew* Hood had been a liar, or at least that he hadn't told the whole truth about certain things until he sat down to write them, but I was going to let Rintrah learn that for himself.

"Sebastien Lemerle is a monster and unre-deemable, a man I will never forgive. If he's alive, he's only alive because he's supposed to be dead."

I watched him grab up the manuscript. I was nervous he would destroy it himself rather than allow it to confuse him, possibly humiliate him. Instead, he tied it up neatly and handed it to me.

"Take it. I will help you, but only so long as it takes for me to figure out what the hell is going on here. And, by God, I doubt very much that Sebastien will reach the end of this here story alive. I doubt it, yes I do."

I packed the parcel into my bag and slung it over my shoulder. "Thank you, Rintrah."

"Aye, boy, you don't know what you thank-ing me for just yet. I still got to think on it. This conversation ain't done. The next time we talk I will come to you. By then I'll have a plan."

I began to walk out.

"Right now you're going to the church to pray for your bloody soul. If this deal ain't square, you may find out you wish you had at-tended to it earlier."

I drew myself up to my full height, which I'd quit counting years ago at six feet. I stretched my arms and blocked the last of the sun. Rintrah fell in my shadow.

"Always the fucking albatross, ain't ya? Now flap on out of here."

I walked with Rintrah down the path, around the courtyard beneath the balconies, and out onto the street through the carriage-way. The lookouts, seeing the boss, jumped up from their naps. Rintrah glared but didn't say anything to them. He turned to me, his hands on his waist.

"No cards until we settle this."

"Yes sir." I saluted.

"I ain't joking. And no liquor. Or not much, leastwise."

"I understand."

"You protect that pile of paper with your life. Don't show it to no one. Not a soul, not even that little Irish girl you're buggering. Even if you're in love, you don't tell her a thing, hear? Especially if you're in love."

I nodded solemnly. I was getting the point, that I was deep into something that I needed to take serious. Rintrah patted me in the middle of my back, gently.

"Go on then."

*　　*　　*

Yes, of course. I knew why Rintrah didn't trust me around the Hoods, at least not about anything important. I had transformed from the man who would have knifed Hood to death, to the slightly older man who would never hurt Hood and who only wanted to read his books and play his cards and tend ice, but among the men Rintrah knew, such changes never happened. Vengeance might take years to flower in full, but it would flower without a doubt. Men did not change, they bided their time. Who was to say I wasn't biding mine? I understood why he didn't trust me. I had stained my hands forever once.

When I stepped off that boat four years ago and onto the wharf, I don't remember thinking anything, I just looked and listened and stared gape-mouthed at the whole thing. There weren't a thing in the world I knew of that weren't sitting somewhere on that wharf, and plenty of things I'd never seen before in my life. But that wasn't the thing. Hell, it weren't even the perfume off the whores who rustled by me without even stopping or the sound of the wharf creaking under the weight of the men and the horses and the pounding of the barges and steamers tied too loose on their moorings. No, it was all of it, all together, the piles and piles of things that blocked my seeing the city and seemed to never end. There was so much, I couldn't picture so many people in the world who could use it all. I could have started a grocery, fifty groceries even, just from the oranges and cans and ladies' hats and little streams of molasses and all kind of other things that escaped their piles and hogsheads and went drifting down the wharf on the breeze jumping off the river.

The captain told me there were seventeen miles of levees. Everywhere there were things moving. Sometimes I'd just squint my eyes and all that motion worked itself together into one vibration of a hundred colors. I knew then I was just one man among hundreds of thousands in that city, each hurrying and scheming and stumbling along, none ever straying far from the river, which was the bearer of all things. I was scared for the first time I could remember since the war. I had never been in such a big place.

Packet boats floated by lugging great piles of oranges and green bananas and bales of plantation cotton, all of the colors looking like they was fighting against the brown Mississippi for the notice of us on the shore. Behind me, I heard the belching and smoking cotton press, five stories high and more than a thousand tons, crushing cotton in its jaws like a great captured beast.

Negro stevedores and roughnecks hauled the boats to the dock with thick hawsers in their hands and thrown over their shoulders, their arms and backs straining and shining. Sailors jumped off them same boats and ran into town, after what I didn't know. Later I knew: to find the last places they remembered being happy.

Clouds of mosquitoes moved together like whining ghosts between the piles of boxes and cotton and vegetables, surrounding those in their path and moving on. All the while the river kept running. Pieces of the country come floating downstream and this place, this swamp with fancy buildings, caught them all.

Then I picked up my bag and moved off, into the interior of the city, down streets crowded by men and women in all kinds of colors. I heard people talking what sounded like nonsense, and then I realized it were words, languages, and there were a dozen of them, and in the air around me all this wild talk twisted and turned on itself until it was one language that sounded like song more than talk. I walked off down Chartres feeling a little scared and also excited to get started, thinking there weren't a better place in the world to set down. I could see the money, I could *feel* it, at every step. They was just throwing it at folks, maybe even me.

Whatever I had known to exist in my short life, New Orleans had more of it, and plenty more I had never imagined.

That night I got drunk and wandered the riverfront again. The great piles, lurid and fantastic and welcoming, had become dark hulking things in the thin lamplight. The lights across the river, right on the Point, danced from poles and in windows, and sometimes they seemed to detach and float toward me. I realized how high I'd become. I stuttered and stumbled my way toward the edge of the levee, toward the lights.

To my right, farther up the wharf, another light drowned out all others. Fire, great leaping and crackling white and orange fire spitting black smoke out across the river, where it was sucked back into the dark. A barge being salvaged for scrap lumber to build houses had caught fire. Barges covered in cotton dust could erupt in an explosion like that, I had known that, but I'd never seen it. I was mesmerized by the fire, and I was so drunk on the flames that I didn't at first hear the men closer to the barge shouting, *Man aboard!* And there he was, a tall, muscular, and bald man trying to muster the courage to run through the flame and into the water. Men were shouting at him to dive out, to get out, to run, to get away, but I could see it was all useless advice. The only thing that fella would listen to, the only thing he was paying attention to, was that fire, and it weren't speaking to him. He would run at the flames, which surrounded him on all sides, and then dart back again. I ran to the edge of the wharf and leaned over the side. The smoke made me feel sick. I shouted, "Don't be afraid, it can't hurt you!" Lying. I wasn't certain I could ever jump through fire, I was afraid of those red licks. But I reckon he believed me, or wanted to believe me: that it wouldn't hurt, that a stranger up on the wharf would know better than those flames and be worried about him. Nothing else to do. He ran through the flames pushing at him and leaped through the air for the water. The cotton dust on his clothes lit instantly, and I could hear him scream. I prayed for the quick relief of the water. But the man landed on a stray raft of old logs and was knocked in the head. He did not move again, and soon he was consumed by the fire and, obviously, blessedly dead. All of us standing up there watching couldn't do nothing. Someone sent for a newspaperman, who arrived as the police began to try to fish the man's body off the raft. They had to cool the body down with water first. The newspaperman began to ask questions, and I fled.

Always a price, and that price always paid by the ass-poor, the simple, the people who weren't known but by a few and would never be remembered.

The next morning I asked for directions to Hood's house. I could have gone anywhere, but he was the reason I'd chosen New Orleans. In my excitement, I'd nearly forgot.

I walked uptown and hid behind an oleander bush across the street from his Garden District house. I watched his brood, his slavering, drooling, laughing, hair-pulling clutch of children gallivant under the magnolias in unthinking bliss, chased by their young and beautiful mother. I became more resentful every minute. For hours I stayed there, watching. *The butcher, the murderer, the*

cold bastard has children? *He* has a family?
If I showed him a picture of my family, would
he care now? Now that he had his own? I still
doubted it.

Hood finally emerged from the house and
climbed awkwardly up onto his horse. I vowed
to follow him and end his life. He rode and
I ran. I cut through yards and alleys to keep
up. Hood made only three stops: at a sawmill
where they turned old barges into wood suitable for building, and at a mason's yard, and
then finally at the cleared and slowly trans-
forming site of St. Geneviève's Chapel, where
a young, gigantic, and very tired priest stood
before it, hammer in hand. I hid behind a pile
of lumber and listened to them speak.

Hood sounded nothing at all like I had
expected. He was icy but deferential to the
priest, calling him Father. They talked about
yellow fever, the work at St. Geneviève's,
but most of all Hood talked about the money
he'd just spent paying off the priest's debts
on stone and wood and medical supplies.
He told the priest he couldn't keep paying,
that the priest would have to finish sometime
soon, whatever his wife wanted. He said this
without malice, just a matter of fact. And
then Hood said something very strange. He

said, *Sometimes I think I will always be a penitent,* and the priest said, *There are never former sins, and they cannot be paid for. Penitence is its own reward,* and then he turned his back on Hood as if he were nothing. Hood merely nodded his head and walked toward his wagon. I thought to myself, *Penitence may be its own reward, but the sins gone get you, Hood.* I was the body of that sin, its arm, and that arm carried a knife.

It was becoming dark, and I slipped through the back gate of the cemetery. The hinges squeaked, and I looked back and could see the huge priest silhouetted in the late afternoon sun against the horizon, turned toward me and scanning the long shadows. I was better than him, though, I could move without being seen, I was a cat. By the time I got around the block and into the intersection, Hood had only just mounted his horse and begun to clop back toward that mansion Uptown. It was not much at all to spook that old horse, nor to pull Hood down off it and out of the intersection, behind a wall. I'd brought a sack for my head, eyes cut out, the word *Broker* across my forehead. He struggled to his feet and I kicked him down again. He never called out, he only tried desperately to see what was behind the holes in my mask, to see my eyes. I kept moving, didn't want him to think that something human had ended his life, but something unfathomable and elemental and straight from Hell, where I would drag his soul. That's what I wanted him to think. *Why didn't he call out?* He finally just sat there, in the dirt and mud, his horse standing off and watching us close. He looked ready for something, and then I knew it was me, and I raised the knife and it flashed, and before I could bring it down I had a premonition.

I saw the body, and the man on fire, and the blood running in the mud after the battle in Franklin, and how I had slipped in it as a boy, and how I had picked my way among the frozen dead arrested in their worst moments of agony. I saw my soul float off, never to be captured again. He bared that bearded neck of his, and God as my witness my knife came within an inch of the pulsing sinew. I'd have done it, and I could have done it, but I did not do it.

All I can say is that it's a whole lot easier to imagine a man's death—the torture before it, the final reciting of the man's sin, the blood and pain, the dimming of the light, the quiet afterward—than to do it your own self with your own hands, the man in front of you panting and snuffling and so fleshy and heavy and real. I seen the dead, I seen a whole lot of the dead. Hood had fixed it so I would never quit seeing the dead, and not just the frozen on that battlefield, piled atop each other, but also the face of my sister dead in her bed. I had been a boy, I played in the creek and in the fields, trapping rabbits and catching grasshoppers and making cat's cradles out of honeysuckle vine. And then *he* came. It was not innocence I had lost. Lost that later. What I lost was any expectation of good and right, any faith that I could know those things anymore. I lost my *innocence* when I realized that I was not alone in thinking that, and that there weren't anyone with any sense who *expected* beauty, or worse, sought it. Beauty was accidental and fleeting, and even if you were on the lookout and caught it at the right moment, that beautiful thing would break your heart no doubt, and all you'd have to show for it was ashes.

Revenge, revenge was one of those beautiful things I had imagined, perhaps the last beautiful thing I kept locked down tight in the deep cells of my mind. But when I stood over Hood, and I could have made that circle closed and taken that revenge, all it looked like to me was a crippled man rolling around in the mud. Could have been anyone. And what's more, once I'd finished him, the thing that would have been left would have been a corpse, a pile of death, the ugliest thing.

I fled. The last I saw of him that day, he was still sitting on his ass, his head cocked backward, throat turned to the dark orange sun.

They would be after me, I knew that much. Someone would hunt me. I wondered if I could get back on a boat. I ran through neighborhoods and black faces stared out at me from candle-yellowed windows. It became full dark. I turned and turned and then there were no houses, and in front of me lay trees and the sweet smell of peat and the sound of tree frogs, and I ran toward it.

I went into the swamp. I skirted the lights of the maroons, the swamp men long ago escaped from captivity and mingled with the Indians. I became lost, permanently lost. I thought I would die there, and finally I sat down between the knobby knees of an old cypress and resolved to get it over with. I watched the water ripple and roil at my feet where something ate something else quietly and efficiently. I fell asleep and I dreamed hard things.

Asleep, I had pinned my hand on a small, sharp cypress knee. When I woke at first it seemed there was no one around. But then there was an old man sitting against another cypress a dozen feet away, looking at me.

"You had a dream, boy. What you doing here?"

"Don't touch me."

"Ain't gone to. But you ain't right, boy."

His skin glowed white in the starlight, a dusty white.

"I'm fine. Got to get out of here. You stay away."

"Son, I watched you dream, and you fighting the Devil, which mean you got something to hate, no? You tell Houdou John, Houdou John knows what he talk about."

I knew no one in that swamp or in that city. I didn't trust the man, and I shook my head.

"Suit yourself."

Houdou John gave me some water from a flask, and we spent the next few minutes looking around us. I noticed some odd-shaped orchids hanging from the branches above, like stars. From the water just two

hummocks over, I could see a twisting, amor-
phous cloud of black lift up from the water
and drift together between the trees toward
us. Houdou John stood up and brushed off
his canvas pants, and I did the same. I could
hear the cloud before I could see it clearly:
mosquitoes. All around us clouds emerged
from the water. The sound seemed to come
from deep within my ears, the whining and
droning that cuts straight into the brain. Houdou John looked nervous. He picked up a bag
of roots and began to march off away from
the clouds.

"Follow me, boy, that is, you want to get
out of here."

"How far is it?"

"To St. Gen's? Maybe a quarter mile. You
lucky the General ain't there no more."

"And the big priest?"

"He the one sent me for you."

We made one stop. I heard a moaning
like wind between houses, only this were
real moaning. It came from out behind a big
white building that Houdou John called the
convent. There was sadness and pain in those
moans, and also loneliness. The sound got to
my ear long before we come upon the source.

I wished, later, that he'd never have taken me that way.

"This is the plague's home," John said, as if that explained anything at all. Out of his pocket he handed me a rag to cover my mouth. We passed through the gates of the convent, below the arms of a large cross.

"We gone to see this last thing before we go back to the chapel where Father Mike waiting on you. You a dumb boy, you need some learning you gone to keep from dying. I myself got what I need right here." He padded his burlap satchel slung across his shoulders, and I saw the knife protruding. *Guess I'm gone to do what you say, old man. Guess I could be dead right now.* Then I caught sight of the plague's home and forgot about him and anyone else.

Nuns tended to the afflicted, who raised up a ruckus of coughs and hacks and shouts and moans that were like an evil choir. We must have been taking too long at the entrance, because soon there was a man behind shouting for us to get out of the way. We split on either side of the path and watched a slope-shouldered bald man and his young, stout-armed, and glassy-eyed partner carry in two people who looked like skeletons already.

They drooled out their mouths and looked at us without blinking, and I started to jump forward to wipe their chins when Houdou John stopped me.

"Don't touch. Yellow jack, or scarlet fever, or cholera, or some damned thing, anyways you don't want none of it. These folks come to die."

"Why here?"

"The nuns will take care of them until they gone."

"And what about kin?"

"Kin? They got no kin. Those who got people, they don't end up here. They die quiet in nice rooms, in they houses back behind walls and curtains. You don't never see *them* until the hearse comes."

Around the side of the building I could hear men hammering and sawing. Reckon they was making boxes ready for when the moaning stopped.

"We all just as likely to end up here as these poor souls. Anytime. You got negroes here, you got white people over there, don't make no difference. Not here, at least."

"Every fella dies one time or another."

"Not like this. You tell me who deserves dying like this?"

"No idea."

"No one. And that's what General Hood and Father Mike are trying to change, and you just nearly killed the man. Now, you can leave me now or you can come with me to see Father Mike. He's got work for you."

I just nodded, and without thinking about it, I kept following him. We turned back to leave, and I looked back over the patients on either side of me, and noticed how the gaslight threw streams of light and shadows across the gasping choir of expiring souls, and one of them in the light caught my eye and raised up. *I know you, I know you!*

I told him he didn't and we left.

That night I met the giant priest Michel, called Father Mike. He scolded me like a child and I let him do it because he held a iron sledge in his hand like it were a twig and it don't do to cross men like that.

"So here's the thing, young'un. What's your name?"

"Abraham Lincoln."

"You're breathing well for a dead man."

I didn't say anything. He went on, ignoring my sarcasm.

"I dislike the constabulary very much, had

my own affairs with them in my youth and would not willingly send any man off to the Calaboose. Now, the General wants your head, but he'll calm down and see the wisdom of what I'm proposing. I'm guessing, knowing who the General is, and you being a right anonymous young fellow, that you got something from the hoary past you want to take up with the General, and my guess is it's the war. Easy guess, of course. So first, I need to know, can you live in this city and not raise a hand to Hood or his family?"

The battlefield at Franklin, its crop of the dead. And then: *Just a crippled old man rolling around in the mud. Nothing to get from any of it.*

"I can."

"Then I suppose that, being a priest, I should extend charity even unto my enemy."

"Thanks."

"It's not as if we haven't all thought of doing the same thing to the man," the priest added.

And that's when I was marched down to the big house of a little dwarf and introduced to Rintrah King. To the big white Spanish house on Chartres with its neat courtyard lined with lovingly trimmed banana trees and palms.

"Do not laugh at him, Abe," said the priest, who still didn't know my name. "I am myself afraid of him, and I'm afraid of no one else except God." Men apparently under this dwarf's command flitted here and there on business that I could tell, after growing up an orphan among the saloonkeepers and hustlers of the Mississippi, was nothing straight or legal. Not my business, I didn't ask. The dwarf and the priest huddled in a dark passageway, and I heard the dwarf laugh. "No, he didn't, really? By God, I could use a man like that." The priest shushed him and scolded him. Then they walked over to where I stood beneath a brass wall sconce filigreed in a wrapping vine like muscadine. The dwarf sized me up and asked me if I knew cards. The priest interrupted.

"Not this one, no, he doesn't, Rintrah."

"Looks like he might. Got those eyes. Bet he's got some cards in his pocket."

I did.

"This one needs to get right, if you understand my meaning, Rintrah."

"Oh, so this is church business, is it, Father Mike?"

"It's my business, and I ain't sending him to the Calaboose. I could make it church business, though," he said, looking around with big eyes, taking in all the activity. "How do you think you would hold up against the bishop, my friend? What you got going now, liquor? Liquor it is. Ah, and there goes the boxes of tobacco. Tax-free, I assume? I could have this place seized and reopened as a convent in a week."

The little man shrugged, as if he had a thousand young cardsharps at his command, losing one wasn't much of a worry. He looked at me steady this time.

"All right then, Father Mike, my *friend* since you yourself were a thug and a fornicator, out of my love for you, we'll send him down to Henri Rouart's ice-making monstrosity. He come up here last week wanting a favor, which I did for him, and now it's his turn. What's your name?"

"Eli Griffin." I told it straight before I had a chance to think.

"Eli Griffin, you go on down and report to Monsieur Rouart, who is a degenerate gambler and owes me money, and tell him that you have a job in his iceworks. And what's more, I want you to tell me what the hell he's got going down there, it sounds like one hell of a money racket if you ask me. Now git."

*   *   *

Rouart was a handsome and silent man, nearly always in a stovepipe. His big bushy eyebrows pushed out ahead of him. When I reported to his factory—a low-slung building on the tracks with what looked like a smokestack poking out the top—he just sighed and waved me over to the others, Italians and Germans bundled up like it was Canada, slicing big slabs of ice formed on iron pipes that ran floor to ceiling. I nearly froze my ass off that day.

Afterward, once I'd got a coat and the hang of the work, I realized that there was no better place to be in New Orleans than among the pipes and the sawdust and the pallets of ice blocks. The ice that formed on the pipes were like something natural, it was the forest of an ice kingdom, or the jagged formations of an ice cave. The light that came in through the windows was spare and filtered, but it didn't matter because the ice itself seemed to give off its own light.

And it was cold in there, when the rest of the city was hammered down with the heat. Wisps of mist flew up off our bodies whenever we moved. I wasn't the only one who saw this as something to recommend the factory. Rintrah came to visit sometimes. I had a chair I liked to sit in, on the north side of the big ice room, where I could sit and watch the ice form when I wasn't cutting it and shaping it and sliding it down toward the pallets and the sawdust. Rintrah would come, ask me if I'd figured out how much Rouart was making, and whether Rintrah could get in on the business, I'd tell him no, he'd curse me, and then we'd sit talking about the heat and women.

My other visitor came at first with Rintrah, but then came on his own nearly every day. General Hood nearly never said a word, except to describe what he thought he could see on the pipes. *Bears, rows of corn, the face of Sherman, angels.* He never once mentioned our first meeting, which I assumed was Father Mike's doing. Part of his penance, I reckon, to suffer in silence and to love his enemy. He would unstrap his leg, lean it against his chair, and let his head loll back. After a while, it got so he'd stay for nearly two hours, and during that time I'd have to get up and cut ice, leaving him alone. There were times I'd pass by a row of pipes and see him at the other end, talking to himself. He was always calm and friendly when he left. He said the cold made his leg feel better. The ice factory was another world, entirely separate from the place outside, and knowing there's a place like that, a place you can get to sometimes, can give a man some confidence. That's what I thought, at least.

It was right odd for me to have General John Bell Hood sitting next to me. He didn't come only for the ice. He came for me, I'm sure of that now, now that he's handed his book, his confession, into my hands for safekeeping. He knew who I was, where I had come from, and what I had thought of him, and why I had done what I'd done. He came and sat next to me, day after day, giving me every opportunity to ask him questions, to insult him, to curse him. Instead, after a while I began visiting him at his house, doing odd jobs. I think he liked me around to remind him of something he didn't ever want to forget.

Still, Rintrah didn't trust me, not even with Hood dead. He didn't believe in such stories, which was perhaps why he is the last one alive, and the most miserable.

CHAPTER 5

From the Journals of Anna Marie Hood

I decided to paint John only a month after we began courting, and once I'd begun we became a family scandal. I piled sketches of ears upon obsessive studies in shade for his eyes, the hollows of his cheeks, the crevasses of his forehead. I drew his lips ten times, which even I will admit was excessive.

John never understood the fuss, but he worried at my mother's outraged whispers that drifted into the parlor from the dining room. "It is not proper for a young lady to stare at a man's face so closely, not even after marriage," she said, whenever she knew we could hear her but not see her. Sound traveled peculiarly, clearly, between the two rooms though they were separated by a hall. Of course she knew this.

"I'm sure you will tell me how it is improper," my father said, barely bothering to whisper. He was no doubt reading the *City Item,* which would disintegrate in his wet, salty hands before the evening was out.

"It is too intimate."

"So is the streetcar." Father had given up hope I would find a different man, and now that he'd made his peace he seemed to want the whole thing over immediately. If he could have married us himself right then—me with paint on my fingers, John dripping in his black vented suit—he would have done it, I was sure.

"I am not joking with you, Duncan. Look at those lips!"

"Which do you mean?"

"His!"

"The ones on the paper or the ones on the man? Dare I be so intimate?"

"All of them. No, don't look. What are they doing?"

I heard the door to the dining room open

and I could picture my father's white head and red nose, each gigantic, poking around the corner. John could see him from where he sat, and he nodded his head as if in shame.

"Don't move," I said.

"Your father is staring at me. It's not natural. This is very strange."

"Yes, they are fascinated by you. Now please stop talking or I shall paint your mouth wide open like an idiot's."

John nodded again at my father and turned back toward my easel. My father shut the door behind him and I heard my mother muffled against his chest as he carried her away into the garden.

"Why would you want to paint me? There are far more beautiful things, Anna Marie, as I'm sure you know."

Perhaps there were. But when the day came that we owned our own bed and knew each other's bodies as husband and wife, I was afraid there would be no time to watch his face so closely, to take down in my mind every pockmark and iris fleck and turn of his ear and the slow downward drift of his big eyes. I imagined much movement, I imagined frenzy and weight and great huffing and pleading sighs, and then some part of him would be lost to me forever. I would never see his face, his withered arm, that head, his chest, in quite the same way as I saw them now, when they were untouched and shrouded. *Now* I could see the man who had captured me, who had made me love him. Afterward, after we had joined our bodies and—yes, I know the word, Lydia; it is a good English word, you should learn it and never use it—he would break through, he would be too close for me to see him as I did now. I didn't want to forget the first John I knew.

In truth, painting a man is as erotic as my mother suspected. That was another reason why we sat there in the parlor, two arm's lengths away from each other. I stared and consumed him, I put him on a canvas.

I was an artist, before there came all the children, and then there was no room for my easel and no time for mixing paints. I was nearly unschooled, but I had talent. It is not so strange, I think. I began painting almost immediately after the afternoon with the old painter who had hoped to seduce me and who had never put paint to the canvas. I remember thinking that I would prove myself better than him, and so I would make something good

out of such a tawdry afternoon. But that's not
it, that's not why I painted and that's not why
I kept painting. I painted because, like the
old man in his tiny apartment, I wanted to
see people as they are without the coverings.
I had no interest in landscapes, especially the
landscape of the city, all smoke and horses.
Studies of fruit were colorful and terribly boring. So I painted faces, usually from memory.
At first I rode the streetcar and stared, and
then I went home and drew those faces on
some of my father's linen stationery I'd stolen
from his desk. I drew with pencil and also
pieces of charcoal I took from the fireplace and
wrapped in a piece of my old baptism dress,
holed out by moths. I worked in the dark of
the carriage shed behind the house, and when
my mother asked me about the black beneath
my fingernails, I told her I had been in the
garden weeding her rose mallow, or pinching
off and pruning back the vines of her moon-
flower. I should have known that these obvious lies—I loved flowers but had never once
helped my mother in the garden—would
cause my capture. One day I was sitting in the
old carriage shed sketching the lopsided face
of a young and buxom chambermaid, who
had been sitting that day next to a nun on the

streetcar and had stared at the religious woman in fear and longing. I intended to sketch the nun's face next, the pleased face of a person who knows she's being stared at. I was so engrossed I didn't notice that Mother had followed me, that she had watched me, and that when she'd seen enough, she marched into the shed. She seized up my pad and I nearly smacked her before realizing who she was. She marched back into the house calling for Father. I stayed in the carriage shed, dreading the verdict.

The verdict was that I should draw and paint on proper canvases, with proper pencils and paints, and cease immediately the sneaking around and stealing charcoal. It was not the behavior of a lady, and it also became clear that my parents loved art. I hadn't known it from the awful cartoons and faded sketches of Roman ruins that hung about the house, or the way they'd hung the portrait of Grandfather, the great judge, in the kitchen pantry next to the dried beans, flour, and lard. I was not to become a *painter,* of course, but merely a lady of talent. "There is nothing wrong with that, Anna Marie," Mother said. "Better than having no talent, mmmm? Or the wrong talents? There will be no laying about cafés with unkempt men, of course. You shall paint in the parlor."

John was the first person I painted from life and not memory. At first I kept starting and stopping, finally stabbing my brush at the canvas. He tried to smile, a smile that was slow and agonizing like a great limb cracking. I think he thought I was nervous, and once he stood up and walked toward me, assuring me that this painting wasn't necessary if he made me uncomfortable. "You needn't fiddle with nature, Anna Marie, and you shouldn't worry about insulting me. You couldn't."

"Sit down, I can't paint you like that." He was standing in front of my easel, scrupulous about not peeking at the canvas, his palms turned up and gently thrust toward me, as if he were giving me something. Permission not to paint him, I suppose. He shrugged and sat back down.

It wasn't any nervousness that had frustrated me. It was the idea of painting someone living. He moved, his eyes gazed at me as long as he could stand it and then shot downward, his eyelids blinked, his neck flexed, his whole body seemed to vibrate. He was a man, a person, how was I to paint him? He moved. Everything moved on him, if I looked close enough I might have seen the blood running to and fro. I didn't know how to paint a person in motion. My memories had never moved, they had not thrummed like this.

The painting is outside your bedroom now, Lydia. It's the one you call *Daddy Under Glass*. I admit that he looks a bit like he's been trapped, his eyes agog. Somehow I managed to paint those big hands not upturned in offering, as I saw them that day we began, but raised at me as if to push against the canvas from the other side. It's a kind face, though, and that first night we had met he had said that kindness was rare. Here, I thought, here is kindness in *your* face, John. I wonder if that surprised him. The lips are right, I know that much, and the luxuriant sweep of gray beard, that's all correct. The way your father's neck descends into muscle at the shoulder, the vast breadth of his chest, that's all correct also. Your father said he loved it and insisted I keep it. Mother was amused by it. "You've really captured his likeness," she said, happy and so *very* proud of her *cultured* daughter. She even forgave me for blackening the piece of my ruined baptism dress with the charcoal. When she thought I wasn't looking she folded it carefully and slipped it into the pocket of her apron. "So glad it is of some good use still," she said, nearly warbling, stroking my hair. Father admired the brushwork.

It's a horrible painting, of course, and yet I believe that John loved it and I love it too. It's the first thing we made together, before we made you children.

I don't think of that picture when I am near him now, or when I am dreaming of him. I have ten thousand others, a million others, that I memorized during those days of staring into his face, and I was able to sneak those out of the house without Mother knowing. By the end of the sitting, John quit posing and simply watched me, especially my eyes. He watched my eyes and my hands, and once in a while he would touch his nose or his forehead to tell me about my paint smudges. I believe he made his own pictures during those days. This scared me at first, as he himself scared me. He was a man who had seen the unnatural deaths of men at the hands of other men, and had made a profession of it. What could he possibly see in the face of a woman who had spent the war riding horses and taking piano lessons? A few dozen city blocks were the compass of my world. He made me shy and hopeful, he made me want to follow him out into the world, battened down in sea storms and riding horses through the Caucasus, or whatever one would do with a man who had no fear. Of course he had fear, as much as most of us and more than some. Maybe the painting isn't so wrong after all. Only later did I see that in his face, and also the love and longing. He hadn't been beaten, it seemed to me, but he *had* been whipped. The thing most people have seen in his eyes is exhaustion. I'd say that was right. He told me he wanted to put down his load. He wanted to sit beside me, he wanted me to sit beside him, and across that parlor and in the center of my world, I saw love and admiration and lust in the eyes. A strong man for whom I was both a mystery and a respite. I didn't paint *that* of course, but a few weeks later we were engaged to be married. Draw your own conclusions, darling.

The only other thing John said to me about that painting, besides describing his admiration for it—a terrible lie!—was that it made certain things clear to him.

"I must live up to it now," he said, leaving on the last day of his sitting, when I'd finally turned it around for his inspection. "That is the face of a different man."

I thought he was insulting the painting, or making a joke. Later, I knew he was talking about himself. *He* would have to become the different man. It was not easy, Lydia, it surely was not. Not for any of us. We assume that when a person sets out to change their life, that person is setting out to change it for the better. I'm not so sure anymore. Or, rather, I'm not sure it's possible to know how you'll come out when you start mucking around with your life. And the hard part isn't the setting off, the hard part isn't the beginning.

You're old enough, Lydia, possibly you've noticed. We've both changed, and the worst of that transformation has only recently come to pass. This is the lie of that painting I made, or at least of the folly of painting it and thinking it would be him, my John, perfectly captured. No one, no one *real*, stays still for very long. Memory stays put, it patiently remains in place while we hang ornaments from it and dress it in finery. But flesh and blood moves, it never stops. Flesh and blood is naked, it is constantly falling and scarring and breaking and getting dirty and picking itself back up. This was true of me no less than of John. I suppose that's what I should tell you about now.

I pray we are through the worst of it. I am too tired now to think. Your little sister is crying, she wants food.

CHAPTER 6

John Bell Hood

How many times did I carry her off to our rooms? One hundred times for every child? Two hundred times for each of the eleven? It would be a low estimate. I didn't have relations with Anna Marie so much as I dug into her flesh, merged with the heat and musky sweat of her, became greater than human rather than less so, as I was in the daytime as an incomplete gargoyle bearing forth only shadows where parts of a man had once belonged. She was pale and smooth, and the muscles in her back stood out as twin ropes descending, flexed in her arch upon me, arms behind her head, her knees dug into my sides. I needed only to imagine that curved back, the arch, the stretch of her arms behind her head, the rough nipples on my tongue, the heat and rankness of her, and off we would go upstairs. Nine months later, a child. Or twins.

Ten years of that, of lying on my back immobile, was the vantage from which I watched the years wrench devilry and lust and joy from her face, to be replaced by duty and exhaustion and distraction. And always I was on my back, unable to take charge of her as a whole man might. After the seventh child, we began sleeping in separate bedrooms.

I came home when it suited me. I kept a cot in my offices for those nights when, having spent hours bent over the maps of old battles, I collapsed and slept, dreaming of messengers and the clank of camp spoons. On those maps I arrayed gravel and river stones for the troops, matchsticks for fortifications, golden pen nibs for commanders. I pushed them here and there, wanting to see the battle again, to hear it and smell it. Never broke through, though. Around me I kept the letters from my correspondents spread over the floor and upon the desk, in the chairs. I stalked from one letter to the next, peering down at them and their reports. *We moved into an enfilading position, but lacked support from the front, and thus could not press the advantage as they were able to wheel toward us on their flank without risk. . . .* I barely understood that talk anymore, that language. Why did you not just kill them? That is what I mumbled to myself sometimes, shouting it other times. Your job was to kill, not to save men!

Could I have talked to Anna Marie about my work, my memoirs? I could have, but I would not. She was a woman. More important, I suppose, she was my wife and I did not want my wife to think I was insane.

Nor did I want her to know what I spent my days doing. When I came home in our third year of marriage and told her that I would be closing the cotton business, I led her to believe that I had been cheated of my rightful business by unscrupulous men, that my partners were dullards, and that had I just another six months we would have been rich on the Tennessee cotton I'd recently cornered in the market.

In short, I didn't want her to suspect the truth. We had failed because I did not bother to lick the boots of the Creole men who controlled the wharf, nor had I stooped to beg business from my former colleagues, the politicians and farmers who still remembered the Gallant Hood. Of course, it was not begging and it was specifically why I had been brought into the firm in the first place. Yes, I had cornered a market in West Tennessee cotton, but only because I was one of the few cotton men unaware that flooding had been worse than usual in the flat country around Memphis, and that the cotton I had purchased was worthless for anything other than the making of nuns' habits and paupers' rags. The truth was that my partners had left me in disgust. They were right to do it, though I hated them.

It was months before I admitted that failure. I stayed late every night, tracing my fingers along the meridians of my failures, where the lives of men had ended. In the hallway on one of those nights I could hear the negro housekeepers sweeping and shining and talking.

"The crippled man, he work hard."

"Not like them fancy men, not like a Creole."

"Not like a *white* Creole."

"Not like any Creole, you know it."

"True, true. Yep."

"Work like an American. Building things."

"A cripple building things. Strange days. And he look like he washed up with the Ark."

"Older than he is."

"How old is he?"

"Don't know, just old."

"Ain't never take a drink that I seen."

"Ain't never seen a woman up in here neither."

"He got a cot."

"Too small for two, though."

I put my maps away for the night and folded up the letters. I went home to Anna Marie, to the unfathomable gabble of children in my house. I had become unspeakably sad as the voices of the negro dust sweepers faded down the hallway. They would have known about the flood. I went home to tell Anna Marie of my failure.

I wasn't a failure long, praise the White League, that ragged, unseemly collection of bullies and paranoids.

They came to all of us, all the Confederate generals living there in the teeming swamp city: Beauregard, Early, Hooker, Longstreet, and Hood. *Where do you stand?* they asked. By which they meant: You, who spilled blood in the war over these very same matters, what will you do now that the city is occupied again, and the victors rule, and the negroes run for office in their brand-new suits?

We all made our vague promises, our assurances of solidarity, all worth spit. Every one of us was afraid of arousing the anger of the Federals, who might charge us with crimes, possibly treason. Who knew? General Longstreet, though, could not help but engage the question posed by the White League: *What will you do?* I'd been around him since serving in Texas, and I knew him to be a principled cuss likely to martyr himself for the pleasure of it, the pleasure of setting a righteous fire to yourself.

Not long after the White League had approached us, the *Daily City Item* published Longstreet's letter exhorting the good people of New Orleans and South Louisiana to not merely accept Federal rule and occupation, but to welcome it in the true and proper posture of the vanquished, which is in obedience and servility to the victors who had, after all, proven the superiority of their will and their culture and their cause by mule-whipping us on the field of battle. The rules of war dictated our submission to our conquerors. It was the only honorable position.

Six months later, after his utter shunning, he came to me. His insurance business, the Insurance Association of America, would shortly fail, he said, because of the boycott. I was not surprised, though I acted so. He seemed pleased by this, perversely.

He said, "John, I trust you, and I would like you to take over the insurance business and save it."

"I couldn't," I said, knowing that I could.

"You must, you are not *tainted* as I, and you have that family."

When he said *tainted,* and declared me clear of any *taint,* I briefly wanted nothing more than to be so tainted. But I agreed to assume the ownership of his business for a nominal charge.

When Longstreet walked out our front door that last time, he turned and said, "I feel light, John, for the first time in many years. Do you know what I mean by that? Do you feel the weight ever? I reckon a general might give up his command, but it's a whole lot harder to shrug off that cursed weight of it and its history. I've been years with it, and now it's gone. Strange."

I *did* know that weight. I kept it in my office, on my shelves, with the maps and the letters. I smiled and waved good-bye to the general.

This is what Rintrah said to me when he found out I had launched into the insurance business.

"Don't fuck up this one, too, General, or you'll hear from me."

"Hear from you?" I bit into one of his tangerines and slobbered on his hat. "And what do you mean, 'this one, too'?"

Rintrah wiped his hat and charged me three cents.

"I know everything, John, and I especially know the failures. I have an ear for it, a touch. I can feel failure wobbling the street and vibrating the banquette. It is a very useful skill, there's money in failure if you know where to find it. And so of course I know how your cotton business failed, *General*."

"And why should I care what you know?" I had only recently learned of his childhood friendship with Anna Marie.

"Because you would not only hear from me if you fail that woman again, our Anna Marie, but you would have to reckon with Father Mike."

A dwarf and a priest. It was the beginning of a bawdy joke, not a threat.

"Father who?"

Rintrah arranged a meeting in the cold and strange wonderland of Mr. Rouart's ice factory, and that was how I was introduced to another of Anna Marie's friends, a giant and hairy priest named Michel, called Father Mike by those who knew him best. After meeting him, had I been told he'd risen fully formed from the rotting leaves and tea-dark water of the backswamp, I would not have been surprised.

Father Mike's beard iced up while I watched. He was some ancient beast of the far north, picking at the white frost of his breath and gabbling on about women and liquor and his nearly erotic love for the Virgin, whom he merely referred to as *Mother*. We ate cold chicken while Rintrah and the priest related their stories of Anna Marie's childhood, which they described as nearly feral. I think this was wishful thinking. Those two were the feral ones, or at least primitives. Hunks of chicken flew from their mouths and seemed to freeze in the air, clattering to the floor. (I believe I'm inventing that, but it conveys the truth of what I remember, anyway. They had poor manners.)

This Father Mike wore a bowler and the

overalls of a stonemason. A fine gray dust covered him from head to toe, except where the chicken grease had absorbed it and darkened his mouth, his fingers, his chin. In the dim light of the factory, shrouded in gray, he might have been a being coughed up out of the dark, a prophet of the icy dark, if not for the fact that he swore and blasphemed with great enthusiasm.

"Why are you dressed as a mason?" I asked, bored.

"I am building a chapel and a cemetery."

"Doesn't seem a priestly occupation. Aren't you supposed to be slinging smoke around on chains and performing the black magic or whatever it is you do with those crackers?"

"What do you know of a priestly occupation?" he asked kindly. He threw a chicken bone at one of Mr. Rouart's ice-covered condenser towers and it stuck fast.

"Don't know much, I suppose."

"Do you know St. Geneviève?"

"No."

"She's the great intercessor on our behalf during times of affliction. Such as when one loses a leg."

"And she grows the leg back?"

He stomped out in a huff, upending his chair

and sending it crashing against the far wall, apparently without his noticing. Rintrah glared at me, grabbed Father Mike's hat, and went chasing after. When he returned, he read me riot.

"You can think of something better to do when afflicted than praying?" he spat.

"No." I was ashamed of myself. Perhaps I was jealous of that great, powerful giant who spoke of my wife with a familiarity I myself didn't know.

"My first instruction to you, General, as you try again to make something of yourself in the business of this city, is this: don't insult the Catholics."

"I didn't mean . . ."

"Of course you did. Give me his chicken."

To make amends, I began giving Father Mike a little money for his chapel, here and there when I was flush, and I have to say that I began to enjoy watching the stone worked into figures and altars, the chapel rising as if it had always been there latent in the soil. And Father Mike himself grew on me, though it would be a long time before we were friendly.

When Anna Marie discovered I'd met Father Mike, I saw relief pass across her face. She eyed me warily, for a moment, I suppose wondering what he might have told me, but when it was clear that she still had her good reputation in the eyes of her husband, she smiled.

"Why have I not met this man, your friend?"

She shrugged her shoulders and walked away toward the kitchen, where the cook was braising ducks.

"I didn't think you cared to know them, John. They are the past and this—" She swept her hands about her, taking in the muddy footprints, the precisely sorted collections of dead snails, the dolls missing the stuffing from their arms, the smudged and scratched furniture, the black shoe marks on the walls. "This, darling, is the future!"

There was something wrong about that answer and I knew it immediately, I just couldn't say what it was. There was something missing, in both the stories Father Mike and Rintrah had told, and in Anna Marie's casual dismissal of the subject. Something missing, something *absent*.

Only much later would I realize that it was a person who was missing, someone dear to all three who, nonetheless, they would not talk about. And when I discovered this person's existence, ten years later, it would be too late.

CHAPTER 7

Anna Marie Hood

Paschal had taught me to fish. He said it was a survival skill he had inherited by blood. He meant his negro blood. Then he would laugh and watch me run the hook under the shiner's spine.

I think you were seven years old when we spent the last summer at your grandparents' fish camp across the lake. They called it The Fish Camp, but it was something more of a small rusticated compound suited for half a dozen families who required that their food be cooked fresh and served daily by permanent staff. There were changing rooms on the beach, and shade for hammocks, and we spent two months there that last year while the city burned with fever.

That summer I showed you and John Junior how to fish. Or, rather, I showed you how *I* fished; your father showed you his way, which involved chicken gizzards and elaborate floating apparatuses made of driftwood. He was an uplander, I suppose that's how they fished in Kentucky. He didn't fish with shiners, but Paschal had shown me how to gather the weighted net in my right hand, line in my left, and spin it out onto the water so that it blossomed before it splashed down upon the water and sank down into the dark to trap the little bait fish. It occurs to me now that John couldn't cast a bait net. His bad arm wouldn't have allowed it. It's odd I am only thinking of that now, years later. At the time I thought only that he was obstinate.

We spent that long summer with my my cousin Henriette, her fiancé Gustave, and my parents. My brothers and sisters had scattered to their own retreats, though occasionally they'd ride over to play cards. Only the Hoods ever went fishing at the fish camp. The others tittered and shouted and dove into the hot water of the lake when they couldn't bear the heat in their hammocks any longer. Henriette read *Tom Jones* to her fiancé and I could hear her giggles across the beach and up the creek all the way to the bald spot along the bank where you and John Junior and your father and I dangled our feet high above the black water. We caught red fishes and white fishes and black fishes, and I don't remember any of their names. Your father knew them. He brought them back for the servants to eat, since no one at our table would eat anything that hadn't been hunted or gathered by professionals and shipped in boxes from the best traders in the city. At supper I could smell our fish being fried back in the kitchen, and through the window across from my seat, past my cousin's bouncing head, I could see the back stoop where the negroes ate the fish straight out of the skillet and nodded their heads slowly, without speaking. It looked delicious, but I never asked them to serve it to me, I never asked them to fry something up for me or any of you. There were rules.

On the days the four of us went fishing, Mother insisted that the youngest children stay in her care, for fear of drowning. Then she would take them to the lake and fall asleep in her lounge where I would find her hours later, the children scattered between the water and the kitchen in the big cabin where there were spoons of sugar and knots of fried bread dough. The children might have hitched up the plus-four and ridden it straight into Lake Pontchartrain without Mother knowing, but they didn't. They were good children, you all were good children.

In the early afternoon at the fishing hole, you and your brother would curl up between the roots of the oak that shaded us, and your father and I would stare for long stretches at the black pinpricks where our lines entered the water. John always yanked his line out of the water first. I could go all day without ever checking my hook. Not John.

One day he whipped the line out of the water so hard it hooked the branches in the tree behind him, and he spent five minutes plucking and yanking at the line, trying to get it loose without getting the hook in his face. His wood foot, which he had removed from his boot earlier, now punched holes in the earth.

"Why do you do that, John?" I had woken with a head that felt pricked by sharp things. Colors were more vivid, people moved slower. I suppose it was Father's wine of the night before, he had made it himself, and so it had to be finished. Another rule. Now all things seemed strange. Even the children's faces seemed thinner and sharper. It made me curious.

"Why do I do what? Try to get the hook out of the tree? Because we don't have many more, and it's right there, almost got it. And then I'll be catching some big fish, I feel it."

"No, that's not what I meant to say. Why do you pull your hook out of the water so quickly? If I were a fish, I'd be offended, surely. You serve up the meal and before they get a chance to pick up their knives and forks, you're whisking it away. Very poor service, John." I wanted him to laugh. The sun had begun to burn away the wine fog and I was happy to be sitting by the creek with my man.

John stopped pulling at his line, which was now hopelessly wrapped and tied in the branches of the oak, and bent his head down toward where I had reclined on the ground with my arms above my head. I hoped he might give up on his hook and take up with his wife. You two were still asleep. John stayed standing over me, nodding his head.

"I want to know what's happened with it,

I don't want any fish getting my bait without my knowing it."

"Just wait until the fish tugs. That's the accepted sign, Mr. Hood."

"But that's not how it always works. They get in there and get out and you don't ever know it. I mean to catch those little bastards, too, unawares."

He pulled a knife and slashed at the catgut finally, springing the branch, hook, and gizzard loose. The hook and gizzard flew off into the underbrush. John looked after them and grimaced. He put the knife back in his pocket and sat down next to me. He took up my hand and let it sit limp in his own.

"If a fish makes off with your gizzard or whatever that is, without you knowing it, does it really matter?" I said.

"Of course it does."

He chuckled at himself. His stinking gizzards nearly always looked as pristine as the moment they'd entered the water. He said he admired my patience and that he wished he had some of it.

"I'm not just impatient, though." His voice dropped so low it vibrated in my chest, and I sat up.

"I can't stand not knowing."

"What, John?"

"What's happened down there, and what's happening."

"You want to be a fish?"

"I don't want to be fooled by fish. Or anything else."

Now he squeezed my hand and I was relieved. And scared.

"Men died because I was fooled, Anna Marie. Sometimes I was fooled and didn't ever know it until it was far, far too late. There's nothing worse than that, Anna Marie, believe me. Because what could I say to the ones in the hospital torn up by ball and artillery? I couldn't tell them I'd made a mistake, though of course they knew it already. Knew it better than me."

I knew nothing about war, but I knew he was waiting for me to say something. His hand began to let loose of mine.

"We are all fooled sometimes, John. That's life."

"And death. And when you've stepped over the pieces of boys, just children some, who died because you were fooled, see if you find any comfort anywhere in the idea."

He put my hand down, laying it carefully where he'd found it.

"Why are we not talking about fishing?" I wanted to cry, and I was angry too. How dare he make fishing into something awful and cruel? "What are you trying to say, John?"

"I don't know. Just don't want to be fooled, and I can't stand not knowing if I've been fooled. The fish, your family, the traders, my clients, who knows who's laughed at me? I understand less and less every day."

I stood up, picked up my pole, and yanked it out of the water. A blue-gray fish (bream, John called it) flew out of the water. It gasped and gaped at the world, it flew in a perfect arc over my head. I saw its beautiful white belly, and to this day I can draw the way its color disappeared into that soft white flesh, and also each drop of water that it left in the air like a track. At the end of its soundless flight it landed on John Junior's face with a wet thump. John Junior screamed and cried and stomped at the fish, which flopped into the underbrush in the same direction as John's old chicken lizard.

When John Junior had calmed down, I sent him back to the cabin with you, Lydia. I remember you looking at us, your parents, for a long moment before taking your brother by the hand and telling him there would be no more fish falling on his face, not to worry.

Late that afternoon, when you children had been dressed and sent off to the dining room, John and I got dressed for supper. We'd spent the rest of the day at the lake, sitting in the shade of the bathing cabin's porch. Your father read the week-old news-paper that had been brought that morning with the day's supplies from the market. I traced circles on a piece of paper.

My family, our family, were not fish out to fool him. But he couldn't tell the difference, and I was afraid of what that meant.

John's blue suit was all he had to wear for supper. He hadn't known, and I'd forgotten to tell him, that he should order a summer suit or two for dining. The other men had white linen suits with open collars that they wore to table and had cleaned every day by the servants. John looked like a man on his way to a funeral, by contrast. He cleaned that suit himself every day, wiping it down and brushing it carefully at night and then in the morning.

The last night of our vacation we ate capons trussed up in red ribbon. Father joked that they looked uncomfortable. John untied his before the blessing and then began to try to tie it back up again before I stopped him.

"What are these?" he whispered, after

Gustave had made the blessing, full of thanks for happy things that had yet to come to pass, and also for Henriette.

"Chickens. Fatter roosters."

"Not pheasant?"

"There are no pheasants here, John."

"Of course, but I thought the Creoles could get their hands on anything and put it in a box to be shipped to their summerhouse."

I kicked him lightly. I thought, *I am glad there will be no more fishing.* John was not one to let a joke go.

"There are Creole tomatoes, and Creole eggs, and Creole peppers, and Creole beef, and Creole okra, and Creole traditions, and Creole water, so surely there must be a Creole pheasant somewhere prancing about."

"No. Well, yes, but they aren't birds." John opened his eyes wide at me, feigned shock at the betrayal of my own people.

"In any case, that's what I thought it was, a traditional Creole pheasant. Now it's a chicken. I'm not nearly so impressed."

"Nor is it terribly impressed with you, I'm sure."

"Ah, it will be." He rested his good hand on the breast of the chicken and pulled off a leg. A piece of yellow fat from around the thigh joint flipped into the air and landed on the tablecloth in front of Henriette. Father smiled, but no one else seemed amused. The rest had their knives and their forks poised in mid-air like musicians awaiting their conductor. Gustave smiled, nodded at John, and carefully placed his fork and knife on the bird, sawing gently and without sound.

After that we were quiet until the dessert, which was imported blueberries from upriver and, as Mother unfortunately put it, "Creole cream." John swallowed a laugh and began to cough.

"Are you all right, John?" Father asked.

"Perfectly," John said, straightening his back and looking fierce. King for a moment.

I listened to the clink of spoons, the slurps, the deep breaths John took beside me.

"And everything else?" Father never ate blueberries.

John had his mouth full, nodded his head. I watched Henriette and Gustave across the table, pulling their berries one at a time to the edge of the bowl and draining them with the spoon, looking up at John. I thought of overturning their bowls, standing on the table, challenging them all. There were only a few times in his life that John ever needed protection.

"Just fine, Mr. Hennen, we're squared away now. I have entirely transferred our assets to the insurance company that General Longstreet turned over to me, and we have just finished our first year underwriting river vessels. Mostly barges, though I was also honored to insure the steamship *Natchez* this year as well."

"Has it been good work?" Gustave nearly leered, a great dark jaw and narrow teeth, big brown eyes. He knew something, they all knew something. Or thought they knew something. They always thought they knew more than the *américain*. John had been right about that. He quietly finished his blueberries and placed his spoon on the table in front of his bowl crosswise. It was a strange place to put it. Gustave looked at it as if it were a pistol. John squared his shoulders, crossed his arms on the table, and leaned toward Gustave, un-blinking. It was easy to forget his size, he was always so sad seeming.

"Very good, thank you for asking, monsieur."

Gustave leaned back and feigned to stretch his arms, as far from John as possible. He turned his head and seemed to be speaking to Henriette's right shoulder.

"I've heard otherwise."

Father stood up, but Mother pulled him back down.

"I've heard the same," she said. "It's a perfectly acceptable question, we are all family here."

"And me, I've heard it too." Henriette, though I have always loved her dearly, didn't know the first thing about insurance or the riverboats or the trade at the harbor. I'm not sure she'd ever been there. She loved her man, but I loved mine.

"Pah, you've heard no such thing."

"I've heard that our dearest John, despite his best intentions, has been associating with the wrong people."

Henriette was fierce, fiercer than Gustave. She said this looking straight into my eyes, aware of John glaring at her and not caring a bit. She knew I disliked her fop, and so she had to dislike my general.

"Who did you hear that from? Our dearest Gustave?"

"Anna Marie." John put his hand on mine. It was hot and dry and tense.

"I think," Father said, "that we should let each other to their own business."

The servants picked up the berry bowls quickly, flitting around the table like black moths. They hurried away and through the door to the kitchen, where I knew they would listen intently to the sport at table and argue its nuances. I used to join them before I became too old to be trusted with their secrets.

Though he had been given the opportunity to end the interrogation, I knew John would not take it. He had to know. I understood him suddenly, and I understood the fish.

"No, Mr. Hennen, I think that it *is* a family matter and I am happy to discuss it. My success is my family's success, which is the success of your daughter and your grandchildren. However—" And here he turned to Gustave, who was caught flicking and rubbing at a tiny blueberry on his linen lapel. He looked up, surprised.

"However," John said, "I must know specifics and facts, numbers and the testimony of trustworthy men. I am not interested in gossip."

"That seems a proper policy, certainly," Father said.

"I do not gossip, sir." Gustave began to raise his voice. It was a lovely voice, he once sang in the theater near Jackson Square before it burned down, before he decided to marry. He was a land speculator, he said to strangers, but we knew it meant that he sold plots of his family's ancient property, which had come to him by death.

"Then speak up, sir, and remember who you are addressing." The General awoke.

"Who I am *addressing*? Oh good Lord. Fine. Who are your partners?"

"Two men recommended at the St. Louis Hotel by a friend. They are insurance experts. And Creoles, though that means nothing to me, it surely means something to you."

"I do not know these men," Gustave said. "They are not to be trusted."

"The second surely does not follow from the first, unless you are the Lord Himself."

The rest of us sat back in our chairs. The argument was on, there was nothing to say. To my shame and horror, I nearly nodded my head with Gustave. *They are not to be trusted*. I knew this in my heart, and had known it from the beginning. Gustave spoke for me, and it made me want to walk into the lake and never turn back. I was a traitor.

"Mr. Hood, you are being naïve. Not every Creole is, say, of the same moral fiber. They do not all come from the proper families, and thus they have not all had the concepts of honor, and lawfulness, and loyalty, imbued in them as it has been in us, and, certainly it must be said, in you."

"Are you accusing my partners of a crime? Of betrayal?" Though he shot back angrily as if to defend them, I believe John sincerely wanted to know. But he was loyal, it was true, loyal to a fault, and he would not act except in their defense.

"I am accusing them of being unknown, either to the proper businessmen of my acquaintance, or to the families of my circle. And that makes them a foolish gamble for you, sir."

"And why?"

"They have your money, sir! They have Anna Marie's money, and Lydia's money, and John Junior's money! They are strangers."

John closed his eyes and sat still, arms still folded on the table in front of him.

"It is something to consider," Father said softly from the end of the table.

And John did consider it. He *had* considered it. He had told me so. But I was not enough.

"They came to me with the recommendation of men I trust. Men I trust to tell me truth and to advise me properly, to be loyal to me.

I am loyal to them. These men, my partners, have given me no indication that they cannot be trusted. And so, because honor dictates it, I shall give them my trust until they abandon it. And I shall do no other."

"They drink!" Gustave hissed.

"That is their business. And, might I add, do you not drink spirits also? I believe I've seen you. For instance, last night."

"You are naïve and obstinate, Mr. Hood."

"General Hood."

"You cannot trust unknown men, even if they speak French and knew the Emperor himself. Oh hell." Gustave leaned back, all of us now in the shadows of the candlelight, hiding from the man sitting at the table frowning. He was quiet for a long time, but no one moved. Father began to stir, but then Hood spoke up.

"I must believe in the goodness of men. I must assume their godliness. I am called to this, we are called to this."

"*Enfant*," Henriette whispered, and I kicked her under the table.

"I will believe men when they speak to me, and I will believe that they will return my trust and loyalty to me. I will believe this *first*, and I do not give a damn who gave birth to them, or who baptized them, or which of their ancestors consorted with Iberville, or which of them paid to build the cathedral. I am as willing to trust the son of the man who built the cathedral as the son of the man who paid for it. I choose to live this way now, because I have seen what comes of men's suspicions of each other. It grows to anger, and anger grows to war. I have given my leg and my arm for the right and the privilege to live my life as I choose, and this is how I choose to live it. I do not want to hear your opinion about my partners ever again. If you think that I will not answer you if challenged, you are very mistaken, little Gustave. I have retired from war, but the war has not retired from me."

Gustave knocked over his chair when he rose to his feet, but instead of challenging Hood for insulting him, he marched out the doors onto the veranda and then down the path to the cabins. Henriette followed him, but not without hesitating for a moment and looking at John steadily. She nodded her head to him and he nodded back.

"Good night, General Hood."

"Good night, Henriette."

Only much later, when Henriette was no

longer engaged to Gustave and he had become barely a memory, did I realize she had not bothered to say good night to the rest of us. Only John. I don't think it is right to say that she ever came to like John, though I dearly wish she had. She approved of him, that's all.

We were left at the table, the four of us blinking at the guttering candles. After a minute John stood up to beg exhaustion. "Tomorrow it's back to the city, and I'll have to get the troops up early and organized if we'll ever make it back by sundown," he said. In his dark suit in that dark room, his face appeared to float above the table on its own.

I said I would join him and began to stand, but he whispered that I ought to sit with Mother and Father awhile, as this was the last night of the summer with their daughter. So I sat and watched him hitch and limp out the same door Gustave had slammed open.

Mother began to cry and Father handed her his handkerchief, which he removed and held out to her without barely seeming to move. She nodded. "They are both so wrong, and that is all that I know," she said. "I don't know what to believe."

I said nothing and neither did Father. Mother looked from one to the other of us, waiting for Lord knows what, and finally she excused herself also. We all stood. Mother went through the door to the upstairs bedrooms, and I waved to Father before walking out onto the veranda on my way to our little cabin where the children, if God was in His heaven, would be sleeping and I could lie awake all night in peace.

Outside the candlelight the stars crowded and receded and flashed, and the more I stared the more the dark seemed to lighten and disappear. On the lake, chopped by a light night breeze, the starlight broke and multiplied. The peaty rot of cypress water drifted in the air, also the sweet rusty scent of grass that's been out in the sun all day. The rocks that formed the veranda's short wall where I sat had been warmed by the same sun.

"Anna Marie?"

Father's voice from the doorway, tentative. Letting his eyes adjust to the dark, I suppose.

"Right here, Father."

"Ah. Yes."

He walked over and stood next to where I sat until I patted the rock next to mine. He thanked me, though it was his wall. He had built it when I was still a baby.

Quiet. Father could appreciate quiet, as

well as the undeserved spectacle of the heavens. John was the same way. Silence was no sin among us. But, finally, Father came out to say what he had to say.

"The General is an unusual man, Anna Marie."

"Yes, he is, but I always knew it. So did you, I think."

More quiet. Father toed the cracks in the stone below his feet.

"I did know it. But I'm not sure I quite understood until tonight what that meant. I thought he was just an eccentric, because a man is never quite like the rest of us when he comes back from war. Never. But it's not just that."

I wondered if he'd been sent out by Mother.

"So what have you learned tonight about my unusual husband, Father? I don't intend to change him, and I know I couldn't anyway."

"Oh, Anna Marie, I hope he doesn't change. I will pray for the world to change around him."

"That's a strange idea, and I'm not sure what it means, either."

"I mean that a man who is willing to face criticism, ridicule, failure, because he prefers to believe that men are good, such a man is

closer to God than the rest of us. He is unusual, he is good. But. But, but, but." He took
my hand and pulled gently so that I would face
him. "He is naïve and you are not, at least not
about life in this city. He has seen more of the
worst of man than you and I will ever see if we
are lucky. He was a brutal commander, Anna
Marie, I know you don't like to hear this, but
it's true. He had no patience for weakness and
he was arrogant. He cost many men their lives
without good reason. He knows it, I heard it
tonight. And I heard a man praying for absolution, willing to suffer for it."

"I heard a man dressing down a loud-
mouthed twit, that's what I heard."

"Possibly. Yes, that's true. He was good at
it, wasn't he?" I looked at Father, who was
chuckling. "I would have liked to have seen
Gustave challenge John. No, I would not have
liked to see that, that's a terrible thought. But
I will always have the dream."

My father had always loved me best. It's not
nice to say, but it's true. And I believed, when
I thought about it, that I loved him more than
Mother or anyone in the world until I married John. I wondered if Father had ever been
jealous.

"If you love him, little Anna Marie, you will

make sure that Gustave, and all the rest, are proven wrong. And if you can't keep him from himself and disaster, you must know that it was the price of loving a man like that. You may suffer, but you must not quit him because he is unsuited for this world. You knew that at the beginning and you loved him anyway. God is love, you know."

I could only nod, for fear that I would betray what I truly thought and ruin those words that still hung between us, ruin his remaining faith in my own innocence.

"I like him, Anna Marie."

"I do as well."

"You would, of course." He stood up to leave. "You were an obstinate, delightful child."

In the cabin the children were asleep and John sat bent over his suit by the moonlight at the window, maniacally brushing it. I was afraid he might rip it and I took it from him and hung it from the wardrobe door. He sighed and relaxed his shoulders. There were fingernail marks on his forehead, bloodless quarter moons, which he got sometimes when he held his face in his hands. I think it kept him from yelling. In all the years I've known your father, Lydia, I've never heard him yell except at horses and dogs, and then very politely.

I sat in the chair opposite his and took his hands.

"You don't believe a word of what you said at the table tonight, do you?"

"I want to believe it. I want to live like that. I want to trust."

"Why, for heaven's sake?"

He looked down at his hands in mine, cracked and red.

"Because I'll lose you if I don't."

"I don't need you to have the blind faith of a saint."

"I know. Still."

"What?"

"I must learn to trust men, to believe in men, or I will never learn to trust you."

"Me? My God, John, what have I done that would make you mistrust *me*, of all people?"

"You married me. Of all people."

I loosened the bindings on my dress and let it slip down. I stood up and it slid to the floor. John tried to pick it up but I fended him off with my foot. Soon I was naked, and I didn't much think about the children in the other room.

"Let's go fishing."

John smiled, and it was good. I suspected he would lose our money, that Gustave would have the last word, and it didn't much matter to me at that moment. And even at the very worst, when I thought John had lost his mind *and* our money, I never forgot that he had sacrificed some part of himself, the vicious and paranoid and brutal part—the part that had always kept him safe—for me.

Back in the city he still barked his confidence, intimidating to his colleagues and the men of his club, but he always suspected he had erred somehow, somewhere, whether at the office or at home, and that he had missed this error, and that consequently people laughed at him when he wasn't looking.

He couldn't help that, it was part of him. He resisted it, he ignored it. Soon, though the world hadn't changed and it was just as petty and deceptive as ever, he himself began to change. Slowly, slowly.

CHAPTER 8

John Bell Hood

In our tenth year together there was a party, a ball, thrown by Anna's cousin Henriette. We didn't go to parties much, and that suited me just fine most of the time. But on this night, a year or so ago, I had decided that we should attend. I don't know why, except that perhaps I wanted to show off my new leg, which allowed me to walk with nearly no limp. I had been practicing.

"They will not recognize you without the hobble, John," Anna Marie had called out from her dressing room. "You have lost part of your character."

"Does a limp form character? I think it is more of an amusement, and I am glad not to be amusing your friends anymore."

"They are not amused by your wounds, John. They are sympathetic and solicitous, I thought. They take pity. You are the warrior in their midst." She laughed.

"I call that being an amusement."

"I call you pitiful, but I'm still fond of you."

We were going to the very same ballroom where we had met, where Anna Marie had so rudely and insistently ingratiated herself to me. God bless that ballroom. Perhaps that was why I wanted to go to the party this time: to revisit the beginning, to remember what had happened that night.

I walked down the stairs to the library. The dust raised little motes out of the deep pile of the Venetian runner that had been in the house since the beginning. We had let our staff go, and the dust didn't bother me. The dust was natural, normal, it made the place seem substantial to me. It annoyed Anna Marie, though, and I knew she'd take a broom to it soon.

I stepped into the courtyard outside the library and had a smoke. There is a kind of Louisiana sky that is so deep and blue and bottomless and bright that the occasional cloud that slips off the Gulf can cast a shadow with the power to shock and startle, before quickly moving off, leaping over walls and roofs and into the next courtyard. I blew smoke and watched a cloud glide over, and quickly the courtyard went black before reappearing again in blinding color. Mockingbirds and sparrows flitted away from the darkness, calling to each other in search of the light. If I had been aboard that cloud, I thought, I could have looked down on one hundred square blocks of the city, each carved into a delicate labyrinth of courtyards and hidden gardens. My wife had mastered these labyrinths, grown up in them. They would always be a mystery to me.

The children had been carted over to their grandmother's apartment for the evening, and so the only sound I heard when I came back inside was the whisper and slip of Anna Marie descending the stairs in her gown. I could see her frowning at the dust, until she realized I was watching her, and then she smiled sweetly and let me take her hand.

"Are we walking?" she asked.

"I haven't sold the trap yet. We'll ride."

"Shall I drive? Or do you promise not to run into any old men on the way?"

"I will try."

Anna Marie was very excited, she bounced in her seat, and I realized how long it had been since we had stepped out. At the ball we danced and we acted as chaperones because we were, now, two of the old people. I rested on the same settee where Anna Marie had perched the first time I saw her. This time, I watched her cut through the guests and greet her cousin, who had been talking to a tall, lanky man with the playful dark eyes of a sprite. He favored his right leg without noticing it, the sign of an old wound. *Ha! Someone else for amusement!* Anna Marie's cousin looked nervous, but I hardly noticed it because Anna Marie looked so happy. I could hear her laugh across the ballroom, her head back and her hair cascading down her back.

Later we went outside to the garden in our role as monitors of the chaste. There was St. Joseph again, he seemed an old friend. We held hands and whispered jokes to each other and looked stern. The moon had come up quartered but bright, and when I looked closer I could see that someone had given St. Joseph a garland of gardenias. *Good for you, Joe*, I thought. I was happy just then.

After a few minutes, I noticed the several

young ladies who had also been haunting the garden. They hurried toward the foyer door, frightened of something, and at first I thought they were merely concerned that their dalliances would be found out. Then I heard angry shouts and laughter from around the corner of the building. I heard the sound of a sword slipping from its scabbard. It was a sound I could never mistake, a hypnotic sound. I lost myself for a moment, and with a nod to Anna Marie, I made for the sound.

I can only explain this behavior of mine as instinctual, bred in and cultivated until I could no longer turn away from the fight, until I was only a dog in the pack for whom survival meant culling the weak. How easily I forgot Anna Marie in that moment. I hurried down the river-stone path and around the corner into a small clearing that opened up out of the live oaks and magnolias, a small green lawn lit by yellow light through the windows of the service kitchen. Five young Creole men—I knew them by their fine features and prissy coats—had surrounded a sixth of their number. The negro servants watched nervously from the back steps outside the kitchen. An old black man removed his neck rag and twisted it in apprehension.

The sixth Creole stood a head taller than the rest, though this did him no good every time he fell to the ground drunk. I drew closer, staying among the trees, taking cover in the dark, preserving my options. I had no weapon. They were all drunk, and one of the antagonists had drawn a curious weapon, thinner than a rapier but equally sharp at its end. It looked like a very large sewing needle, and it appeared to have been removed not from a scabbard but from a false cane. *Such odd people.*

The tall man in the middle smiled and laughed as the others shouted at him. He was drunk enough to think everything a joke. I moved closer. I was a scout again. My leg was flesh once more, and I saw nothing but battle.

"Nigger!"

"Traitor!"

"Filthy bastard."

The tall man held up his hands and smiled.

"Now, now," he said. "Who is this nigger we speak of, this black heart?"

"You sneak in and dance with my sister?"

"I have known your sister as long as you have, Edgar! I danced with her when you still shat your pants. I taught her the piano, for heaven's sake."

The tall man looked around for laughing faces and found none.

"I will kill you! I will tear your tongue out and serve it to the woolly heads you call kin!"

This must have been the brother, who looked every bit as negro as the tall man, which is to say not at all.

I almost turned back then. A drunken fight, with curses. They likely would not even lay hands on each other except to hug and sob and hoist another bottle together. Such a commonplace. I thought to go find Anna Marie, but before I could turn she tapped me on the shoulder. In the moonlight that snuck down through the leaves, I could see her face creased by worry.

"What are you doing?" I whispered.

"I am as curious as anyone." She looked out at the mob. "Oh blessed Mary!"

"We should leave."

A little man had pulled the brother, Edgar, aside and was whispering in his ear. He pulled the young man's head down to his mouth and wrapped his meaty right hand around his face, curiously intimate and violent at once. The tall man entertained himself by making faces at the other men and dancing gimp-kneed with his hands in front of him and his legs cocked out like those of a mantis. He carried a cane carved red and black like a snake, but it didn't look like it would be much help in a fight.

"See, I'm dancing, I'm dancing! Just like a nigger. Who's going to stop me?"

The little man looked up, unblinking, at the dancing man. He nodded and pushed the outraged brother away.

"Just *like* a nigger," he said, offering the dancing man a bottle. "It's a remarkable likeness. *Bravo!*"

"Thank you, Sebastien."

"I wonder if you aren't holding back, though."

The dancing man wiped his mouth and offered the bottle around, but found no takers.

"What you mean?"

"Take off your shoes."

"These are fine, fine shoes. I'm not giving them to you."

"Nigger, do what you're told," Edgar shouted. The little fellow, Sebastien, turned toward him.

"Shut up your mouth right now."

Edgar backed up behind the others, nodding his head, like a cur just whipped.

Anna Marie was still standing behind me, pressed against my back. There was no sweet familiarity in her now, only fear.

I sized up the man who had taken charge of the little farce unfolding in front of me. I would never have given him a second thought except for the way his face never broke, never betrayed emotion even when he blissed out Edgar. A face carved of hard wood, and yet practically placid. *I knew a face like that, once.* The others maintained space around him, wherever he stood, as if they would turn to stone by touching him. This was the sort of man I once had sought out for my lieutenants, when I had needed men others feared disappointing, men who could lead other men into bloody chaos across burning bulwarks without leaving a single straggler behind. Such men were not often imposing to look at, they didn't *look* fearsome. Men feared them not because of what they *could* do, but what they had done and, most importantly, what they *would* do. *I knew a man like that once.* Other men shrank from him while gazing on in fascination.

Sebastien took the tall man's shoes and

placed them neatly on the steps behind him, scattering two negro servants back into the house. I could see that he'd drawn a substantial but tentative crowd. Men peered around the corners of the building and from the trees. Women gathered in little knots, whispering. With every minute it became darker as the stars rolled out of the sky. The dancing man, now without shoes or stockings, moved in and out of the growing darkness.

"I will take good care of your shoes, friend," the blackbird said. He smiled and his teeth seemed to glow.

"They say he took those teeth from a lame Guinea he found begging on one of his boats," Anna whispered. That was ridiculous, of course, but such legends arise from fear.

"Roll your pants up." The tall man, still enjoying himself in his stupor, seemed to think it a game. He rolled his pants up underneath his knees. *Two perfect legs,* I thought.

"Now your jacket. Take it off."

The tall man hesitated, and for the first time he tried to focus his wayward eyes on the man in front of him, to try to get some sense of what was happening, I suppose. *It's too late for that, son,* I thought.

"Why are they doing this to him?"

Anna Marie looked at me angrily, desperately, as if my ignorance was unbearable. At once she was ready to cry and ready to fight. *I knew a man who had inspired that emotion in women. Before he killed them.*

"He is an octoroon, I believe, and he should not have been here."

She was crying and clawing at her hands. I stopped her.

"He is a negro?"

"Such a blunt, unsubtle word."

"He is as white as they are. White like me."

"He may be white, but not like you. These are their rules."

"Whose?"

She leaned away from me against a tall locust and folded her arms.

"All of them." She flung her hands out wide. "Don't you see them all?"

By now Sebastien had succeeded in removing the man's jacket. The other men had utterly surrendered to his command. Even the angry brother, Edgar, so violent and hot minutes before, had sheathed his weapon and stood by obediently. If any of them still possessed the fire and piss that had drawn them outside to confront the negro, they had all handed it over to the little man. They stood now in silent rat-ification of whatever Sebastien chose to do. They had given him the authority to act and to think for them, and I could see in Sebas-tien's face that he was glad of their surrender, and that he despised them for it. *Sebastien, Sebastien. Oh God.* The negro, though, had earned his respect, even if he was also the object of his torment. The negro talked back and did not show his fear. Sebastien was per-versely deferential to him.

"Roll your sleeves up, please."

"This is becoming boring, Sebastien. What are we about here?"

"How else can we counter the slander heaped on you if we can't examine your skin? In fact, take your shirt off entirely. I am pro-tecting your interests here, friend."

"It's cold, Sebastien."

"Fine. You are a black-hearted field nigger who dances with white women."

"That is not true."

The little man finally let his temper boil up.

"Then show us your white skin, or I will burn those clothes off you."

I knew the voice. I held on to Anna Marie

all the harder and shrank farther into the shadows.

The shirt dropped quickly to the ground and the tall man stood meekly before the other men, as if he had suddenly realized his predicament and knew what would happen now. His chest and back glowed in the waning starlight. Freckles scattered in dense clusters across his shoulders like the shadows of those stars.

"Are you a negro?" the blackbird asked.

The tall man straightened up again. He had courage.

"I am whiter than you."

I hadn't seen the poker on the ground behind Sebastien. He raised it into the air, heavy black iron. He was very fast, inhumanly fast. The poker crashed into the tall man's bad knee, caving it in and snapping it. I had seen men with such injuries, and I thought, *He'll need a wood leg too.*

"Stop it!" Anna Marie screeched in my ear.

That man, their friend, screamed until his lungs emptied. He breathed and screamed again. The women hurried off with their hands on their ears. The other men looked grim. The game had ended, something else had begun.

"Stop him." She said it again.

In the interest of perfect honesty I must record the reasons I stayed under cover in the trees, holding my hand over Anna Marie's mouth. She bit me hard, she kicked. I must state the reasons I prayed that General John Bell Hood would not be found at what had obviously become a lynching: I was confused and unsettled by the sight of a white man stripped to the waist and barefoot, abused as a negro; I felt the ache of my leg on its wooden buttress and was unsure that I was still one who could make others obey; I did not know what any of them, even the victim, had done and I understood nothing about them; I had my own problems and it would have been foolish to compound them; I had not intended to witness this, it had been an accident; it was not my business and a prudent man always kept prudence in mind. This, I think, is nearly a full accounting of my cowardice.

I should also say that I was afraid of Sebastien. I had my reasons. I knew him and, yes, I feared him.

Prudent. Oh yes, I was prudent. I was prudent while they bound the prisoner and gagged him with his own stockings. I was prudent when I could see that the little mob hesitated, that none of the young men had either the stomach to kill the man nor the strength to resist Sebastien alone, and that they could have been swayed from violence had someone, anyone, acted for them and relieved them of their burden. I was prudent when they carried the man toward my little patch of woods where I shrank back into the deepest dark. I was prudent and *scared*. Scared, scared, scared.

Bald fear coursed through me, and I felt ashamed and alive. When had I last been afraid? It was the moment before the Comanche's arrow pierced my hand, when I was young and still jealous of life. There had been medicine on that arrow, perhaps. It robbed me of fear, which is a kind of love. A love for breath. *I live, others die.* I had not been courageous in battle, I was not *gallant*. I had been inhuman, despicable, brutal in my insensate way. But now I felt fear, and it was both humiliating and stirring. I did not intervene for the drunk white negro because I preferred the novelty of cowering. My heart thumped and my face flushed hot. Of all the confessions I need to make, this is the one that shames me the most.

*   *   *

As the men approached, I could hear them rasping out questions to the blackbird. *Where are we taking him? What are we doing?*

"Why did you undress him?" whispered Edgar. I wondered if he even remembered that it had been his drunken outrage over the honor of his sister that had set a man on his way to death. With every step he looked more the boy.

"Are you embarrassed by his flesh?" Sebastien asked. "Do you long to touch it?"

"No."

"Don't ask questions. I made him to look like a nigger so that he would be *recognized* as a nigger when they find him. There should be no confusion. In fact . . ." He stopped the procession on the other side of the two oaks that shaded me and Anna Marie. She bit at the hand that muted her.

"Put him down and roll him in the dirt," Sebastien said. "Yes, like that. Now step on his hands. *Step on them!* Grind them into the dirt, break off those nails. We cannot have him looking like a man who belongs in our drawing rooms, can we?"

One of the men quietly vomited at the base of one of the trees, not five feet from my boot. Anna Marie reached out to touch him, to help him, but I held her back. She bit the flesh of my thumb and I swallowed a shout.

"Don't get your nastiness on the General. Or his wife. How do you do, Mrs. Hood?"

Sebastien looked straight at us and I released Anna Marie. She glared but said nothing.

"You've been watching for quite a while, General. We are not trained soldiers, but we do the best we can. I would have thought you'd help, but I suppose you had something more interesting on your hands there." He winked.

"Let him go." I surprised myself, but only for a moment.

"Oh, General, you can do better than that. I know you don't mean what you say, or you would have come out of the trees."

He kicked his prisoner hard between the legs.

"But really, wouldn't you like a lick? These niggers hate you, you know. You, General Hood. They always did."

I said nothing.

"No?" Sebastien smiled. "Next time, then. We're off to see this one on his way."

When they had gone, I escorted Anna Marie down the winding, crunching path, back through our wonder garden, past the statue of St. Joseph with his pleading hands, and on to the foyer door. Before she stepped through, Anna Marie stopped. I couldn't read her face.

"You will not silence me again."

Then she disappeared into the warm light and across the soft carpets. I didn't follow her, I assumed she wanted to go home without me. I was once more the cripple and erstwhile general of the late Confederate Army, alone. My head pounded, my good leg felt weak.

I sat in the garden long after the last light, whispering awkward prayers to the stony-faced Joseph.

CHAPTER 9

Anna Marie Hood

I am walking about the house now, the fever has receded, and yet I feel every bit a hundred years old. My marriage is a thousand years old. I struggle to remember the clothes I wore before meeting the General, the books I read, the things I ate, the people I knew. I carry a rag with me at all times now when once I might have carried a fan painted with pelicans. Noses must be wiped, blood stanched from scrapes, milk sopped from the floor, urine mopped off trembling legs. The midwife laughs at me. She is still here, her name is Hammoloketh, or Ham.

Hammie. She follows me from room to room, sighing and sputtering as if I'm pulling her by a harness. She doesn't leave though I've told her she should. I *want* her to leave, but she says she is well paid by Rintrah only while she is here, and that my little criminal friend has made it perfectly clear she is to stay, so unless I can muster the strength to toss her out, here she stays. John doesn't notice her, never speaks to her. I talk to myself and pick at the holes in the settee where John has forgotten his cigars. I talk to my dead mother, I tell her she should have told me what this would be like, the casting forth of children, the creation of our own army of grabbers and wailers. I would do it again, of course, but I would have liked to have *known*. I might have learned to stay out of John's bed, at least a little more often. I would have been prepared for the isolation, the monasticism of motherhood, and not been forced to learn about it while listening to the screams and fending off the tugging hands. I say this to my dead mother, though I know I am actually saying it to Ham, who smiles and chuckles and waves her rosary at me as if fending me off. I do not know if she has children and I have not asked.

She is my company now, my visitor, my

guest. I still leave the card dish on the table in the foyer, and sometimes I polish it. I have nearly rubbed away the date of our marriage engraved in the center beneath our initials. It was a wedding gift, of course, and once it was always filled on Thursdays, my receiving days. Now I only receive Ham, and she has no cards. But once the multitudes came with their cards, my mother's friends, their daughters, and the wives of the men who curried the favor of my famous husband. How grand, that horrible mob of gossips and critics and spies, my visitors, my *people*! I don't miss them, though I do miss the sound of their voices and the way their crowd of bodies dampened the echoes in the house. Now it is just Ham in the corner, clicking her beads and listening for the crashes and indignant weeping of the children upstairs and in the yard. Someday she will say something, I am sure of it.

Where did my visitors go? The city has grown around our Third Street house, every year become denser and newer. We had been country people ten years ago. The Mussons moved in across the street five years ago, and then our block became crowded and fashionable. You know the Mussons of course. Do you remember when their cousin, the painter

Degas, came to the house to paint Mathilde?
You were only just walking, of course you don't
remember. He sketched you stumbling down
the streets just out of my grasp. I have this
sketch somewhere, he was very kind to give
it to me. I will make sure to find it. Mrs. Mathilde Musson Bell and I traded calls for years.
Her husband, the American William Bell, paid
visits to your father. He cultivated your father,
fawned over him. He pleaded with the General to declare himself against the abomination of negro rule, *which was surely coming*.
The White League, of which Mr. Bell was a
prominent member, needed men such as
Hood and other heroes of the Confederacy to
stand up again and fight. This is what the man
who sat out the war told your father, who left
half his body on the fields of fighting. Your
father turned him down flat, though I know
he enjoyed the flattery if not the flatterer. *I
believe you misuse the word* hero, *William.
I have rarely been called by that word, and
less so every year.*

Monsieur Degas also spied John struggling
to get up in our trap one day during his long
visit, and he strolled over to ask your father if
he might paint him without his leg attached,

and your father refused him also, but only because, as he explained, he had already been painted by his wife and that one portrait of a gargoyle was more than enough for one proper house. I cringe now to think that he turned away little Edgar for fear of offending me.

William Bell became angry when he heard of this latest rejection, which he added to John's rejection of the White League, as if the two were one and the same and directed at him personally. He never thought much of Edgar Degas. Oh William, he who walked down the center of banquettes as if he himself had built them and damn the other traffic, he who combed his beard to a greased point at the center of his chin, he was not used to rejection and pointedly refused contact with us ever afterward. This was the beginning of our long social decline, which William took pleasure in instigating, I do believe.

But the painter, the little man Degas, simply shrugged his shoulders at his rejection, and wished the General well. I heard it sitting in our library, where I was listening through the open window. *I do not encounter many men who do not want their portrait made, it is maybe, yes it is, it is admirable. I do not know how to say it. It is* bon. *I could make a very good painting, but there would be no love in it, no no, not like that of your lover. Ah, your wife? You are lucky, and not so vain, so* américain. He gave John a hearty shake and whistled back to the Mussons. I wish William had heard this.

Now where are my visitors? They've spread out, they've found new things to do. They watch the Opera, they plot the overthrow of governments. To their left and to their right as they look out from their carriages, behold the men maddened by war, mere animals now, shambling along. The old warriors flinch at the sound of the horses, rend their garments, soil themselves. In the market, which has spread up and down the river, widows and their children sit quietly in doorways clutching the last portraits of their men. These men wear woolens and campaign hats and their eyes look utterly white. The pistols they carry, or the bugles or the battle flags, it all looks much to bulk for them.

The *américains* thump and dig their way through the city. They do not call on me either. They spend their days raising buildings and cutting roads, perfuming their bosoms, shooting pistols in the sky. Their houses have sharp corners and picture windows so that anyone might see them eating, arguing, sleeping, making money, bathing in coin.

Had it only been a matter of money, I would still have visitors. The ladies would have brought us things, they would have taken pity on us. We would have been poor, embarrassed, but not alone. John's failures in cotton factoring were not so unusual. Among Creoles, a head unsuited for business was, in some circles, a matter of pride. In the Creole world, there were other things to preoccupy a fine and subtle mind, things that were born and died in a brief season like flowers, love, the taste of a good liquor, the Christ of Lent.

But such things did not occupy the mind of your father. The General wanted only to plead his case before the court of the Confederate mind, to convince those who cared that he had not been incompetent, that he had not sacrificed thousands on the field of Franklin for naught. He muttered about it in his sleep, and he throttled the sheets as if they were the throats of his critics. His businesses failed, whatever he says, because he didn't care as much about them as he did the opinions of men in distant cities, most of whom (I imagine) gave him no thought at all. John thought he was constantly recognized on the street. If we rode through town in our open trap, he would pull his hat down tight and tuck that beard into his shirt. He'd ask me if I'd seen that man staring, the one with the ruined and burnt face, and I'd say no, he hadn't been staring because his eyes were dead. *We must find a closed cab,* he'd say, ignoring me. *I do not like being gawked at.*

Your father hid. He hid in his office, grousing about money, scratching at his war memoir. He hid out in the ice factory down on the wharf. He haunted dark men's clubs, and the corners of hotel lobbies beneath dimmed lamps. He hid in his room, asleep beneath the woolen sheets or pacing—*step, click, step, click*—long into the night rehearsing for debates he would never engage. *Our flank WAS guarded at Spring Hill! That was HUMAN error. . . .* He came to me always deep in the night. The wraiths subsided only then, and he could concentrate on me and on him, on our bodies, on our sharp angles and sweet tingling, on the warm and furious thing of us! If your father had been home more, if he had not secreted himself away until the middle of the night, I might have had fewer of you children. But those were the moments allotted to me, and I craved them whatever pain and exhaustion they might bring later.

Now we are alone together nearly every moment, except when one of you children crashes into the room chasing a wayward grasshopper, or when we all walk along the levee and spot the lights of the riverboats twinkling away up the river toward cities I've never seen. It's an awfully unsettling idea: that there are people who will live and die without ever being aware of you. John would have said this was his greatest wish, but in fact it was quite the opposite. He had known fame and he had known infamy, and he had lost the power to reject either, especially for perfect anonymity

I, however, have become glad of anonymity, if only because it protects me from the chaos, silliness, and violence of my city. Even my old friends talk of nothing but whiteness, of the indignity of deferring to Yankee governors and the humiliation of *our men*. Our *white* men. We have governments and shadow governments now, each claiming sovereignty and willing to enforce it by club and pistol. They brawl on Canal Street, gouging eyes, burning posters, and overturning horse carts for barricades. The *gens de couleur,* the octoroons and quadroons, always the picture of mystery, elegance, and desire, are now merely nigger mammies. All negroes are now possessed of pop eyes, swollen lips, and bent spines, if the newspapers and their artists are to be believed. Occasionally they must be purged, the negroes, and so they are rousted, trussed up, beaten, toyed with, burnt, or worse. And afterward, when the muttering hobos are picking over the remains of the negro cottages and plucking out pairs of pants, some bright cuff links, a ladle—my people scurry back to their parlors and recite the litany of purity, of whiteness: *Father and Grandfather and Great-grandfather never dallied with the coloreds, Mother is pedigreed back to Charles Martel himself, and we have maintained this purity at great sacrifice for the good of our race, we have no coloreds in the henhouse, Amen.* I say bah. I know no such purity. I see the negro in every face, every big dark eye and thick black head of hair, and in every long and graceful hand picking out études on the piano.

This is how my city lives, now. In it, your father and I grew lonelier together. Your father had no interest in continuing the war, and so he turned down the men who came to him to take a position on the negroes and on the Republicans. He turned down the men who asked him to lead them in rousting these invaders. After this, they had no use for him. As for me, I had married the crippled and eccentric and traitorous General, and so I could be safely ignored as well.

And so there we were, orbiting each other, muttering curses at our enemies, hardly ever looking up.

A year ago, your father and I went back to the ballroom where we'd met, for a gathering of swells and toffs and Creoles and mistresses, the usual thing.

"We are going because we have not been invited to a party in quite a many months, and here we are with an invitation," John said. "So, we go."

"It helps that it is my cousin's party."

"I'm not sure what you mean."

Here, darling, you might think that your father was being purposely dense, but it's not true: he really had no idea. Society was not one of his interests, and consequently not something he'd even begun to master.

"You yourself have noticed that we rarely

are invited to the parties, and yet you haven't asked yourself why?"

"No. I assumed there were fewer parties."

"Remember what city you live in, John."

"Yes, true."

"I nearly made a career of going to parties when I was young."

"Yes, I'd heard that."

"Fiend!" I punched him on his good shoulder and my fist bounced back.

We were sitting in our parlor, which was still stocked with liquor. I poured him a brandy and took a dram myself.

"I am saying, John, that we are not being invited, and this particular invitation comes to us only because my cousin doesn't dare to snub me."

John sipped noisily at his brandy, a bad habit.

"We are being snubbed?"

"Yes."

"Because?"

"Have you been to any White League meetings?"

"No."

"Have you written to the newspapers denouncing the Federals? The Freedmen's Bureau?"

"No. But you know that I couldn't."

"Have you burned down a negro house? Lynched a half-breed?"

"No."

"And you're a former Confederate general?"

"I see."

He knew all this of course, that he had failed miserably as a former leader of the late Confederacy. He had not met expectations, and when the notables of our humid, cramped little city wanted a Confederate general—or several—to lead their resistance to Federal rule and the rise of the negro, he had not volunteered. They are people with long memories.

John poured the rest of his brandy out the window onto a pink hydrangea. Another bad habit.

"You're going to kill that plant."

"Mmmmm." He was thinking. "Why would your cousin not dare to snub us?"

"Personal reasons. Family history."

Which meant, in the ancient code of the Creoles, that I knew she had once taken a colored lover, and that now in her first year of marriage it was imperative that no one else find out. I must be kept happy, and she knew it.

But just to make sure she knew it, I invited her lover to the party myself. I thought it a

clever idea at the time, though I hadn't spoken to Paschal in years.

Does it shock you, Lydia, that I can speak of
lovers? I had my own, darling. It's true, I won't
deny it now that I'm gone and I don't have to
see your face. Don't be shocked. Perhaps you
aren't shocked. Perhaps you've had your own
lovers and know the sweet promise and tender violence of an affair. What do you love? I
ask not for my own benefit, of course, since
I am now moldering in my tomb and unable
to hear you. Don't begrudge me my morbid
humor. It's all that keeps me from crying out
for you. I couldn't go on without death's wit.
Death was something that was always present
then, it lingered behind all of us like a shadow
waiting to subsume the body. So many people
died, it's easier for me to name the ones who
lived.

Paschal, as you now know, was once one
of my oldest friends. He was also once, and
briefly and in the distant past, my nervous little cousin's lover. His mother was a quadroon,
rumor was. He had thin, knobby, twiggy fingers that stretched far across the piano key-
board and ran promiscuously and lightly over
the keys. Among other things, he was a piano

teacher, and I have no doubt that during her lessons my cousin had wondered very often about such fingers, each one an independent creature ruling over the white and the black with force and delicacy in turn. She found out in time, though she would tell me nothing.

Are you shocked that one of our family could love a negro? I don't know that there was much love, merely fondness, but I would understand if you were surprised. You shouldn't be, really. He was an educated man, after a fashion, and if you didn't know he'd been an orphan raised by nuns, you'd have assumed he was the son of the finest sons, a gentleman. And surely he was brother to white men unknown, cousin to others, their equal in all but blood, but even blood was less of a barrier to friendship than we might imagine now, now that the lines have been so clearly and cruelly drawn. He had been a friend to some of the men who killed him. My darling, he was their friend *to the moment he died*, I have no doubt. But most damnably, he had been *my* friend. His name was Paschal.

The city had changed. Just a few years after the war and we had all begun to behave like the *américain*, greedy and jealous and so awfully righteous. Paschal had once been trusted with the fairest of Creole blossoms, a misplaced trust in the matter of my cousin, I will admit that, but now he was permitted to teach piano only to his own kind. But we were his kind! Coarse, ignorant, money-mad men were newly admitted to our society because they were white and because they owned the city, but the delicate and talented *gens de couleur libre* who lacked only our *purity* (or what purity we had been able to secretly distill from the dark waters of our ancestries) were banished like common servants, or worse. They looked like us, and that could not be excused anymore. Kin denied kin. It sickened me, but of course I went along. I liked my pretty things, my pretty life. Acquiescence was the price of eternal membership in a society that would swaddle me and give me warmth for as long as I lived. That was very silly of me. I should have known there was no constancy in the new city, no loyalties that could not be forgotten or traded. You know this now, child. You need only look around you, you need only look at us here in our house, alone with the dusty and tarnished things. Where are those lovely and chivalrous creatures of my childhood now? They are not here in our house, not here where there is no money or prestige. No one comes to teach my children to play music, no one seeks our company, no one helps fill the pantry. I have no doubt that, were he still alive, Paschal would have come to continue your lessons, Lydia. *He* would have come. What a bitter thing to know.

This was the real truth of that awful, momentous night: my own ignorance cost a man his life. I had thought that the old rules could still apply if I only wished for them, and that a man like our piano teacher could still, if only for a little while, be allowed the gift of a beautiful night. *I* had invited him, and *I* had convinced him all would be all right. *Your friends will be there, they will remember you,* I said. *My cousin will be there.* For this foolishness my cousin would not forgive me for many years. After all, I think, she still had loved him.

Paschal died that night. I had invited him there, and there he died. He was beaten and dragged off by men who knew him and had always known he was colored, only that night being colored was a death warrant. I watched them do it and I said nothing. It was so very stupid. He danced with a woman, a white woman, and her drunk brother took up her honor, such as it was, and set in motion events that quickly leaped out of his control and into the hands of another, crueler and more blood-drunk man by the name of Sebastien Lemerle. I cross myself when I write his name, may his evil spirit be banished from me. I can't write anymore, thinking about it has nearly convinced me to tear this entire letter up, since it's clear it can only become the chronicle of my sin and loathing. Remember this only: Paschal Girard, the beautiful orphan, disappeared from the earth while I watched.

Shame and loathing and guilt. *Guilt* is not a sufficient word for what I felt, but it will have to do. I had killed a man even if I did not tie the rope. It was because I was stupid and insisted that the world ran according to my rules and my wishes. Who had ever told me otherwise? I could do nothing but flee the scene of my crime, our crime. What pact had that little killer, that Sebastien Lemerle, made with Lucifer? That is not fair to him. What pact had *all* of us made, and for what purpose? So that we might be preserved in amber, never changing? So that we might twirl eternally in our dancing shoes across an endless floor, past dark faces holding out full trays in bony hands?

I never told John that I knew Paschal. What

does that matter? I should have told him *that night,* that first moment we heard the shouts and saw the young women running. I didn't tell him, and then I couldn't tell him for the shame. And why hadn't I told him, why hadn't I said, "John, that is my dearest and oldest friend, you must save him!" John would have done it, for that reason. He needed a reason, that was his sin. And what was my reason for silence? I was like every bystander in every mob formed since God created the earth: I didn't want anything bad to happen, so I convinced myself it wouldn't. *I didn't think they would take it so far.* And if they weren't going to take it so far, then why, I reasoned, should I risk revealing myself as the woman who had invited Paschal, as his friend? I'd never be invited to a party again. As much as I claimed to not care about our snubbing, it had cut me hard. I wanted to go to their parties, so I let them kill Paschal. That's what I did.

I left John that night and walked to your grandmother's house in my bare feet. I left my shoes at the base of a small oak like the one that had hidden me. An offering. Oyster shells in the road cut my soles. I prayed to St. Basil and the Holy Mother, the two who knew the ways out of Hell. I prayed that I might be rescued from my sin, that the pact with evil would be broken, torn up, and burned. I remembered to pray for all of us, too. It was an afterthought. I don't remember praying for the souls of strangers before that night. I have prayed that way many times since. May God forgive me my youth.

I arrived at their house as the moon fell below the trees. It crossed my mind that I might never return to John, to our house and, forgive me, *to you*. I thought of you, though, I thought of you so innocent and sweet, probably asleep in your blue gown, your hair tangled around your face, your chest rising and falling silently while the other girls, Anna Bell and Ethel, snored in perfect rhythm. But I was marked, condemned, I was sure of it, and I could not risk seeing you. I was contagion.

The path to the front door was cool underfoot, lined by squared boxwoods and lavender. I could feel each red brick and each line of mortar, canted this way and that, a pattern I'd nearly forgotten since, as a girl, I'd run that path without shoes, ever in flight from pirates, or alligators, or fish oil, or church. I had known those bricks as well as I had known my own freckles. I had once been able to walk the path with closed eyes, knowing with each step where I was, what would come next, and how close I was to the end. That awful night I closed my eyes and walked. I discovered I had not forgotten. At the end, at the foot of the steps and in the gaslight that wavered behind the wings of moths and an ephemera of may-flies, I stopped and opened my eyes. I watched the last few bloody footprints behind me disappear into the brick.

My mother believed I must have taken ill, otherwise why would I cast off my shoes and my husband, and bloody my feet? No fever, she said, but a spell nonetheless. She sent me to bed and washed my feet through the night. She said I looked like a ghost.

I wished John could have known Paschal. Paschal had not been of this world, he'd been something apart, something blessed and innocent, though not so innocent that he didn't know how to acquit himself with a woman, as my cousin had once reveled in telling me. There are beings not meant to live among the rest of us, I think. They have been lost on the way to Heaven, they live only as an exception, an anomaly. Paschal was born out of sin, and as if to refute that wickedness and the transgression of abandonment, he swallowed beauty whole, infusing himself with it. Art and music, they were all. He played the piano as if the instrument were only incidental, a convenient conduit for thoughts that became music when exposed to air. It would not have surprised me had he made his music from rocks and ash, from the clang of iron on brick.

But this is what a killing does: it proves that safety is a wisp, that evil is strong, and that every moment of comfort and peace and beauty rests on a foundation of wishful thinking and ignorance.

CHAPTER 10

John Bell Hood

I knew Sebastien Lemerle, I had known him many years before, but on that night at the ball, I let Anna Marie think I'd never seen him before. I led Anna Marie to think I was a coward, which was far better than her thinking I was complicit in the scene unfolding before us: in the torture, the perversity, the mercilessness. Better she think me only a coward than a cruel and inhuman coward. Better that she didn't know that I had been shocked to paralysis the moment I recognized him.

I believed Sebastien Lemerle was an evil

blown into our lives from parts unknown, that he was sent by the Devil to murder, terrify, and destroy, and we were not to understand. Only bear it, bear the burden of man's lot and original sin. But it did not fall to us randomly.

On the train into the city, the old man had warned me that I would be remembered. I thought he meant *recognized,* singled out, noticed as I limped and clunked down the street. To be remembered, though, that implied a kind of familiarity I was sure I wouldn't find in New Orleans. This was why I had chosen the city, to escape. These were not my people, these were not my trees and birds and fish, these were not my streets, these were not my churches. I would disappear in New Orleans, lost to memory. I dreamt sometimes, when it was particularly heavy and wet in my quarters, when dreams came as in a fever, that my leg would grow back. Everything else grew in the damned place. The air lay upon me like soil and I felt new.

But I knew Sebastien Lemerle, and surely I was *remembered* by him. He would not have been able to forget, and had I cared to think about it, I might have guessed he'd be in the city. I did not care for Sebastien, though, as I cared very little for the men I ruined.

It was a hundred years ago. A thousand, maybe.

I remember him clearly. He rode with me in Texas before the war. He polished and sharpened his knives when he wasn't eating or sleeping or fighting. He let his black hair grow down in front of his eyes and he never said much to the rest of us, and then it was often in French. He was a corporal, in charge of men. He never raised his voice and still his squad never questioned him and always followed. I wondered what hold he might have over them, but only briefly. I assumed he was a private disciplinarian, meting out beatings and threats when no one was looking. It had been my experience, to that point, that men could be led by fear. I learned later, in the war, that love would bind men, thousands of men, to some generals, but by then it was too late for me. I was the Gallant Hood, riding into danger, damned be the weak and nearly everyone else.

In Texas I was young. I wanted to fight. I wanted to fight Comanche. Sebastien Lemerle and his squad came with me.

We drove for many days over dry country. The horses had little to drink and less to eat as there was very little rain to green the sand

and dirt. The earth there was broken into slabs thrust up in every direction and concealing the dark and narrow avenues of ambuscade. In the daylight we avoided those hiding places, and in the night we sought them out. One morning we awoke to a brief rain, and we all gathered about one man who was holding out an old oilcloth in his wide arms, catching the water in its trough. We drank like dogs.

We were out for weeks longer than I reported. The Comanche were always ahead of us, leaving their curious, light-footed tracks. At least once every couple of days we'd see one watching us. We were always just a half day's ride away, always so close. I wanted them. I didn't realize then, in my cursed and doomed youth, that one killing led to another, geometrically, until the only way possible to escape the massacre was to lead a whole army into the maw and hope for an ending.

The first man to go down was one of our sharpshooters, a Kentucky man like me, but small, blond, and bone hard. He spoke in tongues and thrashed while the other men tried to hold him down. He needed water and there was no one with enough to spare. To share it would mean a sooner death for us. He asked us to give him his birthday cake, he asked us who we were, he asked *what day is the fair gone start?* I took Sebastien aside.

"We'll have to leave him."

"We can send him back, sir. One man could take him back."

"I can spare one man, but not two."

I looked at Sebastien closer then. He had fine bones, and a large and round head, but his face was pocked. He wore his hair long to cover it, I realized. He never looked at me directly, always at my shoulder or my feet or at some imaginary figure off in the short distance. He chewed his words and let them go with a struggle, as if he were afraid of what would happen if he looked me in the eye. Not to him, but to me. The idea amused me, but I didn't know him so well then.

"Yes sir. But we can leave him a horse and what food and water we can give up. He can have mine."

The more he talked, the more righteous I became.

"We leave no food or water behind. We can't spare it, Corporal, and you know it quite well. He can have the horse, she's in worse shape."

"We have to spare it. The food. The water. He'll die." He pushed the hair out of his eyes.

"We don't. And we won't."

He looked at me with sudden and unhappy understanding. I had given the order: leave the man to die alone. This is what I believed I had been taught to do. It had always thrilled me at the Academy to hear an instructor describe how we would have to make hard decisions, to eschew popularity for right, comfort for necessity. I had wanted to be that man. What I hadn't realized then was that every decision didn't need to be so damned hard. Hard-hearted, that is.

Sebastien walked away and ordered his men to mount up. They fell in with me, and we went off. Perhaps the boy would gain his senses and make it to safety. Perhaps he would die with honor, fighting Indians. Perhaps he would die and never be found. I would later declare him missing in my official report.

Sebastien let us go and walked back to the boy. I saw the smoke and the birds fleeing before I heard the shots. Two shots. Some of the men turned to go back, but I urged them on. They didn't know what I had said to Sebastien, and some of them cursed him as a murderer. I let them think it. I had nothing to say. I could feel my hands shake. I had not thought what would happen to our little sharpshooter after we mounted out. Sebastien had, and the shots rattled me. My first kill, and it smelled of dust and horse sweat. Tasted dry.

He caught up to us a half mile or so down into the next valley. He rode at the back and said nothing for two days other than *yes sir*.

I had bound him to me. I knew he disliked me, perhaps hated me, but I was his only friend now, after those two shots. He would not explain himself to anyone, though some of the smarter men figured out what had happened and approached him diplomatically, with forgiveness. *Go fuck yourself and get in line*, he'd say. He didn't speak to me, either, but when we bedded down he stayed close, and when we rode we rode together. He wasn't afraid of the others. He simply couldn't be one of them anymore, having killed their friend, no matter what the reason. He could put a gun to their heads and pull the trigger, and that made him an outlier. He wasn't one of them anymore. He was one of me.

It was three days after the killing that I realized how I could beat the Comanche.

I nodded off in the saddle and jerked awake periodically. The rest of the men were in worse shape, and I knew that we had only a couple more days before we'd all be dead of starvation or thirst. Two men had deserted, riding off toward civilization, and I knew I had to act quick to finish things off or risk being recalled to the post and humiliated.

I was awake when we passed a strange rock for the second time. I remembered it because it had resembled a very large, bloody red liver. Birds had perched on it, streaking the rock with their dung. I had seen the rock seven days before.

A circle. If we were being led in a circle, what were we circling? There was something at the center very dear to the heathen Comanche.

It was only a day's ride to the center. I was glad for the drought then, for the dust. We moved faster than we had for a week, raising a great cloud. I wanted them to see that I'd solved their riddle and that I was riding for their children and their wives. I wanted them to stop me. I wanted them to fight.

Sebastien rode beside me, shaking his head and pulling his slouch hat tighter down over his eyes. I knew this to be his one outward gesture of anger.

"You are not satisfied with the plan, Corporal?"

He scratched his horse's neck slowly, gathering his words.

"I just would like to know what we're going to do when we get there."

"That will be up to them."

"We're going to beat them there."

"Yes."

"Then what?"

"We shall see."

I believe Sebastien was afraid. I believe he was afraid of himself. I believe that Sebastien was afraid of what I would allow him to do, what I would encourage him to do. The killing of the sharpshooter was the beginning. While riding beside him and observing him, I decided I had misjudged him. His men obeyed not because he disciplined them, which he didn't, but because he was unknowable and therefore capable of anything. His silences contained possibility, and after he put down a man and his horse, those possibilities turned dark. If he was not insane just then, he would become insane under my tutelage. I pulled it out of him, used it for my own ends.

The camp was dirty and chaotic. The women, children, and old men lay in the shade of deerskin shelters, nothing more. They had little. The twisting breeze of the lower valley

pulled the smoke from their fires into whirling cones that danced from shelter to shelter.
I watched from an overlook with Sebastien
and two scouts. The men, crippled by age,
ambled from fire pit to fire pit, each built in a
hollow part of a rock wall, or under an overhang. They had seen our sign and struggled to
put out the fires slowly without releasing too
much smoke. Too late, of course.

They were all dressed as vagabonds. They
wore torn shirts taken from trash heaps,
leather shoes and boots that didn't fit, snap
brims and slouch hats. They had accepted our
refuse, made it their own. A strange people.

There were eleven old men, eighteen
women, thirteen children. Their warriors had
discovered our gambit, and I could see their
own dust trail moving toward us like a snake.
They were no more than an hour away, and
I reckoned they were fifteen strong at least.
We were an equal force, though starved and
weak and feverish. I decided we would fight a
defensive fight to multiply our strength. Make
them attack.

Sebastien stared down at the encampment,
mumbling to himself. I had seen him do this
while writing letters home, to whom I have
no idea. He scratched at paper with a nub and

chewed his fingers, searching for the perfect word. I guessed it was a woman. Someone who made him anxious, twitchy. He mumbled to himself then, as he did now.

I sent the two scouts down to where the rest of the men had found cover. They were to get them up and prepared, ready for a fight finally.

"Corporal, what do you think?"

"The Comanche will be here soon."

"We'll have to take the camp. They'll fight if we have their women."

I could hear him grinding his teeth. He put his hand up to his head and brushed his hair back. The pocks on his head looked as if someone had taken a carving knife to him. It was a landscape, now furrowed.

"Take their camp."

"That's right."

"Then what?"

The question again. I smiled. Why did I smile? Why such joy? I felt every drop of blood cascading through my body, I was aware of every thing around me. I could see with my hands, with my skin, I could feel sound on my cheek, I sensed the earth and the air move, turning and turning. *You'll have to make the hard decisions.* The hard decisions were cruel and necessary, they marked the man who knew the world from the man who lived with gauzy hope for beauty. One could not know good without knowing evil. The hard decision.

"We'll see."

He pulled his knife and I thought he would attack. I was surprised he hadn't tried sooner, and I rolled to my feet and drew a pistol. But he was only pulling it to sharpen its blade, which he spit on and tested on the dark, wiry hair of his arm.

"You're going to finish this, aren't you, sir?"

"If by 'finish' you mean defeating the enemy, then yes."

"You mean for us to do more than that, even if you don't say it. Even if you don't know it yourself. You mean for something else to happen."

"I don't know what you're talking about."

"You will. You'll know it when you see it, sir, and you should know that you did it."

"Go back to your men."

He held the knife up in the sun and let it flash in his eyes.

"Yes sir."

We took the camp, it wasn't difficult. No

shots fired, no one hurt. We divided the men from the women from the children, three small groups seated on the ground in the shade of rock and scrub. They were silent, no one spoke, which I found odd. I imagined screaming and yelling, I had dreaded it actually, but it had all gone well.

When we were done we took our defensive positions—there was really only one way into the camp, the rear of the camp was blocked by a boulder field. Not long afterward the Comanche were standing above us in the rock a couple miles away, looking down. There were more of them than I'd realized, perhaps twice as many, but we had the defensive position and the advantage. We had set the terms of the fight.

For an hour we remained like that. Our captives barely moved, never spoke. Our men became restless, or fell asleep. The Comanche didn't move, just stared and stared. It was shortly after noon, the sun fell down upon us and pressed. I felt rooted to the ground. We had set the terms of a fight, and there was no fight.

Sebastien came over, head down, kicking pebbles out of his way. Everywhere Spanish bayonet plants grew up out of the ground as if the earth had armed itself.

"They ain't coming," he said.

"They'll come."

"No they won't. They'll wait us out. They know we can't stay here forever, that we've lost our strength. They've been watching us for days. Weeks. They know it. They'll wait us out."

"We have their camp."

"What do they care, sir?"

"The women and children."

"They look comfortable to me, and to them up there with their arrows and rifles and lances. They haven't even taken a shot, they haven't moved."

He was right. I'd known he was right before he said anything. I suppose I had wanted it to happen this way, but couldn't admit it to myself. I was glad to have someone else to say it for me, someone else to do it. When it came to it, someone else made the hard decision for me.

"We'll have to stir them up," I said.

"You want me to do it, don't you see?"

"Yes, Corporal."

"You knew this would happen. It was the only thing that *could* happen. When we turned off that track and came to this camp, there was only one way this would end, no? You'll understand someday."

I registered his insubordination, his snarls, the glancing look into my eye. Full of disdain and hate.

He dragged the first woman out into the clearing, visible for miles around, and cut her throat like he was butchering a hog. She was dead quick. One soldier started to run but thought better of it when Sebastien rounded on him, knife flashing, growling. The rest of the men stayed put, averting their eyes.

The Comanche stirred but didn't charge. Sebastien took the woman's child and killed him the same way, laying him gently next to his mother. Their blood mingled and was absorbed into the ground. Still the Comanche did not charge. Sebastien shouted at the men that they would die if they didn't get busy, and when the men saw that the warriors were willing to suffer the sacrifice of a mother and child while waiting us out to our deaths, they understood. I watched.

Once the massacre began, there was no stopping them. *One killing leads to the next, and so on.* A man changes when he's killed someone, so much of what was possible for him in life becomes impossible: innocence, grace, forgiveness, sweetness. A killer is always a killer, and once the possibility of redemption disappears there is only anger: at a world that led to damnation, at the dead themselves, at whoever was at hand. The anger is contagious, it moves through groups of men instantly causing frenzy. I didn't involve myself. I watched the Comanche ride hard for us, screaming.

We shot, stabbed, and beat the women and children. We ripped their shirts off and mutilated them. Some of the old men, old warriors, fought back and were struck down quick. Some others of the Indians ran off, chased by others of my men. Some escaped. Soon it was over, thirty down. The Comanche were close and I ordered the men back to their positions. They were slow to move and I rode in among them, slapping at them with my sword. *Get on and get down!* Only Sebastien remained, eyes bright and body bent, putting his knife to each throat of the fallen, just to make sure. His shirt was brown with blood, as were the heels and toes of his boots. When he stood up I could see the tears running down each cheek. He didn't look sorry, though, for what he had done. Some part of him wept while the other part brandished his knife and licked his lips. I'd never again see him weep, or show remorse for anything.

The battle was quick and hard. They drove off our horses and we fought on foot. Our rifles and pistols overwhelmed them ultimately. Our men fought for their lives, and they were maddened temporarily by bloodlust. We chased them down the dry draw of an old stream until it was clear they weren't coming back. An arrow pierced my hand, a wound I can still see and sometimes feel in the night as a hot flame. I heard a man hollering something godawful down among the boulders and sage of the old streambed. When the shouting was done and the howling was over, Sebastien returned from the streambed with a blank look upon his face.

Twelve dead Comanche, and though we suffered no deaths during the battle, I wrote down in my notebook these words: *One dead, the Kentuck fallen honorably.*

When we were returned to the barracks, I wrote a report that described how we were tricked by the Comanche into a fight and how they used their squaws in battle. From what I remember of my official report:

Meantime, the Indians quickly as they discharged their arms, handed them to their squaws, who ran to the rear, reloaded and returned them. At this juncture I was pierced in the left hand with an arrow which passed through the reins and the fourth finger, pinning my hand to the bridle. I instantly broke the spearhead and threw it aside. Unmindful of the fact that the feathers could not pass through the wound, I pulled the arrow in the direction in which it had been shot, and was compelled finally in order to free myself of it to seize the feathered in lieu of the barbed end.

Thus raged this hand-to-hand conflict until all our shots were expended, and it was found that owing to the restiveness of the horses we could not reload while mounted. We then fell back about fifty yards and dismounted for that purpose. Soon afterward arose from beyond the burning heap one continuous mourning howl, such as can alone come forth from the heart of the red man in deep distress. These sounds of sorrow revealed to me that we were in little danger of a renewal of the assault, and I was, I may in truth say, most thankful for the truce thus proclaimed.

* * *

Several things happened the week we returned. I received a letter from the commanding general of the Department of Texas, describing our horror this way: "Lieutenant Hood's affair was a most gallant one, and much credit is due to both the officer and men." Thus was born the Gallant Hood legend. I received a promotion and a new command and our unit broke up. Every other man requested a transfer.

Sebastien Lemerle came to see me off as I was packing the cart that would carry me over to Fort Mason and my new duties. He had cut his hair nearly to his scalp. This time he looked at me directly, coolly, almost without blinking. He was looking for something.

"Back where I come from, Hood, they say the mark of the Devil can be seen. You got to look close, but there it is, always. On marked men, that is."

"You should rest, Corporal."

"Your secret is safe, *Lieutenant*."

"I have no secrets." A lie, but I had already begun the march to becoming the great disgraced General Hood, and I would become an excellent liar.

The Comanche had fled from me, and my men had feared me. They had marched until they were starved and dry as the sand in their boots. They did this because I told them to do it. The Comanche stopped to fight because I had driven them to it. Men shot each other, clubbed each other, sent arrows into our hands and hearts. I had ordered it so. The skies fractured into so many mirrors, each reflecting back my great glory. I did not notice this then, as I was fighting for my life. But I remember the light, numb feeling of watching the fight spread out from me like cracks in glass, and as man tumbled with man to the ground with knives and teeth flashing, I was myself enlarged to contain it all. I was its cause, its mind, its soul. The arrow that pierced my flesh had already been part of me from the moment I'd been born, perhaps before. The pain was extraordinary, perfect, a point on my body in which everything—warriors, soldiers, magpies, brush, rock, blood, the unintelligible language of the savage—was stilled and made known. I was simultaneously the boundless and ancient battlefield and the point of one arrow in one flesh. I was young and I had destroyed worlds. I was ruined and awed by myself. I required obedience.

"You have no secrets from yourself anymore, that is true." His voice sounded as if it were coming from the bottom of a very deep well. Distant, and yet reading my thoughts.

"Step back, Corporal, and shut your mouth."

"You and me, we are like brothers."

"I have no affection for you."

"I have none for you. But we are, what you say, *the same*. We are reborn from the same womb, out of darkness. Twins."

"You've been drinking."

"Never. Not once in my life. But I will admit the world looks much different now."

I mounted and rode off.

"See you later, Lieutenant!" he called. My hand began to bleed on my saddle. Soon it was dripping onto the ground, which absorbed it quickly as if it had never existed.

So, yes, I knew Sebastien Lemerle, native of New Orleans, son of Creole whores and privateers. I didn't at first recognize him that night at the ball. He dressed fine and he talked with grace and power, nothing like the stoppered and shifty young man I had seen kill silently and with resentment. I saw a man enjoying himself, a man in command. He had become something greater and more awful than I'd known back in Texas. I had known him as a skilled but reluctant killer, a man who knew what he had inside and had wished desperately to keep it screwed down forever. I had forced it out of him, and then there he was, beating a colored man with a poker and making sport of it.

Can a man say he has created another man? Once a stranger but now something remade, a piece of a man's neglected and rotten soul broken off and given form, life? Would that man be a brother, as Sebastien had suggested ten years before? I denied it then and convinced Anna Marie I'd never met the man. But now I am not so sure. I believe that the presence of Sebastien in my city—or, more precisely, my presence in *his* city—was not so much of an accident as I at first suspected. When I pray to God and when I dream, I hear the howl out beyond the scrub, in the streambed, and I wonder if the events that followed that night at the ball, and the people caught up in them, weren't somehow sung into existence by the beast who gave forth that howl. Poor Paschal, Rintrah, Father Mike, Anna Marie, Sebastien, me, and even that amiable idiot Eli Griffin. Something was loosed on the world, and there in New Orleans it fell to us to silence the howl somehow.

CHAPTER 11

Anna Marie Hood

I sometimes walked out to the levee where the cannoneers fired their guns each night to ward off the miasma and the fever. I brought them bonbons as I'd once brought them to the runaways in the swamp as a child. You must remember this, Lydia. I brought you with me many times, and now I regret it. I regret having scared you, and I know I did. The men at the cannons were rowdy and wore uncombed, curling beards. The colonel in charge of the battery wore his nut-brown uniform as if he had a grudge against it, twisted and wrinkled and shoved beneath his belt here and there. The colonel stepped lightly around the cannons and appeared afraid of them. He did not join the others in shouting *hurrah* with each fusillade. He looked pained.

The noise was suffocating, heavy, and lingered on long after the dirty yellow flame shot out the end of the tube. There were no cannonballs, only sound and fire. Even so, we all watched out over the water for the effect of the shots to become apparent. What effect could there be? I didn't understand the theory of the cannons, how they could stop the disease from calling on our houses and in our public rooms, how the smoke and fire could dampen the bright, hot fevers. Regardless, the cannoneers had ringed the city and each night a dozen guns blasted forth, sounding in every direction. We looked out at the mist above the brown water and above it to the slip of clouds that snuck past the moon. We expected to see something. The sound of the cannons made you cry, Lydia. You held your perfect little hands over your perfect little ears and you cried out for me. You grabbed at me, you took my skirt in your fists and looked up to me for help and explanation. All I could tell you was that this was the world, and in it men died and men fought death, much like you fought sleep at night from your trundle bed. This fight was loud and ugly and waged by men who burped and drank and leered at your mother. *These are our heroes,* I told you there, standing on the levee watching the cannon rock back in its carriage. I had no business telling you that. This world you must discover for yourself, and in *your* searching you may find that the better world of your soul, in which there is only truth, contains no such ugliness and despair. This is not what your mother discovered, but you may discover it still. It's not what I saw when I watched the men pull their fraying lanyards and let loose the explosion. It was not what I saw when I imagined the disease wafting in on river winds, pushing back our cannons and armies and superstitions. I saw faces in the mists, gargoyles and demons, so sad and brutal and resigned. I didn't tell you that, thank God. I spared you something at least.

I suppose one might call my interest in the cannoneers an obsession. I thought of it as my own enlistment in the war, my contribution. The men thought I was for sale, I'm sure, and they grabbed at me when their prim colonel wasn't watching. I didn't acknowledge their fumblings, and later they quit trying. I never told them I was Mrs. Hood. The last time I visited the cannons I overheard one young, skinny cannoneer with syphilitic eyes. *She's got no sense,* he said. *She believes in this, sure enough, and if that ain't sign of the galloping crazy, there ain't nothing crazy. And I know* that *ain't true.* I missed those boys when I retreated back to the house in shame and for good, just in time for the birth of the epidemic.

People began dying in late May. You could tell because the streets emptied of all but the clock-clock-clock of cart teams pulling their dead-heavy loads, and the cassocked priests hurrying up one street and down the other, from sick house to cemetery to funeral Mass, a thin-lipped and endless parade of piety and grim faith.

Paschal might have died that summer had he lived to see it. I asked myself many times while chasing after you children and boiling your potatoes whether I would have felt the same way about Paschal if he'd died pale, dry, and afire in a comfortable bed, rather than at the end of a rope held by strange men in the dark. Would I have felt the same anger, remorse, and dread had the miasma taken him? If Paschal had died at the hands of God, pushed down by the contagion, His own inscrutable messenger? Had that been the cause of Paschal's death, I would have blamed God. I would have avoided Mass and refused the Eucharist. But who did I have to blame but myself? I had led Paschal to his sacrifice, and I had watched it proceed. God had not arranged it. Or, if He had, I had been His willing accomplice, His conduit. I had to accept the blame. I could have resisted. Yes, I might have resisted even God. Instead, he disappeared by my doing and penance had to be paid.

I began with you children. You were innocents who had no need to know of their mother's fall, and who did not deserve to suffer from it. Alas, I believe you *did* suffer. I removed you from the world and set you on hard wooden chairs in the parlor like so many porcelain dolls propped up and staring at me. I had emptied the house of every other adult but me. This was not the mother you had known, but then I was not the Anna Marie *I* had known. I could do all, solve every problem, sing every nonsense song, polish every fork to its last tine, cosset my children in discipline, answer every question, and be loved again. I saw the wonder and anxiety in your eyes. I noticed that Anna Bell no longer carved her letters in the plaster walls of the room she shared with the twins, Marion and Lilian. I saw Ethel trying to cook a *gombo z'herbes* in the fireplace as the cook used to do it, though my little daughter had never picked up a pot except to beat it with a spoon or to hold toads captive.

Finally, there was quiet. You all played silently in your rooms. All I could hear was the wind in the windowsill cracks and the groaning of the floors as they settled, always settling. This silence drove me out of the house. I was so drunk with my own ideas about blame and sin and death, when I left I didn't think I'd done anything notable once I'd locked the doors from the outside and shut you all in. *As long as nothing can get in or out, all will remain unchanged and as if I'd never left.* I think I believed time would stop, otherwise I never would have left you all alone, invulnerable to the future so long as the doors were locked. Perhaps you were safer, really; safe from me. Did I tell you when I would return? I don't think I did. I didn't know myself, truly. I saw Duncan pressed up against the glass window in the parlor, watching me. He looked relieved, his face slack and open, eyes bright. It is only now, as I write this, that I see the tragedy in his face, which was the face of a son glad to see his mother go away.

I would never be right again, I thought, if I didn't face the fact that I had helped to kill my friend. More than that, I had to admit that this friend, this man who had been part of my history since I was a vain and adventurous young girl, this *colored* man had been an utter mystery to me. I knew nothing about him, nothing about how he had lived in the convent orphanage, nothing about the family that had abandoned him, nothing of what he did when he was not with us making jokes and playing the piano. I grieved for that man, but also for my own cold heart.

I vowed to change, and to change I had to understand. I had to understand Paschal, and Michel and Rintrah and John. Myself too. How ignorant I felt.

CHAPTER 12

John Bell Hood

The mark of the Devil on me, as Sebastien had put it all those years before, was *cowardice*. What terrible outbursts of cruelty and horror have been committed by man in the interest of concealing that terrible secret, our cowardice. From the moment we crawled out of our caves on our bellies in the dirt, seeking fire and foraging roots and insects, man had been plagued by cowardice. Left to our cowardice and its power to consume, we would have starved happily in the dark, chalking our names on cave walls. But cowardice must be beat down and concealed, and it is by the transmission of fear, the distribution of it from one man to another, that this cowardice is most effectively muted, though never truly overcome. This is what I think, anyway.

I was afraid to fail Anna Marie, and yet I knew the insurance business had been a foolish idea. I had no head for such business, and yet I sought it out anyway, damn the fear. Now it was failing.

I was afraid of the men who governed the city, and so I became a knee-walking sycophant around them, currying favor down at the Pickwick Club, listening to my voice pitch higher only to be swallowed up in their thick blue carpets and red curtains.

Long before that night at the ball I had become an anonymous man, rarely referred to as the General except by men with mischief in their eyes. I was a simperer, a sniveler. I depended on the charity of other men, my new business partners and the men who might give me their business. This trust was misplaced, my dependence a disaster. I lived in fear of what men thought of me, and so I continued to write my letters and to re-create the battles of my youth, searching for that unalloyed courage I thought I'd find in my past, some evidence for it.

But I was not a courageous man, and so how could it be that *I* should be called upon to silence that howl, the cry of the Comanche and the damned? How could I think it would ever cease to ring in my head, that wail of outrage. And yet I began the task. I fought it. In the days after the ball I became deathly tired of it, the howl, and I knew I couldn't live with it anymore. This is what General Longstreet had meant when he'd called it *the weight*. I had to put it off, stop it. I set out to silence it. I set out to become a man again, which is to say, a human.

There was much to overcome. I was a streetcar man, cramped morning and night between broad shoulders. The city passed by cloudy windows, it was soft and beckoning. I knew it was neither, that it was hard as most places and perversely cruel, but it was also Anna Marie's home, and when the facts of the city stand against the allure of that woman, I can't count the smokers blowing their choking, decomposing clouds into the air of the streetcar, or the flower sellers drumming their product without cease or subtlety, or the mumbling and lost people staring after us as we passed. As long as Anna Marie was somewhere in the city (currently at her parents' house for a long visit) and my platoon of children, the city was brilliant and I its master. There were no lynchings, no old enemies.

Had that only been true. I was a master of nothing, a bearded and dour troll with a dead history and a future in hot-air schemes and greed. In the mornings I stepped off the streetcar, tossed a coin to Plato once he'd shined my shoes on his old lemon box, and walked over to the office on Common Street. Most days it was Plato, sweating, knock-toothed, and black as swamp water, whose conversation, irrational and soothing and confident, saved me from the grim fear of failure during those moments I had on Common Street before entering my cursed office rooms. All other conversations during the day would be disappointing or humiliating.

"Shine it right up, General?"

Someone might have told him about me, but more likely the title was merely one of several he used with his customers. Others were "colonel," "captain," "duke," and "marquis," the latter reserved for other negroes. He fit us each with titles he believed appropriate to the man, and I took some pleasure at the thought that he'd picked me for a general merely on the way I appeared. I had supped at the finest tables of Richmond, courted the loveliest flowers of the Confederacy, and been the confidant of President Jeff Davis himself, and yet it is the shoe-shine man I think about now, the one man who owed me nothing, who had nothing to gain from me but a coin or two.

"Thank you, Plato."

"Gone off to make you some money today, right, General?"

"As much as any day."

Plato was smarter than I had at first believed, much to my discredit. "No sir, today's it. Today is the big day, I see it. Smell it. Can't mistake the sign, got to march on off down there and take it when it comes, 'cause it coming."

"What signs?"

"You still here, ain't you? Every day, there you are. Ain't dead yet, so the Lord got plans for you. And the Lord likes a man who got patience. A man who does his work every day. A man who humble. Not like the rest of this city, everyone spending they hours figuring what they gone do next, someday, once they's got around to it. The clouds are looking good for you, too."

"You read signs in the clouds?"

"Nah, just saying that shine gone stay on

you all day. No rain to run it off. It gone be a pretty day. A *moneymaking* day."

It was never a moneymaking day. There were money-hoping days, and money-needing days, and money-promising days. I hung my hat on the hat stand every morning, sat at my desk in the quiet corner of the big wood room, and listened to my partners tiptoe around behind me. On the blotter I laid one piece of paper every morning. On this paper, engraved with my initials, I would write another of hundreds of letters to the men I had once known when I was a commander and a warrior. I had to force myself to pick up the pen and write the first words, clever and dignified words. But however I worded it, the letters always said this:

April 5, 1887

> *Help me. Let me insure your cotton, your boats. Give me your money. I know no one. Once, you favored me, perhaps admired me. Now I find myself unsuited for everything respectable, and unable to make my way in the business as I once made my way across*

battlefields. I know nothing and am uncomfortable in all things now. I depend on the kindness of old friends and whatever dim memory of loyalty from long ago. Have pity.

My partners whispered to each other and mewled at me. They were rarely in the office, always out *soliciting business*. They had many meetings. I was naïve. But not so naïve that I couldn't be pushed to anger. On that April day, I began to end my suffering and humiliation.

Felix was alone when he finally arrived, and God knows where Alcée was. In the late afternoon, the sun through the windows melted orange on the cypress floor. I had been writing letters all day but had just run out of ink. My mind wandered, spiraled down. I became angry.

"Felix?"

"Yes?"

"Felix, why are you and Alcée always whispering? What is it I may not hear?"

"Nothing, General, for you to worry about. Minor matters, clerical details."

"It has been clerical details that have marked every loss, every penny of mine that disappeared somewhere into those wharfs, and so I do not consider them minor. Tell me."

Felix was tall, stooped, and sallow. He paid a disturbing amount of attention to his mustache, black and gleaming and thrust ahead of a bony face and sunken cheeks. His jacket was too broad for his shoulders, the waist of his pants too loose.

"We discuss how to run off with your money, of course!" He grinned and I frowned. "A joke, General, a joke."

Why did these men, Felix and his friend, Alcée—built fat, short, and fidgety like a beetle—think they could joke with me? What had I ever done to encourage *that*? I knew jokes, and could laugh, but not with such men, and at my own expense. I demand respect, but I am not without humor. Humor. Laughter. Innocence. I understand it.

Oh hell, I *was* without humor. I *am* without humor. Who is this man writing on this page? So weak, so ingratiating, so worried. I do not recognize him. I should have broken the skinny one's neck. He had stolen from me, I was sure of it, but there I was, negotiating with the bastard, listening to his joking barbs. Filthy Creole, no doubt a fornicator and possibly a sodomite. God had struck him down, and would continue to strike him down. Why else would he look like a man already dead, bones awaiting their tossing into some great common grave for the worthless. Or into the river. I was humorless, yes.

I wanted to eat his heart, remove his eyes, cut him in two. My hand ached where the arrow had marked me. I had tied my lot to this man, this goblin. I had been weak.

I took him by the front of his shirt and pulled him down to the floor by my chair so I could look into his eyes. His eyes were nearly black, and I thought I detected fright. This fed me, made me bolder. I slapped him and he cried out. He tried to get to his feet and I pulled him down again. *I am still strong,* I thought. He waited for another blow, eyes closed, but I held back. I savored the look of anticipation in his face. He was terrified, and I had terrified him. *Good.*

"Do not ever take a liberty with me. Not again. You won't do it again."

One end of his mustache had found its way into his mouth. He tried to spit it out while keeping an eye on me. The moment could not last, but for now he was mine. I could feel my leg growing back, I could feel the muscles again. Power flowed back into my arm, my muscles grew taut and whole. I nearly jumped to my feet. Foot. I thought better of it. But I knew I still had power, that I could command a man to sit on his knees before me.

I wondered if I could kill Felix, who remained quiet and kneeling during my reverie. He breathed heavily, a thin and whiny rasp wrenching from his chest. He watched me, and in his eyes I could see the fear had passed and all that remained was puzzlement and growing impatience. I swept my good arm across my desk, sending papers and glassware to the floor. The letter I had been writing (*May I be forgiven the imposition, friend . . .*) fluttered down between my feet. I must have seemed insane.

"General, this is not necessary. I was merely making a joke, a bad one, yes, but still a joke."

"Is it a joke that we have no money, that we are believed fools in every lounge and club up and down this city?"

"I do not know this. Who speaks of this?"

"Liar."

"Perhaps it is only the jealous who speak this way."

"Jealous of what, for God's sake? Perhaps it is only *me* they speak of."

Felix's eyes narrowed to nothing. He was not stupid, nor was he entirely without courage.

"What are you suggesting?"

His head was very hard. The metal knob of my cane cracked against him and then vibrated so painfully I nearly dropped it. He fell in place, keeled over, and curled on the floor like a puppy. I sat and watched him, peaceful and still, until I could see his chest rise and fall.

My head began to ache, caving in at the temples. (My head hurts as I write this. My heart is pushing against my chest. No more cigars.) I surveyed the room: a riot of paper and ink and ledgers and broken glass extending out from where I sat. I contained all of that also, but I felt no thrill in it. Just pain in my head.

I stood up, gathered my hat, and hobbled over the casualties. There lay the record of my fortune, all of it empty or illegible. There had been no fortune, only a childish trust and childish fantasies.

Lord help me, but in that moment I gave serious thought to killing the man. I required a sacrifice equal to the loss of my standing, equal to the humiliation of being deceived by two godless French twits, equal to the horror of knowing I'd been the financier of their descent into the underworld. I knew this, yes. I had followed them, tracked them, made a reconnaissance of their movement, their activities, their lives. I do not beat men without reason.

On several evenings I had pursued my prey from glass of liquor to hanger steak at Arnaud's, to more liquor in the clubs and the negro music dens, to (most unnerving) the little cottages off Rampart Street where the two kept their colored women. Pretty little cottages. My partners walked arm in arm, point to point, holding each other up. Too drunk to notice me clunking from shadow to shadow. Drunk on my money. I had been defeated without ever engaging, without meeting the enemy until it was too late.

Felix lay on the floor, quiet. One side of him, the side that lay against the hard, old bargewood floor, had become white in the dust, as if he were disintegrating, ashing away, restoring himself to his original state. I left him there. I walked into Alcée's office and broke open the locked drawer of his desk, where I knew he kept the true book on our business. I took it and ripped out the first page. It said, in thin and angular letters, *Défense d'entrer.* I thought, *Oh, of course it's private, and thank you for reminding me or otherwise I might have taken it or violated its secrets. Forgive me!* I stabbed that page through with his sterling letter opener and pinned it to the desk. I had their record of crime, and I left my own, bleeding and foggy-headed. We were square. Our partnership would take months to sever cleanly, but I was free from that day on.

I walked out and down onto Common Street. Behind me I could feel the heavy, moist river breathing on me, pushing me on and away. I slipped through the shadows that chilled the wood of the banquette. I passed Plato and said nothing. He sat on his box drawn back between buildings that leaned against each other. He had pulled his hat down over his face. His eyes followed me, and he smiled.

The more I walked, the less my head hurt. I went down unfamiliar streets and saw nothing I knew: strangers, galleries, screeching children throwing old fruit, screens of graying sheets floating in the air from lines cast between houses. Dogs sniffed at me, interrogating the stranger with the limp. Water crashed from a basin held in the window above to the courtyard three stories below. It sounded like breaking glass.

The less I knew of what I saw, the calmer I became. The known world contracted, all was simple. I sat in a nearly abandoned café and watched my hand stir the syrup of coffee clinging inside the cup. My hand was steady. I was steady again. Now I could feel remorse. Sparrows dipped in at my feet, where the remains of old bread lay dried and disintegrating. I admired the birds, like brown brushstrokes on slate. They reminded me of my men rushing across dark fields. I flinched at the memory and downed my drink. What were my prospects? I might hunt sparrows and serve them up fried on the street. Silly. I could not decide whether to get up from my seat or stay counting the grinds in the bottom of my cup. I stood up and sat down. The old man at the counter danced slowly to the music in his head. A palm put me in shade of a sudden, a breeze cooled my face. I walked out.

I found my friend Rintrah on his corner packing up his merchandise for the day. He had artichokes, ghastly things. I walked so slowly toward him, so deliberately, like I was swimming down the street. He saw me and I saw the alarm on his face. He said nothing and offered me an artichoke for free. I held it like an egg, afraid of what might hatch from the barbed, dark thing. He rocked on his heels, his hands in the pockets of his vest, and waited for me to say something, but thought better of it. For a moment I entertained the thought that he already knew what had happened, that behind that thick beard lay the face of a seraph. Everywhere at once, nothing unknown to him.

"General?"

"May I sit?"

He gestured at the stoop behind him. I watched the street go by. I had hardly ever imagined such places during the war, certainly not the vibrating, growling, clanging street presided over by a dwarf on his fruit box. When I thought at all of this other world, it was always something like a tableau containing houses and streets, neat, trim, and empty. *Empty.* I had not thought of people in this paradise beyond smoke and rifle fire and shouting. *I had thought of an empty place, one in which I could walk alone, undisturbed, amid the achievements of man, his monuments and landscapes, without having to hear anyone else jabber on in my ear.* So many damned people on the street.

So many people everywhere. I suppose had I thought of a woman, the place wouldn't have been entirely empty. Yes, I had, an Eve to my Adam, only without the will to disturb me nor the means to lead me from my happiness. I thought of Anna Marie then. *No Eve like that, for damned sure.* Nothing was what I had dreamed, not even love. Some things were more interesting.

"Are you well, General?"

"Silence!"

I was listening to the spies passing by, down the alley, carrying their bombs in grocery sacks. *That's Hood! I'm sure he's looked better, but how would you know? I heard he's made of wood, not just his leg, but his head and his heart too. But I am cruel.*

They would report back to Washington. They would report my weakness. I thought I should fall in and show the colors, show that I would not be crossed or defeated. There were no lieutenants, I would have to do without them.

Maman, who is the man talking to the air? Does he talk to insects?

They are all enlisted, all maneuvering. Flanking me!

Don't look, cher.

Rintrah had finished packing up his arti-chokes and stood quietly next to me. He re-moved his short straw hat and scratched at his tangled and dense black hair. My head began to hurt again. I noticed that my shirt had stuck to my chest in sweat. I whispered.

"Clear the street."

"What?" The dwarf leaned his ear toward me.

"Clear the damned street!" I shouted. Women turned and hurried on, pulling hats close over their eyes. I watched their feet click-clacking away from me, thin heels and thick heels, brown toes and yellow toes. *No respect*. Had they been respectful they would have arrived for forma-tion in matching footwear. Nothing conformed now, there was no standard.

"Keep the whores out of camp, no exceptions."

Rintrah sighed, as if he'd seen people like me before.

"Come with me, General." He took my arm and tried to pull me to my feet. "Let's get you out of here before you make more of an ass of yourself."

I tried to stand up on the brick step, caught the edge with the kindling I called a leg, and toppled over. Rintrah fell with me, cursing me. A crazy quilt of eaves and corners reared up against the sky above me, General John Bell Hood, and among them I saw two brown thrashers twisting together in flight. I lay heavy on Rintrah and he jabbed at my ribs with his sharp, fat fingers.

"Get up, you're killing me."

"I wouldn't kill you. Don't have it in me anymore."

"General. Christ."

The thrashers disappeared behind a narrow coal chimney, and I rolled off and stood on my knees. My leg had been queered and I straightened it. When Rintrah got to his feet he stood taller than me. Fierce, broad, craggy browed.

"General, you're drunk. Let's leave the street."

"I am not drunk."

I followed him. He looked back at me, suddenly curious about something. A thoughtful look passed his face.

"Does Anna Marie know where you are?"

"No."

"Come with me."

It was an order, pure and clean and without deception. There was no answer but to follow, and I did so thankfully.

*   *   *

The garroters, Rintrah said, *they been sleeping all day, but they just getting up now, so you stay close, General.* I didn't understand him, so he made a sign with his hands around his neck. He made his eyes bulge out farther, until they seemed about to pop out of his head, and I told him to please stop. As the light left it got dark quickly between the buildings and along the sidewalks. The sky was still lit up warm, but we were in the dark as if sunk in a pit. Rintrah slowed down some and was careful about looking around corners and down alleys. We walked down an alley so narrow I could barely get my shoulders through, and at the other end was a courtyard greened by date palms and a great, fraying mass of hibiscus, where the cobblestones looked as if they would never dry.

In the dark, it was a different city. I didn't see anything of the city I'd seen earlier. The noise of the day, what I had once thought was like a song, was a fine wailing. Like something in pain giving up, or someone sad knowing the sadness was forever. The dark had done it, I thought, nothing to worry about. Things are strange in the dark, sounds and shapes and lights come out of places all of a sudden, places you can't see and so you think they come from nowhere, out of the air, ever present. But then in the day you see where you've been and you aren't afraid and you laugh at yourself and you have a nigger shine your shoes.

The dark buildings seemed like they were leaning over the wet street, about to fall in on us, Rintrah and me and the pickpockets, fancy ladies, sick and insane who drew around us. I stumbled into a hole in the street and cried out, but Rintrah was there to catch me. Ladies in purple and yellow dresses leaned out from their balconies on the second floor above the street—it was Burgundy Street—and waved their kerchiefs. I watched hunched men in tight hats duck into the dark doorways beneath those balconies. I was blinded by each quick shot of light that hit me and disappeared as quickly as the doors could be opened and closed. I stopped walking and let my eyes get themselves back and righted, and when they did I looked down the street and I saw block and block and block of women raised up high above the black stream of men and boys and dogs in the street. They were leaves that had been taken up by the wind and never let back down. I stood still long enough that some of the whores right above me took notice, and they called for me. For a moment, just a moment I swear on my Bible, I wanted nothing else but to be upstairs with them, surrounded by all that color, raised up and laid down by all those soft hands. They called to me with lewd words, and I thought they sounded sweet. They leered at me and I saw only kindness. I stared up at them and they began to poke fun at me. I looked stupid. I was stupid. What did I have anymore? There was no money, and I was a fool for all to see. I let the whores have their fun with me.

Rintrah had gone on down the street without knowing I'd stopped, and when he saw what had happened, he came rolling back up the street on his bandy legs, shook his fist, and roared at the whores.

"This here is a good man and you ain't getting in his way. I'll make sure of that, don't you cross me. He got himself a woman, damned if he don't."

His voice was deep and loud, and it shook me until I was awake again. The ladies he was shouting at flicked their tongues at him, but they did quit shouting at me and turned their eyes up the street. I reckon they were looking for what else the street would bring their way. Rintrah took me by my elbow. His hard, sharp hand was painful and I told him so. He didn't speak until we'd gone down the block a ways, and then he let me go.

He lived in a large white house four blocks away, close in on the street, approached through a small arbor woven with trumpet vine. Gargoyles smiled brightly from the brick above tall windows. We let ourselves in at the back, the courtyard entrance. Behind us water trickled slowly from the mouth of a lion, down the brick wall, and across the slate. Parakeets twittered from a twisted fig at the center. It was cool back there, the sun hid behind roof tiles.

We sat in a room overlooking the court-yard on the second floor. There were no rugs, no mirrors, no tables, no paintings, just two wooden chairs on a wooden floor newly swept. The walls bore nothing but a perfect coat of whitewash in which there was no variation or error. The sun threw no shadows. All was uniform, spare, and perfect. I removed my hat and saw that my shirt had begun to dry.

Rintrah brought a pot of tea and two white cups. He set them on the broad windowsill near our elbows. He said nothing, just pointed at the tea, and I drank. He climbed quickly

into his chair, swinging himself up and flex-
ing powerful shoulders.

The tea was bitter and chalky, but it calmed
me.

"What have you been doing?" Rintrah's
mouth moved slowly. "Why did you come
find me?"

I had been destroying, fighting, routing
the past and the future. I had been defeated
by the present. I was at a standoff. I had
beaten a retreat. I had nearly crushed Rintrah, an old friend of Anna Marie's and my
new confidant. I had made myself free for
the moment. I had been doing one hell of a
lot, but at the moment I had nothing to do
and no desire to do it.

I told him what had happened. I told him
I was on the run. He swung his legs against
the bottom rung of the gray oak chair. Then I
told him I *wasn't* on the run, that I had done
the honorable thing by tearing up the office
and beating my partner, and that I would have
been well within my rights to cut his head off.
I told him I would have me jailed for dishon-
orable conduct had I been in charge of me. I
told him my head hurt. He squeezed his eyes
and popped them open again and again. He
looked irritated.

"Drink the tea," he said.

I did as I was told. I calmed, my heart slowed. I slumped in the chair and balanced my cup on my stomach. Rintrah did the same. We stared at each other for many minutes. Occasionally I studied the baseboard and noticed that someone must have scrubbed at the joint with a needle or a very fine wire. There was no mortar of dust and hair and dirt that always collected in such places after moppings.

"Thank you, Rintrah."

"You frighten me, General. I reckon you're not well. You're not yourself. Breaking up businesses don't usually involve the cracking of skulls. You know this."

"Yes."

"Something has taken your head."

"Yes."

"Fever."

"No."

"Yes, a fever."

I felt very sleepy. Rintrah put his teacup on the windowsill and hurried out of the room. I threw the bitter drink down, hoping to stave off sleep.

I woke several times, a few seconds at a time. I lay on a pallet made of old wool blankets.

Rintrah must have dragged me into the corner, the strong little bastard.

Later, I don't know when, I woke and through the scrim of just-parted eyelids I saw that the poisoner, that damned dwarf—I had been drugged!—had pulled a small table into the room where he wrote furiously on blue paper. He scribbled and crumpled, scribbled and crumpled. He swore at the paper, and at the ceiling. Paper piled up around him, and only occasionally would a page make it to the blotter and into the small collection of pages he finally stuffed in an envelope.

Again I awoke and watched him swinging my cane like a club, round and round, vicious and untiring.

Again I awoke and he stood over me, still as a rock. All I could see were his shoes, shined and gleaming. I looked dead in the reflection and dared not look up.

The last time I awoke I saw that he had made a pallet for himself in the corner diagonally across the long room, an identical pallet to mine. There he lay with his back to me, facing the wall. *Where was his bedroom?* I thought. *Does he have a bed? What is this place?*

The priest who sat at my foot smiled when my eyes finally focused on him.

"Father Mike," I said.

He never looked much like a priest. He was a childhood friend of Anna Marie's, though we rarely saw him. He was someone Anna Marie had known but almost never talked about, someone I thought she had outgrown. In the priest's case, I had always assumed he was insane, a suitable explanation for avoiding him, in my mind. He looked like a mason or a carpenter, sun-browned like an old vine. His boots were heavy and caked with mud and he had unbuttoned his shirt down his chest. Such a chest. Broad and sowed with black hair so thick he appeared, in the candlelight, to be disappearing into the darkness through a hole in his center. A beard like a wire brush, a head wrapped in a nimbus of sweaty, stabbing locks. The little poisoner asleep in the other corner needed my attention, a boot on his throat perhaps, and I rolled over to see about getting to my feet. Father Mike wouldn't be ignored.

"Want to kill him, do ya?"

"Hadn't thought about it."

"Maybe he needs killing. Some do, you know."

What day was it? I thought. The battering I'd given Felix seemed as distant as the mistiest memories of my boyhood. Another life. It was dark, no moon. Mike's eyes shot gold sparks in the candlelight. He looked amused, like there was something funny about me. This made him look more the priest. That is, smug.

"Don't know about killing."

"Go on, John, kill him. Look at him, he's an abomination. If *that* was made in God's image, the rest of us are doomed. Kill it. He poisoned you. Go on."

I hesitated. One thing in his favor, he talked like no priest I'd ever known. Those men had been mainly simpering tea-sippers and natives of the righteous salons owned by the rich and the generous and the lonely. This priest, Father Mike, would not have been welcome in such places. He wouldn't have matched the drapery.

The other reason I hesitated was that my leg had disappeared.

"Where is my leg?"

"Ah, yeah, don't know about that."

"Liar."

"That's no way to talk to the man who's been tending you through your illness."

"What illness?"

"Some would say that the Devil had taken you, and although that is a favorite explanation

among my colleagues, I don't generally sub-
scribe to it unless I see horns and fire and that
sort of thing. I think you're just mad, crazy
like a damned mumblestumbler."

"Give me my leg back."

He tugged at his beard and split it into two
spikes. *Who looked the Devil now?*

"I'm not lying when I say I don't know where
Rintrah put it. Can't say it wasn't smart of him.
But don't worry about that now. Hop on over
there and kill the runt. Drag yourself if you
have to."

He was scheming me, and I wasn't going to
fall for it. Didn't know the scheme, but I could
see it, anyway, in that smug smile. I was sensi-
tive to schemes now, wasn't going to be taken
again. That was my intention.

"Think I'll leave him alone for the moment,
Father."

"Aye, a shame, John. Another day."

He stood up. A huge man, hands like knobs
of oak. He walked to the head of my pallet,
dipped a rag into a basin I hadn't noticed,
squeezed it, and placed it softly on my forehead. Water ran into my eye and it stung. He
mopped that up with a dry cloth. I blinked.
His fingers were gentle, and I was soothed
against my will.

"You made quite a mess back at that office of yours. I don't think you'll be welcome back there soon."

I wondered who had told him. Rintrah, obviously. Can't keep secrets, had to remember that.

"Why did you go there?"

"I wanted your partners . . . are they *Arobin* and Felix? *Alcibiades?* I didn't catch it. Charming, though. Felix needed a change of clothes. Blood on his shirt and so on."

"Why," I growled to reiterate, "did you poke into my business?"

He nodded his head and began braiding his beard.

"Yes, yes, forgive me. The first reason is that Rintrah asked me to go over there. He told me your situation, and his answer to every trouble is to call for the priest, meaning me. It's been that way for many long and irritating years. The second reason is that it seemed amusing and I welcomed the diversion from my regular duties."

"What use is a priest?" The cloth felt very good on my head. I counted the boards in the ceiling, not a single one gapped or bowed. I wondered how Rintrah reached up there.

"I'll assume you're asking what use I might

have been in this particular case, and not generally."

"Hmmm." I felt myself falling asleep again. He changed the cloth and I noticed that he knelt on his knees upon the bare floor, which must have been painful for a man his size.

"I thought it would be an amusement to tell Messieurs Felix and Alain . . . I hope I have that right . . . to tell them that you would not be calling the constabulary to report them for attacking you and vandalizing the office. I told them, in the considered opinion of a priest of great size and belligerence, that they might begin to make peace with their Maker by clearing out, not returning, and keeping their own counsel in these matters. I believe I told them, specifically, to get runnin' and gag themselves, or I'd gag them for good."

"Why would they listen to you?" Silly question, I just wanted to hear the answer in his own words.

"Sometimes I wonder, really, why anyone listens to me. It is because I am a priest, of course, and this is a town in awe of its priests, but really, what does that say about the state of our Church? It seems an impoverishment to me, this willingness of the herd to follow their shepherds without question, as if we had secret knowledge. I've found this tendency very convenient in my work though."

"And what is that work? I've meant to ask. Don't see you in church much. Don't have a church, right?" Why, I thought, should I be the only humiliated one?

"I minister to the dying. It's my specialty."

"And this includes acting as a thug?"

"No, no. As I said, that was just for fun. And I wanted to see what damage a one-legged man could do. Very impressive, I should say. However, if you miss those two so much, it's not too late to invite them back! Shall I go find them?"

He knew the answer to that question, and he also wanted to hear me say it. He smiled. I felt around me, hoping my leg had merely been misplaced. I could use it to club him and escape. He was a strange man, getting bigger and more bearish by the minute. He made me anxious. *Why had he helped me?*

"No, I suppose it's best we all parted ways."

"Mr. Alcée . . . that's his name! . . . said something about a stolen ledger."

"I don't know what that might be."

He pulled the very ledger from the floor beside his chair.

"Not this then? Because this makes very

interesting reading. Had I been the poor, stupid sap buggered in these pages, debit by debit
by debit, I might have broken a neck or two."

I drew myself up until I could sit. Father
Mike, odd he may be, was an equal. I wanted
him to see me full. Or as full as I could be at
that moment, missing my leg and wrestling
around among the blankets.

"And you a priest? Breaking necks."

"Still a man, though I'm better than most at
confessing my sins."

He left the room for a few minutes, taking the candle with him. Rintrah wheezed in
the corner, a black lump in the faintest starlight. My anger had passed. All that remained
was curiosity and emptiness. I had no more
expectations.

Father Mike returned with a cup of water
and a jigger of whiskey. He stood over me
while I drank, and he was still there when I
slumped back down into black, dead sleep.

In the morning Rintrah had gone and Father
Mike sat in his chair, great head slumped over
his chest and cushioned by the thick chaos of
his beard.

My leg lay beside me. It had been sanded
and cleaned. I strapped it on and stood.

Flights of small brown birds dipped past the closest window, tall and narrow and so clear I thought the birds might fly into the room and alight on our shoulders. I still did not know precisely where I was, I couldn't remember all the turns Rintrah and I had made to get to the house. The room faced the courtyard, and into the distance all I could see were roofs broken periodically by the tops of trees drifting slowly back and forth, and drifts of gray streaking the sky above wash fires.

I felt strong. I *was* strong. I *am* strong. Lord, I thought, I could stomp out there through the puddles of morning dew in the cobbles, past the wrapping vines concealing a hundred years behind thick and twisting arms, and through the city. I could beat and break my own path, straight and wide, no wall or alley or fence able to withstand me. This is what the city needed, a man to put the bulwarks in order, to clean the trenches and dig them afresh. How many men had been lost in those streets, tripped up, swallowed in blind passageways, disappeared through unmarked doorways?

How could that house be so clean, and why would anyone care so much?

"You're up, lad, and clomping about like a draft horse. Reckon you're feeling better."

Father Mike had arisen and folded my blankets without making a noise. I stood tall on my feet and still I had to look up at him.

"Where is Rintrah?" He was big, but he was a priest and I was not intimidated.

"Still like to kill him, then, the unnatural creature?"

"No."

"Sure you don't want to even kick him around a bit, have a little sport? Ah, he'd make a good sound bouncing down the stairwell, *Help, Father Mike, I'm bumpity bumpity owww.* Can't say I haven't thought about it myself, obviously."

Before I got to know Father Mike better and realized he was having fun with me and that, in truth, any man who raised a hand to Rintrah risked his holy terror and wrath, before I understood this particular priest's peculiar *methods,* I became fully convinced of his insanity. *Insane with the love of Christ,* he would have said.

The priest walked toward the doorway and beckoned me to follow. We walked down a hallway lined with cabinets, some containing dozens of tiny drawers labeled in French, others containing a few large doors big enough for a man to crawl into. At one end of the hall a small metal door had been fitted, like the door to a coal stove.

"Incinerator," Father Mike said, noticing my puzzlement. As if that answer didn't raise more questions. Everywhere the floors were bare. The treads of the stairs were short, rising only a few inches at a time. Each landing had been reinforced underneath with cypress beams angled floor to ceiling. We walked up to the third-floor landing, so many tiny little steps. Four piles of wooden cots, broken down and stacked, rose from the landing to the ceiling. Hundreds of them. I heard a faint voice.

"The boys are down this way," he said, turning left down the long hallway cut through by bright, white light admitted through thin windows in each room. Every door had been opened, every window too. The place was being aired out.

"What boys?"

He said nothing, just kept striding down the hallway as if on the march, swinging his long arms and whistling. At the end of the hallway we turned into a room on the right away from the street. I expected to see Rintrah, but there was no one. Along the wall to the left stood piles of white washbasins, like the one Father Mike had used to cool my head, and also a couple dozen cases of what appeared to be whiskey. A violin leaned over in one corner, gathering dust.

I was angry and confused. I had been led through a twisting rabbit warren of white-washed walls and emptiness. I was no one's plaything, and whatever Father Mike had intended, I wanted no part of it. But I followed.

"Right through there, Cap'n."

The priest pointed at a small door in the wall. I kept looking and realized it was much bigger, only painted to look much smaller like a child's door. The rest was disguised as part of the clean, white wall.

"Father, this has become too tiring for me. I shall see Rintrah another day. Thank him for his company and trickery, which I will take up with him later."

Father Mike took a deep breath and turned to face me full. He bowed his head and for a moment I thought he might whisper a prayer. Perhaps he did.

"Hood, I must insist that you accompany me into this room. Rintrah is in there, you may speak to him about his behavior yourself. But there is someone else with him you must meet."

He said *must* in the tone of a man who was making a statement and not a request. Then he opened the door and disappeared into the dark. From inside he called, "Follow or leave, bugger, but you will never know that woman of yours until you come through that door."

Presumptuous papist. I went through the door.

Inside was an empty room, darker than the rest, lit only by thin, horizontal windows that I later realized were hidden by the eaves of the house and not visible from the street. A secret room, exposed rafters and beams and studs. I saw manacles attached to every other beam, bolted deep into the wood, awful and black and rusted.

"What place is this?"

"It was one place once, now it is another."

His mysteries were tiresome, but I would become used to them. They were Rintrah's great joy. I looked toward the voice I recognized as the dwarf's. He stood on his fruit box naked to the waist, an apron around his middle. He had posted himself at the side of a sturdy wood bed. There was a patient, a man entirely nude and unmoving. I had never studied a man as closely as I did this one. His skin was perfect, pale smooth and hinting at a color thwarted only by the darkness of the room. His legs and arms were long, his torso muscled. I couldn't see his face. A fly walked up one of his legs and posted itself at the concavity of the man's stomach. The man didn't twitch, his skin did not goose bump. Rintrah killed the insect with a towel, leaving a quick welt on the flesh, and the man never flinched. Rintrah bathed him with a wet rag, never stopping except to wipe the sweat from his own neck and chest.

It was not as hot in that room as I would have imagined. I remember the open windows everywhere. I didn't understand the manacles, and I didn't understand the scene at the bed.

"Is he dead?"

"I may be only a fruit man, but I ain't a fool, General, and I don't waste my time bathing corpses."

"Don't smart off at me. I've got business with you."

He nodded.

"He ain't dead, that's what I'm saying."

I felt the two of us falling back into our old banter, as if the events of the last day had not happened. I considered telling him what a pretty little nurse he was, but then he stepped down from his fruit box and I had nothing more to say.

The man on the bed was not dead, by God. I saw his chest move and his eyes blink. He was not dead, and he was not entirely alive either. He was between worlds: between the living and the dead, and between what I had believed and what I knew.

The naked man on the bed in the middle of the secret room of a rambling and strangely immaculate house, tended by a hairy and impetuous priest and a caustic and duplicitous dwarf, that man, *that man* . . .

That man had been dragged off to be killed by a man called blackbird. I'd seen him go off to die. I'd heard him speak when he could still speak. He was the very same man. I knew his eyes and those long fingers. They grasped nothing now, moving nowhere.

"And now you've met all of Anna Marie's friends," Father Mike said ruefully. "Too bad for Paschal."

There was a hospital at Franklin, where the hundreds died. Several of them, actually. They hadn't been hospitals before I rode my army up into that town, but for weeks afterward those houses and mansions and churches were the refuge of the maimed and hopeless, my casualties, the men whose names we'd have to strike from the rolls. Their absence would be my handicap, my burden. When I walked through the Methodist church that cold day in November 1864, I was *angry*. Not at myself, never that, but at them. Them in their neat rows of improvised cots. Blood and piss ran between the floorboards, there were men who would never wake up from their slack-jawed sleep, there was a man missing his tongue and bottom jaw who flapped the sagging skin of his bottom lip at me.

I studied their faces for signs of malingering. I poked men at their wounds to ascertain the degree of their pain. The churchwomen gaped at me and finally, tired of my harassment of their charges, took to rattling the bedpans against the bed frames in protest. Had they been my troops I would have had them locked up. Instead I left, disgusted. *How had they let this happen to them?* I remember thinking of the men in that hospital room. *Why did they let it happen?*

I had spent my time in hospitals. I'd woken up in a hospital ward suddenly missing a leg. I hadn't noticed until the nurse turned down the blanket to dress the amputation. The air had been foul, its stink and corruption nearly visible in the air wafting over me, but I would not despair of it. I had demanded to be sent back to my unit, I had demanded a leg or a post or a piece of kindling to strap on, I had left as soon as I could sneak away. I'd gone back to fight. I despised the sick and, truly, anything prostrate and passive. Such things—such people—were meaningless for being cast aside and passed by, for not being able to act on the levers and pulleys of this world, for not making the world *submit*.

I can barely remember what is true about the battle at Franklin now, what I've invented or warped or twisted to protect myself. I knew that my saving might be in something as simple and small as making amends, making a confession, an apology. But I had been terrified of what would happen afterward, the humiliation and finally the forgetting, the anonymity. I did not want to be forgotten. I used to tell myself, I am a good man, I love my wife and my children, I am a good citizen, I was a good soldier, and so why should I be ridiculed and forgotten and judged? How few men have been in my shoes, yet how many would step forward in judgment? I wished to be left alone.

And then I found the man in the attic, and immediately I had will for nothing else but to submit myself to the levers and pulleys of the world, to submit to them and whatever I was called to do.

I was, indeed, surprised to see Paschal alive, though in some state between life and death. I didn't know his name before, of course, I knew him only as the victim of Sebastien, the tablet on which Sebastien had written his private note only I could see, only I could read: *I am still here and I have grown large, greater than you can imagine.* I was responsible for the body in the attic. It seemed a miracle he was not dead, but his living corpse was even more of a rebuke to me. I was *still* responsible for him. I dared to tell no one.

That day I spent hours sitting with Father Mike and Rintrah, bathing the patient's brow. Rintrah told me their story, about the orphanage and the very brutal way the two of them had made the acquaintance of the priest, who had not been a priest but some sort of Creole berserker back in those days.

I learned the sleeping man's name. They both described a man not made for this world, a grown man who believed in magic and pixies and beauty and grace, who refused the baser truths of this life. He played music, they said, that sounded like people whispering and giggling. He could spend a whole day eating nothing but squash, so taken by the perfect curve and color of the ripe yellow vegetables he bought by the basket from the Italian vendors in the French Market. He was puzzled by the idea that such behavior was odd. He believed it was only paying proper respect to beauty, and in fact was required of him. I watched him in the bed as they told these tales, and all that moved was his chest, up and down, the sheet slipping down his thin arms with each breath. *Obviously a lunatic. A beautiful, chivalrous, and gracious lunatic.*

Still, I was responsible. I went back to my office high above Common Street. I stripped to nothing before lying on the cot under my office window. My body felt diffused, dissipating in the air like dust, reconstituting itself, changed. I wondered if Anna Marie would ever return from her parents' house. Someone, Father Mike probably, had cleaned up my desk. My partners had cleared out, their desks were empty. Mice skittered in the walls, and I knew they were mice because the rats tread slower and liked to screech. The floor, old barge wood, was gray with age.

I had little money, and what money I had

we spent on clothes and entertainment and lessons for the children. Appearances, appearances. Perhaps Anna Marie would never come back. The room faced west, and in the late afternoon the only admirable feature of the room took over, the fanlights over the tall windows. I could see to the river and out into the green wasteland behind the city and over to the great inland ocean called Pontchartrain.

That day I lay and let the heavy breeze pass over me. It had been two months since the ball, and it felt like years. The man was still alive. He was a ghost. He was my ghost. *I don't believe in ghosts.* I had made him as surely as I'd made Sebastien his executioner. One thing from another, the endless piling of bodies.

I had thought that my reckoning would come, if it came from anyone, from some soldier who had been with me during the last, failed campaign of the late Army of Tennessee. Surely those would be the losses that would be counted against me. Many thousands died during those few months while I drove them on and on and on. (I have the exact figure around here somewhere, but it doesn't come to mind at the moment.) That's the sort of thing they hold against a general.

But Indians? And, hell, we *won* that skirmish. Of all the men with grievances to lodge with me, and there must be many thousands roaming around the Southern states, why would it be the corporal from the old Texas campaigns who rose up to smite me? This is the way I thought of it: he had lynched a man because of *me*. I had no good reason to think that, no reason to think he had even known I was there at the ball. But I believed it nevertheless, because what I saw him do I'd seen him do before. He had taken the squaw in hand just the same way.

While I lay there, stewing in the endless me and me and me, a note was slipped under my door. I was by myself, of course, so I didn't bother with my leg. I crawled across the floor to retrieve it, crawled back, and hoisted myself back onto the bed. I picked the dust and two dead bees out of my beard. The note was in Anna Marie's handwriting.

> *I hear you made an ass of yourself yesterday. Congratulations! We await your report! Please trim your beard and come home. You*

are wanted. Lovingly, AM and the
Hood Brigade
    p.s. Watch out for Rintrah, he's
a mean one.

I strapped on my leg and got dressed.

CHAPTER 13

Anna Marie Hood

Before that sickening night, your father insured the lives and cargo of other men. He paid them for dying or being destroyed. *How much easier war would have been had that been the arrangement, just a series of transactions in a ledger book,* I said to him once. In the months after the ball, during that spring last year he became a ghost flitting through to and from the house filled with our children, and I rarely saw him. At first, when he was gone for days at a time, I thought perhaps he had found a woman. I didn't care. But he was instead a mopper of vomit and a burner of bedsheets, a benefactor, cavorting among the afflicted under the command of Father Mike. He had been smitten by a priest, and this infuriated me. He became the hero and savior of the sick and the dying. He dared fate among the ill, and most important, he had little need of us. You and me, Lydia, and the children.

When we were married in the church, John had said it *stunk of smoke and wine,* which I was to understand applied to the entirety of the Church and its thousands of years, its art, its music, its saints. Smoke and wine and the Devil, that's all it was to John. He was such a perfect Protestant, such an ornery and joyless defender of the faith, his faith, the faith of discretion and chaste glances at the Perfect Christ, who was never human and rarely spoke. The crucifix above the altar of our wedding embarrassed him. He spoke the wedding words through that apostolic beard of his, which moved as he spoke as if trying to block the sound from his mouth. John would have climbed up and put more clothes on the muscular and bloodied Christ, maybe a uniform, if there had been time. But no, there He was above us, half nude, a man. Once, long afterward, in our courtyard sharing a flagon of

Father's wine and crowded upon by hibiscus, he told me he could die like that, nailed for his sins, if the Lord asked him. I asked him if he would die for the remission of *our* sins, and it took him two days—two days!—of pondering the question to arrive at an answer, which he delivered as if addressing the Congress instead of the rolls, the marmalade, and the sleepy eyes of children at the breakfast table. *No,* he said, in short. I think he was ashamed to say it. I was surprised that he had thought much about my question at all. I had meant it as a joke, I'd meant to make him laugh at his own portentousness. This will tell you much about how each of us treated the Everlasting. I was in love with Christ and the Holy Mother and did not fear them. John obeyed God.

Now, in those strange days after they hauled Paschal away, John became filled with the stink of smoke and wine under the tutelage of my brutish friend the priest. I was angry with him often, I wanted him all to myself. That's not true: I wanted more of him to myself. But he had taken up with the fallen angels Rintrah and Father Mike, the bug and the beast, and I knew how they could take over a life, several lives.

It was Rintrah who introduced them,

Rintrah who has done everything and been everywhere. He always had his little fingers on everything. The first day John disappeared, I received this note from Rintrah.

Dearest Anna Marie,

Your man lies at my feet, which is to say he's sunk mighty low. I found him on the street jabbering off like a monkey in heat. I have brought him back to the old place, you know where, and here he lies. I've drugged him so he would sleep, and that, lass, is one of the good things about living in a charnel house. There is concoctions and tinctures and potions always about if you know which drawer in which chest to pull on.

It was right nearly too much to be asked of me, Lady Hood of the Uptown Hoods. Too much to be asked to befriend your man, this oaf, this half-feathered peacock, the battlefield murderer. Yes General, no General, aye, that's funny General. *I will admit he amuses me from time to time, and after a while he may even be tolerable. But now, must I also drag him off the street so he ain't picked up by the constable for being pickled or brained or mad or whatever it is that afflicts him? Must I also nurse him, must I make him a bleeding bed and tuck him in nice and sweet like? Why have you thrust this man upon me? Is it not enough that I know you are gone from me, that my infatuation was fool's gospel? I thought it was my deformity, but now that I see you mooning over this dour, insufferable, and foolish cripple, I know that it was not the way I was born but the man I became. Regret and recrimination now, that's all. And Lord knows how you bed him but apparently you do, forgive me my coarseness but I must say it, it's been on my mind. All those children. I would protect them with my life, but damn, woman.*

Your peckerwood general snores. I'll wager you're dozing right now in

*the silence of his absence. I have no
such luxury, he's loud like a boar.*

*I could have very easily poi-
soned him, and you know this.
You also know that I am very capable of that, I am not squeamish.
I have not poisoned him, however. You may consider this my
wedding present a few years late,
lucky there was anything at all
to get from me. I considered poi-
soning him, and I also considered
beating him with his own cane.
It hefts nicely. He is spared. Come
get him.*

*Your little friend,
Rintrah*

Before I could arrange for a carriage, I received a second note:

A.M.,

*Disregard letter of morning.
Was drunk. All forgiven. A fine
man.*

Even so, need to sleep. He'll be
back soon, I reckon.

R.

A very odd set of letters indeed. Not unexpected though. Not from Rintrah. Not from Rintrah, in the presence of Father Mike, the bear-headed troublemaker. We were one being in four parts, we had known each other since we were children. Three parts, three parts, three parts. I sometimes forget that they lynched the fourth.

For months afterward John only occasionally came home to change clothes, though he always smelled as if he'd just washed, reeking of sour water and lye. That spring I saw the flashes of his anger that must have terrified his troops, and I found in myself the corresponding urge to sting and stab, to cause hurt. Most of the ladies I knew were glad to have their men off somewhere else so that they could command their worlds undisturbed. Finally, he didn't speak and I didn't either. I had you children to attend, I was too busy! Noses to wipe, lessons to administer, and above all, protection to give. Protection from animals and their teeth, strangers in the street, sharp knives, mosquitoes, snakes, illness, sin, melancholy, rotten bread, broken toys, cruel humor, and death. I forgot to sleep and when to eat. I dismissed the cook for serving tea too hot, and the chambermaids for laughing at John Junior when he fell from the porch into the roses, scratching his pale and flaking arms. I would not let a thing inside, nothing would touch you children.

Toward the beginning of last May, John came home briefly and told me he would be spending another day with Father Mike, wiping drool from the dying. I thought we had plenty of drooling children he could stay home and help.

"They aren't dying, Anna Marie," he said, drinking the last of his coffee, grounds and all. His horse was already saddled and ready, I could see it sweeping flies away and twitching its ears just outside the dining room window. His clothes didn't match and were threadbare at the elbows. Why hadn't I noticed that? I should have fixed it, or had someone fix it. I wanted to take them off him just then, tie him down until I had patched them.

"Would you wipe their drool if they were dying?"

"Of course."

"But not until."

He put his coffee down on its saucer with a small, gentle clink, as if restraining himself.

"The disease, the fever, it's starting, and I am needed. There are families dying. This one is not. The children are safe. I am being a Christian."

"Not much of a man, though."

"Because I do not do a woman's work here at home? Because I do not nurse the children?"

"No, because you do a woman's work out of the home, nursing strangers with a crazed priest and a dwarf."

"Your friends, or so you say."

"They have been my friends since I was a girl, and will remain so. They have been your friends for a month. And yet you court them like someone lovestruck."

"I work with them. Do not be insolent with me."

"You work like a guilty man."

"I am not guilty."

"So you tell yourself."

I'm not sure what I meant by that. I suppose I meant that he ought to feel guilt for abandoning his family who loved him. But that wasn't the guilt he felt, and I knew that. (What man *did* feel such guilt?) No, the guilt I meant, I believe, is the guilt of having presided over the killing of young men, thousands and thousands. And that's one of the ways I learned to cut him down.

"I'll have no more of this," he said. "Know your place."

"Oh, I know it quite well. I know every inch of it, and every child who runs through it. But do you know *yours*?"

He stood up, wiping his mouth and tossing the napkin carelessly to the floor, watching me.

"Mine is with the sick right now. I can do good there."

"Yes sir, General."

It was as if I had been conjuring, working spells. The minute I mentioned the General, there he was standing before me. His eyes on fire and wide open, as if to take in every detail of the situation before attacking. His chest rose up, his fists flexed, and his spine straightened. He cast his eyes down at me as if from a great height.

"Do not call me that," he said. "Not ever again, not once. You will obey me, and shut your damned mouth. I make the plans here, I carry them out. You are to support me. No more talk."

He was daring me to talk back to him. What punishment he thought he might administer, I don't know. But he expected to be obeyed, and I was never a woman who appreciated being told my place.

"You go to the sick house as if you are going to war, John. You talk of the yellow jack as if it is something you can overcome, something you can pin down and defeat. Something you can attack and fight. Is it any wonder I call you by your name, General?"

He ignored me and gathered his coat. I didn't care, I talked to his back.

"You forget, I've lived with that sickness all around me, with the yellow jack and the cholera and the measles, I know them better than you, and I know they don't stop and they certainly don't go away because a man—you, Father Mike, a hundred other men like you—thinks he can beat it down. It's always with us, it's part of us and this place."

"People are suffering." He spoke with his back turned, poised at the door.

"I thought you'd be used to that."

"Never used to it. Never get used to it. You would not know what I'm talking about, and I don't care to discuss it with you now."

He turned back around and his face was

hard like stone, his beard like moss. He was a mountain, a rock, not a man.

"I thought you might understand penance. But you understand very little outside your gilded life, your flowers and petit fours and whatever the hell else you concern yourself with. You are a brat."

Had I a rock, I would have thrown it at his head as he rode out, but I was frozen in place. Petit fours? Flowers? Where? In this house? And then I knew how sharp and mean he could be. There were no candies here, no flowers, no fine parties and dancing, but he knew how much I craved them and how much I loathed myself for it. How dare he? How dare he find the gap in my own armor?

The first of May I marched down Burgundy without a hat or an escort, collecting old lettuce leaves on the bottoms of my shoes, brushing the flies off my face, and wondering how in the Lord's name the sun could come so close to the city without burning it, or at least instantly drying the pools of wash water and whatever else it was that collected here and there against the banquette.

I rapped on the door of the convent and soon a small wraith had opened the door, pushing the drapes of her habit back from her bony, veined wrist. I said I was there to ask about Paschal Girard and she quietly closed the door on me. Through the thin parapet windows on either side of the door I could see a whirling of black, sisters coming together and conferring and flying apart again. I pounded on the door but they did not answer again that day.

I went back once a week for three weeks, and on the fourth week they admitted me to the foyer. This time a big red-faced sister took me by the hand and into a chapel, where a funeral service was being conducted. All the nuns sat in rows in front of me. A repetition of black against candlelight, reminding me of the shadow lace casts. No one spoke to me, not even the red-faced nun who disappeared among her sisters. *They're testing me,* I thought. But Mass didn't scare me, and neither did the plain oak coffin at the front before the sanctuary. I began listening to the priest just as he spoke to Jesus of our crushed and dry hearts. *Oro supplex et acclinis, cor contritum quasi cinis: gere curam mei finis.* The nuns remained still, but I could see tears on some faces. I assumed this was a sister they mourned, but then I noticed that the coffin was oriented feetfirst before the altar. A layman, loved by nuns.

Then Michel, Father Mike, stepped out to assist the older priest with the Requiem Mass. I had been so thoroughly transported into another world, all smoke and light and silence, that nothing, not even the appearance of that great hulking thing at the altar, surprised me.

Together he and the priest attended to the business of the altar as if the rest of us weren't in the chapel with them. If he saw me in the back he gave no sign. I don't know how he could have missed me, clad in festive green and purple, my hair sprung in every direction. Had Father Mike asked the sisters to invite me in? I was still too young to believe in coincidence. The Mass ended and none of the sisters approached me, so I glided out of the chapel and down a hall to the side of the building. There I could see Father Mike hurrying out of the vestry toward a set of doors. I called out to him and he stopped as if someone had yanked a rope. His face lifted up toward the ceiling before he turned and faced me.

"Anna Marie."

"Michel."

"Are you joining the sisters?" I walked toward him until I could see the stubble on his cheek and smell smoke on his cassock. He hadn't slept, I could tell. "You'll have to explain your children, of course, but they've taken in fallen women before."

"You are not funny, Michel."

"No."

"Whose death did I just mourn? Whose body did I just commend up to the Lord, with my prayers?"

"A friend of the order's, that's all. They wanted the Requiem Mass held here, and so here we are."

"Where is this person's family?"

He stroked his beard, cupped his chin in his big paw, and frowned. His mouth puckered and relaxed over and over. Michel, though smart, had always wrestled with thought. Then a light came up in his eyes, and I knew he was about to tell me a lie.

"They didn't miss anything." He gazed at a marble seraphim cast as a wall sconce as if it might lift off and bear him away.

"It was lovely. Of course they did."

"They didn't."

"Why won't you give me the name?"

Here he smoothed his robes and straightened his back so that he loomed over me. I knew that gesture. *I am a priest. I open the tabernacle and bear the body. Don't question me.*

"It's church business, and it's best that it remain private."

"Why did the sisters bring me there, if it wasn't my business?"

"Ask them."

"Have you seen my husband?"

He couldn't keep his chest puffed out any longer and the air went rushing out *whoosh*. He shook his head.

"I don't keep track of the General."

"Tell him I am looking for Paschal." The words came to mind just as I said them. That's what I had been doing, looking for Paschal. Studying him in his absence, in his death.

I thought I could disturb Father Mike with questions. My eyes said, *Had Paschal been here? Was he afraid? Did he die alone?* I had assumed he was cast into the river and never found, but now in the mysterious world of the church, I had begun to have my doubts. Here were the nuns who had raised Paschal, and the man who had beaten him nearly senseless on meeting him. And there, on the altar during the service, had been the paschal candle, the Light of Christ Risen. None of it meant anything. It was not unusual that Father Mike would conduct a funeral at the convent, and perhaps the sister had mistaken me for grieving family. The candle was not Paschal. Even so, the mystery of what had happened to Paschal after he disappeared into the woods, and why, and who he *really* was, became an obsession that day.

I *did* disturb Michel. He puffed out his cheeks and let his jaw drop as if he were staring at something horribly deformed. Some of the sisters brushed by us and tittered at the big priest once they'd floated by.

"Do you know anything of Paschal?" he said.

"He died. He was murdered. He was never found."

"Then why would you look for him?"

"I've begun to have my doubts. Because that is not a complete answer."

I turned my back on him and left him standing there in the hall. When I turned the corner toward the motherhouse, I looked back and saw him still standing there, eyes closed.

It comforted me to pretend it was *his* body in the coffin. I pictured him there, his body blessed, his death properly mourned. I preferred the lie to the truth, which was that he had disappeared and been subsumed in the air and soil and water, little parts of him floating through us, breathed in by us forever, never seen. Now I had seen him offered to the Lord and I was happy.

Even so, I was still angry with the sisters. I would not be treated as an impertinent dog. Nuns did not frighten me. I'd known religious all my life and, anyway, Michel the Terror had become a priest. They all had feet of clay. I hurried toward the room of the mother superior.

Sister Mary Thérèse, I discovered when I pushed through to her small office chamber, was the tiny and dried up little woman who had first shut the door in my face. She did not look surprised to see me. She betrayed no expression, or perhaps it had become impossible to form an expression with a face crossed and chasmed with so many lines: worry lines and laugh lines and crow's-feet and an impressively beetled brow. Was the absence of expression what one called *beatific*? Hers was a face only God could love, and I suppose she knew that.

She greeted me by name.

"Anna Marie Hennen Hood. You are a persistent woman. A blessing on you, child!"

Her face remained only a puzzle, but her

thin, rasping voice sounded genuinely pleased with me.

"Sister, I'm confused. Why have I been allowed here today, after being barred so rudely? It's troubling, Sister. I wonder what you're up to."

"Up to nothing, dear. Persistence is sometimes rewarded. The first time we met, I did not know you, and when you mentioned poor Paschal's name, I had no reason to trust you. Surely, knowing what happened to him, you can understand the mistrust. I am still trembling to think of it."

Behind her head hung a thin crucifix. The emaciated Christ hung limply except for His head. I had never seen Christ's face turned to Heaven. Every crucifix I had ever seen portrayed Christ at His death, His head hung in temporary defeat. But this Christ was fierce, His eyes burned. It scared me.

"Sister, I suppose I should tell you my business."

"Oh, I think I know your business. I've learned much about you, *chère*. You would not have been admitted otherwise. I know your friendship with Paschal and that little devil Rintrah, and I know about your husband, this Hood."

Spied on by nuns! Did they follow me, or did they have informants? This was a desperate and treacherous town, but even the nuns? Ah, darling, there is nothing sacred.

"Perhaps, Sister. Or perhaps I just want to know what happened to him."

"Surely you know. You were there. Or so I've been told."

"Yes. But I only saw him dragged off."

"And you watched."

"Yes."

"And you did not stop them?"

"What could I do?"

She stood and gathered her missal. There were prayers to be said, psalms to be sung.

"I believe you must answer that for yourself before I can tell you any more. Please see yourself out. You may come back tomorrow."

I wanted to stop her, to grab her, to make her answer my questions. I could feel the tears burning behind my eyes.

"You mean I should have died instead."

"Come back tomorrow."

And she disappeared through a small door behind her table, off to prayer.

The hell I would come back the next day, or any day, at the direction of the old woman.

I was the hope for the species, I had done as the Lord had instructed and brought forth life. I didn't answer to barren old women married to the unattainable, the unimaginable. I was too new to marriage and motherhood to know what I meant by these thoughts, which dogged me the next few hours while wandering the streets of the old quarter. I was not too naïve to realize what *bringing forth life* had meant after bringing forth life for ten straight years. Still, there was the ache of superiority. I flounced in and out of the milliner's shop (where I demanded they make me a dress), and knocked over a colored boy with twelve pairs of shoes around his neck, tied in perfect small knots by the laces. I sat in the café behind St. Louis and had a snuff of port. The old men leered at me and I was repulsed by them when once I would have been pleased. I no longer accepted any idea of myself that was not my own. I suppose that was what I had wanted to tell Sister Mary Thérèse, but I didn't have the words.

One moment the café rattled with laughs and dry coughs and shouts, and the next it was quiet. I was too busy sipping my port and watching the liquid ease down the side of the glass to notice at first. When I looked up, the dozen café loungers were each staring toward the bar, where stood a man with scars on his neck. Bad skin, rotted and pitted. In his hat he wore a yellow feather. He was a common sort of dodger, poor hat and worn soles flapping against the bar rail. He ordered two drinks for himself, both amber and thick in short glasses. Both went down quickly. The fascination was a puzzle to me, but the two old men beside me who had been watching my legs leaned together and whispered loudly an explanation.

"It's Hector. He looks as if he's been busy, no? I believe it is time to leave, friend."

This Hector, I understood, had killed two colored teachers at a local colored school during the recent White League riot. He was a killer, a hunter of colored flesh, the one old man told the other. The attack on the school had happened the week before. Colored, Creole women teaching colored, Creole children their French lessons and their piano lessons. Huh? what's going on now? she didn't see it, did she? is she imagining, remembering, what? [It was reported in the newspaper, it was spread as gossip, she heard it from a cabdriver. She could have heard it any number of ways, and the way is not important.

I'm starting to get irritated now.] I turned up Dauphine and saw the air melted by the fire and the children waving from the top floor, jumping out, falling and falling. The women had been murdered first and laid neatly in the foyer in their blue dresses and white aprons. The children had no one to help them. Such a great victory for the White League, though they somberly denied that those were their thugs, their torches and knives. What did it matter? This was their city, and that fire was no contradiction of that fact. I took a wrong turn and tripped over a man playing cymbal in the street and singing wordless songs. I thought I saw something black flash by at the edge of sight. Something black and liquid. I thought I was being followed. I heard no screams, only the rush and snapping of fire. There could be no more dreadful sound. The children's shouts burned and were carried up in the fountain of ash, unheard.

"Thank God for him, but I would just as soon he stay on that side of the room. Or on the other side of the city," one of the old men chuckled. Here was a man who acted on impulses they only indulged between glasses. I knew them, these strangers. They plotted without acting, lectured without understanding. The colored man's time was over, it was agreed, but let others attack the women and burn the schoolhouses. Others not fit to share their liquor. Who did I despise more, the murderer or his audience with its clean hands? I don't know. The two stood, donned their felt hats, and walked out through the arched doorway into the glaring afternoon light where they disappeared until next time.

The man called Hector took his seat at their table. He twiddled the yellow feather in his fingers. I looked for blood on him, some stain that could not be sloughed off, but of course there was none. Unlike the old, recherché Creoles, he didn't stare at the sight of a woman alone in the café. He looked everywhere but at me. He nodded at some of the others but said nothing. I know he must have felt my eyes on him, but he only remained hunched over his two glasses.

I was back at the ball, only I was watching the moments before Sebastien took hold of Paschal, before Paschal had been seen, before the urge to destroy had taken hold. There he was, just sipping his drink. No rope, no cruel jokes, no insanity. It was before I had caused the death of my friend. Everything went back to that night. I was angry, I was about in the city searching for Lord knows what, I had observed the requiem for a stranger, I had berated a nun, I was drinking in a café alone.

"He's going to die, you know." I spoke without intention, or at least a plan.

"Pardon?" He slowly turned his face toward me. It had been slashed on his left side, his neck scars were livid with the first flush of alcohol and looked fresh again. His eyes were gray, his eyelids drooped. He had no interest in me, not as a woman or as a companion in the café.

"Do you know Sebastien Lemerle? He is someone like you. He is going to die."

"And what is someone like me?"

I raised my voice so the others might hear.

"A murderer and a devil, bound over for Hell."

No one looked at us, but everyone listened.

"Murder is a matter of opinion, madam. Though I don't know why you would call me such a name, in any case."

He was coy, playful, like a cat. He waved his yellow feather toward me, feigning to tickle me. He was enjoying himself, he knew precisely what the others in the café thought of him.

"The school."

"A terrible injustice."

"Yes. Yes it was."

"Giving those girls hope, that's a crime. Not murder, but bad enough. Hope of being white, of having white things, of thinking white thoughts. They tease the dumb creatures."

I had nothing to say to that, I barely understood him.

"He's going to die."

"Lemerle? And who shall do the killing? I have no particular love for Sebastien, but I wonder who wants him dead? He is a hero to some, and certainly he can take care of himself."

He had leaned toward me so the others couldn't hear, but I nearly shouted my replies to foil him, to embarrass him. When he looked around the room he did so apologetically, as if he were concerned for the opinion of these men for whom he was a necessary monster.

"I am the wife of the General John Bell Hood, of the late Confederacy." The words echoed in the room, as if I were announcing John's arrival.

"My! General Hood! I would pay to see that, though I believe the cripple would be at a severe disadvantage."

I threw my port into his face, but there was only a drop left and he licked it off his lip.

"Your husband must be a very courageous man. But I must ask you, Why don't you kill him yourself? You drink like a man, and talk like one, and you issue challenges like one. I wonder about General Hood. He has his woman going about the city drinking with men and making threats on his behalf. It is strange."

I stood and brushed past him without a word. The owner of the café walked over to the man Hector and told him to leave. He had watched the whole conversation without intervening, I suppose for his own amusement. Of course it wouldn't do to have a murderer *without chivalry* in the café.

The murderer didn't follow me, though I thought he might. I heard him laughing as he walked down the alley past the church before turning down toward the Place de Armes.

I walked back toward the convent. I nearly called out for Sister Mary Thérèse to come save me from the cold Hell I had begun to glimpse in each crack of slate banquette, in the gawking, nattering, toothy, passing bursts of yellow and red and indigo who jerked past as if hung by string and twittering on about the

weather and the Opera. It was Hell that had
been waiting for me all this time. How many
years sitting in the window of my mother's
room, watching men and ladies and horses go
by down the avenue? How I had believed in
their grace and goodness, the warm and fasci-
nating righteousness of their lives beyond our
garden, how I had imagined a wide, wide horizon. I had dreamed of this even in those days
after Michel's behavior in the swamp, even
after knowing how he had ended the one possibility of escape for two who had so ardently
wished for it themselves that they had left
the pious women who had saved them, the
women who I hoped would save me now.

I took the correct turn, straight toward
the convent, and then I knew I was being followed. Women in black glided past cisterns
and under dark galleries. They knew what I
had done. They closed in, sweeping toward
me, faces white and featureless.

Then I was at the convent door, shouting
Sister Mary, Sister Mary. I could hear the
sound of my pounding echoing down the
stone hallway. I waited for the ghosts to set
upon me, but Sister Mary Thérèse opened the
door before they could pull me back.

"I killed Paschal."

"Surely not," she said. She stood before me in work habit, brown homespun and bare feet. The hem was wet as if she had been cleaning something.

"He was there at that ball because I told him to go there."

"You invited him."

She took me by the arm and marched me into the chapel out of the hearing of the others. I had surprised her, and she was not used to surprises. She knew me, she had thought, but now? The back pew was rough-hewn and different from the others, full of gouges and sharp edges, and I could see where distracted nuns had scratched crosses and crude cats and bleeding hearts lightly into the wood.

"Yes."

"To cause trouble."

"Yes, but not real trouble."

"You get to choose? You play with your friend like he's something you bought on the street, and then you think that you can choose what happens when you abandon him?"

"I never abandoned him."

"You abandoned him like he was just another nigger to you. This is the house of the Lord, child, do not blaspheme with your lies."

"It's more complicated than lies."

I thought she didn't understand my point. But she pressed on. Her face cracked and split as if to release something terrible within, terrible for her. Anger, violent thoughts.

"You stupid girl, you are no mystery." She shook. Her pale brown hands gripped the pew until they'd turned white. "And you know little about the man Paschal, this man who haunts you, the man you called friend, the man you used as a pawn in your silly little games. Oh, I know why you invited him, do you think Paschal does not talk to his old mother Mary Thérèse? Hmm. In the end, you cast him off and confess your guilt. I suppose you want absolution? I cannot give it. *You* know nothing. You don't even know the person to whom you're confessing."

Just as quickly as she'd spit that out, she recovered herself. Her face gathered together again and became unreadable. She put her hands in her lap and lowered her head, mouthing words. When she looked up again she reached over to hold my hand.

"Why?" She sincerely wanted to know.

How could I tell her that, late at night, I felt the horror and shame of not knowing my man entirely, not understanding him completely. I had married a man who had led an army. I was horrified that he had killed, that he had likely whored, that he was both the bearer of news from the outside and its cautionary tale, broken and brooding. What kind of man ordered other men to their deaths? I imagined he strode through the underworld like a prince when the light went down and he was out of the sight of proper folk. Where else could such a man find a home, who had ridden over bloody roads and watched the deaths of boys and old men? I believed this was the reason I had been snubbed, removed from guest lists all over the city, looked on with pity. *Fine,* I had thought, *but you all aren't without your little shames either.* And so I had set out to remind my cousin of her own shame, just in case she had forgotten.

This is how I thought of my dear friend: a shameful dalliance, something to be ashamed of, an embarrassment. I had changed. I had become a horror to myself.

How to tell a nun this? I coughed out something and she seemed to understand. She twisted her hands in her lap and got to her feet. I wanted to ask her what she meant, but she was gone. She walked down to one of the front pews and knelt, genuflecting in long, sweepingmovementsfromherheadtoherchest to each shoulder. She entered a pew and knelt, her hands clasped before her, elbows on the pew in front. I don't know why I stayed, nor why I, too, got to my knees and prayed to the Holy Mother. There were moths in the air above the tabernacle, drifting up toward the window in which Christ reassured His mother and Mary before leaving them again. *He was always leaving,* I thought, *and no one thought to comfort those two who had always waited for Him.* I watched the back of Sister Mary Thérèse's head, and I could see she was praying furiously, working her rosary and pausing now and then to talk directly without the beads.

I was staring at the Resurrection window when the old mother superior appeared again at the end of my pew.

"There is someone you should meet. I will get her. You've come for information about Paschal. Don't ask her anything, she won't answer. But you should meet her."

It felt like those moths orbiting the head of the Magdalene had temporarily taken residence in my stomach. I read that somewhere in some jungle or bush the natives believed that the place where a child first stirs is a place that marks the child's character and destiny. A new understanding of the life I'd chosen, bound in its old and hard-spun chrysalis, first stirred in the back of an old convent chapel while nuns brushed quietly by down long stone hallways. I hope that means something.

It was the red-faced nun who had brought me to the Requiem Mass. She stood over me and then sat down at the very end of the pew and did not speak. She only looked at me, and then to the candle at the altar still lit from the Mass. She looked afraid it might snuff out, or more likely, that I would snuff it out. She was tall and green-eyed, and only by looking closely could I tell that she was much older than I'd first thought.

"Who are you?" I said.

She only shook her head.

"Why did you bring me in here earlier? Why did you let me in at all?"

She stared wildly at me, as if she were trying to get me to do something. Her eyes never left my face. I looked at her hands, long, elegant, and supple fingers on calloused palms. Farther up her wrists I studied long, thin, faded old scars. I looked up in her face and it was Paschal who looked back at me. Paschal's face, his nose and eyes, his laugh lines, his sad mouth.

When she saw that I understood, she stood and left me alone again.

John was not happy that night, one of his rare appearances for supper. I suspect he came to supper only to confront me. How did he know the spectacle I'd made at the café, or what I'd said? I didn't ask. On my way home the streets had filled with gawkers staring at the crying woman walking straight and without sound. I passed them without looking, but I noticed the boys running between the bananas and the fan palms, off on errands I couldn't guess. I suppose some might have carried the news of my disintegration to John, no doubt scratching at a ledger with his pencil or lounging in the winter of the ice makers. Or they might have merely offered news to the network of clubmen and potbellied traders who, I knew, would pass the word along without fail until it was known by all. I bought shrimp from an Italian woman and she smiled sadly at me when she handed over the tightly wrapped packet of soggy, fishy newspaper. A woman could not have a secret, so why bother to hide tears, or anger, or a slight wobble in the step? I'd have as much luck hiding a goiter. That's what her smile said.

Mother, who had been looking after the children during one of her brief sojourns back into the city, boiled the shrimp for supper. The house on Third Street seemed older than it had three weeks before. The two great bay windows on the second floor like eyes in a pale red face, a white gallery at the front like a yawning mouth. Sitting with my husband for supper *was no longer* new. The flatware was not new, the china was not new, the crystal not new, especially not the old glass I insisted remain at my place, carried over from my parents' house. The mosaics of yellow candlelight upon salmon walls, so light and trembling, reminded me of the butterflies my father and I used to collect a lifetime before. Here I was the wife and the mother. Out there, across Canal Street and among the Creoles, the mud was deep and I was always who I had been.

I don't know exactly how, but your father could eat anything without getting a speck of it in his beard. His sad blue eyes always stared down at the table at something a few feet in front of him, usually the salt dish, and with that beard his entire aspect at table was that of a daydreaming, fastidious Moses. He had once been a great talker, and more romantic than I had imagined, but his eyes never lifted

from that point in front of him on the table. I
wondered if there was something beyond that
point, something beyond the table and the floor
and the earth that he could see, something
that he wouldn't let go. When he was silent for
days, I was convinced of this. On those days he
seemed to make his own weather. No candlelight could illuminate his face, nor dance upon
the walls. This was untrue, of course, but it's
what seemed to be true.

That night, when he finally looked up from
the tarnished salt dish and points beyond, he
said I had most offended him by implying that
he was a murderer, a vengeful man.

"I do not seek out men for revenge, I do not
kill because my wife, or anyone else, tells me
to."

Oh, such cant! I thought. *You don't do it*
now, *now that I need you.*

"I know," I lied.

"This man, this Sebastien Lemerle, as I've
heard he is called, he will not like these
threats. And as you and I both know, he is a
dangerous man."

I watched him speak, the gray and the black
of his beard moving back and forth as he spit
the words out, and I could tell that fear did
not bother him in the least. He was lying.

"Surely you're not afraid of him. I am not."

He brought his good fist down on the table, making the candles jump and gutter.

"Do you think," he snarled, "that we are the only two in this city? That you are the only one I am responsible to protect? That we are the only two he might wish to harm?"

I had no earthly idea who he was talking about. His eyes drifted off again. He seethed. I thought he might weep.

"Just keep your mouth shut about Sebastien Lemerle. I do not want my name and his uttered in the same breath. Ever, by anyone."

"Don't talk to me like that, John."

His head drooped and his shoulders hunched.

"It's important," he said. "Just remember that it's important."

In the long hours after supper John sat out on the front gallery sipping an old cognac, one of several his old friends from the army had sent him after our wedding. They were squat little bottles that he lined up in two small rows upon the sideboard. They were each different, but he drank them in turn, on down each row as if one was the same as the next and it was his duty to treat them without favor. Had I not spied him through the porch

window nodding gratefully at the passing menagerie on Third Street, holding a glass and
cigar in one hand and propping his bad leg on
the rail, I might have fallen out of love with
him that night.

CHAPTER 14

John Bell Hood

My days became alike. I left the house, I went to the attic, I stood vigil, I wiped Paschal's head and neck with a wet cloth, I fed him tepid soups and watched him swallow unconsciously. I looked for signs of life, waking life. I quit going to the office entirely. I left word of where I could be reached, and occasionally Alcée rang the door and left papers for me to sign before scurrying off under Father Mike's glare. They were invariably papers authorizing the payment of claims, and I signed them all without inspection. I did not care to argue with anyone with a claim against me, even though I knew the money wouldn't last. I was involved in more important things, I thought.

Sometimes Paschal moved, and at first I would limp out of the attic and down the stairs to summon Rintrah or Father Mike, who trudged dutifully up the stairs behind me, leaving the first of the season's sick lying on their cots, rigid like cordwood in the throes of their fever. I hardly noticed them, only the smell, which was sour and peaty. Each time they followed me into the attic and watched for a few minutes as Paschal twitched and then lay still, and then they'd leave me alone again. I came to learn that the body is not entirely ours, and sometimes it does as it pleases without our knowledge. Paschal never woke up, but I stayed there, watching the silhouettes of the windows meander around the room from morning to night.

Father Mike argued with me.

"I don't understand why you come," he said to me after three weeks. We stood out back of Rintrah's house, in the overgrown courtyard. Untended banana trees browned and crumpled at the edges, and the orange trees gave up tiny, mean little fruit. The house was enormous, and from our vantage point I could tell that the sick ward was not its only function. Across the courtyard from us I could see the shadows of men walking by windows, carrying great, heavy boxes here and there. I could hear the faint sound of glass clinking. Someone kept shouting profanities, and every few minutes I could hear the sound of a horse cart pulling up on the other side of the house, out of my sight. Father Mike said Rintrah had won the house in a card game when I asked how an orphaned fruit vendor could find himself in possession of such a house. He didn't bother to gild his lie, he seemed tired. I decided the men in the other part of the house carried the explanation, but I didn't much care. I didn't care for anything but that attic.

"I come because I'm supposed to come, that's the best I can explain it, Father," I said.

"I think you are not right, you're touched in the head," he said.

"You and Anna Marie," I said.

He looked quick and hard at me, and then looked up at the roofs, a brief smile on his face, like he was remembering something.

"She is not a stupid woman," he said. "You should not worry her."

He removed his boots and let his big yellow-tipped feet dry out in the sun and unbuttoned his shirt to his waist. He was unselfconscious about himself, like a dog.

"I would like to tell her what I do here, but you've sworn me to secrecy," I said.

"Why don't you do what you tell her you do? That would solve the problem."

"I should take marriage advice from a priest?"

He blew air out from his cheeks.

"What you should do is notice what the hell is going on around you. How many sick do we have in the ward?"

"A couple dozen?"

"More. Do you know any of their names? How many coloreds?"

I didn't like being quizzed, but I answered. He was commanding, compelling. He could have been a general like me, I thought. *He would have never stooped to that*.

"I don't know any names, I'll admit. I'd say half colored, half white."

"All colored. And their names are Antoine, Jeremiah, Lucille, Katharine, David, Nicholas . . ."

"I understand."

"No you don't. If you did, you would leave Paschal alone and help us with the sick who actually know pain, who know what is happening to them, and that they are dying. You would help with that. Instead you have made our friend Paschal into a voudou fetish, something to protect you. You are weak."

I slapped him then and was on my feet. The sun burned the back of my head, and in the bright light I saw the red come up in his cheek. I was once his physical equal, and if I wasn't anymore I could still make him hurt. He shrugged.

"Slap me, shoot me, stick me with a bayonet, it's all the same to me."

And then he walked back into the house, barefoot and bare-chested, leaving me standing under the banana tree.

I didn't spend all of my time in the attic. I spent some of it at Mr. Rouart's ice factory, watching the ice form on the pipes and letting the chill restore my calm. I took walks. I usually arrived home very late.

On one of those walks a few days after Father Mike's lecture, I stumbled across the funeral in Congo Square. I watched women dressed in white smocks and white tignons leading the coffin, and the men in white following behind with the coffin on their shoulders. I heard wailing and shouts and watched mourners prostrate themselves in grief. And at the moment when the coffin was raised up to depart the square for its final journey to the colored section of the cemetery, the wailing became more intense. Men and women strained to place their hands upon the coffin one last time, and when the coffin finally departed and the crowd was left behind, I heard the cries. *Cut the body loose, cut it loose!* I hadn't noticed the drums, but immediately they began to pound a syncopated rhythm that each of the mourners picked up and set down. They whirled and shook, jumped and laughed, sang and grimaced. One of the mourners, a woman about Anna Marie's age, twisted her hips and held her hands to the sky, spinning and gyrating, her eyes closed and her mouth half open as if letting a ghost escape through her lips. I was mesmerized. She was so beautiful and so terrible, terrible for having her beauty brought out by death. *Where did she come from? Why is she here?* And then, *Where was she when my boys were dying at my command?*

I knew nothing about death, only killing.

I walked back to Rintrah's house, lightheaded and preoccupied. I didn't go straight up to the attic. I sat in one of the sick rooms, where fourteen people lay on cots in two straight lines. I sat across from an old colored woman, her skin as thin as a moth's wing. Her nose and mouth and throat were inflamed and swollen, and I thought that if the fever didn't kill her starvation surely would. Even so, her eyes were clear, and they stared darkly at me. I silently confessed my sins to her. How I had betrayed, how I had brought chaos to a world with no shortage of it. How I had brought unexpected death, tragic death, death without sense. I had struck without warning, and there could be no resistance. I had helped to design these deaths, and I helped to spread them. And when the dead lay on the ground, I had ordered shallow graves and then a march onto the next killing.

The sun filtered through the long curtains of white linen that had been drawn against the heat, and I imagined the woman across from me might be swallowed up and lost in the diffused light and weightless dust. She seemed so insubstantial at that moment. I became agitated. I watched the willows and the tulip magnolias gently shake outside, casting shadows across the window, the room, the woman's face. I had always thought that willows were beautiful, and they were no less so in that moment, but for the first time I noticed their imperfections, their asymmetries and browning leaves. I blinked and when I looked again I thought I could see every wrinkle in the bark, every vein in every leaf, and the segmented bodies of every insect upon them.

The woman in the bed moved. Drops of perspiration ran down her temples. She reached up and, with some effort, pulled a long brown braid from behind her neck and stretched it out upon the pillow next to her, letting the air cool the back of her neck. I watched her lie back and die.

The next day I didn't go up into the attic. The man on the bed in the attic was not the man who had been killed, he was not Paschal, but some other man made of the same flesh but residing in another world. My business, my *penance*, was to be had in this world. My business, as it had always been, would be to fight.

CHAPTER 15

Anna Marie Hood

After my argument with John, I decided the next day to take my father's carriage back into town, since we had no horse ourselves and no working carriage. I wanted to wander far, and so I called for my father's driver, George. I was five months along with the baby, I could still get out when I wanted, and I wanted to ride hard, to slip through the air and the miasma and the muck and not be touched by any of it, I wanted to see all that I had missed and was missing. For the first time in that city I felt an outsider.

Paschal's mother was a nun. A red-faced,

silent nun. She had perhaps even raised him without his knowing. She had cut her wrists. Every day he had lived as an orphan with his own mother nearby. I could not possibly understand what that had meant, I knew that much. It was a tale bigger than anything Paschal himself had ever spun about himself, and far more true.

We careened down Esplanade and over Rampart until we came to the big trees at Royal. George cut the reins hard and we swung to the right, slowing to squeeze down the narrow street. Women in coarse brown frocks hurried down the street with loads of vegetables in grass baskets strapped to their backs, intent on the market. Had I eaten their vegetables? Would they have recognized me as anything but someone who ate vegetables? It would have never crossed their minds to ask such questions, I knew. Negro men swept the gutters and the sidewalks, and negro women in purple, yellow, red, and blue tignons shook rugs and sheets out windows, as if hailing a parade. Negro men in heavy boots and thick trousers scaled roofs to repair slate. I didn't know where the slate came from, nor did I know how it stayed there laid upon the steep roofs, and why the roofs did not slough it off at once. Negro women hurried lazy white children along the sidewalks, steering them around harm and toward the errand of the day. Negro men drove the horses that carried the people who watched. Like me. Negroes everywhere.

Toward Dumaine we rolled. I looked back at the scene on the street. I watched as the wheels of our carriage spit mud and water and all manner of corruption up into the air and onto the fresh sidewalks.

I stared intently at the back of George's head, which did not move while we rode. I knew this was a matter of pride for him. His body absorbed every jolt and dip, every violent wrenching of the carriage by the treacherous street, and still his head never wobbled. I tried to think of the last time I had seen his children, and I couldn't remember it. Where was his wife? I had never met her. Did he have one? Was she alive? I didn't know. There had been no wedding invitation, at least not one for me. What color were George's eyes? Brown, certainly, but what shade? I knew the back of his head better than I knew his face. The back of his head was broad, and curved gently down to his thick neck. There were often bumps beneath his skin where he had shaved his neck. There was one dark mole on the left, and another that occasionally disappeared on the right only to reappear months later. His hair curled tight against his skull, and gray hairs had begun to make their way up and through the black. The gray hairs were lazier, less tightly wound, wilder. I saw where someone had snipped the stray hairs back to a manageable length. George had been with my father for thirty years, and like my father, he was vain.

The carriage twisted sharply to the right and onto the sidewalk, scattering a pile of trash and a box of oranges. I flew against George's broad back and he held me back with his left arm while gaining control of the horse with his right. A boy had dashed out in front of our carriage, and we had almost run him right over. He carried some shoes around his neck tied together by their laces. He stood in the middle of the street, his boots in a puddle, entirely undisturbed, as if he had expected our carriage to come along and run up on him. The shoes swung against his chest, and for a moment I thought they would drag him down. His skinny white legs looked too thin to hold him up, especially with the shoes knocking about and swinging. There was no fright in his eyes, and what's more, he stared straight at me, unblinking and unflinching, as if trying to see something about me. As if he knew me, and I him. He was not afraid of me. I saw this, and then I guess George saw it too.

George had righted the carriage and stopped the horses along the curb, and was now descending the step to the ground with his switch in hand.

"You know better'n dat, boy. You make way for ladies. And what that look on your face? Don't you sass."

But this was a white boy, a defiant boy, yes, but a white boy. I was angry about the way he looked at me, but I also didn't want George in trouble.

"I don't think that's proper, George," I called.

He turned back to me, his hand now on the collar of the boy, switch in hand. Why the boy hadn't run, I didn't know then. A small crowd of negroes and Italians gathered to watch.

"Oh, it all right, Miss Anna. I know his papa, he got that colored cobbler shop up on Burgundy. This here is Homer."

He was colored. My God, I should have guessed. I had been chasing colored ghosts for days, and yet couldn't see in front of me. *So*

white, his arms are burned red from the sun.
While he awaited his licking from George, as
if he'd been waiting for it since birth, he kept
looking me in the eye. This, perhaps more than
anything at all, infuriated George. George did
not look strange white people in the eye.

I felt a knot tie itself up in my stomach, and
pressure like hands pushing in on my temples. Something broke, and I could not allow
George to beat this little colored boy, even
though I'd watched him clear the way for me
and mete out punishment to the insufficiently
deferent since I was a little girl being taken
to church. That day I couldn't allow it. *And*,
I thought, *I can never allow it again.* Everything had changed in a day and a night, and I
was new.

"George, wait."

George stopped dragging the boy to the
sidewalk, where he could properly switch
him, and looked at me. We had stopped traffic on Royal, and the cart drivers behind us
were shouting. The crowd on the sidewalks
got bigger. I stepped down from the carriage
as quickly as I could, picked up my skirts, and
walked straight to the boy.

"George, enough. Let him be."

Now *I* had made George angry. Enforcing

the rules gave George great pleasure, I suppose in knowing that there *were* rules and that he had mastered them. He was a man eager to discipline those weaker than himself. I had interrupted one of his pleasures.

"But Miss Anna, he a disrespectful little nigger boy, and he insulted you now."

"I want you to leave him alone."

"His papa would want me to switch him, ma'am. Just so you knows. Somebody else gone do lot worse someday, he don't learn."

"And I want you to get back on that carriage, please."

There *were* rules, and because George was so absorbed by them, he could do almost nothing but obey. Almost nothing.

As he let the boy go, he cuffed him across the back of his head, as if to say they weren't finished with each other, and when he turned back toward the trap I slapped George hard and loud against his face. I slapped him again when he looked at me in surprise and hurt, and I slapped him again when he didn't move fast enough toward the carriage for my liking. When he got back up top, his hurt had become a crooked, knowing smile at nothing in particular.

Before the boy ran, he whispered, "I will

find you, don't worry." And then he ran while I stood there slapping my negro driver in the street like any other proper and imperious white lady might have done. I slapped him like I'd slap a dog that had messed the floor, or a recalcitrant horse that would not get into its stall. George took it, and now he smiled a little bent smile. He held out his hand to assist me.

It was horrifying, so *I* ran, too.

I flashed by open windows filled with gawkers, drawn to the spectacle of a frightened, proper white Creole woman in hard shoes click-clacking down the banquette without concern for propriety or the filth of the street. *I will find you, don't worry.* I turned this corner and that one until I began to pass the small yellow and green cottages of the quadroons. *They* knew better than to stare, and *their* pity I didn't resent. To them it would have appeared I'd lost my mind, but they also would have considered insanity a privilege of my station. I was as clear and certain of myself as I had ever been, however. I came to the corner of Conti and Royal and let a scream loose—a deep, raspy scream at the heavens—which caused the old apothecary on the corner to hobble out of his shop waving his hands as if to ward off the demons so obviously besieging me. I relieved him of his worry with a bow and a smile, and finally I felt in control of myself. I straightened my soiled frock and replaced the veil that had flown backward from my face and hung like an empty net over my shoulder and began to walk back down Royal to Dumaine.

George searched for me, of course, and a few times I saw him pass by in the gap between distant blocks, moving his head from side to side. He passed by me on Royal but did not see me pressed into the portico of a house whose mistress peered out at me with abnormally wide eyes set in a powdered face behind the wavy gray glass. I wondered whether she had ever been out on those streets alone. She looked like one of the thousands of women who lived above the streets in this city, secret and silent, the last of old families long dead.

But I was out on the streets, aware and exposed. It was thrilling. The kindling carriers, bent over and bearing great bundles of tree limbs tied to their backs, waved and called out to me as they passed on the street. I walked as if I belonged there, as if these, and not the woman in the window, were my people. I waved to the fruit sellers and the praline ladies, who bowed to me no matter how loose I carried myself, or how familiar my greeting. I even loosened my tongue and spoke the French I'd heard spoken beneath the stairs among the servants since I was a little girl, the patois my little girlfriends and I had spoken to each other for amusement, all of us losing ourselves in giggles, imagining ourselves in tignons, scrubbing floors and cleaning up after babies.

The boy stepped out in front of me then, out from a small alley onto the banquette ahead of me. The shoes around his neck, brand-new, swung around him when he turned to look at me. He showed no surprise and didn't speak. He turned away from me and began to walk down the street. I followed, calling after him. *Boy!* I said. *Boy!* But he never said a word. Every once in a while he looked back after me, as if to make sure I was following. He looked at me as if he knew me, as if he could see through the sinew to the center of my heart. He looked at me as if he knew *what* I was, and why I had protected him. He did not look impressed or grateful.

We passed the convent and he stopped, looking up. An ancient hand appeared in an arched window and waved, he nodded, and then he continued on. When I passed, the curtains had been drawn again. I let myself be led. I understood that I was to follow.

We made an odd pair, the cobbler's son and I, walking up toward Rampart, crossing over the busy street, and into the little neighborhood around Congo Square. I kept walking closer to him until finally we were walking together, side by side. I noticed he was careful not to get so close that I touched his shoes. There were a pair of petite boots in light calfskin for a lady, a pair of formal shoes in black leather for a man, and a small pair of lace-ups in horsehide for a child. Each shined, sometimes even picking up the glancing and trembling sun off the water puddles we walked between. He did not fall behind me, nor did he take the road side of the banquette. He walked as if I were his equal, and that he owed me no special consideration. *He is a courageous boy,* I thought.

We stopped in front of a small cottage painted white with green shutters. The shutters were drawn and the green doors were closed. The house looked asleep. The boy, who George had called Homer, opened a side gate and beckoned me through it.

At the end of the damp, bricked walkway overcome by vines climbing over the wooden fence, we mounted a set of stairs up to a back porch. Homer tied a handkerchief around his mouth and nose, and then handed me one of my own. I did my best to tie it tight. When he was satisfied, he walked through the back door and held it so I would follow him.

We walked straight into a room empty of everything except a table upon which sat three rotted turnips. My eyes adjusted to the low light, and I could see that there were low cupboards against one wall, flung open and empty. Homer took up the turnips and flung them out the door into the back garden, where three cats descended upon them for a moment before slinking away.

"Don't like turnips, I guess."

Finally, a few words.

"Who?" I asked, thinking he referred to the people who lived in the cottage. Or maybe the cats.

"Thieves," he said, and I thought I could detect anger behind his kerchief. "Cupboards ain't always been empty. Had some nice plates in there."

I began to think I understood, which made me all the more fearful. *Why had he brought me?*

"This house is abandoned then," I said.

"No. No it isn't." He walked out of the room, through the high doorway, and disappeared into the darkness of the next. Why did I follow? There had been a reason the Lord had put that boy in the way of my carriage, a reason I had slapped George, a reason the boy had appeared again, a reason for the hand in the window of the convent. If I left I would never know. I went through the door.

God forgive me for crying out at what I saw, for surely I will never forgive myself.

A man, a woman, and a child. Homer looked at me, not surprised at my cry, or at the tears that spilled from me. The Thompsons, he said. Each had turned ashen and anemic, their eyes yellow at the edges, their skin as dry and as thin as corn husks. All three gazed upward, their mouths open, their hands by their sides. I noticed the little girl held her mother's hand. The thieves had not stolen the fine blue coverlet that had been drawn up to their chests. *Tiny graces,* I thought.

They were negroes, not as dark as George, not as light as Homer. Or as light as me. Mr. Thompson's hands were not terribly large, but they were thick and calloused and peeling. Working hands, skilled hands. Homer told me that this was their house, that Mr. Thompson had built it himself when he wasn't working at the forge making filigreed iron rails, and that the fever had come on them all very quickly.

"I have never seen dead people before," I said to Homer quietly. "Why did you bring me here?"

He looked at me as if I was speaking in tongues.

"They're not dead."

God forgive me for crying out again, and this time shrinking to my knees. I prayed for deliverance, and for the salvation and protection of us all. I prayed for the health of the Thompsons, and for all of our souls.

Homer straightened the coverlet. He picked up a wet cloth from a bucket beside the bed and began to wipe each of their faces and drip water between their lips. I saw their eyes flutter, and their throats move to take in the water, but not a single other part of them moved.

"They will pass soon," Homer said. "My papa thought they might pass on before I got here."

I motioned for him to be quiet, afraid the Thompsons would hear his morbid talk. He smiled bitterly.

"They can't hear us," he said. "They're most of the way to the other place, and they listening for them angels. That's how it always is."

Now Homer turned his back to me and flipped up the coverlet at the bottom to reveal three pairs of feet. Mr. and Mrs. Thompson's feet were bare, cracked, and crisscrossed by old blood. The little Thompson girl still had her lace-up shoes on, but they were worn through at the toe and the heel, and could barely have been useful. Homer took the shoes off his neck.

"What do you mean, 'That's how it always is'?" I said. I was angry and I only dimly understood why. This young boy thought he had something he could tell me, something he could teach me, and I resented it. But I didn't know what it was.

He didn't answer me.

I felt only pity for those three coloreds, in their pretty and neat little home built board on board by the shriveled man now lying on the bed before me, unseeing and unmoving.

"Why, they need a nurse! A priest!" I said.

Homer kept unlacing the shoes, his back to me.

"Yes ma'am, they did. But that cost money. Most folks got their own kin to worry about. And now it too late, just about over."

"What about their family?"

He looked up but didn't say anything.

"Who doesn't have a family?"

Why was he fiddling with those shoes? I was enraged.

"What are we doing here?"

"I know what I'm doing here," Homer said. "You followed *me*."

There was a dust-covered stool in the corner away from the bed, and I sat on it. I stared at three pairs of feet.

"This is how it always is?" I whispered, afraid of my voice.

Homer understood that I had been defeated, and was gentle with me.

"Not always," he said. "But a lot."

"Why did you bring those shoes?"

Homer looked down at his papa's work, the fine shoes, and smiled a little.

"They steal shoes too. Always. They alive, but too weak to fight back, and them thieves take the shoes. They won't take shoes off a dead man, but living people don't scare them none."

This was my city, strange and unknowable.

"And Mama says," Homer continued, "it ain't right to be buried barefoot, don't matter who you are, nobody ought to be seen in their bare feet at their own funeral, like they didn't care about who they were, like they didn't have pride, like they didn't deserve respect. Can't go off like that, Mama says."

"Who will bury them?" I said, noticing that I had given up on them as Homer had. Perhaps I would stay to watch them die. Perhaps they had already died and I had not noticed. *I had not noticed*. The things I hadn't noticed, an infinitude.

"There other men who take care of that. Papa knows them. I'll tell him that they ought to get sent soon."

He knew I would never die like that. He had seen into me, he knew who I was. He had not once asked my name, and I was confident he never would, nor would he ever mention this day to anyone. He was a smart boy, an unusual boy. I leaned forward on the stool and looked down at the pine floors. I traced a line in the dust with the toe of my shoe. I wondered if the three people in that bed had said good-bye to each other.

Homer was putting the first shoe on Mr. Thompson.

"Wait," I said.

I stood up and walked to the water bucket next to the bed. Homer sat back and watched, as if he had known this would happen. I took the bucket, full of old water and dirt, and tossed it out into the garden. I saw a cistern full of new rainwater, and I used it to rinse the bucket and fill it with clean, warm water. I walked back into the room.

Homer was now sitting on my stool. He said nothing. He waited.

I removed the clean handkerchief from around my face and dipped it into the water.

Homer got up and stood by the shuttered window.

I knelt and began to wash Mr. Thompson's feet. *Hail Mary, full of grace, the Lord is with thee, Blessed art thou among women . . .*

Homer opened the window and pushed out the shutters. The sunlight warmed my back, the breeze cleansed the room, and in my bones I knew that the Thompsons were dead. I could feel it. I washed Mrs. Thompson's feet, and the sun dried them quickly. I came to the little child and hesitated.

"I'll be giving her a new pair, ma'am, though she already got one set," Homer said from the corner. He sounded very far away. "I reckon she would like a nice pair."

And so I unlaced her little shoes, and pulled them off, and washed her unblemished little feet.

"The nun says you were friends with Mr. Thompson's cousin, or uncle, or some such," Homer said. "He ain't been around, he would be the last of the family, I reckon. You know how to tell him? My father would call on him, you wouldn't have to do it. You busy, I'm sure."

I shook my head. He looked disappointed but not surprised.

"Them nuns are strange," he said. "They all love them mysteries."

I nodded.

"Well, you know, she, the nun in charge, she said for me to tell you you ain't to go around the convent no more after this, that they now told you everything you wanted to know, whatever that was. I ain't nosy."

Of course he knew the entire story, I had no doubt. He stood up.

"And now I got to do my work, ma'am."

I left Homer to his business and went out of the house. I wandered the Quarter, stopping in the little shops I knew, having conversations I would never remember. I was not in myself, I floated above. Nothing was the same, as far as I could tell.

Hours later, when I had emerged from my

reverie, my mind again reunited with my body. I took the streetcar back home. Our rooms were lit by warm yellow light through the tall French doors that faced southwest, toward the river where it came twisting down toward me. I threw open the doors and stepped out on the second-floor gallery. I willed the good citizens of New Orleans to look up, to see me as I was at that moment, but they kept their heads down and their eyes forward, marching grimly down toward St. Charles. I soon lost interest in this entertainment and went in search of my husband, my general.

I knew, I think, by faith alone—it amazes me that I would even write that, I had already changed I suppose—who had been in the coffin that day in the convent chapel. It's what I chose to believe, anyway. I only wish they'd thought enough of me to let me know the truth.

CHAPTER 16

John Bell Hood

Soon I was a partner in the operation of Father Michel and Rintrah, tiptoeing among the cots and the patients on the floor, sending sheets to the burner and cooling the fevered. On the other side of the house, Rintrah's men received, stored, and shipped off thousands of boxes of contraband and stolen goods, the exact nature of which I scrupulously avoided knowing. I knew only that the shipments came in beautiful carriages made up as hearses, and that the horses often smelled briny and sour when they arrived, as if they'd been washed in Lake Pontchartrain.

Sometimes I heard the men talking about *the fish camps,* but I was fairly well convinced that it was not lake trout in those boxes. I suppose I had become part of a criminal enterprise, and then only because the sick ward operation needed money, and who would give money to comfort the indigent afflicted, to keep alive the half-dead negro man in the attic? I accepted the arrangement, though I must have shown my distaste on my face. One day I caught Rintrah laughing at me as he counted out all manner of struck coinage in gold and silver, which he placed in an old, blackened bull sack and cinched up before leaving it for Father Mike.

"You always were a sucker, General. Steal or be stolen from, that's the thing. I would have thought you'd learnt that already."

"I don't accept that."

"Ah, I suppose it's better you don't, mate. You'd make an ass of yourself as a thief."

It was yellow fever season though I had no talent for nursing. I could not think of anything to say to those lying at attention in their cots, rigid and red-hot dry. When I felt obliged to say something I would turn away and go to the walnut blanket chest where we stored some of the linens I kept buying, and there I would polish the smooth, tight-grained wood until I felt the need to talk subside. I had come out of despair, found hope in a half-dead man, and stayed on in the hope of finding someone I *could* save if I couldn't save Paschal. I gave every spare hour to the work at the house.

I'm certain I lost money by abandoning the insurance office for hours on many afternoons, though I might have lost that money anyway, and I know I lost money buying linens I knew would be burned in the incinerator or buried with the dead. I begged Michel and Rintrah to let me tell Anna Marie about her friend Paschal.

"She brings attention," Michel said. "That mob will be embarrassed that he is still alive. Embarrassed they failed. Who knows what they do?"

"She is not a gossip," I said.

"She brings attention whether she opens her mouth or not," Michel said. "Her whole life. I know this my whole life."

And so when we talked of Paschal, I talked to my wife of a dead man who was still living. At times we talked about him at supper, barricaded from each other by those damned flickering candles and their shadows, and I heard the sound of genuine grief, and began to catalogue the characteristics, habitats, and subspecies of that grief. I heard a guilty longing for childhood, the wistful memory of the glittering and faceted world of light imagined in that youth, anger at the man who had turned a beautiful creature into mere meat before hiding him forever. These are all griefs, and from them I came to know Anna Marie Hennen Hood. I knew her mind as if it were mine when, her words in my head, I would go to see Paschal every once in a while and look into his face. She gave him life in those moments, he was not merely something destroyed and pitiful.

I wonder, then, whether it was the circumstances of Paschal's second death that lifted me into a murderous madness, or whether I would have strapped up and gone hunting in any case.

What must a man have done to deserve two deaths? Or, I suppose, what is he owed in Heaven, what special provisions are made, after twice offering up his body to God and suffering the pain of death? I pray that Paschal Girard is comfortable now, and that the other seraphim look on him in awe and bring him grapes.

He died once at the end of a rope strung from a pawpaw tree. It should have been his one and only death. But the tree was old, and though the branch was thick it was also rotted and dry. This would not have been obvious on a dark night even if Sebastien had looked closely, which I doubt anyway because I know the excitement of crowds that smell death; they push and urge, they are impatient. I went to see the tree several times after discovering Paschal in the attic, after Michel explained how Paschal had come to be lying there alive. The branch was at first yellow, slick, and jagged. Later it dried, the broken spikes at the edge of the break dulled into gray, dead fingers pointing. Michel told me he threw the broken part of the branch into the river, an accursed thing best carried far away.

Who had sent word to Michel that night? He never knew. The colored boy who came to his door ran off after shoving the note into Michel's hands. Michel had no reason to doubt the truth of it. He had told Paschal to stay away from those people, *his* people, the people who had raised him a cruel and violent boy who, only by the grace of God and his own fear, had found refuge in the Church. Michel knew they were charmed by Paschal, but only so far as people are charmed by trained raccoons. They would never take such a beast home, never make it theirs. They would eat it first, put it in a pot with savory and root vegetables. Paschal never understood this, Michel said.

Michel rode out in his nightclothes, armed with a knife and a pistol, angry and keening. He willed the hanging tendrils of the tupelos to strike him, he prayed for the coach-whip snakes to drop on his head. He told me he wasn't sure what he would do with the pistol, and considered the possibility of turning it on himself. *Had I ridden up on that clearing in the woods, and seen him swinging among the pawpaws, I believe I would have died there with him. I was so tired.*

Instead, Paschal had fallen and was alive, as far as a man who can't speak or move or see is alive, as far as a man who can only breathe and swallow and shit and piss is alive. In the clearing, lit by the dropping moon, Paschal was a pile of discarded clothing, arms bent back underneath him, his legs tangled in the creeper that choked the wood. The mark around his neck glowed red, and there were drops of blood seeping from the rope burn like honey from a comb. His face, Michel said, was neither calm nor agitated. Puzzled and disapproving more like, Michel said. Michel dismounted and walked over, expecting to see the distended and crooked neck of a properly hanged negro. Instead he saw the supple, blushing face of a living man and heard the rattle and rasp of a dead man taking his breath back. The branch had broken, and the noose had been tied loose, awkwardly. The cruel executioner had denied Paschal the quick death of a broken neck, and thereby saved his life. Saved some part of it, at least. Michel carried him back to Rintrah's house on the front of his horse.

Why did I care about all that? I felt guilt over the death of another man, that's certain. Not for the first time, Lord knows, and I thought I was inured to it. I had walked over corpses during morning inspections and slipped in the blood of boys and old men twisted together upon the slope at that accursed place, Franklin, Tennessee. I had ordered the digging of many thousands of shallow graves that I knew would soon be unmarked and forgotten. This was my business, this was my profession. The dead were not human and had not lived. They were creatures best put out of sight and forgotten, abominations that would threaten a man's sanity if allowed to live on in dreams, in diaries, in memory. And so I purged the dead and I never knew a man who kept his sanity during the war years who didn't do the same. And if they didn't forget the dead they would soon be dead themselves. They would wander about in battle without purpose or conviction, out of their minds, baring their chests before the enemy, charging into suicide. These were the men who quit talking, you could always tell. The Devil had their tongues, as they say. I am alive now because I refused to acknowledge death even while I urged men on to it. I cheated demons by becoming one.

But this time I had created the killer as surely as if I had carved him out of chestnut. I had given him life and, later, when it was more convenient to be silent, I watched him do his work. That's what a demon does, I suppose. But this man, Paschal, was alive again, and I had visions of angels. I could be an angel! He stared at me with eyes that had to be closed periodically and moistened with briny water. I thought he could see me and what I was, and that with his gaze he could transform me. I had been given a chance to reverse the course of my sin, a meandering creek with headwaters at the spot the arrow pierced my hand, a creek that had become stream, river, and ocean. If the last of the dead, if Paschal could rise again and suck back the life that had escaped him there lying upon the leaf mold among the crickets and beetles, if he could do *that,* why couldn't the rest of them? I pictured a long line of men each standing up in turn and disappearing into the night. It was a comforting vision. All that I had to do was to save Paschal.

We dismissed the servants, and I sold Lydia's pony, Joan, to pay for medical supplies. I slept at my office. Anna Marie and I rarely spoke.

She sent me a message, "To Be Delivered to My Husband by That Dear Bastard Dwarf Rintrah," informing me that she was pregnant with another child. I heard about the impending birth of my son from a messenger. I spent some hours in the attic fuming to the silent Paschal about his old friend my wife, before I was able to remember that last time I had gone to Anna Marie's bed. I went home to see her and express my congratulations, but she was out in the garden pulling pokeberry and was too out of breath to speak. I told her a woman in her condition should not be out working in the heat, that the heat and the weeds and the bugs would ruin her child. I said, *her child*. She looked at me as she might look at an idiot slobbering on the carpet.

"Nine children, John. Now ten. Please don't start giving me advice now."

"I'm sorry."

"About the child?"

"No, about insulting you with my advice."

She viciously ripped a pokeberry out of the ground, accidentally pressing it awkwardly to her cheek where the berries left a red and thick stain like blood. She wiped at it thoughtfully and looked at her fingers.

"Well, *I*, I the mother, *I*, am sorry about the child."

Two days later Paschal was murdered and I don't remember much more about that summer until she was nearly ready to give birth, a great ball of a woman, crying and biting at my shoulder.

I found him dead in his bed one morning, peaceful and still. On the bed, where I found Paschal with the pillow over his face, was a small arrow cut from a cypress branch, carved with heathen designs, its delicate leaves left on for the arrow's feathers. The mark of a devil, if not *the* Devil.

Suffocation, a pillow, a funeral. Rage. I waited for Lemerle outside his old cottage on Dauphine, knowing he would see me and that he would understand why I had come. He would want to know what I thought of his handiwork. *Murderer.* And so he walked out of the house and paused at the top of the porch stairs, eyeing me and pulling his black trail hat down close over his eyes. He disappeared down a porte cochere choking on clematis and trumpet vine and soon rode out on his crazy-eyed gray. He had his Winchester with him and I carried my Colt. He didn't stop until he was halfway to Grand Isle, and when he did I had already abandoned his trail to make my own. I pushed through the scrub and wet, staying hidden, hunting him. Old broken stumps and sharp-thorned things cut my horse but she, good as gold, never whimpered. We tracked and plotted together. I could see for miles, I could hear the work of ants, I smelled viburnum miles before seeing it, I felt the vibration of the ocean against the earth a day's ride away.

I hunted a man. Time to end it. I heard his heart, the sound rattled the scrub pines around me. I pulled my pistol.

I had let the man finish his work. I had let him sneak into that house, that holy and God-bright house, and desecrate it. I hadn't only allowed it, I had led him there, I was sure of it. I had brought him to that house as surely as I had brought myself. He was a part of me like my leg, an appendage strapped on and redolent of the past, my bloody past.

He stopped in an old clearing, probably part of an old fish camp. He sat quietly on the horse, not looking in any direction. He was listening for me. I had dismounted a quarter mile before, and now I stood twenty-five feet away, watching from cover behind an ancient oak. I heard nothing, not even the birds. Perhaps they had quit chittering, content to watch. I cocked that pistol, the *snick* of it echoed. He turned his head slowly toward me and frowned.

"Come out, Johnny boy."

A man, an arm, a weapon, a will? I was condensed and simplified then, I felt the capacity for speech disappear. Unnecessary. There was only one thought. The hunter and the hunted, the creator and his mistake, the murderer and the inevitable vengeance that must, *had to,* fall upon him swiftly and without hesitation, or God was a lie. At the very least, He needed to be doubted and kept at arm's length, if He did not mete out swift and fair punishment. I was willing to be His hand, and if He were to reject my offer, I would forever mistrust the pleadings of the faithful on behalf of Him, that He has a Plan and that we must trust that the Plan is good even when it seems utterly broken and nonsensical. I knew of Plans, I had thought them up and written them down, I had turned them into sound and fire. If need be, I would draw up another Plan and execute it to the letter, starting right then in that clearing with Sebastien, who leered at me from atop his horse.

"Get down," I said. I didn't recognize my voice.

"No. Shoot me down."

"I give the orders."

"I stopped taking orders a long time ago, Lieutenant. General. Mister. *Américain.*" He spit. "Mr. *Américain,* I like that. I shall call you that."

Then I had him in the air, falling into the soft swamp thatch. There is an advantage to being a gimp, and that is that no one bothers to notice your healthy parts. I knocked him off his mount with my good arm and cracked him across the skull with the pistol as he fell to the ground. He moaned.

"Mr. *Américain*. You don't understand!" Now he spit blood, hunched up on his hands and knees. "Mr. *Américain*, John, General, I *admire* you!"

That enraged me, and I kicked him with my good foot. I didn't understand why we were talking, why I had said anything to him. A bullet through the head had been the plan. I raised the pistol and slipped on my bad leg. We lay on our backs, face to foot. I kept the pistol on him.

"Yes, yes, this is right, it is perfect. We have come the entire circle, coming back, you and me, we will settle this? Yes, we will! It is over, bless the Lord!"

He confused me. I shook it off. I engaged my primitive mind. Pulled back the hammer again. Stood up.

"Yes, yes, I *did* kill your nigger up there in the attic, I certainly did. You found the little arrow? Good, good. You knew who had done this immediately, no question. That's perfect, that's how it had to be."

I didn't pull the trigger. He looked up at me out of the corner of his eye, smiling some, like he was glad to see me. I was disoriented, I felt the whole creeping swamp around me shifting, taking new angles on me, waiting for me to stumble so that I could be wrapped up and carried high into the treetops for devouring. Which one of us was a part of the swamp, which one was the agent of its will, its tooth and claw? I meant to be, but I didn't know. He continued.

"I don't mean to call him merely your nigger, General Hood. I know who he is. Was. And I know that he is much more to you than a nigger. I know what kind of man he was, I knew him before that night at the ball. That is not something I'm proud of now, believe it or not."

"I don't believe it."

"It is true, nonetheless. I have done two things these last few months, one that makes me proud and one that makes me think I shall burn for eternity, and both of them were for you."

The little slippery, greasy, backwoods hypocrite and liar. Put it on me? I was a god, the God of War and Vengeance, I could not be blamed. I did not move on a plane subject to the judgments of mortals. And yet I listened, listened as if playing with the mouse before biting its stomach out.

"You admire me, and because you admire me you lynch a friend, badly, and finally come back to finish your work with a pillow? That's admiration?"

"Let me stand."

"You may sit."

He sat on his ass, his knees drawn up to his chest, rocking, still trying to get his breath back. I watched his pants go dark from the wet seeping up from the ground. He had scratched his face, or perhaps I had scratched it, but in any case the blood ran down his face in thin, straight streams and clotted near the edge of his mouth. He looked painted for Carnival.

"I sit. And I say, *I admire you, Hood, because you are saving yourself, though you were the Devil and you damned me, damned me, damned damned damned. You ascend to Heaven now.* And I, I only, I wanted to help you."

He held up his hand not to protect himself but, it seemed, only to delay what he had already decided was the inevitable. Again I didn't fire.

"You had no business keeping that man alive, General."

"You botched the job, not me. I only helped to clean up your mess."

"Oh no, General. I didn't botch, as you say, the job. I did it too well! I meant to tie that knot, and the knots on his hands, in a way so that he could slip out once we had gone. I told him, I whispered it to him. He nodded his head. I said to never come back, and he nodded his head again. He was a brave man, though a nigger. Among other things."

"The branch broke. That's what saved him, not some absurd gesture of goodwill."

"Yes. I tied the knots too tight! These hands"—he looked down at them, caked in black silt and brown mud—"these hands are very good with knots, much practice. They work on their own."

"You're a liar."

"If he could talk, he would tell you."

"That's not at all funny."

"I mean it sincerely. If he could have ever talked, he would have proven my innocence."

"Then why string him up at all? What were you doing?"

"That was for your benefit, Lieutenant. You

could not intimidate me. If you were coming for me, I thought, I would rip your world apart, throat to gut, beginning with the octoroon spy you'd sent after me. He had no business there."

At that moment I successfully entered his world, distorted and blinkered as it was, and understood what he had done. He was describing a demonstration, a feint, something to scare me away. Why would I come for him? I suppose he assumed I felt guilt for Texas, for chasing down the Comanche, that I would need to have him killed. I didn't feel guilt, but he thought I did. *He thought it*. He felt it. He was a better man, if more brutal, for crediting me with an emotion I should have possessed but did not. I did not. I thought I didn't, anyway.

"So why would you try to spare him?"

"I am not an animal," he said, showing me his hands. Thick, horny skin broken by ragged calluses. "And I had begun something, I will admit, that I couldn't stop without risking *my* neck. Things get out of hand, slip away. They get bigger than what they're supposed to, and far worse, no? And I became angry when you pretended not to know me. Me!"

He was raving now, spitting out the sides

of his mouth, trying to get it all out before
the inevitable. He clutched his knees. His
legs were entirely covered in dark mud. He
looked like something just emerging from
the swamp.

"And then why would you kill him?"

"Because he was my responsibility, and not
yours. I had made him that way. He collapsed
on *my* march, and had to be left behind. All
you and your midget and your priest had done
was extend that man's pain. Not enough to
live, not enough to die."

"He showed no pain."

"Life is pain. If no pain, there is no life,
and yet you wouldn't release him. How do
you know what he felt, did he talk to you?
Make hand signals? No. So I did it for you.
You didn't have the guts, and I do. Perhaps
you were afraid, or sentimental. The kindest thing was to let him go. You never did
understand mercy. Never. You left it to me
to end the pain back in Texas. I put an end
to the pain you caused. But this time it was
pain I had caused and you were prolonging
it, perverse bastard, and so I took control.
And I did it knowing you would come after
me, so here we are, and I am about to die."

I raised the pistol.

*   *   *

How had Father Mike found us? And why
hadn't I heard him? He must have ridden behind me, and yet I hadn't noticed. I had been
so intent on my quarry, I hadn't heard a giant
priest on a mule clomping behind me. But
now he stepped into the clearing and I finally
understood the stories Anna Marie had told,
the stories of the brawler and the sensualist,
the boy who made men afraid. Here he was,
older, the sleeves on his shirt rolled up above
the elbow, his forearms near as big as my leg.
My good leg. He stepped between us and we
both looked up. His hair, always long, was now
wrung with sweat and whipped about his huge
head. He glared down at both of us, but mostly
at me. It was impossible to imagine him pre-
siding over the Eucharist. He looked fit only to
preside over the wrestling of alligators.

"Put the pistol down."

"I won't."

"Fool, I'll take it from you and make you
eat it."

I lowered the pistol.

"Give it to me."

Sebastien called out, desperately. "Show
me the mercy! End this now, Hood. The
pain! Don't listen to him!" But I could see in

Sebastien's eyes that he was relieved, that he knew he wouldn't be dying today. Even so, I didn't hand over the pistol.

"What about Paschal?" I asked him.

"Paschal reconciled himself to the Church through me, he has been relieved of his sin, and now he is at peace. And now I'm here to make sure that another of my friends, though I'm not sure why I call you *friend*, that another of my friends doesn't do something very stupid he'll regret later. You are a Christian? Then I command forgiveness from you in the name of Jesus."

"You're commanding me?"

"It's the language you speak, unfortunately."

And then he had the pistol. I don't know how he moved so fast, but first it was in my hand, and then it was in his, a tiny thing against his palm. He pocketed it.

"Are you otherwise armed?"

"No."

He lifted Sebastien up by the back collar of his shirt, like a man picking up a kitten, and fished through his pockets. Out came four knives and a small-bore pistol. These went into Father Mike's pockets also.

"I followed you, John, because this man is damned by you, but you can still be saved.

God is here, God is *right* here. I will help you see Him, but you must forgive. I will help you, but you must ask. There will be no more killing today, or I will break my vows and have my own vengeance. I hope I am not being ambiguous."

Then he walked into the woods and, a few minutes later, I heard his mule clop-clopping away, back toward the city, like some country friar off to talk to the birds. He made me afraid, he awed me. I never thought to follow him, and I never thought to ask him about his appearance in the swamp that day. He was some other kind of being, something born in the muddy woods to which he returned. When I saw him again he was just Father Mike, but in the swamp he was mysterious and lethal, like the alligator.

I went over to a log and sat down.

"What will we do now?" Sebastien said.

"Reminisce, what else do we have?" I said.

And we were there for three hours. After some time I relaxed. I tended his cut, and tied up his horse, and holstered my weapon. I spared him. My head flooded with thought, language, the complexities of expressing life in words and sentences. I was no longer the General, and I hoped the General was gone for good.

The city disintegrated around us, and we knew it to be our fault. Reconstruction was over and we had not been reformed or reconstructed. Men had become, perhaps, more vicious for having thought of themselves as the conquered for so long. We were the conquered, as General Lee said, and we owed obeisance to the conquerors. If only the conquerors had possessed greater will, for now that they were gone, along with their Freedmen's Bureaus and their garrisons and their sham legislatures, our people asserted themselves brutally, as if they could take back what was lost and more, as if they could make time reverse itself.

Sebastien had hanged a colored man no blacker than himself, and had witnessed the burning of the colored school in the Vieux Carré a few weeks before. The appeasers and collaborators, the Republicans and the other opportunists, kept their heads down. The White League—old French Creole reactionaries and other white Southern nationalists—met and plotted in the open. Elections had become occasions for battle, and we had endured the ignominy of two competing legislatures and governors set up in nearby hotels. My friend General Longstreet had been trapped in that conflict, and had made the impolitic—if also honorable— decision to denounce the violence and the resistance to Federal and Republican rule, and he lost his position in society and his insurance business. The rest of the Confederate generals in New Orleans—Hooker, Beauregard, and me—knew enough to keep our heads down, to bide our time, and for my canniness I was given General Longstreet's insurance business. Let it not be said that cowardice is without reward.

So here we were, fighting the war again and again and again. When I mentioned this to Sebastien, he nodded. He'd been to Shiloh, he'd ridden with General Forrest at Fort Pillow, he knew what we'd done. *I don't know, Hood, if I'm suited for a world where there ain't killing to be done. No sir.* And I told him that was my fault, and he nodded his head.

Things that weren't my fault: disease, heat, floods. At the periphery of the city the cannons sounded each night at dusk against the coming miasma, that unseen mass that carried yellow fever and malaria and cholera and houdou things. I told Sebastien that the report of the cannon made me flinch, and that its echo rang in my ears long afterward. Firing out into the night at the unseen and unknown. That seemed right: we were a city under siege, cut up and slowly murdered from within and without. All we had was the river, and Lord help us if it quit carrying the packet boats and the barges to us.

"The cannons," Sebastien said, touching the clotted blood curtaining his cheek. "The cannons are my friends. We can still fight, that's what they say to me."

"I don't care if I never hear the sound of a cannon, or a rifle, or a pistol, or a sword unsheathed, ever again."

"That's not what I would have expected you to say, General."

"What do you mean?"

"I mean, what else do you really know?"

"I am a husband and a father. I know that. I sell insurance."

"Are you good at any of those?"

I paused to think about that. Might as well be honest.

"No."

"What else?"

"I take care of sick people when I can. I buy things for them, blankets and medicines and such. I help."

"And that? Are you good at that?"

Another pause. It crossed my mind, not for the last time, that I might have spared myself much anxiety and trouble had I just killed him outright like I'd intended. Was I good with the sick? Was I a healer?

"No. But I refuse to fail at that. I refuse."

"But your wife, your children, your business? You do not care?"

The admission, finally. I could make it, now that my quarry had become my counselor.

"I don't know. I don't think about those things so much."

"But disease, yes? Disease you think about often."

"Always."

It killed without discrimination, and death by yellow fever was excruciating. It came on the body so suddenly that even in death the victims seemed incredulous, unbelieving. They were healthy, walking the street and chasing their children, and then they were down. I cannot say whether it was my experience of war that drew me to the diseased, or the disease that helped me understand my war. In either case, I had been overcome by an obsession. I could not tolerate even one death, and yet I was bedside for hundreds. Each death brought me one step closer to

Hell, I was sure of it, for they were my fault somehow. I had never stood on a battlefield holding the hands of the dying or burying the dead, the men whose last moments had been conceived and ordered by me, and yet I could not leave the diseased alone, and every rattle and rasp, every towel of sputum, every pine box, I added to my own tally, which was the tally of my transgressions, the things I would have to explain to God. I never turned my head to the heavens and thought *Why?* because I knew there was no sense, just as I now knew there had been no sense in my pursuit of the Comanche, or in that bloody charge at Franklin. It was all part of my lot, the bringer of endings, blithe and stupid destroyer. I told Sebastien none of this, but I had the feeling he could hear my thoughts. He looked at me kindly, and this frightened me.

"I don't want to see you again, Sebastien. I'll kill you next time. Or Rintrah will. They were friends, he and Paschal."

He blanched for a moment at the mention of Rintrah's name, but only for a moment. He patted my shoulder. I wished he could stay, that I could allow him. It wasn't possible.

"Not if I see you first, friend. But you'll not

see me in the city again. Only in that next life."

He mounted up, picked a scab from his face, and wheeled around and out of the clearing. He may have been my closest friend, or at least the man who knew me the best, and I disliked him some for this. Even so, he was spared, and I wondered if God would credit me that mercy. I don't know what difference it would make, but I like to have the books square, the maps precise. Not that it ever did anyone, me least of all, any good.

I didn't love the disease, the dying. I loved Anna Marie. How could a maniac have seen that while I remained ignorant of it myself? I mounted up. I sensed the last battle approaching. *Be proud of me, Anna Marie.*

When I returned to town, I rode straight to Rintrah's house. Rintrah and Father Mike sat in a small pantry they'd made into their war room, the secret room to which only a few were admitted. They bent their heads over a pine-stick table, rickety and bowlegged, on which Rintrah had laid out a sheaf of papers. They looked up when I walked in, they nodded, and turned back to what I now understood had been an argument.

"Can't do it, Michel. There is no money for this."

Standing around them were three colored men, two of whom I recognized as Houdou John, Father Mike's friend, and the coachman who has worked for Anna Marie's father so many years, George. I didn't recognize the third colored man, but everyone in the room, even Rintrah and Father Mike, deferred to him and called him Mr. Plessy.

"You mean," Mr. Plessy said, "that there is no money you would spare."

Rintrah narrowed his eyes at him. "Don't get any ideas, Plessy. I've been very gener-ous. Look at this house, it's a blasted stor-age shed for colored castoffs that even *your* people won't look after while they die, so don't be getting high and mighty with me. I've done put down plenty of money for you people."

He said this nearly without anger in his voice, which he kept soft and steady, as if still trying hard not to offend even while of-fending. I wondered who this Mr. Plessy was, exactly.

"We all have made our sacrifices, in our own ways, this is why we here today together," said Houdou John, always the peacemaker. I leaned against the wall and tried to remember his last name. I realized I never knew it.

"Who is this?" Mr. Plessy nodded his head at me, as if I were a servant.

"That's Anna Marie's husband, the General Hood," said George, looking at me nervously. I didn't know his last name either. Mr. Plessy nodded his head.

"Your wife knows my stepson, Homer, General Hood," he said.

"I know nothing about that. Anyway, I am here on other business."

"I reckon you have the same business here as the rest of us do, General Hood."

I stood up straight to register his impertinence, but he wasn't looking at me. He was looking at Father Mike and Rintrah, who had stopped fiddling with the papers in front of them and had looked up at me.

"Perhaps you do," said Father Mike. "Have the same business, that is."

"We might have a proposition for you, Hood," Rintrah said.

And so, though I had intended to tell them I could no longer spend my days and nights there at the sick house, that I had obligations as a husband and a father at home, I listened to their plan. I listened out of friendship and respect, but at first I had no intention of seriously entertaining any scheme for any purpose that would require me to be away from Anna Marie and the children anymore. I had been shamed by a killer into recognizing my obligations to my family. Then, as I listened, and the perverse brilliance of their plan unfolded, I couldn't help but be drawn in to their madness.

They intended to spirit from the city as many colored people as they could come high summer, when the yellow fever would be at its height. Father Mike had become tired of always tending the dying, and I came to understand that Mr. Plessy, Houdou John, and George had become tired of burying their dead.

Escape from the city during the summer had always been the luxury of those with money. They had the carriages, the servants, and the houses up north of Lake Pontchartrain where the yellow fever nearly never appeared, and when the summer was over they would return to the city as if they'd merely been on a holiday and not in flight for their lives. They never saw the city that was created in their absence, the suffering, the heat, the constant parade of coffins, the despairing insanity of those who had nowhere else to go. That was not their city.

Father Mike and Mr. Plessy, I learned, had decided that it would no longer be the city of the poor colored either. Where the others had their houses and breezy verandas and cooks and maids up north of the lake, Rintrah had his fish camps, where he had been storing his goods for many years. And in the city, he had his fleet of hearses.

"You got the perfect setup for moving people out of the city," George said. "It ain't like you never moved contraband before."

"They ain't contraband, you can't just stack the poor bastards up like pallets and bottles," Rintrah said.

"They aren't contraband?" said Mr. Plessy, to no one in particular.

The problem was the money, always the problem in everything. Rintrah had the means to move people out of the city, and a place to send them where they could stay a couple months, but he didn't have the money. He would lose all the money he'd be making moving liquor instead of people, first off. Second, most of his men wouldn't likely have any part of it, and the rest would want an unconscionable amount of money, more money than he had in the world. "They ain't going to take kindly to the idea of moving negroes out of the city ahead of white men," Rintrah said. "And neither will anybody else in this damned city." The rest of the people in the room nodded their heads sagely, and yet they persisted with him.

I suggested that they move poor blacks *and* whites, so as to partially assuage the concerns of Rintrah's men. Mr. Plessy chuckled bitterly.

"That might make things easier on Rintrah and his boys, but it wouldn't do a lick of good for us," he said. "When it came down to it, no white man, poor or not, is going to let a nigger go on ahead of him, and so we'd have riots and the only way to end it would be to take the whites out first, all proper like, and when that's done, and once the whites had taken up all the fish camps, what would we then do with the coloreds? Half them be dead by then anyway. That's not what this is about. Understand me, General Hood, I am here for *my* people."

"And what about those whites who have no way out either?"

"They better get to planning and scheming

they ownselves, I do believe. They on their own."

So, the money. When Rintrah looked up at me and said, *We might have a proposition for you, Hood,* this is what he meant: he wanted my money. At that point, I asked if I might be excused to talk with Rintrah and Father Mike in private. Mr. Plessy, Houdou John, and George filed out slowly, watching me, and went into the hallway, closing the door behind them.

"This is not why I came here," I said.

"Nevertheless, it's the question at hand," Father Mike said.

"I don't have such money, such resources."

"But, I believe, the Insurance Association of America does."

"That's not my money. That's someone else's money, that's everyone who's bought policies."

"It's money, and it's in your possession," Father Mike said, leaning so close I could smell the vinegar on his breath. Collards. "They're going to break you with those policies, we all know that. Your business is just about done, anyway, we all know it. They're going to bleed you dry with their claims. All those riverboats you insured, all that cargo? All those profits? They're gone and you know it. This is a plague city, friend, there isn't going to be any business here soon. And they're all going to come running to you for their claims, for some money. So you got to decide, who gets that money."

"It's a matter of honor, Father," I said.

"It certainly is."

I promised to think about it. Rintrah snarled and said I'd have a week to decide, or else they'd have to scrap the whole idea. In the confusion of it all, I forgot to tell them I was leaving them for Anna Marie and the children. The point had become moot, I guess.

I began to get up to leave, but Rintrah held me back. His strength, the size of his hands, was always surprising.

"I have other business to discuss with you, Hood," he said. "I know what you been doing."

"Calm down, Rintrah," Father Mike said. "Just ask your question and get it over with."

Rintrah sucked air into his cheeks and blew out. He looked me straight in the eye.

"You went after him. You went after him without telling me. Without my men."

"Yes." I saw no use in lying about that.

"What happened?"

I *did* see some use in lying about that, however.

"He's dead."

"Where?"

"I said he's dead."

"Sebastien Lemerle is dead. And you killed him."

I didn't answer, I only returned his stare. I was tired, and my heart had gone black momentarily. Rintrah looked at me suspiciously, but then relaxed.

"That's it then."

"That's it. It's over."

I walked out, nodded to the three colored men lined up along the hallway, and mounted out for the house. Rintrah was weeping the last time I saw him.

CHAPTER 17

Anna Marie Hood

John never told me about what he'd done to Sebastien Lemerle. I heard about it much later, and even then I never told John what I knew. I decided that if he didn't want to tell me about it, he had his reasons. I'd come to trust him again, don't ask me why. I will admit this, though: I was ashamed. Or, rather, I was saddened by the realization that what I had prophesied in that café, something I thought was the most terrible thing I could utter, this oath I had sworn in anger on Sebastien Lemerle in the presence of another ugly and laughing killer, that those words of mine had been made hard and true. I was shocked to know that my husband could kill a man. Is it odd to say that? Yes, I was shocked that my husband, the Confederate, the man known even among his detractors as a vicious fighter, could end one particular man's life. I was responsible, I thought. I had wished it to happen, I had prayed for it, I had uttered the words, *Sebastien Lemerle will die*. And so he did, and I was not at all unburdened by that knowledge. I was not set free, I did not feel that there had been justice. It just seemed one more killing, nothing greater, and did not bring any greater order to the world. Perhaps this is why I never mentioned it to John: I could neither bring myself to congratulate him or condemn him.

He came home afterward. It took me three days to realize he meant to stay, and that he wasn't running out the door to carry water for Michel and Rintrah. It was unexpected, Lydia, not least because I had come to understand, I thought, his obsession, and I had been prepared to accept it. Instead he bumped around the house, noticing things for the first time in many months. He saw that the oil was out in the lamps, and he rode off to get some. He fixed John Junior's door, which squeaked. One day I watched him from the doorway as he slowly spun around in the middle of the living room, as if memorizing it, crinkling his brow now and again when he saw something new, or something old he'd never bothered to notice. He tested the red upholstered chairs, all three of them, and the blue couch, unmatched but comfortable, and spent the rest of the afternoon leveling the legs with a plane. He was very neat, I noticed. Meticulous about picking up the wood shavings. Then he took a nap.

He carried you around on his shoulders, Lydia, like he used to, hunting spiders and wren's nests up in the eaves of the porch. He lingered after supper, even as the sun went down and it became dark, and we talked. Not the talk of giddy lovers, but talk between a man and a woman who had been tested and had decided that they could not go through with the days alone. This was love, too.

I didn't ask him why he never went to the office, I was too glad to have him at home. He seemed preoccupied in his quiet moments, and at night he mumbled to himself. *I have obligations, I have made promises.* I thought he was talking about us, you and me, Lydia, and the rest of the children, and so I would put my arm over his chest and draw myself close. We slept in the same bed for the first time in several years, without any discussion.

Should I have questioned his return, should I have forced him to explain it, to justify it, to argue why he *ought* to be let back into my bed? Should I have made him prove himself, should I have forced him to make various admissions of fault and sin and recklessness and coldheartedness? Another woman might have made him earn his way, but I thought I could see in him, and feel in the knots of muscles in his back, that he had already earned something, that he had already suffered for his absence. Had I wanted to be right, I would have made him argue his case. The truth, though, was that I just wanted things whole, this family and this man and our bed.

I let my fingertips drift across his chest, stirring him only just enough to set the nightmares flitting off into air and nothingness. I would soon learn that his *obligations* weren't only just to the family, but in that moment I was particularly content.

On the fourth day John went over to Bayou St. John with John Junior, and they brought back five large catfish. The fish lay on the back porch slowly turning from dark blue to gray while John showed Junior how to skin and fillet the big cats. We ate fillets fried in cornmeal and pepper, with okra from Rintrah. The okra came with a note to John, which he didn't show me.

During supper, and after you children had left the table to play among the weeds and vines in the backyard while the sun still shined, John kept pulling out the note to unfold and fold again, each time creasing it tighter and tighter. He looked at me over the last few of our candles, and he cleared his throat.

"I have a decision to make," he said, stroking at his beard as if he could yank it off and become someone new. "Or, rather, we have a decision to make."

The words themselves were enough to make my heart beat in my throat. The confusion in his face nauseated me. Perhaps I had been wrong to think that he had changed.

"Yes?" I sat very straight in my chair. The candles blocked his face at the other end of the table, and so it seemed that his voice came out of the flames.

"I have not been entirely honest with you," he said.

Another woman. I was silent, my hands clawed at each other in my lap.

"I am a failed businessman, now twice over."

I was so relieved, I nearly said, *Well, of course you are, darling!* I thought better of it. "Oh dear," I said.

"I have failed you and the children, we are on the brink of disaster. I never cared much for the numbers, the money. I was foolish. Soon the insurance company will have paid out all of its capital in claims, which are coming all at once because of the damned epidemic that seems about to break open here in the city. Did you know," he said, spearing a piece of catfish as if it had personally thwarted him and his plans, "did you know that up and down the river the boat captains have been instructed not to stop in New Orleans for fear of taking aboard the contagion? The cotton docks are nearly empty, same as the molasses sheds. And now the factors and the traders and the importers come to me, their insurer. They have their hands out and demand to be paid so that they might continue to live as if nothing has happened."

I kept staring into the flame, looking for meaning in this talk of his. I understood what had happened, but what decision was there to be made?

"This is what you do, of course? Pay out money? They are not wrong to ask for it."

He leaned back in his chair, hands behind his head, looking up at the ceiling where flies and other insects had left their trails. I could see his face, and it had suddenly relaxed.

"I need to clean this ceiling tomorrow," he said. "It looks as if someone has tried to draw a fresco up there in insect shit."

I giggled at his profanity. It was a weakness of mine. He looked toward me, searched for my eyes.

"Yes, that is what I am supposed to do. I am supposed to pay out such claims so that rich men may remain so. I do not insure poor men against poverty, only wealthy ones. I do not insure poor men against death, only the ones with the money. On and on."

"You sound like an old abolitionist all of a sudden," I said. "What have you against the society men, the people with money?" I had plenty to hold against them, but that was personal. John was talking as if there was something more basic at stake.

"Perhaps I do. In any case, I have been asked to think differently about my job as an insurer, and to consider turning what money is left in the company over to another cause entirely."

The note from Rintrah. Of course Rintrah would be involved.

"And that would be?" I didn't care much what he did with the company's money. If we were to be bankrupt, what did it matter how it happened. Soon I would learn that it mattered quite a lot.

"Father Mike, Rintrah, and several negro men have made plans to evacuate great numbers of coloreds, those who could not afford to escape otherwise, from the city before the epidemic gets much worse. They are sick of watching these people die, Anna Marie. It looks particularly bad this year, and so they think this is the year to secretly move these people out and away from the yellow jack."

"Secretly?"

"They believe that they would be prevented if whites found out about it."

"And they need money."

"All of it."

I had yet to tell John about the day I watched the family of Paschal's cousin die in their tiny Treme cottage, how I washed their feet and how Homer had fitted them with shoes. I saw them now. I had never been the same person since, and yet I had not told John. I had kept it to myself. I was possessive of them, those moments standing in that dark room, because I had not been the same woman ever since.

"Where will they take them?"

"To Rintrah's fish camps, north of the lake."

"By horseback? Cart?"

"Rintrah's hearses. No one bothers a hearse, Rintrah says."

Rintrah's hearses, Rintrah's sense of humor.

"So you will give them the money?" I assumed he would, simply because he was having such trouble deciding what to do. The John Bell Hood I had first known would not have hesitated, he would have paid the claims of the insured and let the rest fend for themselves. If he hesitated now, it was because he had changed also, and powerfully enough to overcome a lifetime of subservience to authority. He just needed a little urging. I felt no hesitation, I cared nothing for the money, but if it could keep another father, mother, and daughter from dying alone in a dark cottage foraged by thieves, then I thought there was no question what had to be done. John was shocked.

"Anna Marie, think." The excitement in his eyes betrayed him.

"Are we too good to be poor?" Had little Anna Marie, daughter of the great jurist Duncan Hennen, flower of a thousand balls, just said such a thing? I had.

"No, we are not too good to be poor. But the children! And if I were to abandon those insurance claims, any hope we would have of finding a place in society again, where a general and his lady ought properly to be, would be ruined. They would bear that grudge against me, who gave away their money to negroes. We would be lost to them."

Perhaps it was the staring into the candlelight, or perhaps it was simple anger. In any case, I felt the edges of my sight closing in, red spots floating in front of me.

"I give not one damn about those people. Where are they now? Where are they with their money? Do they help us? Do they even come to see us? And what do they do with their money? They build monstrous, half-empty pillared homes while across the city men die, and then when it's convenient they run their carriages over the unmarked graves on their way out of the city. Dying of the fever is not for them but for the benighted and unlucky. I say to hell with them and their money."

John stood up, came around the table, and

took the seat at my right hand. He stared into my face as if he were watching a new species of insect unfold from its chrysalis. Something dangerous.

"You don't believe that."

"I do."

"These are your friends."

"No longer. I have none, except for you, and these children, and Rintrah and Father Mike. And had I been thinking correctly, as I am now, I would have still had my friend Paschal, I would not have allowed him to be offered up like a lamb at the sacrifice."

His face turned stone hard. His sky-blue eyes burned hard, almost becoming gray in the low light. You stumbled in then, Lydia, to show us a clematis bloom as big as a dinner plate, and when you saw us you slowly backed away. Do you remember that?

"I cannot afford the luxury of being so flippant about our responsibilities and future."

"Flippant? You know as well as I do that I speak the truth." I had passed some test, some point, and now all I could think about was getting rid of that money, giving it away. It was dirty and it tainted us, even if it wasn't ours to give away. I could sense the anger in the room and it made me desperate.

"And now, Anna Marie, that I understand your point of view and what you wish for me to do, I believe I need some time to consider the matter alone."

He stood and went for his coat. It was all I could do to keep from jumping up and wrenching the coat away from him, to keep from dragging him back to the table and tying him there so that he would not leave again. But I had to let him go. If he could not see the truth of what I had said, and if he could not see the true path, the righteous path, that he had been called to take, there wasn't anything else for us to say, and certainly no future together that needed protecting. The last four days had been nearly perfect, and they would remain so even in distant memory, if it came to that. I watched him thump down the steps of the front porch and unhitch his horse.

Four days later I opened the door to find the giant priest waiting for me. Father Michel. Father Mike. My old, clumsy, strong friend.

"Anna Marie, why is this door locked?"

"Good afternoon to you, Father."

He pursed his lips and crossed his arms. I must have acted drunk, and he sniffed my breath. He shook his head and gathered himself up like a proper priest. He had come for other business.

"John has sent me for you and the children."

I now noticed the large four-in-hand in the drive behind the house, captained by a bored seminarian perched up on the box.

"Sent *you*? Why, then? And why you? Has he lost the use of his other leg?"

I hated myself for saying such a thing about the man I loved, but I was not entirely whole at that moment, as I've told you before.

"He is engaged in the sick ward and cannot get away at the moment."

"Bah."

"And he thought you'd more likely listen to me than to him."

I do not know when the tears began to slip down my face, and I only became aware of them when Father Mike stepped over and put his arms around me. I buried my face in his cloak, which also smelled of lye, like John himself.

"You must all leave the city. You cannot give birth in this city, Anna Marie, however stubborn you are. Look at your stomach, that balloon! That child could come any moment, and he *must* not come into the world with the fever everywhere. It is very bad this time. Believe this."

Ah, Michel. So tender and so primitive, a rough sculpture of a man who had never ever become very comfortable with other people and their passions, so afraid of his own. Thank God for the Church. And now he stood in my foyer, no longer the satyr in altar boy's robes, but a man pleading for my safety, concerned for my health and the health of my children, no leering anger, no bravado, no threat. He dressed modestly now, his clothes loose and threadworn. He had quit cutting his hair long ago, and his beard had become long. He had banished his vanity, the pleasure he had taken in his powerful body, his fists, his cock, his mastery of the brutal side of men. Now he breathed out only a kind of true love, rough and innocent and pure. He had become a priest after all.

It felt as if we were all coming to the end of something that had begun nearly twenty years before in that swamp, when Michel and Rintrah and Paschal and I had come together. Whatever had been set in motion that awful night was coming to its final stage, and either we would pass through and be forgiven, or we would fail and live always in fear and doubt and regret.

"What of the others?" I said, showing Michel

to the blue couch. He sat at its edge nervously rubbing his hands, which flaked skin from a dozen calluses.

"What others? Who do you mean? We have no room for others. Your friends will have to fend for themselves, I'm afraid."

"You know who I mean."

He knew who I meant, but I think he was surprised that John had talked of them to me, and more so that I cared.

"I do not know what the plans are for them. We shall see. I have come for you and the children, it is imperative that you leave now. The others we can talk about later."

"I'm not leaving without knowing that they are going also. I want to know those plans you claim you don't know."

We had not mentioned their names, who they were. *The coloreds, the negroes, the field niggers, the octoroons.* I sat down in one of the red chairs, newly solid on its legs, and crossed my arms as if I was perfectly willing to stay in that seat forever. Would I have put the children at risk to make my point? No I would not. But I was ready to die myself, and if not for the life growing inside me, I might have done just that. I sat on my seat, immovable and insistent, because I wanted Father

Mike to know that I had changed. I wanted
everyone to know.

"They are coming with us also," Father
Mike said.

"In hearses?"

"In hearses."

"Why have we a big carriage to ride out in,
then?"

Father Mike rubbed his fingers through his
greasy locks, leaving behind what looked like
tilled rows of hair, a crop upon his thinning
head. He smiled at me out of one corner of his
mouth. Sardonic.

"The others will disappear and no one will
notice, but you are Anna Marie Hennen Hood,
your husband is General John Bell Hood, and
you cannot just vanish. You must be seen leaving the city, like the rest of the gentry, or the
gentry will become nervous."

He knew that word, *gentry,* would stab at
me, and he smiled the old twinkling altar boy
smile, before sobering again. I ignored his insult for the moment.

"And so we go," I said.

"And so you go."

"It will never be the same after this. Our
lives will change."

"And this is so bad?" he said, gesturing at

the rags he wore, at the unkempt beard. He was calm, nearly happy by my reckoning.

I said nothing for a while. Then I turned around and shouted into the house that you children were all to prepare for vacation. Before going upstairs to oversee the chaos and the fights and the packing, I remembered something and turned around. Father Mike had taken to staring out the window, where a mockingbird plucked at pokeberry fruit.

"Why you?" I asked.

"Hmmm?" He was engrossed.

"Why did he send you?"

"I am his friend," the giant priest said.

We fled the city before the plague could get worse, and we did it knowing we would return to utter poverty. There he was, sitting on the box with the driver, scanning the terrain and squinting into the distance as if leading us into battle. We spoke very little, but I do not mind saying to you, Lydia, that I was at once overjoyed and apprehensive. I was anxious about what we would become now, and how we would feed you children, but I was confident that we would get through that. I was more apprehensive about the people we would soon meet, with whom we would soon share cabins and food. I was scared of them, of what they thought of people like me. I wasn't sure I wanted to know.

I will never forget that ride out to the fish camps. Do you remember what the city was like? Don't forget it, you must remember it to tell your own children. (May I live long enough to meet them!) Priests hurried across streets here and there. The carriages of undertakers got in our way on the narrow streets, and when the breeze lifted up off the river as it always did, it collected and carried the stink of the dying and their sweat-yellowed sheets, now burning in barrels across from courtyards where young families still took their late lunches and did not stir at the shouts of the undertakers' men, or the moans of the grieving in the little rooms above them. The city is not for the fainthearted, of course. *We* would sip wine at our own executions. On another street, I watched families lined up along the sidewalk with tiny coffins at their feet, waiting for appointments with the daguerreotype man who would preserve the last expression on the face of their children. Ghastly idea, I would never do that to you children. God strike me down for even thinking that!

But there was nothing else to think about. The smoke drifted across every street, the mud grabbed at the carriage's wheels, the sewers ran with the same abominable muck, and yet the only noteworthy thing was the long procession of the dead trundling over the cobblestones toward cemeteries across the city. I remember it was hot, and I draped my hand and arm out the window and down the side of the carriage, where a mighty sow snuffled at it before I could snatch it back. A woman sweating beads down her head and clearly out of her mind, her face a rictus of fear and joy, ran at the carriage and I pushed her away. I didn't think of how brutal that must have seemed.

Or perhaps it didn't seem brutal at all, to cast aside the unlucky and forgotten. It was no ordinary fever season. Those who remained in the city, and those of us who had waited to the last moment to leave, could not help but be changed by the effects of isolation and constant reckoning with mortality. This, you must not forget, Lydia: epidemics, whether of disease or of violence or of heresy, rob the living of a sense of the past or the future. All is compressed into *this* day, and *this* night. The living become paranoid, at first vigilant against strangers and outsiders, and then suspicious of neighbors and friends. The things that once seemed important seem insignificant. The formerly pious crave bacchanals; the formerly dissolute make their way to Mass every morning to cower before the Risen Christ. Superstition runs riot, especially in our city of ghosts. Catholics see the voudou priest. *What can it hurt?* the living say with a shrug, once they cease to care.

I wish you hadn't seen those things, that hellish tableau. The bodies tossed out on the street, the men fighting each other over the spoils of the dead, the women praying for forgiveness and their own speedy deaths. After a while it began to rain, do you remember? The water ran over the banquettes and made it seem that we were galloping out on a mirror multiplying the afflictions of the city.

I'm sure you remember the month out at that fish camp, one of a dozen or so that Rintrah had strewn around the lake and also down the river into Plaquemines Parish. We slept out in tents, where they came from I never knew. We looked like a small army strewn among the cottonwoods and cypress. We used the shack to cook meals and to house the frail, the rest of us slept out on the ground. There were so many children, and at first they were wary of you and your brothers and sisters.

They treated you as if you could hurt them, or order them to be hurt. Thank the Lord that John Junior had the sense to wrestle one of the young boys and, when he lost, to jump up with a face full of river mud and throw his arm around his conqueror, declaring him king of the camp. After that, I rarely saw you children. You learned new games, and sometimes you'd sleep in other tents with your new friends. I considered whether you could live like that back in the city, but I resolved not to think about it. It would be impossible, of course, to live like that.

I saw the boy Homer soon after our arrival. He said hello to me. We didn't talk about that long afternoon that seemed a lifetime in the past, though it had only been a couple months. I watched him move about the camp, I spied on him. He did not join you children in your games and wrestling matches and fishing expeditions. He spent most of his time quietly sitting at the edge of men arguing their fates, and what this escape from the city could mean for their futures. Were they obliged to the Church now? To that underworld fiend, that dwarf? To a *Confederate* general? There was a man who often sat in the center of these discussions, on a stump he dragged from place to place. He was graying and clear-eyed, he sat straight and said little, but when he spoke it was as if there could be no other person speaking in the camp. He kept his voice low, and only on one occasion when the wind was turned just right did I hear what he said. *There are no obligations, and there is nothing that will come of this but your lives and another year of health, the Lord be willing. We are men, and so we should remember the sacrifices these others have made to help us, but we are not indentured to them. They are men of free will, they have their reasons for the things they do, and they do them. God's gone to separate the wheat from the tares, didn't He say? We got to live like we believe that. Don't worry about nothing else.*

Homer most often sat behind this man, listening intently with the shadow of a smile occasionally crossing his face.

Finally, after nearly two weeks in the camp, I was carried into the little shack and laid on one of the cots. An old woman with hands sheathed in thin, tan skin, crinkled like crepe paper, tended to me and called for water and the least dirty rags that could be found. She smiled at me, and in that riven face of wrinkles and cracks, I saw worry. She needn't have worried. After nine other children, I knew when there would be trouble. All I felt was relief, lying there on the cot and watching the spiders string up their webs in the corners for the mayflies and the flying ants. I knew that the child would be safe, that he would be a boy, and that his name would be Oswald. The rest didn't share my confidence. I suppose I looked old and frail to the young girls who came and went with pails of water on their heads, eyeing me furtively. The graying man brought his stump to the front of the shack and informed the rest what was happening, that they needed to stay out of the way, and that someone ought to go find General Hood, who was at that moment inspecting one of the other fish camps. This man also said that the child would be a blessing on all of them, life before death, and he picked out three women to take care of my children while I was in the bed. "You done took care of white children before, ain't no different now. These are good people now, you seen that yourselves. Be good on them too." I listened to his speech through the chinks in the shack and was brought nearly to tears.

Oswald came just as I expected, much to

the surprise and delight of the old wrinkled woman who had detached him and scrubbed him and swaddled him off to a wet nurse nearly before I realized he was out and in the world. The pain had been sharp, piercing, and short, thank the Lord. Even so, I was very tired and I slept once John had arrived at the shack. He held my hand.

A day or so later I was still in the cot, still light-headed and in and out of dreams, when Homer and the gray-haired man came into the shack and sat down at the foot of the bed. Homer said hello, said he was glad I wasn't dying, and then introduced the man as his stepfather, Mr. Plessy. The man was not at all uncomfortable around me, as so many of the others had been. He sat there as if there was nothing terribly special or scary about a white woman in her bed. I found this surprising, and then comforting.

"Homer says you the lady who went to see those three poor folks die in their house, the day I sent him with the shoes. Was that you?"

"Yes."

He nodded his head.

"Do you know who they were?"

"I don't remember their names."

"They dead, names ain't important. But do you know who they were, to you that is?"

"They were my friend's family."

"The friend you call Paschal Girard, yes. That was his cousin and his cousin's wife and daughter."

The friend you call . . . "Did he have another name?" I asked.

"Sometimes he called himself David. No last name. I believe that had been his given name, but this was something he figured out only a long time after. After the war, after he was sent down to niggertown."

"Sent where?"

"That's how he said it. *To niggertown.* No one else I knew called it that, but he did."

"Sent down by whom?"

Now he *did* look nervous, but only briefly. Homer got up and left us, looking back at me through the closing door before shutting it.

"I come here to tell you truth, not to make trouble. I come because you and your husband have done a good thing, a godly thing, and because I know that you been wanting to know about your friend. I come here only to help you, and I reckon I won't have no other good time to do it except now."

I felt cold of a sudden, and he saw it. He

took up a green blanket from the corner and laid it over me daintily, not wanting to touch me. Not wanting to be too familiar.

"Go on then. You can't make trouble in telling me about Paschal." And now, *David*.

"Not so sure about that, but I already got a foot in, might as well put in the other." He settled back down in his chair. "When he said, *sent down to niggertown,* what he meant was that he had been sent down by you. You and your friends, the priest and the dwarf. And please believe me, Mrs. Hood, it ain't easy for me to tell you this, now that your friends have done for us what they done. They're saving our lives, no mistake. But Homer told me about how you wanted to know about your friend, so there it is."

"I sent him to *niggertown*? What does that even mean? And how could I have possibly had the power to send him anywhere? If you knew Paschal, as you say, you know that very few people sent him anywhere he didn't already want to go."

"That's true, that's true, he was a willful man. But you got to see, a man like that is a complicated creature. He ain't like you and me, we know who we are just by looking at ourselves in the mirror. But more than that, we know who our people are, who we come from and where we come from. But a man like that Paschal, he don't know none of that, the mirror don't tell him nothing and there ain't no family for him to ask."

I closed my eyes and shivered, pulling the covers up. I must have lost some blood, I felt clammy and nauseous. I knew what he would say next.

"So you get your family where you can when you a man like that, and I reckon you were his family. You and the priest and the dwarf. It sure as hell weren't his cousin, he barely knew him and that family until the end, and then he died."

"And we were always his family."

He nodded his head.

"True, true, but families change. They go cold and hot, you know what I mean, you don't always feel the same way about them, sometimes you don't always treat them right. You just hope and pray you got enough time to make it right in the end."

I was losing my patience. I wanted to hear his verdict, hear the recitation of my crimes. I didn't need to hear his fuzzy-headed wis-dom, not right then. That's what I thought of it right then, *fuzzy-headed wisdom,* but I knew he was right. I was impatient to know how right.

"And our family?"

"All I can say is what Paschal said to me, and I only knew him as a man who came around the neighborhood every so often, always wanted to talk."

"Say it!" I screeched, and he flinched. Homer began to come back into the room, I could see his face in the doorway curious and scared, but when he saw me he backed out.

"He said y'all would have nothing to do with him. After the war. When no one wanted to have anything to do with a nigger no more, the white Creoles especially, who were our kin but tossed us out. You know what I'm talking about. When the *américains* took over. To them we were nothing but niggers, even Paschal. And y'all, you believed them. They had the power, see. You know this."

I would not be accused of crimes I didn't commit.

"I *never* cast Paschal out, never thought of him like that."

Mr. Plessy closed his eyes for a few seconds and then opened them.

"You didn't invite him to play piano at your wedding."

What? That was so long ago. An oversight, I almost said, and then I realized how much worse that would sound. My friend, the oversight.

"He didn't even bother to come to our wedding."

"He said he wasn't invited."

"No one was invited. They just came."

"All I know is, and this is what he said, *I knew then she didn't want me around anymore, when she kept me from touching her piano on her wedding day.* That's what he said."

"Well, I never saw him after that, or not very often. Where was *he*?"

"Did you go to see him? Did you invite him in?"

He was right. I had to quit arguing, but I couldn't. I looked for any opening, any glimmer of light.

"He was busy with his real family."

"You didn't know that, ma'am, and anyway he weren't very busy with them. They didn't know him, and he didn't know them. Sister Mary Thérèse thought it would help him to find out who his cousin was, but it wasn't nothing like that. It wasn't good, he got hisself in trouble in that neighborhood. He was

going to take them out of the city this summer, to Pass Christian, but then he died. And
then they died. And that was the end."

I had begun to cry without noticing. I felt
the tears on my chin and wiped at them. Mr.
Plessy looked at me steady, impassively, and
for the first time I had the feeling that he was
angry. Anger came up in his eyes, flared his
nostrils.

"The dwarf and the priest, they didn't want
him around much either. The dwarf wouldn't
give him a job, even when Paschal begged.
Said it weren't no life for him, but Paschal told
me he'd have taken any life from Rintrah, just
to be around him. And the priest, well, the
priest wouldn't take his confession. Said he
didn't want to know Paschal's sins, said there
were negro priests who would be better to
hear them. And when a man says to another
man that he won't listen to his sins, priest or
not, he means that he doesn't care."

I thought I would gag at those words. I saw
the picture Mr. Plessy was drawing, a picture
of a man cast out, *sent down to niggertown,* a
place where he wouldn't have been comfortable, but at least a place where he wouldn't
be reminded of our betrayals. And he was
right, it had become difficult to explain our

friendship with a colored man. It had never
been mere familiarity, never just acquaintance.
He had been our intimate, and when the war
ended and the negro came to be thought of as
a traitor, we became suspect, possible traitors
ourselves. It was best, I suppose we thought,
to be more guarded, more circumspect. But
secrecy and circumspection can quickly become mere abandonment. It's easier.

"You've come in here not to help me, but to
punish me," I said. "You are a terrible man."

He shook his head slowly, but knew well
enough to get up and begin to leave. He was a
very smart man, I could tell, and very keen on
his own intelligence, his knowledge. He carried it on him like armor. He knew more than
me, and he'd proved his point. But in his face
there was no spite, and I realized his anger
had not been at me, or at Rintrah or Michel.

"He forgave you, I should tell you that, mis-
sus. He didn't think he would have done anything different if it had been him, and for that
reason he had to forgive you. I think he was
right about that, and it makes me hellfire hot.
We would have all done what you did. That's
the evil, you see. He was a very sad man when
I knew him, which was only when I tried to
intervene between him and a white man who

lived down in the neighborhood with a colored girl, who he called his wife. Your friend was a very handsome man, and that's all I'll say about that."

Then he left me alone with the image of Paschal strung up from a tree, alone as he'd been for years.

John came to stay with me in the shack during those final weeks of seclusion, finally satisfied that all the camps were running in proper order. In the nighttime I tried to tell him what I had done to Paschal, but he didn't want to talk about it.

"There are others who have more to answer for than you and your friends. You didn't kill him."

I wasn't so sure. I hid, engulfed in your father's arms, vanished in the heat of your father's body. I wanted to be nothing, air, ether, something not bound by the laws of this world, the arbitrary and cruel laws. But I was not ether, I was flesh. Nine months later the littlest Anna was born. Nine months later we were as poor and as ostracized as anyone in *niggertown,* and though I'm certain Paschal would not have wished that on us, I felt closer to him then. He had always said he loved my name.

CHAPTER 18

Eli Griffin

That was one hell of an operation they pulled off that summer, and of course, old Rintrah had come to me demanding that I help. When I asked how much I would be paid he hit me in the shins with a red-and-black cane carved with twisting snakes on it.

"I ain't paying you a damned thing, and if you know what's good for you and your *job* and your *lady,* if you can call her that, you'll take yourself a vacation and help me haul these negroes up to the camps."

He had come down to the ice factory, but instead of sitting down for a spell like normal, he fidgeted and picked at the ice on the big tubes, flicking shards here and there until I had to tell him to quit before someone slipped up and hurt themselves.

"What am I supposed to say to Mr. Rouart? 'Sir, I've got to leave for a couple months so I can smuggle negroes out of the city, I'll be back for my job directly after.' Is that what I'm supposed to say?"

He tried some of the ice and spit it out, rubbing at his yellow-and-green teeth.

"Have you seen Mr. Henri Rouart around these parts recently?"

"I have not, no. He's a busy man."

"Busy getting hisself the hell out of this city. Henri Rouart isn't even within a hundred miles of this city at the moment. He's not dumb, he ain't going to die with the fever. So, first, Rouart wouldn't notice if you decided to swim to Ireland. Second, Henri Rouart does what I say, in certain cases, and that includes giving you a job. And third, you ain't to tell anyone, not one single soul, what we doing. Don't test me. Keep your mouth shut."

When Rintrah put things like that, it was hard to resist him, and so I packed some things and wandered out over to his house on Chartres, and Holy Christ it was like an army had decided to shack up in Rintrah's house and in his courtyard. Men, mostly colored, strode in and out of the house, piling supplies here, lining up women and children over there, and greasing up the hearses by the carriageway. And who was in charge, who barked the orders and took the reports, who inspected the lines of escapees, who examined the quality of the horses? General John Bell Hood, CSA. I could see that this chapped Rintrah's ass, but Hood would just look at him and say, "My money, my operation, step back," and Rintrah would storm off. Father Mike thought it was quite funny, and he chuckled while he took down names and examined the refugees for the telltale signs of the fever.

I had only imagined what Hood had been like as a general, and I will admit that it wasn't an entirely favorable image. But now, when he was standing on one of Rintrah's fruit crates, I could see why he had been able to send men into battle though they faced death. He was still when all around him was flitting and hopping and screeching. His eyes saw everything, and those eyes had become even lighter in his excitement, they looked barely human. He spoke in low tones, and the lower his voice went the more attentive people became. Nothing happened without his knowledge or approval. Most important, he looked as if nothing could go wrong, his face said that there would be no problems and no mistakes and that all would survive and return safely, and under his gaze the people of that house and in that courtyard were encouraged and assured. When Rintrah had told me about the plan to move negroes to the fish camps in hearses, I had thought it unlikely. No, impossible. But now, I stood in the courtyard with my adventure sack slung over my shoulder and not only believed that the plan would work perfectly, but I was eager to put my shoulder to the wheel and help out. I walked over and reported to Hood.

"Lieutenant Griffin, good of you to finally make muster. We've got people who need to be escorted into the transports and made comfortable, though you need to pack them tight. Don't know how many runs we're going to be able to make, so we have to maximize the use of space. But be gentle, dammit."

"Transports?" I was already confused.

"The hearses, son. 'Transports' is a more accurate name at the moment."

And so it became my job to take the lists from Father Mike, call the names one at a time, and see that the men and women, fathers and grandfathers and grandmothers and aunts and mothers and sisters, all got into the hearses in some degree of comfort. The line of them never seemed to end.

The plan was not only clever, it seemed a little poetic too. In order to not attract attention, the refugees arrived at the front of Rintrah's house coughing and bundled up, as if they were in the final stages of their illness and had come to be comforted unto death by Father Mike and his helpers. Nothing unusual there, and nothing unusual about the constant convoy of hearses leaving out the back of Rintrah's house. Either they were filled with the dead or Rintrah's liquor, either way they were nothing remarkable. And between the two, the afflicted cast off their blankets, cleared their throats, and marched bright-eyed to the staging area where Father Mike got them prepared to leave.

It was perfect, and Hood saw that the plan was executed down to the least detail, and he was the last to leave the compound before going to meet Anna Marie and the children, who would be riding out of town in a carriage. I rode out of town on a mule that was in bad need of the services of a mule skinner, ornery bugger.

*   *   *

At the fish camps, Hood was in constant motion, only stopping to attend at the birth of his new son, Oswald, and then only briefly. Somewhere he had requisitioned old U.S. Army tents, and he supervised their raising in the woods and open spaces around each fish camp. He directed the digging of latrines, and he identified scouts and foragers who would root through the countryside for food. On his horse, moving down the paths, he was a man shoring up his defenses, shouting orders here, encouragement there.

I fished most of the time, alongside the others. I had a pole out of cane and some line and a hook made from a sewing needle bent in a campfire. I looked like I was sleeping most of the time, except when I pulled up some bass or a cat, but mostly I was listening through the canebrakes and the winding webs of creeper.

"Why you *think* these people of a sudden gone to help us out?"

"The white men? One, he a priest, he got to. God got a straight line to him, that one got a boss man that don't get talked back at. So that's him."

"The priest, all right then."

"The dwarf, he love him some negro ass, he just protecting his interests, get me?"

"The dwarf is a god*damn* criminal and you know it, and I say he got plans."

"What plans?"

"You see if they anything left at the house when we all get on back. You'll see."

"Aw, hell."

"You see."

"They gone to rob *us*? They rob me and what they gone get is a piss pot and my extra pair of trousers. They gone get shit, what I'm saying. You not right in the head."

"You see."

"Mmmhmm. You got one on that line there, maybe you oughta quit running your mouth and fish."

I listened to the sounds of the man pulling in his catch. It thrashed at the surface and dove briefly, a nice catfish. After that first burst of fight, it rolled over on its side and let itself be pulled in, fighting one last time at the end in the shallows, sending the men cursing. Then I heard the sound of a branch or a club brought down hard on its head. A wet thunk and then nothing. Before long I watched the innards go lifting up over the water, glistening green and red and yellow and black, before falling to the water and disappearing again.

"Fry that one up nice."

"Sure will."

"What about that other one, the colonel?"

"General."

"Wit the leg."

"You mean no leg."

"Mmmhmm."

"He done a good job getting this thing together, that's what I think."

"I think he got plans for us too. I think he and his cracker friends gone to do something."

"You an ungrateful man, need to pray for your soul."

"What I know is, when niggers get rounded up all at once, ain't nothing good gone come from it. And I ain't never been, I ain't gone to be, grateful to a white man for nothing. Nothing."

"Who rounded you up, boy? I seen you running down the street with your little ones and the woman just as soon as you heard they taking negroes out the city, tongue out and pumping them legs like you running out a burning house. You yelling, 'Wait now, wait on us now.' "

"You a lying nigger."

"Seen it with my own eyes."

"Outran your ass, now, didn't I? Fat boy."

"I don't run nowhere. I knowed they'd wait. And I also know this. Someday you gone to be thankful for this here fish camp, and when you start telling them tales about how you were saved that summer, and Oh Lord Praise Our Rescuers, I'ma tell tales on you, no mistake."

"All I know, I don't trust a cracker, but Plessy and Houdou John, they good men. And they colored. I'm here 'cause of them."

"Another fish, now."

"That's right, they know who's got it right. They throw themselves at my hook, I so right. I got the fish on *my* side."

"Shit."

When I wasn't fishing, I was running errands for Hood. He called me his adjutant, but I reckoned this was a joke. I took head counts, checked to see if anyone was coughing or fevered, hauled blankets and food here and there as it came in on Rintrah's hearses. All the while I rode on that brokedown old white mule, and the people who saw me going down the paths or delivering vegetables began to call me Lightning. Or maybe it was the mule.

"Won't ever go the same place twice."

"Unless you give 'em two weeks to get there."

After the birth of Oswald, Hood eventually returned back to the central fish camp, a larger place on stilts clad with tin and heart pine. It was the camp closest to the center of his line, as he called it, the string of fish camps under his command. From there he was no more than an hour from anyone who might need him. He spent his days at first pacing around the shack and having quick conversations with the people camped around. I think he was hoping someone *would* need him, but there was never any report of trouble or crisis, except when Anna Marie took to the bed and even then things seemed to go smooth. After a few weeks he finally sat down and tried to teach himself to carve little figures from some of that hard pine. Oh, he was terrible at it, and he nicked his fingers often, including one time I thought he'd torn his little finger right off. I was running around looking for something for a bandage when I heard a rip, and turned around to see that he had ripped the cuff off his shirt and had applied it to the wound.

"That, my boy," he said, giving me a shit-eating grin, "that ain't nothing."

"How about I show you how to carve, General?"

"That would be fine."

And so we made little figures for each of his boys and girls, and then two more for him and Anna Marie. I carved General Hood so that you couldn't see that he was missing anything. I began to carve in a uniform, buttons and stripes and all, but he stopped me and told me to put him in a suit. So I did.

Finally we run out of people to carve—Father Mike hung his from his rosary, and Rintrah tossed his into the fire and cuffed me on the head. I will admit, I had carved his hardly bigger than a splinter, and his ears weren't near that big.

The last one I carved was of M., who I was surprised to find that I missed. She wasn't so squinty-eyed and suspicious in my carving, and she didn't look like she was ever ready to run. She looked happy, I reckon. General Hood noticed, though I tried to hide her.

"Who's that, son?"

"A girl I know. She comes around every so often. No one, really."

"Hmm. And then there she is, carved up and sitting in your lap, after you worked on her two days."

"You been watching."

"I see everything." He laughed.

We sat there, whittling and watching the sun ripple through the ranks of cypress and poplar and cottonwood, orange bending to red as the fiery globe disappeared.

"We haven't lost anyone, have we, Lieutenant?"

"No, we ain't. Not a one."

"That's good. That's exactly right. It's very different."

"Yes sir?"

"To be sitting in camp and not hearing men moan and cry. It's very peaceful."

"Not so much noise."

"Not so much pain, is what I meant."

If I ever thought I'd confront him about the battle at Franklin, the deaths and the pain he had caused that day, that was the time. I'm sure I could have made him apologize, made him apologize to me personally, right at that moment. But by then I'd lost any interest in hearing such things out of his mouth, I didn't need it anymore. That sun, that camp, those blankets, that bearded man carved up in only his suit and not a stitch of rank anywhere, that was some kind of apology I reckon.

"Now go take evening muster."

"Right now?" I was feeling mighty peaceful there with my good thoughts and my belief that all had been made right, finally. I felt calm for once.

"Right the hell right now, Lieutenant. Mount up."

"Ain't much of a mount."

"You can walk."

"Reckon Lightning will do fine."

I was up and about to ride out when Hood called out.

"You forgot the girl."

The carving was standing up on my seat next to Hood, watching me. He took it in his hand and carried it over. I took it and stuffed it in my sock.

"Any girl who comes around every so often ain't nobody, hear?"

I nodded and rode off into the trees, ducking limbs and spiderwebs. When we were out of sight, I moved M. from my sock to my breast pocket and buttoned it tight.

CHAPTER 19

Anna Marie Hood

There is freedom in poverty, I discovered, and the first freedom I indulged was the freedom to feel pain and helplessness and not have to try to explain it, either to myself or anyone else. Explanation was not necessary.

But pain goes numb, and in God we are not entirely helpless, so these feelings, though they never went away, receded.

I was also free to watch you children with the eye of a naturalist. I saw you grow, establish territory, flaunt your talents. I was free to hope that you would escape us one day, escape our poverty. I hoped that when you did you would not despise us.

With my freedom, I did one good thing that seems worth writing down. I went to see Eli Griffin's girl. He never told us her name. I don't think he was ashamed of her, I think he wanted to save her from us and our prying eyes. Smart boy. But I found out who she was anyway, her whole name and the story of her family, and how she lived the first twenty-five years of her life, none of which I plan to relate here. I will respect Eli's desire to protect her, so I will call her M. I never told Eli this, he wouldn't have believed me if I told him I was not offended by her profession and found her delightful. I was afraid that if I told him, *Don't let her go, she is a fine woman,* he would have run away. He was a contrary boy too.

I had much to say and had run out of people to listen. I had so little to give except what you've read here, Lydia: the long, strange life of my marriage, which I cherished as my last possession, the only thing that could not be taken away or claimed as payment of a debt. I was still in debt, though, possibly to God. I prayed, I went to Mass. I prayed to be told what I could do now, when I could barely do for you, my children.

During those prayers, Eli appeared to me. My mind kept coming back to him and the mystery of his life, especially when I prayed the rosary. It must have been Mary, the Blessed Virgin, who called him up to my mind, and Mary who caused me to weep at the thought that Eli would not find anything, or anyone, to care about. He was Paschal also, he was an orphan too. It came to me in a rush. There was a second chance for me.

I found Margaret a month ago. She was cleaning Eli's little apartment above Levi's factory. I had walked the two miles from our house, and when I knocked at the door I expect she saw a disheveled beggar. She opened the door wide, her face wary but placid, and without saying anything she seated me at a small table near the window, drew some water from a pitcher, and served it to me in a tin coffee cup.

"Mrs. Hood."

"You know who I am?"

"Eli has described you, and I seen you from time to time about in the Quarter. You used to drive in carriages, I ain't mistaken."

"No more carriages for us."

"That's what I heard."

She could not have looked more Irish. She had the freckles, the hazel eyes, the light brown hair that streaked red in the sunlight. She had the Irish way of looking suspicious and ready to hear anything, all at the same time.

"Eli has told you our circumstances."

"Yes, he has. I am sorry about your money. But you done good, you done a Christian thing with that money of yours, and ain't no one with sense gone to fault you for that. Not me."

"Thank you."

"Why are you here? Have you come to see Eli? He ain't here, he's in the card houses."

My business was with her, not Eli.

"Do you love him?"

She scowled. "I ain't thought about it, and it's no business of yours, no matter who or what you are."

"That's true. I just wanted to make sure someone cared about him."

She walked to the pitcher and poured herself some water. She sat back down across from me.

"We talking as women? Not fancy lady and poor Irish whore?"

"Yes."

"I care about Eli Griffin, more than I care

about anything else. I don't always know what *he* cares about, but I care about him. Yeah, I reckon I love him, too, though I ain't at all sure what good that's gone to do him or me. He's getting hisself lost in this town, he may know cards and grifting, but he's as innocent as a lamb. Naïve, sure as I sit here."

He was not the first man I knew who had been described as naïve about the city. I'd married the first one.

"Does he love you?"

"I wouldn't know."

"I believe he does."

"Then you'd be a smarter lady than me."

"Don't let him get lost. You know what I mean. Lost in this city. Don't let it happen."

"Got no way to stop it."

"You can. You'll know how when the time comes. Help him then, don't leave him be."

"You a seer? Because I don't reckon you could know the future otherwise."

I drank from my cup and tasted the tin. It made the water crisp to the taste. Outside the wharf gangs shouted and unloaded. I finished the water and decided I'd better go. I'd said what I'd come to say.

"He loves your General Hood, that's certain," M. said, so softly I thought she might be talking to herself. "Hated him once, now he loves him. He'd die for him now. Strange how it all comes out."

I slid my chair around the table so that I was sitting next to M.

"Don't talk about dying." She'd begun to cry silently. Her head drooped a little, and only her shoulders shook.

"Got it on my mind, Mrs. Hood. But you don't want to know that. You came to visit with Eli's whore, tell her what to do and how to live."

"No, that's not why I came."

Her face had turned red, and her eyes shot open.

"Then why did you come?"

I knew the answer to that question, I'd been rehearsing it during the entire walk down the river to the apartment. I'd been thinking about it since Mr. Plessy described for me the last days of my friend Paschal Girard, the other orphan.

"I came to save Eli."

"From what?"

"From being abandoned. I suppose I've failed, but at least I said it. Now I'll go, thank you for the water." I pushed my chair back to the opposite end of the table and walked to the door. M. held her head in her hands.

"You walked all the way down here just to say that?" she called without looking up.

"Yes. I don't have much else to do anymore."

She stood up and smoothed her dress in front of her. It was a more modest dress than I had expected. She looked ready to chase children and tend chickens.

"It was good of you, ma'am."

"Please call me Anna Marie."

She nodded her head and, reaching behind me, unbolted the door.

"I don't know what you mean for me to do, but I reckon I'll do it."

She paused to hear what she had just said. I smiled.

"That may be the most beautiful thing I've heard said in a long time," I said.

The sun was setting when I walked back to the house. I walked along the river and listened to the slap and crumple of the waves against the bows of the riverboats headed upstream. Across the river, in the wilderness of Algiers, some houses poked through the trees. Men on the quay stood back as I passed. I was content with all of it, even the mosquitoes that landed on my arms and on my neck, soon covering me with red welts. I didn't brush them off, I let them go about their business. They were God's creation, too, after all.

When I came in the house, John was in his library crumpling paper and swearing. You, Lydia, were telling the other children bed-time stories you'd invented about gnomes and lions and peanut vendors. I went into the library after kissing you all good night.

"John."

"You're back. You look parched." He was scratching at a piece of paper. At his elbow lay a growing pile of sheets covered in his tight letters, and at his feet a bigger pile of crumpled paper mounded against his legs like windblown sand.

"I think you shouldn't give that book to Beauregard to read."

"It's too late, I've already done it."

"Not the war book."

"Then I don't know what you're talking about."

"The other book, the one you're writing right this second." I stamped my foot and pointed. I felt giddy, like a child. He slipped the paper to the top of the pile and then tried to move the pile into a drawer as if I couldn't see him. "That book, John."

"It's not a book."

"I think you should give it to Eli to read when you're done, and let him work to get it published."

"Why would I do that? Assuming, for the moment, that the book you're talking about exists."

"I think he's the only person who would care enough to do it."

"Well, it's moot, because it can't ever be published. And what does Eli know of publishing?"

"Probably nothing, but he can figure it out. Why can't it be published?"

"There are problems with it."

"Have Eli solve them."

His eyes drifted to the window, where the mockingbird was fledging her two babies. She was unusually quiet.

"You've read it, have you, Anna Marie?"

"No. And I don't intend to read it."

"How do you know, then, that Eli would want to help me with it?"

I removed the sun hat I'd been wearing since the morning, pulled two pins from my hair, causing it to fall down my back. My head felt cool again, and I knew John liked to see my hair come down. He sat up straighter. I thought of M.

"I think he would do anything you asked him to do, and I believe he could use something to do. Something important."

"I'll consider it."

I walked out of the room. "Consider joining your wife, also."

I heard him scraping to his feet and coming after me. "Already considered."

A week later I became ill.

CHAPTER 20

Eli Griffin

Rintrah came by the factory a week after our meeting in his jungle paradise.

"How's the ice?"

"Still cold."

"Right."

He climbed up on Hood's seat—I had come to think of it that way—and pulled out a pipe.

"Ain't supposed to light up in here. Chemicals."

"Well, can I chew on it at least? Or has *Monsieur Rouart* banned that too?"

"No, I think you can chew on it."

"Thank you."

He worried the pipe from one side of his mouth to the other, staring at the files of icy pipes, white ghosts receding into the depths of the building.

"I loved her, you know."

When a man says that to you, you know to keep your wise mouth shut.

Rintrah said he had loved two beings in all his life. The first was the colored man Paschal, who I only know of because I've read about him here in these pages. He was the man who ended up in the attic under his care. They were brothers, or at least Rintrah considered them such. They were not brothers, no one knew where either of them had come from. They had been babies on a doorstep. They had lived in the orphanage together, tended by colored sisters, growing up side by side. Life afterward had knocked Rintrah up one side and down the other, but still he felt protective of the man, his *brother*. The man Paschal.

The second love was for Anna Marie Hennen, and in that he was not entirely crazy. It was not crazy, once, to have thought that Anna Marie Hennen might love a dwarf. She was that sort of woman, he said. But instead, she had married a crippled general. "I hated him. I don't no more, but I hated him. And I hated that she'd prefer a gimp to me, a killer to her loyal and loving Rintrah. When that wedding went off, I reckoned I was going to have to fend for myself. That was the beginning of my career, if you can call it that. But I didn't stay mad and hateful. I came to like Hood well enough, and even to respect him. But I couldn't never see the two of them together, it just ripped me up."

He went silent for a while. "And now it's all falling apart," he said, after a long time. "We're all falling apart. I'm the only one left."

I knew nearly nothing about Rintrah, and so I didn't know what he meant. His face cracked, his mouth slid into a wide slit, the mouth of a man trying not to cry. His light blue eyes welled up. He spit fiercely onto the ground in front of him and recovered himself a little. We sat there for two more hours. I went and got Rintrah a coat from Mr. Rouart's office, and when Mr. Rouart came to fetch it and suggested that Rintrah leave, Rintrah swore at him and Mr. Rouart walked back to his office. He was angry but he left us alone.

When I was done, Rintrah had his head

cocked back on his neck much like Hood liked to do. He was staring unblinking at the ceiling.

"So. Sebastien Lemerle." His voice was low and dead.

"Yes. I should start looking for him real soon, I think."

Rintrah jumped up and began to pace. He grabbed his hair in his big fists and pulled at it, twisted it. Something between a groan and a growl escaped from the back of his throat.

"And then we kill him."

"That's not the plan."

He rolled his eyes. "Well, of *course* we will seek his considered judgment on the literary and spiritual merits of the manuscript. And after that we will kill him. You keep your word, and I finish my own business. Right neat and tidy, I say."

"Why would I go and do that? I don't want any part of no killing, not anymore."

He stopped, goggle-eyed, like I had just admitted I thought the world was flat and that I intended to jump off the edge on my invisible horse.

"You would do this because this man"—he spit again—"this man killed Paschal, and without Paschal there would have been no priest to save you from the Calaboose, and no Rintrah to take care of you and get you a job and keep your ass from getting into trouble. This city would have killed you long ago without me. You'll do it because you owe me. And if Hood was at all honest in that damned book about what Sebastien was to him, you'll know that you ought to do it for Hood too."

I was fairly certain Hood had not meant for me to kill this Sebastien Lemerle. I stood up, towering over the little man. I was getting tired of being ordered around, and I was about to tell him this, though I knew it would earn me a certain beating by one of his black-bearded associates. But then I thought, *What else do I have to do?* I worked in a factory slicing ice. Chasing a villain was bound to be more fun. If avenging the death of this Paschal would relieve some burden, either Rintrah's or Hood's, maybe I was willing. There was something I didn't understand though.

"Why now? Why didn't you go kill him before, if it was so important?"

Rintrah had already begun walking for the door, preoccupied and mumbling to himself. He stopped.

"Because John Hood told us Sebastien the Crow was dead. He said he killed him himself."

He remembered the coat I'd given him, took it off, folded it neatly, and placed it on his chair. "It's a puzzle," he finally said. "The truth is, I'm not sure I trust any of you sumbitches."

And with that, Rintrah put his old black bowler back on his head and walked into the sunshine.

The job of finding Sebastien Lemerle, the hard job, I reckoned, fell to me. I objected since, hell, that had been the thing I wanted Rintrah to help me on. If he, the *master* of the underworld, couldn't find him, how could I?

"Well, of course I could find out where he's at, now that I know he alive," Rintrah said one day while loading up his fruit, on his way out to survey his domain. "But if I were to make the inquiries, or one of my known associates, word would get back to the Crow and he'd flee. Escape. Run terrified, soiling his britches. And we can't have that, see? We need to keep him right where he's at, wherever the hell that is, probably in a pirogue swamped in some fucking lost bayou. If he thinks Rintrah King is after him, there is no chance he will stay put. Hell, he might kill his ownself in self-defense."

He tossed me an artichoke he'd got off one

of the arab boats, and I cursed him when it sunk its teeth into my palm. He laughed. I thought he might be overestimating his reputation, but I kept quiet.

"You, on the other hand," he continued, showing me how to rip off the flesh of the artichoke and suck it good through my teeth, "you are not one of my known associates. Instead you are an unknown young buck, obviously a country boy and probably an idjit, a God-eater who *willingly* goes to see nuns to take instruction, a callow, fearful, and no doubt harmless git that no one will bother warning Lemerle about. Hell, you might be awanting to sell him some ice subscriptions for all anyone knows. No, you're perfect for the job. Now get to it."

He took the artichoke from me just as I was getting the better of the infernal fruit. He pointed to the door.

Rintrah hauled me in regularly, dragged behind two big men who never spoke but only grunted in some language the two of them understood but that sounded like what cave paintings might sound like. *Where's Sebastien?* And each time I had to say, *I don't know.*

And I didn't know. It hadn't been hard to
find his last house, just outside the Quarter
in that negro section they called Treme, on a
street named Marais. He'd had several houses
during the last ten years, I found out from
files at the Cabildo, what they called town
hall down here. Always got to be different,
these people. I found out each of the houses
was smaller than the last, and each street a
little more ragged than the last. Finally, when
I found the Treme cottage, I watched the entrance from the porch of an abandoned house
across the street, rocking in an old gray chair
as if I belonged. No one came out, no movement, and no lights. After a couple hours, I
crossed the street.

The door was unlocked and I walked in,
closing the door behind me. The place was
an old cottage with four rooms, each opening
onto the other. It was rustic, no doubt about
that. The air was stale, trapped between the
rough-hewn cypress planks in the floor and
the dark overhead beams. But in between, on
well-kept whitewashed plaster, hung some
landscapes in oil and half a dozen silhouettes
of a rat-faced family. *That's his, I'm sure.* On
an unfinished cedar side table lay a fine lace
cloth, and on that a slightly tarnished silver

snuffbox. Other than those objects, there was nothing else in the house: no beds, no linens, no pots in the kitchen, no food. He had once had money, that was clear, but here he'd been poor. And now he was gone.

The man at the Cabildo, ink splotted below his eyes like blue freckles, said he had no idea where Sebastien Lemerle had gone, it wasn't his job to keep track of every person, just every property. There had been no sale, Sebastien Lemerle still owned the little cottage in Treme. If there was a sale, he'd let me know, he said. I'm sure you will, I said.

I was quite sick of arguing with Rintrah, who I had once counted as a friend. Now he was the man muscling me to do his work for him. If I was going to go back to my quiet job at the factory, I was going to need to find this Sebastien maniac and also figure out what the hell to do with this book Hood had given me. I began to sit around the old Creole cafés and saloons, hoping for someone to mention Sebastien's name, but it never happened. I asked bartenders if they knew him, and if they did they wouldn't say, but they most always kicked me out right about then.

* * *

There wasn't more to do but keep asking around, so I did. And though I had no success flushing out Lemerle, I had better luck with a separate set of inquiries I began to make secret, under the nose of my all-knowing partner.

I had by then read both manuscripts straight through maybe a half-dozen times, and with each reading any hope I had that the two sets of writings would work together to explain all the mysteries, well, that hope disappeared. They didn't fit with each other, they didn't complete each other. Whether this was true of their marriage I can't ever know, since I wasn't there to observe every little moment between them, every touching, every glance. They may have fit like a puzzle in life, but the written record was missing a whole lot of pieces, words, thoughts, explanations.

The only mystery that really still mattered, though, because a man's life would likely soon be taken because of it, was the mystery of Paschal. He hung over everything that had happened and would happen, as if he were secretly conducting things even now, in death.

I read about him, and I notice things. He is absent for a very long time, and then he suddenly appears: at an orphanage, in a swamp, at a ball, in an attic. Everyone who knew him professes their eternal love for him and a certain marveled gratitude for his friendship, as if he were not entirely of this world and they were all better for it. Father Mike, Anna Marie, Rintrah. They talked about Paschal as if he had changed their lives, as if they were lost without him. Even Hood himself, who knew Paschal only as another nigger off to get lynched and then as the breathing corpse in the attic, even *Hood* swore up and down his life was changed at the lifeless feet of Paschal of the Attic.

And yet. *And yet.*

And yet where was everyone? Why was Paschal at the ball alone? Even with the Hoods at the ball, even at Anna Marie's invitation, he was alone. Unapproachable, untouchable. Where is he during the courtship of the Hoods, and during the ten years since? Where are Rintrah's stories of drinking and gambling with Paschal, of going to the club to hear Paschal on the piano ragging away? I had never heard him tell any such story about Paschal, or any story at all about the man that wasn't in fact a story of the child Paschal. Rintrah would tell stories in great detail about a steak he'd had at Arnaud's, or a madam he'd beat at chess in 1867, but never a story about Paschal the man, his friend. Father Mike had never said a word about him, either, except to say that he'd been the most beautiful dancer he'd ever seen, and that it was Paschal who really should have been the priest, that he would have brought far more souls into the Church than the great belligerent bear Father Mike had become, suitable only for lifting things and long hours at the altar rail praying for forgiveness. *Paschal had grace*, Father Mike used to say.

Paschal was also a negro, the whitest of negroes but still a negro. They rarely mentioned *that*, but I reckoned it was the place to start.

I went back down to Treme, looking for anyone who might have known Paschal recently. In the dirt streets of the neighborhood, ditched but unguttered, colored women walked home with baskets of food and wearing the tignon on their heads, indigo and yellow and green and red and every other color I had no words to describe. Carts passed by, the horses old and swaybacked but the carts painted and greased and running silent below their cargoes of fabrics and lumber and sugarcane. The cottages here were small, but built on thick posts and beams and painted as if it were always Carnival. There was an apothecary's shop, a butcher, a bank. Churches everywhere, small huts and steepled palaces, Catholics and Baptists and Methodists all squeezed in. I saw a man selling fish on Marais Street. He'd iced the redfish and bull cats down, and I nearly told him I'd made that ice but thought better of it, afraid he'd think me crazed and have me run out of the neighborhood. I meandered on, past Lemerle's old house, until I'd gone across the street and around a corner, where I surprised a gang of cats that scattered grudgingly and with hate in their eyes. Down two houses an old man on his porch sat watching me and smiling.

"Lost." It sounded like a question.

"Oh, nah, just looking round a bit," I said.

His face cracked open like a rock split in the heat, a thousand tiny cracks that slipped together as one big grin.

"No, believe me, you lost. But I'll hep you find your way home again. You don't want no trouble, now, I'm sure."

"No."

He was very tall, taller than me, and so dark his airy gray hair seemed lit from inside. His eyes smiled, wrinkled permanently that way, and he wore denim overalls faded to nearly the color of the sky, white at the knees. He waved me up and onto a stool beside him. He had been peeling shrimps from a pail containing a little more of my ice, no doubt bought over on Marais Street at the fish cart.

"Only got shrimps for me and the wife, sorry to say."

"I ain't hungry, thank you."

"At all?"

"No."

"So, you saying that if I bulled them shrimps up right now, you ain't gone to eat one?"

"Not if there was only enough for you and your wife."

"Didn't say *that*. Said they were *for* me and the wife, meaning not for wandering white men lost on their way to the brothel. But now that I see you up close rycheer, I say you ain't one of them. You just lost, any count."

We were quiet for a moment, only the sound of the shells snicking into his trash bucket. I looked in and a few dozen heads stared back at me attached to white shells, ghosts of their former hosts.

"I'd give you a shrimp, it come to that."

"And I weren't lying when I said I weren't hungry."

"All right."

He went silent again, but he looked straight

at me, expecting something. His eyes had yellowed. I decided to start with this old man.

"Are you from here?" Sliding into the questions, make it sound like just talk.

"Do you mean, am I a Louisiana nigger? A New Orleans nigger? No, I ain't. I am a Mississippi country negro and until the war I had me a nice little place near Vicksburg, cotton, hogs, and vegetables. I was a free negro like my daddy, case you wondering. Well, Vicksburg weren't no place for a negro, free or no, come the war, so we come on down to hide round here, with all the rest of the free negroes, except they all French and they polish their nails. The jens culyoor, it's French, you look it up. I build houses now, and the children, they had been good hardworking and churching country negroes, but now they *Creoles,* and they wear funny hats and pray up there with the Catholics. No, say, I am *not* from here."

"I see, well . . ."

"But I got eyes, I see good. What you want to know?"

He had stopped peeling shrimp. He wanted to talk, I could tell, he wanted to show me how much he knew, how nothing got by him. That's how folks get around strangers sometimes, they want to let you know this here's their territory, you just the smallest speck of it. I could be that speck.

"Did you ever know a man named Paschal Girard?"

"Colored?"

Could I be that lucky? I prayed I was.

"Yes, yes!"

"No. Not a white one either. Don't know any Girards, truth is."

I rubbed my eyes, got some dirt in them, rubbed them some more, and finally had to wipe the tears from my face. The old man handed me his handkerchief, but I waved him away. This was hard work, no doubt.

"He was, well, hmmm, maybe not as black as you?"

Shrimp peeled, *snick*. Head never moved from the job.

"You mean he looked white?"

"Yeah."

"That's a thousand niggers right here in this neighborhood, don't know how many more in other places. It don't describe much is what I'm saying."

"Played the piano."

"That makes it, reckon, two hundred."

"Long fingers."

"You kidding?"

I realized then that not only did I know no stories of Paschal since the war, I didn't have the first idea how to describe him in any way that might have added up to a whole fella. All I had were his skin, his music, his fingers, and something about *grace*. And then, maybe, one other thing.

"Might have been friends with a priest and a dwarf."

He stopped peeling and looked up at the rafters of his porch. Then he continued peeling.

"Now that there, that do narrow it down considerable."

Snick, snick, snick. He peeled faster now, fingers moving quick but never more than they had to move. He became more efficient as he got more riled up. He looked out at the street and I looked too. Men carrying burlap sacks over their shoulders walked slowly down toward their houses, home for the day from whatever it was they worked at. Most of them were covered in cotton, though some had got tar on their boots. Every few houses one turned up and onto the porch, took off his boots, tossed his bag inside, and set down on whatever chair, stool, or stump he had handy. Most of them lit themselves a smoke, a few drank out of flasks buried deep in the pockets of their coveralls. And all of them, every last one, were watching us. Not *us* so much, but *me*. They could have picked me out five blocks away, I shone in the sun like a beacon. I had to ignore them, press on.

"You knew him then."

He ran out of shrimp and began to fiddle with the ice, to arrange the peeled shrimp in perfect circles.

"If you know that much about the man, you know what happened to him. And that ain't happening to this negro. Hell, I didn't even know his name until you said it."

"He lived here. In Treme."

He shook his head no.

"Had family down here. Cousin I heard. The man and his wife and daughter died a year ago, yellow jack. And now you got to go."

I *couldn't* go. Not right then. He stood up, gathered his two pails, shrimp in one hand and shells in the other. A powerful old man, I wondered why he didn't throw me out. But he paused before going inside, deliberate, like he might could answer a couple more but make 'em quick and sly.

"He was down here a lot, since you know so much about him."

"Yes."

"Where did his cousin live?"

"On Marais."

My head began to pound hard, a hammer up in there. I had to sit back down to sort it out, but there was no time.

"A man named Lemerle lived on that street," I whispered into my hand, which I pretended to be rubbing over my beard. Not very sly, but the best I could do at the moment.

He opened the door quick, as if to get out of the way of my words.

"And now you got to go see Sister Mary Thérèse at the Holy Family Convent, she knows, I don't know no more."

"What's your name?"

He shut the door. Locked it. I walked out of there under the gaze of every single man on every single porch, all the way into the Quarter to Maspero's, where I drank.

Sister Mary Thérèse. Maybe I should have gone to her first, that's what Anna Marie had done. But what could I do to gain an audience? Busting in and demanding information about Paschal had not worked real well for Anna

Marie, so why would it work for me? I had to figure something else out. Some other reason, some way to slide on up in there, get in her good graces.

In the front of Maspero's, at a large circular table dotted with red candles, sat the last of the great Creole warriors, a half-dozen at least. Shouting *vive!* at this, and *vive!* at that, all the while looking like someone had pissed in their drinks. And too old to be up past sundown anyway. Their world had shrunk until it was only as big as that table, all the old wars were over and who cared what the hell relation of theirs had slept with Bienville? I stood at the back of the café, leaning against the bar as far as I could from the men, who now got up a toast to Napoleon. Their world shrank while mine was being split wide open, accelerating away from me. I was scared, I don't mind admitting to it. I had knowledge I could not possibly share with anyone, least of all Rintrah. Rintrah would either think I was lying and have me strung up, or he'd think I might be telling the truth, in which case he'd have the old man tortured, and every other man he could find, until he'd confirmed the truth of it.

Paschal and Lemerle had been very familiar

with the same street and the same block of the same little neighborhood *at the same time*. Lemerle had seen Paschal, Paschal had seen Lemerle, they had talked, they were friends! Speculation, yes, but possible. And not a possibility anyone else knew or wanted to know. Except for, perhaps, this Sister Mary Thérèse.

The bartender waddled over. His belly, encased in a crisp white shirt, would only allow him so close to the edge of the bar. He talked leaning back, as if facing a hurricane.

"Whiskey again?"

"Yessir. And maybe you can answer me a question right quick."

His eyes drooped, expecting some kind of idjit drunken wiseassedness.

"When is the public Mass at Holy Family? It's just up the street, right?"

He smiled, relieved, I think.

"I go every day! It's quiet in there, people normally afraid of nuns, and so not so many bead rattlers making scenes of themselves. Just quiet on in there. It's half past nine every morning."

Now I knew how to get in with Sister Mary Thérèse.

"Thank you, brother."

"God bless you."

I thanked him again. Blessings, I needed a whole mess of them.

Two days later I rode through the woods and beneath the vines way down in Terrebonne Parish, south of the city, the last parish before the coast. I was on my way to either save Sebastien Lemerle or kill him, and I wasn't sure which. I had a better mount now, a black pony that danced through the brush like a deer.

It began with Sister Mary Thérèse, of course. All roads led back to the mother superior, seemed like. Thanks to the bartender at Maspero's, and my own brief education in the way of the Church, I had figured my way in.

The morning after I had learned of Paschal's life down on Marais Street in Treme, I was in the third pew of the chapel at Holy Family, the first two reserved for the sisters. I arrived early and kneeled and prayed the creed, and a prayer of redemption, and began to pray the rosary with some beads I'd carved while up in the fish camps the year before. I had meant to give them to M., but she had her own and, as she pointed out, I'd left out two Our Fathers, one Glory Be, and one Hail Mary. I remember getting hot and telling her it didn't matter, dammit, and she said that it weren't the beads themselves that mattered, it was the fact that I'd forgotten.

Now I prayed over them hoping that I would be noticed, even if the rosary itself was a mess. I needed those nuns to notice me, especially old Sister Mary Thérèse, and I knew that the sight of a man praying the rosary would be unusual enough to grab their attention. Rosaries were for women, at least that was my limited understanding of the matter. And so I prayed hard over them, my lips moving fast, my eyes squeezed tight. After each Glory Be I paused and looked up at the window Anna Marie had described, the Resurrection window. Christ seemed at peace as He ascended, but His poor mother looked as if she might shatter from grief. For a moment I thought that maybe, had she her druthers, she would have yanked Him back to earth to be a boy again. That was the expression on her face.

Then I bent over the beads again and worked them until my fingers were numb. I found myself forgetting why I had come, the plan. I was just praying, it was like I was hypnotized and kept thinking about that mother and son, parting on earth. I didn't notice the nuns when they filed in, and it was only when the priest began that I got up and took my seat.

Back to the plan, I thought. I knew that it was beyond the power of a nun, not in her makeup, to ignore a strange penitent who prayed so fervently with them. And more importantly, I knew that if that penitent went to the altar rail for Communion, but crossed his arms so that he would be given only a blessing and not the Eucharist, no nun (and, I hoped, no mother superior) would be able to keep from speaking to someone so obviously tortured in his soul. The priest might not notice, but the nuns would.

And so it was that, after the service, while I was pretending to be lost in the corridor of the convent, Sister Mary Thérèse approached and said hello.

"Hello," I said. "Sister."

"You are new here, hmmm? It was a pleasure to have you today, but shouldn't you be at Mass in your own parish?"

I said I didn't know, that I wasn't from New Orleans. I hadn't thought about this exactly, but of course the plan meant I had to lie to a nun. And now I had gone and done it. What kind of Catholic was I going to be? It wasn't a good beginning.

"Where are you from?"

"Tennessee."

"Hmmm. Must be Nashville."

"Thereabouts."

"Have you met Father Donegal?"

Oh hell, she was testing me. Maybe she'd noticed the beads that looked like they'd been carved by a blind Mohameddan. I took a stab at it.

"Never met him, but I'm scared of priests."

She chuckled. "Hmmm. Well. With good reason sometimes, I'd say. I'm about to have some tea, would you like to join me? I take it in my office. It's weak, but nice and warm."

Ha. It had taken Anna Marie weeks to break through to Sister Mary Thérèse, and here I was about to have tea with her. Why Anna Marie had never thought to come to Mass, I don't know. Women don't plan so well, I thought to myself. They go running off half-cocked. Got to be smooth, precise, wily. That was me.

When we got to Sister's office, she shut the door behind us and offered me a seat. Her desk was entirely clear except for her missal, and behind her was the unusual crucifix Anna Marie had described, Christ in agony.

A novice came in immediately with a pot of

tea and one cup. Sister sent her off for a second cup and then turned to me.

"How are you enjoying your catechism lessons with Sister Anne?"

What?

She went on. "You do know, of course, that Sister Anne is a member of our order, and though she is out in the parishes, she attends Mass here once a week? It's her way of staying in touch with her sisters."

No, I did not know that.

"Too bad for you, Eli Griffin, that today is typically the day she comes. She is so very proud of you, I should say, Eli. She says you are a wonderful student, and she even confided in me this morning that you might, how did she put it, *Have the calling*. That means she thinks you might make a priest. Do you think you will be a priest, Eli Griffin?"

I was saying to myself, *The nuns won't hurt me, the nuns won't hurt me*, and praying for time to speed up. "I doubt it, Sister."

"Me, too, though the calling is a mysterious thing. You might be a religious yet, but first you should start by not lying to old nuns."

Here she smiled, took a cup from the novice who had just then arrived back in the room, and poured me a cup. She had me cold.

I thought I should just leave, give up on this plan. But I stayed, and I think I stayed because I really felt guilty, and I thought I owed her an apology. I wanted her forgiveness. I wanted this nun to tell me that I was forgiven, and that I was not on my way straight to Hell.

"I'm sorry, Sister. I wanted to speak to you, but I didn't think you'd want to speak to me."

"Have they not heard of *asking* back where you're from? Tennessee. Are you really from Tennessee?"

"Long ago, when I was a boy."

"Praise His Name, the man isn't entirely a liar."

She blew on her tea, both cheeks puffed out, and then put it aside.

"You were a friend of General Hood's. And therefore you probably knew Anna Marie, also, I'm guessing."

She must have had spies. Or she was magic. I was scared now.

"Yes."

"Don't look so frightened. Sister Anne told me you knew General Hood, and that you had attended Anna Marie's funeral last month. You had asked her how to behave at a Catholic funeral, do you remember?"

"Yes, now I do."

"And since there was ever only one subject any member of the Hood family ever wanted to talk to me about, I'm going to guess that you're here to discuss Paschal Girard. Poor Paschal."

I remained silent. What was I to say to that? She should have been a police officer.

"Come, come," she said. "I am in a good mood, and I have a feeling that your interest in Paschal is, I don't know, *purer* than Anna Marie's. Anna Marie was a good woman, a good Catholic, but an imperfect friend. She knew it, and so her questions about Paschal were always weighted with guilt and sadness and suffering. You have some other purpose, you did not know the man. So out with it."

So I told her. That is, I told her only that Hood had told me a strange story about one of his wife's friends, someone he had also known, and that he had always wondered what had become of the man who killed him. I told her that, on his deathbed, I promised I would look into the matter. That's all I told her. She looked at me skeptically, tested her tea with her little finger, and then gulped half of it down.

"So what have you found out, detective?"

This time I didn't lie, and I told her about

what I had seen and heard in Treme the day before. I told her everything and then sat back, waiting for her to put the pieces together. She frowned.

"Do you have a question?"

"Is it all true? The man said to come find you, to ask you about it, so I reckon you know whether he was telling the truth or not."

"Of course he is telling the truth. But that is not your question, is it?"

"What do you mean?"

"Ask the real question."

I had put this question to myself a hundred times since the night before, testing out different ways of phrasing it, and yet I had nearly forgotten it when it came time to ask. Nearly forgotten, but still remembered.

"Was Paschal the lover of Sebastien Lemerle's wife?"

"Not his wife. Sebastien Lemerle still believes in *plaçage*. She is, what, his mistress? Concubine? Though, I will say, my understanding is that he loves her fiercely and has no interest in any other woman."

"And Paschal?"

"Paschal was nearly irresistible. He was very handsome."

"So it's true."

"Do you think that I peek into the bedrooms of others? I do not know that it's true. But I do know that Sebastien Lemerle thought it was true. And perhaps that's all that mattered."

She finished her tea, which I took to be a sign. She thumped her thumb on her missal, which was embossed with a fine, thin gold cross.

"I do not believe your story. I do not believe that a young man goes chasing after other men's ghosts only because he heard of them on a deathbed. You know more than you say. That is your right. But I will say no more about this now. I believe, I'm not sure why, that your heart is pure in this, if in little else. You do not trust people, perhaps with good reason, but your mistrust makes you small. Too small, Mr. Griffin, to judge another man's heart. We have all done terrible things, and you do not possess the wisdom to decide which of us deserves your punishment. Do not try to take that from God, the punishment is His. Do not become one to be punished."

I stood and began to move toward the door.

"I understand you carved that rosary yourself."

"Sister Anne told you, I reckon?"

"Yes. And she told me where you carved it. Out at Rintrah's fish camps, no? Of course I knew of it! What happened out there, Eli, was a blessing, a grace before God that will be remembered. Don't ever forget that. Let me see that rosary."

I hesitated, thinking she would count the beads and laugh at me. Then she snapped her fingers and opened her palm, and I figured I better drop them in. She closed her other hand over them and mouthed a prayer over them. I couldn't understand the words, but she squeezed her eyes tight, and the color came up in her face. Then she relaxed and handed them back over to me.

"Don't lose those."

"Thank you, Sister."

Outside it had begun to rain. I held on to the rosary in my pocket and ran for home. The streets ran dark with the water, the cypress gutters roared with the rising water. Soon it was over the banquette and over my shoes. I stopped running and trudged on, shoulders hunched. I watched the men on the wharf covering their open crates with oilcloth. I was tempted to sneak under those cloths, into the crates, and let myself be shipped off someplace else, I didn't care where. The task I'd shouldered seemed too heavy now, and it was dirty too. I wanted Rintrah to leave me alone, and I wanted Hood to leave me alone. Anna Marie too. They were all on me, pounding at my head with their arguments and pleadings and grievances. I was becoming tired of them, and yet I was still obliged to carry on, at least to do something with Hood's book. Sister was right, the rest of it was beyond my understanding.

When I got to Levi's factory, I went around back and climbed the outside stairs to my front door. Next to the door sat M.'s tiny lace-ups with the square heels, newly polished. Anger got up in my throat. No one would leave me alone, it seemed. I pushed in.

"I ain't got no money, if that's what you're wanting," I shouted, kicking off my boots. I didn't hear anything, so I looked up.

M. sat at my table under the window, her hair up in a loose knot that she kept twisting while bent over the papers on the table. Papers neatly stacked, each page laid gently down upon the next as she made her way through. There was Hood's manuscript, tied up in one of her bow knots, and also Anna Marie's ledgers, also tied up in a bow. The papers she flipped through now, almost lovingly, were the extra pieces of ledger paper filled with my own scrawl. I stood in the entryway, listening to the water drip to the floor, wondering what I should do. She looked up at me, pleased with herself, and something else. Pleased with me.

"I told you I could read," she said. Her hair glowed golden red in the lamplight, and she'd gathered her mouth up in the kindest smile I think I'd ever seen up to that very moment. I should have tossed her out, cuffed her around, exacted her silence about the manuscripts with threats. Instead I just watched her, saw how she had folded her legs up under and primly drawn her skirt down over her knees. She was wearing a modest dress for once, plain cotton, night-blue. She rested her head in one hand and stared right back at me.

"What I didn't know," she continued, "was that you could write stories."

I went over and sat down at the seat across from her. I turned up the lamp so I could see her better. I didn't say anything still, just counted the perfect little freckles under her eyes and across her nose. *What the hell was happening to me?*

"You read it all, then?" I said.

"Yes. I came looking for money and found this."

"You came to rob me?"

"Borrow, more like. And anyway, I found this and I couldn't stop reading it."

"I'd have liked it better if you'd robbed me."

"Oh, I found the money in that arm of yours, but I didn't take none."

"Why?"

At this she breathed deep. She twisted her hair, rearranged her legs. She looked at me with sad eyes.

"I'd already begun to read these papers, and after that I didn't want your money. Not no more."

The clouds outside piled up and bruised, lightning struck out by the lake, the lamp ran down on its oil, my little Irish bedmate talked low and sweet, she reached out for my hand, and we let ourselves sit silently and let the sadness wrap us up. It was the sadness of change, I reckon. We weren't no longer who we were, pervert and whore, but now something else. A moment of silent sadness was called for, I reckon.

In the morning she stayed and she never left.

* * *

Out of the tangle of sheets and rambling twists of red hair came a voice.

"You need help, you know."

I had got out of bed early, as usual. Washed my face, combed my hair, put on my white shirt and blue pants and black boots, which I polished. I was sitting at the table ignoring the three neat piles of paper lined up in front of me. I stared out the window across the tin roofs of the warehouses, all of them streaked in delicate lines of rust. I saw the first slips of smoke took up into the air above the molasses sheds, first black and then a pure white. The wharfs began to wake up, first one shout, then a hundred. Everyone awake.

"I got help."

"Rintrah ain't your help. Rintrah is your boss, boyo."

The night before, before we'd collapsed into the bed, fully clothed for the first time that I can recall, I had told her what would be soon written down on my own scraps of paper: the deal with Rintrah, the discovery of Paschal's life in Treme, Sister Mary Thérèse. M. seemed not at all shocked to hear that this man, Paschal, so *worshipped* by the others, by a general who attended him in his attic as if he were attending at the mouth of the cave, that this man might have had his own sins to confess.

"He was just a man," she'd said. "And I don't mean *just a nigger*, either. Just a man. Maybe they fell in love, that would be sweet, right?"

"Maybe they didn't do nothing." I glared at the man firing up the cotton press down on the wharf, but he didn't notice. I wanted to protect the memory of Paschal for reasons I didn't understand. I had become attached to the man though I had never known him. I reckon it wasn't Paschal I was so concerned with, but those piles of paper in front of me. I didn't want them to be the records of fools, of the deceived.

M. lifted herself from the bed as if she were carrying five others on her back. Groan, curse, creak. But she was thin as a whip, and I watched the muscles flex in her back, admired the hard curve of her waist. Her hair rolled down and brushed across her hip like curtains. I had never watched her so closely. When her feet touched the cold boards, she sprang up and over to a bag I'd not seen in the corner, and soon she was back in the bed with a comb pulling through her hair. She'd never brought a comb before, never brought anything but herself and her breasts and her ass before. Where did that bag come from? And because she's Irish, she reads minds.

"I always bring a bag, you know, so don't look at me like that."

"Never brought a bag."

"Every time. You just don't never see it."

I stared down at the piles of paper. Was I going to have to put M. in it now? What did she mean, I needed help?

"Rintrah and I are partners in this, M."

"So, what if you told him to go fuck himself, mmm? He gone say, Oh, you right, Eli, I shall! And sorry for the intrusion?" She snorted and started to giggle. I tried not to smile.

"We want the same thing, M., and if he thinks he got to threaten me and insult me to get it done, I don't mind much. It gone all be all right in the end, and I can't do this alone."

"Hmmpf. Now I'm just a stupid streetwalking tater eater, that's true, but I read them papers right there and I don't see where you come to find that you and the dwarf got the same interests. Seems the dwarf wants the man Sebastien's head served up to him, and he gone use you to do it. You gone to lead that man to his death? That's what you in it fer?"

I put my hand down flat on Hood's manuscript, like I'd get the answer up through the pads of my fingers and into my blood. No use.

"No."

She shook out her hair and wrenched it up in a knot on her head quick, nearly too quick for me to see how the hell she did it. She frowned and stepped out of the bed and into one of my shirts and a pair of my pants. She looked as if she'd been swallowed up in my clothes. She glared, and then let her eyes soften a little, like she'd temporarily forgotten that the world had changed overnight. She came around and sat at the edge of the bed nearest me, her hands soft and still in her lap.

"No, that's right, I reckon. You made a promise to a dying man, and I reckon that you don't got no business with anything else but seeing that you keep that promise."

"When did you start thinking you could give out orders to me?"

"I'm just saying what already writ down on those papers. You made that promise, not me."

I liked her ordering me around. She was prettier than Rintrah, looked better in pants. She went on.

"And from what I can tell, whatever or

whoever this Paschal was, he ain't no concern of yours. You're just stickin' your nose in."

"You saying you ain't curious?"

"I'm curious as you, but we ain't talking about me."

"All right."

"And, I reckon I should say, you don't got no cause to be turning that man into Rintrah, doing Rintrah's dirt for him. Hood told you to bring that book to the man, and that you should do. That was your promise. If you want to get him killed, too, that's got nothing to do with Hood or your promise. That's just you thinking you know the truth about what happened, that you can sit like a judge on the man. Can you?"

You do not possess the wisdom to decide which of us deserves your punishment, Sister had said. "You been over to church, M.?"

"Every day."

"I can tell."

"Don't mean I'm not ready to sin," she said, moving her knees to touch mine.

She was right, of course. The promise I'd made had nothing to do with Paschal Girard. The question of what to do about Sebastien had become more complicated. I didn't know what to think about him, nor what I would do about giving him over to Rintrah, and so I decided to put that part of my promise to Hood aside for a bit. I still had that other book to go get my hands on, the war book, at the moment in the possession of one of the city's leading citizens, General P. G. T. Beauregard. I reckoned it might be smart to start there, him being a friend of Hood's and an important man. I thought General Beauregard might have some idea what I was supposed to do with this other thing, the secret memoir. I left M. snoring away happily in the thin afternoon light. She looked happy, anyway.

Beauregard had several houses, including one on Chartres all the way down the street from Rintrah's house, near the edge of the Quarter. I tried that one first. I had been impressed by Rintrah's house, but holy *damn*. Two staircases curved up from either side of the entrance outside, like arms reaching out to grab you in. Four thick round pillars out front, scrolls at the top, and a front door closed in at the top and sides by windows cut through with circles and rectangles, strange patterns with meanings I didn't understand. The place looked like the mausoleum of a prince, or a government office.

A colored man in straight black pants and a white servant's coat answered the door. He was shorter than me, but near as thick as the doorway. He looked up at me with his eyes half closed, as if I'd woken him and he reckoned he didn't have to wake up entirely because he'd be back to sleep soon enough having tossed me out.

"Yes?"

"I am here to see General Beauregard. Is he at home today?" I looked past his shoulder. He moved slick, nearly unnoticeable, and blocked my view.

"These are not his at-home hours, sir."

One of the things I'd learned about New Orleans was that one could be *at home*, which meant folks could come see you, and that meant you could most of the time be at home without being *at home*.

"But is he here?"

"What is this regarding?"

"I am here on business for General John Bell Hood."

"And so?"

"And so how about you go tell him that? And quit staring at me like I just shit on your shoes." I had also learned that the formalities could get you all tied up in knots if you didn't sometimes break on through and throw it down, man-to-man. I puffed my chest out and he narrowed his eyes even more, this time a squint meant to see right into me. Then he stepped back and had me sit on a long black bench against the wall of the center hall while he went and mumbled something in a room off to the right, down the end of the hallway. And after a minute, here came General Beauregard, no servant to be seen.

He was tall, twiggy but strong-looking, his beard still black and clipped neat, his hair still slicked back. He didn't say anything to me, only gestured down toward a room on the left, where the man in white was busily building a fire, laying each log gently as if afraid to make any noise.

Portraits of himself and other generals lined the dark walls. Battle flags framed in gilt rested on small stands throughout. On his desk stood a small Confederate battle flag and a bust of General Lee. Behind him tall bookshelves held hundreds of books on the war, other wars, military strategy, and history.

This is the library of a general, I thought, remembering Hood's strange, airy, and cluttered room where he kept his desk.

"I don't have much time, boy, but I understand you're a friend of General Hood's, and so I have a few minutes."

He sat straight in the chair behind him, crossed his legs, and occasionally sipped something hot from a saucer he kept filling from his cup. I'd never seen that.

"While I'm thinking about Hood, have you been to see him recently? I have questions about his war memoirs."

"Well, that's what I came to talk to you about."

He didn't seem to hear me.

"They are, of course, tendentious and coarse, as Hood is himself, and they will do little to improve his reputation, but I am a man of my word and I will cause them to be published if he dies. Why he thinks he's going to die is a mystery to me, though. There is very little fever this year, though I understand his wife has died. Mary Anne, correct? He should go out to the country and take his children, breathe the fresh air. In fact, you're lucky to catch me here. Only here for some business this morning, and then it's off to the country myself."

He turned in his chair and stared out the window, in his own thoughts. One of his hairs sprang loose and curled down the side of his head. He let it stay, unaware.

"Sir."

"Yes."

"He did die. A week ago. He and his daughter Lydia. I'm sorry to be bringing that news."

I am usually good at reading a man's face, but this face moved too quickly for me. Eyebrows lifted and sank, corners of the mouth jumped and sagged, his forehead was like waves on a lake, chopped up and rough and then suddenly calm. A whole story passed by right there, and I didn't get the first word out of it until he'd finally gathered himself and his face froze, sad but not sad enough as far as I was concerned.

"I am sorry to hear this. When is the funeral?"

"Already been. Days ago."

"I should have been notified."

You should have been paying attention.

"I'm sorry."

"Yes. Well."

He rubbed the bridge of his nose, where there was a mark from a pair of glasses.

"Is there an inheritance?"

A very strange question.

"I wouldn't think it, they were right down in the world at the end, I believe. Left nothing behind except maybe that book you got."

He wasn't listening to me.

"How did he die?"

"Yellow fever, got hot and died." Why ask such a question?

"No boy, I mean, what did he say? How was he at the end?"

"In pain, reckon. Groaning, so forth."

"That won't do, but I'll fix that."

"How . . ."

"That's my business, boy. Now. What is *your* business?"

The ceiling seemed so far away in that room, so tall. The ribbed molding around the door, the eight-paneled door, it all seemed to loom over me, asking me what the hell I wanted, threatening to crash in on my head if I didn't get it right.

Before I could say anything, Beauregard spoke up.

"You know, he once told me I had no right, or rather, that I was stupid, for wanting a report on the disposition of his scouts. That is, *my* scouts, the insubordinate son of a bitch. He wrote me to tell me that such a report would inevitably fall under the eyes of spies, derelicts, and disaffected persons, who would only give away his positions and strength to the enemy. In other words, *my* staff was lousy with turncoats."

Beauregard began rummaging through his bookshelves, finally pulling out a scrapbook and flipping furiously through it.

"Yes, here it is, my reply. 'My Dear General Hood,' I write, 'You must have a low estimate of the intelligence and judgment of your wily adversary, if you suppose at this late day that he is ignorant of the position of your army and the strength of your corps.' And that was Hood, boy, he always had a low estimate of his adversaries. So low, in fact, that he sometimes couldn't recognize them."

By now the hairs at the back of my neck had pricked up. This was not going as I'd expected, though the delight that Beauregard took in telling me that story made me think I might have an easier time getting that war book from him. He was no friend of Hood's, that I knew now, so why would he want to mess around with Hood's war memoir? I decided to chance it, come right out with it.

"Sir, General Hood made a request before he died, and that was that I should go find you and retrieve his war memoir."

He frowned.

"And do what with it? I've already begun to make inquiries about its publication. The book is perfect. It is an arrogant and blink-ered pleading, but that is what we expect of Hood. It is Hood! How could you improve it? Can you read?"

"I can read. But he didn't want me to im-prove it. He wanted me to destroy it."

Beauregard drummed his fingers on the desk. Then he gestured with them, palm up, as if he were presenting the rabbit bouncing out of the hat.

"Well, yes, any sane person would have wanted that destroyed, it is obvious, no? It was something a child would write, so absorbed in himself and so outraged by punishment! But you will not convince me that a man mad from the fever could make such a rational judgment, and I will not carry out the ravings of a madman."

"But sir, I know that he was sane when he told me this. I have been around the yellow jack, been around them dying ravers, and he wasn't one of them when he gave me these instructions. He was very specific, very cold about it."

Beauregard waved his hand, stirring the dust in the air, dismissing me.

"It shall not happen, and I shall not discuss it any longer."

"It was his wish."

"It is not *my* wish."

"He would be very unhappy."

"He is dead."

He said this, and then he relaxed and slumped back in his chair. He even seemed to smile warmly at me, as if I had been beat at something and he would gladly play the gracious winner. There was nothing more for me to do about it at that moment. He believed the discussion was over, and I let him think it. I nodded my head and looked at my shoes, all the while thinking, *We'll have to break in. Rintrah might be good for something anyway. I wonder where he keeps it.*

"Is that all you came to talk about today?" He roused me from my thoughts, my acting the grateful loser. That *wasn't* all I'd come to talk to him about. I had the other thing right there, in my bag. I didn't trust him, and especially not to tell me what to do with it, but there was maybe some information I ought to get out of him anyway. I decided to test him.

"Have you heard of a man named Sebastien Lemerle?"

Beauregard began to laugh.

"Of course, though I don't know the man. Insane, wasn't he? He's of an old family, though they've dissipated in every conceivable sense. I don't believe they have a dime between them anymore, though the first of the Lemerles was a mighty fighter, a favorite of Bienville. Why do you ask?"

"He owes a friend something."

"Your friend will never get it. Sebastien Lemerle . . . He was an army man, I believe. If a man could only fight, if he didn't need to live or eat or move among other men, Sebastien might have been a success in the army. I believe he was discharged in, hmmmm, Texas."

"Just wondering where he might be."

"I do not have knowledge of such men, of course."

I took a gamble and prayed I wouldn't end the day run through by the general's saber, mounted above the bookcase behind him.

"General Hood thought you might know where he was." An utter lie, of course, but I had to see.

"Why the hell . . ."

He spun around on his seat and leaned across the desk, first looking at me and then grabbing for a silver letter opener in the shape of a bayonet. He tapped it quickly on the blotter and concentrated.

"Hood was in Texas, not me. I don't know what went on there."

Didn't say anything went on there, General.

"I don't know nothing about the army, only what Hood said. He said you were right well acquainted with this Lemerle, close friends. He said you and Lemerle were cut of the same cloth, the same people. Cousins possibly, he said. He said Lemerle didn't do nothing without talking to you about it, you was that close. Like brothers, maybe he said. Don't know all exactly what he meant, you Creoles are still a mystery to me mostly, but he seemed to think you'd know where the man would be living now."

Sitting in front of me now was one red-faced Creole, veins popping out his neck, fingernails gouging into the desk.

"You insult me, boy."

"Not me! And I didn't think it sounded so much like an insult when he said it. And I might have got it wrong anyway. It was hard to hear, what with all the groaning."

"I believe you have. Got it wrong, that is."

His color went down a notch. "What did he want with Lemerle?"

"I guess, sir, he just wanted to say hello. Too late now, of course. I guess maybe they served together, if like you say, they both served in Texas. Or maybe he meant you. Are you sure you weren't in Texas?"

Beauregard grimaced.

"I sure as hell was not in Texas with that animal. And I know this much, Hood would just as soon cut off his other leg than have a nice little chat over tea with someone like Lemerle. Now you stay sitting in that chair while I puzzle this out."

He stood up. I could see that the years after the war had been good to him. He had a belly that poked out some, but his eyes were dark and deep and expressionless, as if they were trying to reach in and take something out of me.

"How do you know about Lemerle?"

"He told me about him, like I said."

"He never would have. Never. Sebastien Lemerle is dead, and your great friend the General Hood killed him. That's a fact, and I bet you know it, too."

It wasn't a fact, but at that point I wasn't volunteering anything.

"What are you trying to tell me, with this nonsense? Are you speaking in code? Is this Hood's code? He was always a supercilious bastard."

He called for Henri, his manservant or whatever the hell the man in the white uniform was, and I stood up.

"What are you doing here, boy?" He looked down at my feet. "What the hell is in that bag. Is that paper? *Henri! I need you!*"

And I needed to leave. I'd lived among gamblers long enough to know when to get the hell out of the house. I ran for the hallway and Beauregard tried to step around the desk to head me off, but he tripped over an artillery shell he'd turned into an umbrella stand and went crashing down on his face, black umbrellas piled around him like kindling.

And before Henri could get to me, I was out the door and down the street and over three walls, deep into the city.

That night I talked it over with Rintrah, who laughed at my description of the general falling over his umbrellas. He said he had some idea what was on Beauregard's mind. He made me an omelette in the back kitchen of his house, standing on an old fruit crate.

He was an expert chef, and that surprised me. But his hands, thick and large, were delicate with the eggs and shells, and he could flip an omelette in the air and get it to land perfectly, sizzling just enough to make a whispering sound.

"He's a fucking cheat, that's one thing. He's a fucking lottery cheat, and believe me I know. Takes one to know one. I wish he'd been run through by one of them umbrellas."

"What do you mean, he's a cheat? What about the lottery?"

"Don't worry about that now. I'm asking the goddamn questions. We need Lemerle. Ask him questions, he'll know. That murderer will know, and if he says he doesn't, I'll have it cut out of him."

We ate our omelettes in silence, watching the gaslights flicker outside in the courtyard. I didn't know who to fear more: Lemerle, Beauregard, or Rintrah. I looked over at him swallowing his omelette nearly whole while continuing to swear and lay curses on nearly everyone in the city.

"I wish Michel, Father Mike, were here. He'd love to hear that story."

I was shocked to hear him say that, and knew that it was a sore subject. Father Mike.

Big old Michel. The burly priest who had disappeared not long after the adventure at the fish camps. Not long after . . . oh Lord.

"The lottery."

That was the first and last time I saw Rintrah cry.

Later he got up and gave me a cane encircled by a carved snake and painted black and red. He didn't say a word, just held it out, and I took it.

A few days later I went into the Cabildo and the inky man told me that Lemerle had sold his house, leaving only the name of a parish as a forwarding address.

"He's gone way on down into Terrebonne Parish, young man. Bring a rifle."

CHAPTER 21

John Bell Hood

In October 1868, I approached the lottery building from the west. I had not lost the habit of reckoning his location by the sun, though local custom referred to the river. The carriage rolled downriver, but the sound of the word *downriver* nagged at me, making me think of debris washing down. I had been General John Bell Hood, CSA. How had I ended up there? Rolling downriver through a city that seemed at the end of the world, hoping no one would recognize me, traveling in a borrowed rig behind a borrowed horse just for the sake of propriety *in case* anyone recognized me, harboring the lunatic hope that we could be saved by the slip of paper in my hand.

If only salvation and protection could be contained in a piece of paper. I had spent years searching through papers, letters, journals, and maps, looking for proof that I had not alone ruined the Army of Tennessee and led thousands of boys off to needless slaughter at Franklin and Nashville. But there had been no salvation, no relief from the sting of criticism and loathing that I felt, perhaps too often and too strongly, in the way other men greeted me and talked to me. The instruments of my torture—newspapers, the memoirs of other generals, cartoons—had been paper. They were the means by which I was known and reviled by the many thousands who would go to their grave thinking John Bell Hood was an impetuous, crippled laudanum addict who, if I had not actually pulled the trigger, had caused the death of many young men by fighting the war as if it could be won on courage and audacity and purity of intent alone. I had begun to think they were right, but it was too much to conceive. I shook my head as I approached the lottery building. *I will salvage my reputation. But first, the business.* I shifted my broad hat down over my eyes and slid down in my seat so that I would not be recognized. *What the hell would they say if they saw me? "There goes that Hood, playing the lottery. Thought he had money? Guess he's not much of a businessman, either."* I wouldn't stand for that.

Of course, that is exactly what they said about me when one of the most recognizable men of the late Confederacy stepped down from his carriage, cane in hand, and walked slowly through the crowd, which parted before him. I was recognized. I was always recognized.

Didn't they know that I deserved their respect, not their ogling? I was not a gambler! I was a Christian, a man of God, saved. Who were these men staring at me, these thick-browed, loud men in dark suits speaking their barely literate twaddle? They were gamblers, of course, degenerates and drunks and fornicators. They were not there because God had instructed them to be there, as He had instructed me. They were there for the amusement, but I had arrived for the torture and humiliation that might burn away my sin and misfortune, and perhaps save me. I was there to be tried, sanctified, and rewarded. I was there with a forty-dollar ticket in my hand, with a chance on $600,000.

I stood in the middle of the lobby while the little Creole men scooted around me. I was still tall, despite my wooden leg and vacant sleeve. I had been through the fire before, I thought, I could do it again. My beard had grown long, longer than my official portraits, and had turned gray. I had once entertained the thought of growing my beard so long and thick that my entire face and torso might be obscured and unrecognizable, but I knew it would be futile. *My eyes, damn it.* My eyes were so pale they seemed merely orbs of light in my photographs. I've been told that in person they are sad and unmistakable. Don't know about that.

"Hood!"

I looked around and here came Father Mike and Rintrah, dressed in their work clothes and wearing identical black bowlers.

"Father. Is the Church shutting this gambling den down?"

"Lord, I hope not."

Rintrah gazed around and commented on the beauty of the lobby. The lobby was repulsive, of course. Decadent. Red carpets and settees the color of blood, fat and cackling angels cavorting above the windows.

"How is the hospital?"

"We're in bad shape still, John. I don't know if we can keep going, after this past summer. We have nothing left, the dead took it all."

"Perhaps the Lord will provide."

Then Rintrah piped up from under his little black hat.

"Or someone else, maybe! Lady Luck, yes sir!"

"Don't hold your breath, Rintrah."

"Around you, always, General."

We laughed, and then the bell rang for the next drawing, and we parted ways. As they walked off, backs to me and dressed nearly identically, they looked like father and son. I never saw Father Mike again.

I had business to conduct. As I made my way toward the entrance to the great hall, feeling my wooden leg sink deep into the carpet, kicking up puffs of dust, a thin, yellow-faced Creole slid before me and bowed. He was as tall as me, but bent slightly to the side, as if his spine had slipped off center. It forced him to look up at me, even when he had stood up again. His eyes, bloodshot, made me think he might collapse at any moment.

"Monsieur Dauphin begs the honor of your

presence in his private room, if you please, Monsieur Hood."

Monsieur Dauphin? A ridiculous name.

"I am not familiar with Dauphin."

"Forgive me, Monsieur Hood. He is the organizer."

"Ah."

How did he know I was here? And then, *Silly question.*

"Will you accompany me? It is just up these stairs."

"Yes, I suppose."

I could escape the indignity of standing among the crowd of onlookers and gamblers, perhaps, by sitting with this Monsieur Dauphin. And so I limped along behind the tall Creole, who stood crooked even when he walked, and looked as if he was always preparing to turn a corner.

The stairs were narrow, and gave me trouble. At the landing, the man waited patiently for me to clunk my way up the stairs. When I had gained the landing, the man folded his hands in front of him, bowed again, and made off down the corridor to a small door. He gestured to me, beckoning me as if calling to a reluctant pet. He was rude in the way that Creoles could seem rude sometimes: presumptuous and brisk. *I could snap this man in two. Or I would have, once.* Instead, I ducked my head through the short doorway and entered the private room of Monsieur Dauphin.

The little man did not remove his hat, but sat with his foot on the railing of the overlook, awkwardly massaging a cigar between his lips. He looked up and smiled, and gestured toward a chair like his. I took it, and leaned my cane against the rail. Below I could hear the burbling and crashing of many voices.

"General Hood, I am sorry if I have surprised you. You don't know me, but I know much about you."

Thousands of people knew me, and why wouldn't the little lottery man be one of them? I sighed a little, and rubbed the inflamed callus where my thigh met the wood of my fake leg.

"May I get you something? A drink, perhaps."

"No. No thank you."

"Tea?"

I nodded, despite myself.

"Tea then." He rapped his knuckles three times against the door and the yellow-faced man appeared. The two whispered in their odd French, and then the servant disappeared.

This was not the kind of situation I liked. I was used to being the one with the information, with the intelligence, the man who possessed the power of knowledge. Now I was no more than a penitent in this man's house of sin, an entrant into the lion's den, helpless except for the possibilities contained in the little slip of paper. I patted my breast pocket and assured myself it was there. The tall man returned with the tea in a silver pot, flanked by two chipped porcelain cups. It was too dainty for my taste, but I took it anyway.

"Have you been here before, General Hood?"

"No."

"You cannot have missed the hoi polloi milling about down there, of course."

"No."

"They are fools."

I almost nodded in agreement, before realizing that the little man might be insulting me. The little man seemed to know what I was thinking.

"You are not a fool, of course. I know of your wager, and your ticket. You have bought one ticket, just one, for a drawing that occurs only twice a year. Most men buy as many chances as they can, but you have only bought one. I am curious. Why? You are not a stupid man."

I would not tell this stranger of my dreams,

of my prayers, of my conviction that I had put my fate into God's hands and that God would not fail me.

"It was only for amusement, Mr. Dauphin. I have no hope of winning, of course."

I hope beyond hope that I will win.

"I see. But then, why spend so much, and why wager on the biggest prize? Surely it would be just as entertaining to risk only a little for one of the small prizes. You are not," he said vehemently, gesturing down at the crowd, "like them. They are dreamy and superstitious men."

I didn't answer, and Dauphin broke off his questions.

"Let us take in the spectacle, shall we?" Dauphin said, waving his hand out toward the crowd and the stage at the opposite end of the hall.

A negro, a dark and giant man stripped to his waist, pushed and pulled at the handle of a giant glass wheel while the men at the front of the crowd hooted and urged him on. I noticed how the negro contorted and expanded his body with precision, neither speeding up nor slowing down despite the exhortations of the men who stood close enough to touch the wheel themselves. None of them dared. Off on either side of the stage stood two men with rifles, watching them close. I wondered where they had acquired those rifles, and whether they had been taken to the war, and whether the men carrying them had ever been under my command. This was a notion that often possessed me now, that any man who passed me on the street could have once been subject to my whim, my orders. *Nobody owes me that anymore. Got to quit thinking about it. No one is going to walk into fire for me, not ever again. Hell, it's damned hard to get a man to cross the street for anything but money. Money is honor now. Money is courage.*

I admired the organization of the drawing, the symmetry of the stage, and the discipline of the negro turning the wheel. I was about to congratulate Dauphin on his achievement when the two boys walked out onto the stage. I closed my mouth.

They were young, perhaps thirteen or fourteen, I didn't know. They wore identical uniforms of blue cotton trousers, white collarless shirts, and heavy black boots. *They look like they can't barely lift those boots. Why are they so thin?* The two boys moved slowly, at first holding on to each other and grimacing each time the shouts got loud. Finally they lost contact with each other as they stumbled into chairs and tables that seemed to surprise each boy as he fell to the floor.

"Hurry it up, boy, get us our numbers!"

"Who you looking at? Get to work."

"See your daddy? He just right over there. Right there."

I recognized the uniforms now, I had seen boys and girls like this around the city every once in a while. When one of the boys turned his face up toward the back of the hall, as if beseeching me for his help, I knew I was right.

The boy's eyes were, from that distance, almost perfectly white. I knew that if I were closer, I would see the faintest hint of a pupil beneath the haze of whatever foul thing had grown over the boy's eyes. The boys were blind and had been orphaned because of it.

"Mr. Dauphin, why are there boys from the asylum here?"

"They are here to assure our patrons that the drawing is perfectly square, and unable to be rigged. This is why so many people give us their money, they know that when they lose it they'll lose it fairly. Why it matters I do not know, but it does."

"Those boys look like they're the entertainment."

"There's that, too. It is a spectacle, after all."

I had a mind to beat the little Creole down, but knew this would cause more trouble than I could handle now. *Remember the money.* But I could not let this *spectacle* go unchallenged.

"Do you think they are funny?"

"No."

"Do you think it is amusing to watch two blind boys stumble and fall over themselves, for no fault of their own?"

"They share some of the blame, as they volunteered for the job. I pay well, and the blind boys at the asylum know this. But no, I do not find it amusing."

"I believe you think it is funny, sir."

"I only know that *they* think it is funny," Dauphin said, sweeping his hand out over the crowd. "And they are everything."

I massaged my bad arm. Then I was up and on my feet, my coat off, showing the little Creole my stump, pulling up my trouser leg so that he could see the fine wood. I moved so suddenly, Dauphin half leaped over the back of his chair.

"Perhaps *I* should be down there on the stage, sir, giving your patrons their amusement," I said. "Would this be funny also?"

The little man got control of himself and took his seat, gesturing for me to take mine again. I was on fire, breathing out my nose like a horse, but finally I calmed and took his seat.

"It would not be funny, General Hood."

"No."

"But I *have* thought of you on that stage. It's why I asked you up here."

The drawing ended for me up in Mr. Dauphin's overlook with the last number drawn by the blind boys. It wasn't mine, and when I looked down at it I realized it wouldn't have mattered anyway: the ticket had disintegrated into a pulpy mush in my hot, tight hand. No salvation. Why should I have expected different? Did I really think God had told me *to gamble*? That God would fix the game for *me*? Why? Why me? *Why, because it's always for me, isn't it? The great general! Damned fool. God is not my lieutenant. I have no lieutenants.*

I looked out over the rail and watched the gamblers shuffle out of the hall, kicking little clouds of paper into the air as they went. I watched Generals P. G. T. Beauregard and Jubal Early collect up the money that remained, seal it, and carry it together out of the room.

"I believe General Beauregard and General Early will be joining us momentarily,"

Dauphin said. "You know them, of course? Yes, I'm sure."

"I know them both quite well."

"Well then, a reunion! Wine?"

"I think not."

Dauphin was silent for a moment. Finally he turned square to me and leaned over, so that we were face-to-face.

"May I be so bold as to talk business, sir?"

"I am a man of business."

I looked for the smirk, but found none.

"Yes, I know you are a man of business. And thus I feel free to discuss matters with you directly."

"Proceed."

"Yes. The generals. Messieurs Beauregard and Early. They are fine men, yes? Men of honor? Respected men? Valiant men?"

They were. And this little man knows nothing of how they were on those battlefields, swords drawn, riding the lines. He does not know how they slept on the ground with their men, how brilliant they were over campaign maps, how bold they were to face death most days, and even in the pit of fear and sorrow and longing for home, how they still rode the lines. They gave men the courage they had even when they had none for themselves.

And now they lived in peace and they could not survive.

"I know them both from the war, yes."

"I employ them, of course. They give the proceedings a certain distinction, the promise of honesty. They are like the blind boys."

That was the most sensible thing the man had said to me. They were precisely like the blind boys. They were wounded. They were dancing monkeys. They were entertainment. My God, if we had known such men would dance about onstage like harlots, would we have even bothered to fight?

"I pay them thirty thousand dollars a year to appear here, twice a month."

Perhaps we would have fought harder.

"In addition to their *reputations*, they also are adept at keeping control of the crowd, as you saw."

There had been a disturbance just before the end of the drawing, but I had been too far away to see much before the crowd collapsed on what I assumed were troublemakers. Disgruntled losers, I thought. The only peculiar thing I had noticed was the pockmarked man moving out of the crowd as everyone else was moving *in*. He had been expressionless.

I had admired the way Early and Beauregard had commanded their few troops to bring order to the crowd. So few men, and yet they had commanded as if they had been a division, waiting for precisely the right time. It had been impressive. *It was the only impressive thing.* Down below, the only evidence that there had been any disturbance was a dark streak on the parquet, like a smudge on clean glass.

I said nothing. But now I looked the little man square in the eye. Thirty thousand dollars was a fortune, it would make me a wealthy man, or at least a man who could keep his wife and children in a manner befitting a general and continue the work I had begun with Father Mike. The work would not be hard.

"I would like you to join them. The same terms."

Here was the offer that had been coming for hours. I had known it. I stared at the little man. There was a knock at the door and the tall Creole let Beauregard and Early into the little room. I stood slowly, and each of the men patiently waited until I had reached my full height before extending their hands. *They still know what honor and dignity is.*

"General Beauregard. General Early." I

inclined my head and shook their hands. The two returned the greeting, and as if we had all arrived from our own far-flung command posts to receive orders, we sat down as one, on the edge of our chairs, spines straight, hats upon our left knees.

Mr. Dauphin stood, put his cigar back in his mouth, and put his own hat under his arm.

"Gentlemen, I'm sure you have much to discuss, so I will excuse myself. General Hood, it's been a pleasure. You are a remarkable man, and you deserve remarkable things. This is a generous city for the smart man, a brutal one for all others. I'm sure you know this. I look forward to our next meeting."

Before I could say anything, the door had been pushed open by the unseen hand of the tall Creole assistant, and Mr. Dauphin had slipped out into the dark hallway. The three of us surveyed the great hall's floor, strewn with the lottery's waste, and remained silent. Early looked distinctly uncomfortable and fiddled with the brim of his hat. Beauregard looked sad. He turned his eyes to me.

"We've made a mess of it, haven't we?"

"What do you mean?"

Beauregard was no longer the expansive, joyous master of ceremonies. He was drawn inward, brooding, but also in no mood for coy games.

"Oh, Hood, for God's sake. I have to say it, eh? All right: I am broke. So is Early here."

Early turned to Beauregard in anger, but did not immediately contradict him.

"Bone-dry, Hood, my friend. Without a nickel."

"I was not broke," Early said. "Just poor."

Beauregard nodded his head. "I speak hastily only because we all know why we've been gathered here, and I'm eager to make the situation perfectly clear."

I rubbed my knee and looked past the two men, to the windows far above them. It was blue turning to orange. Sunset.

"I understand," I said.

"I lost nearly everything for that war. I will not speak for Jubal, he can tell you his own story. But it is not much different. We came back to our country, to our people, and we did not know them and they did not know us. They knew money, and what did we know? How to dig entrenchments? Maneuvering to enfilade? The likely range of a cannon? How to feed ten thousand men maggoty tack and make them like it? That was useful knowledge once, and no more."

Beauregard began coughing and waved his hand to keep anyone from speaking while he hacked.

"And yet, we were *the generals*. You are one of us too: the proud warriors, the brave and honorable losers. We are an example to these people," he said, swinging his hand out over the empty hall, "even if we don't like it, even if we only want to hide. We cannot hide. Which means we cannot be poor."

"There can be honor in poverty," I said, surprised he'd said what he'd been thinking, and almost sure for the first time that I believed it. I had reservations. *What do I know about the honor of poverty? I came here to win a fortune.*

Beauregard hung his head and shook it. Early stood up and leaned against the rail, watching the negroes sweeping up the mess.

Beauregard measured his words. "There may be honor in poverty for *them*," he said, again pointing out to the hall. "But what of us? How much humiliation must the Confederacy take? What will they force us to? To the sight of our generals sweeping gutters, or robbing men in the Vieux Carré at night? Is that the price of losing, of all that blood that was shed for, as we might have put it once, *honor*?

I do not mind picking cotton. But I do mind a Confederate general picking cotton."

I understood perfectly. I had thought the same thing before. No longer, but there was a time when it had driven me entirely. Part of what had once made me desperate for money was this, this horror at the idea of failing the Cause by becoming an embarrassment. But I had also wanted the money because I wanted to be comfortable, and I wanted my family comfortable. I wanted status. And I knew Beauregard wanted all of those things too. I just didn't think that anymore. I wanted money for other things now.

"You want me to join you in the lottery."

Now Early spoke, Beauregard having exhausted himself. The old Creole soldier patted his forehead with a handkerchief and watched me with dark eyes.

"We want you to consider it, John," Early said. "I myself have found few ways to make a living for which I am suited. I see no reason that the reputation I built, over many years of fighting and suffering, should not now be the source of my reward. I have worked for it."

"You worked for the victory, for the nation," I said, again surprised that this is what he, apparently, believed.

"That is true, and as a result I am left with this reputation that is mine."

"It is not yours. It belongs to the Confederacy."

Early's eyes widened.

"I did not think you were naïve, John. Do you truly believe that? That anything belongs to the Confederacy now?"

"It does not belong to you."

"I am patronized for it."

"You have sold it."

Beauregard sighed, picked up his hat, and stood.

"I told Dauphin it was no use, General Hood, that you would be too vain to put on a show for the crowd. This is what I told him. But what I was thinking, is that you're too pig-headed to do what is right for you and your family and the rest of us. I may be wrong about that. I hope that I am."

And Beauregard left.

Early stared after Beauregard. Then he sat down in the chair across from me and closed his eyes, as if he were waiting for something.

He is waiting for me to decide. He thinks I will change my mind.

Was there honor in poverty? Here was an

opportunity to provide, and live in comfort, for many years. How could I make this decision for my family? I was a failure. I did not know how I would make a living now. Beauregard was right; he had only one thing to offer anyone, and that was his place in history. He knew that this was the only thing he could sell, the only thing of value he had to sell. It was all anyone wanted from him anymore, and why shouldn't he give it? To do otherwise would be to live with uncertainty and, yes, perhaps poverty, for the rest of their lives. *I have no lieutenants.*

"You will die in the poorhouse, John," Early said.

I will die in the poorhouse. And where did all my men die? I have lost count of all the places. In fields, in woods, in creeks, in muddy trenches.

"You will never be offered something like this again," Early said. "This is it."

I will never have my leg again, and yet I still walk. I have some blessings still. Those men, my men, they do not even walk now. They are lost.

"You are a prominent man, there is no shame in taking patronage," Early said.

I was their patron, and they died. I am owed nothing. I owe much.

"John?"

I stood up and faced Early and smiled grimly. I got my cane set, and put my hat on my head.

"Thank you, Jubal, but my answer is no. Will you tell Mr. Dauphin?"

Early nodded his head and seemed relieved.

"I knew you would say that, John," Early said. "Not everything has changed, thank God. You're a bloody fool, but you're our bloody fool."

Outside, I felt the last warming moments of the sun on my face, before the shadows swallowed the rest of the street. When my carriage lined up for me, I pulled myself in and took time settling in. *This may be one of the last times I get to ride like this. Donkeys after this.*

I was elated. My life stretched out ahead of me, dark and perilous, but not yet over.

"To the poorhouse," I told the driver.

CHAPTER 22

Eli Griffin

But that was not how I remembered it, and sitting there in that kitchen with Rintrah crying over his lost brother the priest, and then later riding out into Terrebonne Parish to do whatever the hell it was I was going to do with Sebastien Lemerle, this is how I remembered that day at the lottery.

New Orleans was a city of crowds. It was not a crowded city, but a city that yanked people along from spectacle to spectacle, into groups that formed and disappeared just like that. Every day the web of spectacles, all them places here and there where you might get to see something special, every day it shifted and wove itself new, so that the tight, straight, and regular city streets only barely intersected the path by which men and women navigated a far more twisted-up maze of beatings, amusement, intrigue, prayer, politics, greed, and charity. Folks formed up around old Creole men arguing the hows and wherefores of a revolt, as if they could; they formed up around drunken *américains* asleep with the pigs; also around a young bride presenting her first child to the world; around the old Creole couple who were torturing their negro servants in violation of the code; around men picking out bawdy tunes on hollowed boxes strung with wire; around the Italian vegetable hawkers; around a young man choked dead in an alley off Dumaine, the dull black bruise of the garrote around his neck as if it had been delicately drawn on his skin, a tattoo. Crowds gathered in cafés to hear the old men of the great families hollering the outrages of a history so distant that no one recognized the names or the places, only the old sounds of pride and loneliness that were the words and the sound of their native tongue.

If the city were its stages, its performing platforms, there existed no bigger stage than the one at Union and St. Charles, just three blocks down from Canal in the *américain* section.

That October, after we'd all been out at the fish camps, the city just weren't the same. It had been crippled, thousands had died of the fever, so many that it made our work seem insignificant, nothing more than a whole lot of shouting at the Devil, him with his deaf ears. I say that, but them that lived because of those fish camps would tell you a different story, and I should include myself in that number. I was grateful. I wasn't ruined, and I was alive. Along with the lives, a thousand fortunes had been lost, but new fortunes called out to new makers. Roll, river, roll. Opportunity acalling.

A crowd had been gathered outside the three-story office of the Louisiana State Lottery Company for hours. It was a building carved in scrolls and cherubs and gargoyles. The people wandered in and out of its doors as the mood took, watching the proceedings and then strolling on back out to the street to gossip and to wait some more. Thousands of men and a few women danced along the narrow boards laid on the mud and sand of the banquette, trying not to slip into the muck.

Liquor passed from hand to hand. It was cool for October, so their faces were not streaked with sweat and their handkerchiefs were not stained with dirt. But it was hot enough that most of those waiting to hear the results of the drawing shuffled toward the building, where the building's eave threw down a few inches of shade.

A little man in a tiny black hat every once in a while come and stood in the doorway, peering out at the multitudes of us. He looked both afraid of the fidgety mass, but also real happy about their reason for standing there outside his building. *I have their money in the vault*, I reckon he was thinking. He was a rich man, I knew, and he had made a whole lot of other men rich the last few years, after rescuing the lottery from failure. None of *them* men would be standing in that crowd waiting patient, hoping, praying, for the news that their number had hit. The rich men, the men who owed that little man a lifetime's worth of favors, knew where the money could be found. *Providence is for the foolish and the dull.* The little man, he was the lottery director.

The little man turned back into the grand foyer, guarded by some hefty stone angels staring blank and dumb down from the fancy carved window arches, and walked quickly up a small set of stairs until he had disappeared. I imagine he peered down upon the entertainment he had dreamed up and gave birth to, an imaginary place in which all the riches of the world were stored up nice and tidy and neat in two large, transparent, and spinning wheels, which I reckon we were supposed to think were magic and not controlled by little men in their secret rooms high above the floor.

I moved through the crowd outside the lottery building without disturbing it. *And why would they notice?* I was invisible because I looked like the rest of the men and was also unknown to them. That had always been one of my talents, getting lost in plain sight. I dissolved into the crowd, I was only a face seen for a moment, a shoulder, a hat. This made me feel powerful, invincible. I was a pair of eyes, ears, a mind. I had no weight on the earth.

I had money in the lottery, knowing I would lose it. I was not stupid. And yet I could not help myself. I couldn't stay away from a gathering of all them people, I had come to love the grotesque and the ridiculous, the absurd: men milling about watching other men pull numbers out of piles, hoping that somewhere down in there were fortunes with their names on them. Maybe it was the summer, the ridiculous things we'd had to do just to save some lives, what with the hearses and all. It had been a circus, and it would have been funny if it hadn't been sad and deadly serious. Maybe this had made me cynical. Or maybe it had made me come to enjoy those ridiculous things, like I had become a connoisseur of the ridiculous, the brutal, the sad. I don't know. No matter, I'll just say that I loved the dramatic and futile gesture. How could I avoid watching the lottery, then?

Now, I did not despise those people, the criollos, the natives white and black and brown. I could see that they were powerful men, men with energy, who reckoned they could become anyone, make anything. Ingenuity and luck. Here at the lottery they paid their respects to luck, and there weren't nothing wrong with that.

I could learn something here, like as not. I had ambitions. I was not dead yet.

I pushed my way to the front of the building, squeezing in between the broad shoulders, ducking beneath chins and stepping around floor-slapping large feet. I congratulated myself on being so nimble, so damned quick.

The cherubim above the windows cheered me. The thick, dusty carpet cheered me, and the gilded archway into the great hall, decorated with carved magnolia leaves and pelicans flying in straight lines, it all made me wish to go on and see the coast one day. I could hear a dull sound beyond the archway, it were like the crashing of waves. Every once in a while I heard a roar, and then the sound subsided. I heard laughing, I heard shouts of anger. I heard the voice of one man, above the rest, commanding attention. The voice was met with cheers, and the man received them gracious, like it were his due. I recognized some words. *Patriot, charity, wealth, responsibility.* There was laughter. I heard the man bark a command, and soon there was no sound coming from the room. I could hear a regular creaking, the rattle of things in a jar, and then the same voice, this time mumbling and groaning as if praying, or making a sacrifice. I couldn't resist temptation any longer. I wanted to see the men who thought they would gain the treasure they deserved. *I know the feeling.* I plunged into the crowd.

It was more than I had hoped to see, it was a fantasy. Every sound and vibration and color settled into a vision I had dreamed, usually drunk, countless times. There was the giant negro! He shone like swamp water! His shirt had been removed! His muscles strained under his skin, tied down by the dark lines of their mooring: the muscles of his chest traced a precise and bold curve up and then down again; his arms disintegrated in a mess of smaller muscles whenever the wheel reached the bottom and he began to pull up again; his thick neck disappeared smooth through an arch into the flesh of his shoulder. He was as black as anything.

The men in the crowd shouted and waved their hands and threw papers at the negro, who never looked up and never quit turning the large wheel. I wished he would stand up, take a break, face his harassers, let an expression cross that great broad face. But the man moved like a damned machine. There was no dancing, no singing, no comedy, nothing like he knew there was a crowd there; just endless repetition of his task. The faces of the negro's tormentors in the front row occasionally flashed back at me as they turned to laugh with their friends, and in those faces I saw smudges of feeling, of hate, of joy; streaks of black hair and pale skin. At the edges of my vision, I saw a hundred different faces, each a daub of color drained of anything unusual. They spoke with one voice, and frowned with one face. I rubbed my eyes, sure my vision was failing, but there it was again: the negro in every way a real person, a collection of details clear to the drop of sweat rolling down his belly and the weird angle of his broken nose; and the men in the audience rolling and growling as one. I had lived in or around the docks, and the streets, and the bordellos, and the saloons, and the cafés, but here was the essential thing about my world, even the part of my world that got all twisted up among the Creoles: here was the mob and the nigger. There was always a mob, and there was always a nigger. Always.

And then, *the blind boys!* They were something to watch. I knew they were blind right off, I could see their eyes. I had lived among the blind and the otherwise afflicted and discarded, I had wondered at the kinds of cruelties that would never be known to the victim, only to the observer. I knew them right away. I did not care for their entrance, and I thought it a hell of a rude thing to put furniture in their path and guffaw when they fell. They were not clowns. But, yep, *the nigger and the mob.* Got to have it. I guessed they were paid fair well for their pains, and that it was a blessing they could not see, and so they couldn't see the men with spittle in their beards shouting with wide eyes and open mouths like chimps. They would have thought far less of their race, I was sure.

There were two wheels on the stage, each one transparent and containing small black cylinders that tumbled over each other as they turned. One was very large, turned by the negro. It contained a hundred thousand numbers stuffed in their little capsules. These were all the chances that the men in the crowd had purchased. The other, which stood by itself on a table, contained a much smaller number of capsules, each representing one of the 3,434 prizes that could be awarded.

The two blind boys finally took their places by each of the wheels. They wore identical blue trousers and white shirts with black boots. Just like me. The boys looked as if they were watching the ceiling, their heads angled up just so. I wondered if they thought they had turned their heads toward the crowd. The noise was deafening at times, it echoed up and around the room, and I reckoned that they might think the men standing before them were giants. Or that they, the boys, were most incredibly small.

So unsuited to the world, and yet there they were in the middle of everything, taking their place. They were so pale, as if they had never left the confines of the asylum for fear of becoming lost forever. There was pride in their faces, too, something I hadn't noticed until they brushed themselves off and took their places. *They know they hold our fates in their hands!*

I climbed up on a chair along the wall and prepared for the drawing to begin. I leaned back against the wall, both hands bracing me on either side, feeling the painted fleur-de-lis pattern on the paper covering the wall. I was content.

When the first man in uniform marched out onto the stage, I thought nothing of it, but when the second, heavier man in uniform joined him, I became nervous. *What is this? Who are these men?* What business did the army have with the lottery? It was all wrong. This was chaos, and here they were putting order on it, two men, their sabers and buttons polished and gleaming, shouting at the crowd as if they were in command. *And the crowd listened!* My eyes hurt.

The taller of the two men addressed the crowd, and I heard the words *Beauregard, General Beauregard,* hiss through the crowd. He was a tall and thin man with a neat beard and long hair brushed back and wetted down. He smiled as if he had just told the crowd a joke he knew to be the funniest they had ever heard. They cheered, and he said, *Attention! We will begin momentarily.*

I couldn't hear every word, but I understood the meaning. Men began to press even closer to the stage, which prompted General Beauregard to hold up his hands for order. The pushing stopped.

The other man in the uniform stood by the smaller wheel and silently watched his companion slide up and down the stage. He had no interest in either Beauregard or the drawing, that was clear. He stared at a spot on the wall at the back of the room. He was a hard-looking man, rigid in every way that Beauregard was flexible, like a cat. Beauregard straightened the cloths upon the table and picked up the chairs where the boys had knocked them over. He swung them up into the air above his head and turned toward the crowd to acknowledge the applause. *A showman, too,* I thought. I wished the general would smash the chairs upon the stage and interrupt everything with a dash of violence and disorder. *He had been a general, he could reckon with chaos. He had made it and used it and et it up, hadn't he? Don't look like he suffered much from it. And here he is, pretending to be the Order itself. What bullshit.* I much preferred the dour general who kept his mouth shut and watched the crowd with disdain. *That one's honest about it anyway.*

As Beauregard put everything in just the right place, and patted the two blind boys on the head, and made a show of urging the negro on in his labors, I looked around me. There had been confidence in the room before the drawing had resumed. Men in their sweaty hats had jawed at each other, slapped backs, teased the weak and told jokes to the strong. Every man had seemed sure he would emerge from the room the better for it, but now that the moment had finally arrived, I could smell the insecurity. They crowded together and they reeked. They removed their hats and fished for their tickets in hidden pockets. They all looked the same direction without blinking. What I had imagined was power and independence had become something else. They were just a lump, a mass, tempered by fear. *The money.*

The general quickly explained the rules and the procedures, which some of the men repeated to their companions in French. I sensed that these men already knew the rules, that they already had spent days standing in the room staring at the stage. There must have been comfort in hearing it again, though, and I could see the men nodding their heads each time the general paused. Light streamed in from the upper windows and fell in lines of dust on the crowd and on the slowly fading wallpaper. In the great hall there was no carpet, nothing to relieve the press of heart pine on hobnailed boots. The men shifted their feet, and on the floorboards I could see stains, which might have been either blood or tobacco. I could imagine a church in the building, or a trading floor. *A little of both, I think.*

Finally Beauregard began the process. He stopped the negro from turning the big wheel and directed him to stand next to the silent general. He opened a small door in the side of the wheel and gestured for one of the blind boys to reach inside. The boy came closer, holding out for the general's arm, which

Beauregard brandished with a great and chivalrous flourish. Guided to the door, the blind boy reached inside and pulled out one of the little cylinders. The silent general stepped forward and took the object from the boy, who seemed startled. Then the general opened it, and in an echoing low voice called out a number. A shout from the center of the crowd. Then Beauregard turned the other wheel a few times and gestured to the other blind boy, who reached in and pulled another number. *The prize! Twenty dollars,* Beauregard roared. In the middle the crowd stirred, and I could see a head bobbing toward the side of the stage, where the prize awaited.

This is how it went for hours. Men gathered their prizes and returned to the crowd, perhaps because they had other numbers, perhaps to lord it over their unlucky friends. Occasionally Beauregard would announce that the ticket in question was eligible for a very large prize, but it never failed that the cylinder pulled from the prize wheel awarded only a small consolation prize. I knew this was one of the twice-yearly drawings at which it was possible to win $600,000 if in possession of the correct and very expensive ticket. I had no hope of seeing that happen.

Then there was a commotion across the ballroom. A large man in a black bowler pulled tight over his face pushed through the crowd. I hadn't been paying attention. Beauregard had called a number. The big man across the room, just a black head bobbing along, pulled a small boy along with him. They were dressed identically, dust-covered stonemasons. Beauregard kept calling the number, bored, and looked as if he were about to decide the ticket holder was absent, when he noticed the man and the boy—father and son?—waving a ticket above his head. I strained to see the look on the man's face. Was there shock or joy? What does a man do in such a situation? But I couldn't see that far and the sun was in my eyes. All I saw was movement, height, the black hat. I was glad for the man, whoever he was. I listened to the crowd.

The three hundred thousand dollar prize! Mon dieu!

He is rich! Bastard.

Beauregard had stopped, and watched the big man cleave the crowd, dragging his boy along with him as if they were part of the entertainment. The boy also wore a black bowler, pulled down low.

At that moment I noticed, as if for the first time, the red accents on the walls, bright like new blood. And the upper reaches of the room, unfinished, bare and crumbling like some kind of ancient ruin.

The crowd, at first, made way for the two winners, falling back from the sight of a man bearing a ticket to unfathomable riches. Men leaned back from the pair, knocking into the men behind them, losing their hats in the fray.

Then the murmuring began. I could hear it, in that guttural and imperfect French, the growling of resentment and anger and calculation. The big man looked, to some in the crowd, to be *ungrateful* or *arrogant*. I heard men talking, gathered in small groups within the crowd, angrily pointing at the big man in the distance, accusing him of being a foreigner, insulting them by not acting glad to have their money, appearing to want someone to take the burden off his hands. I wondered how they could see that, when all I could see was that hat.

I sensed the danger. I recognized this sort of crowd, I had been lost in the middle of such crowds before. I knew such a crowd could turn easily, eat anything.

The big man and his companion had gone halfway through the crowd. The little one kept losing his footing, either jerked off balance or his feet slipping on the thousands of discarded tickets, cigarette papers, and newspapers. Beauregard stood impatiently, his arms crossed, one finger lazily tapping at his chin. I noticed the other general had moved from his place in the background and stood next to Beauregard. He looked out at the crowd, and drew my eye toward a clot of young men moving quickly through the crowd, pushing others aside with shouts, moving toward the prize winners. *He sees it too!* I thought, careful to stay on top of my chair, out of the roiling and flowing of the crowd. The generals whispered to each other. They waited. *Hurry,* I thought, but they would not. They watched.

The two winners had been surrounded by the crowd. The boy had gained his footing. I saw the two black hats bobbing in the middle like things caught in a river eddy, I saw a swirl of men shouting at them and pulling and grabbing at them. Briefly, I thought their backs looked familiar. *Turn around,* I thought, but they didn't, and I reckoned I had seen men like them a thousand times. Something about the hats, but I'd forgotten what it was. I couldn't have been more stupid, Lord forgive me.

I could see that it was the young boy who now had the ticket clenched tight in his fist. Two large and bearded men—*did they all have beards?*—kicked and punched and grabbed at the two, and meanwhile another man crawled through the legs of the onlookers and began to pry and bite at the boy's clenched fist, the fist with the ticket.

The big man received two blows to the head by a man with a cane, and soon he was down on the ground, disappeared. He dragged the boy down with him, unwilling to let go of him. I heard a shout of pain. Soon more onlookers joined in, those passive and cowardly men I knew every mob required, men who, having held back out of fear, now would try to outdo each other. I began to feel sick, and leaned my head against the cool wall. *The mob, I am tired of the mob*. The mob caved in on the two black hats, swallowing them.

Finally the two generals decided to act, and for the first time Beauregard looked as if he had actually been a general and not a circus barker. The two men scanned the crowd and began shouting orders to the wings, where a few men with clubs had been standing out of sight. They began to point, ordering the hired thugs into the crowd, but they were too late.

The men with the clubs, on their errand from the generals, cut a row through the crowd by cracking the skull of anyone who dared stand in front of them. They enjoyed their work. I watched the lusty way they swung their clubs, and the almost tender way they kicked the unconscious aside. It was nothing personal. Never personal.

They clubbed the crowd aside and when they did they revealed the two men, slumped on the floor, blood pooling around them. They dragged the big man into the swallowing crowd, facedown, off and out a side door. The young man saw the glint of a blade in the man's back. A trail of red followed him out, as did the boy, slumped between two guards, nodding his head up and down, trying to look up but having no strength. He must have said something to a man standing in front of him, because the man spit in his face. The guards, to their credit, cracked the spitter's skull for him.

Perhaps the winners had seemed familiar to me because they had seemed so common, so unremarkable. So much like me.

Up on the stage, the lottery continued, no winner declared, no ticket claimed.

I hurried out, skirting the crowd huddled along the wall in the shadows. I imagined they reached out to me. *I am imagining things now.* I was confused. I turned left and left again and left one more time before I had oriented myself. Then I strode through the city, straight toward home.

So that's what I thought I saw. Now I realize that what I had actually seen was the murder of a priest I knew.

CHAPTER 23

Anna Marie Hood

I cannot explain to you, Lydia, how it is that I know that I will die soon, but I've had that premonition and I am sure I am right. I have developed a head cold, a cough, and I feel cold though it is August. A hundred times I've felt this way in my lifetime. This time it is different. God has visited me, I have felt the Holy Spirit upon me, comforting me, preparing me, assuring me that you will be safe and happy. Light is brighter now, the things of our house have sharper edges. There is beauty in the dust and also in the clear sweep of glass that admits the view outside, where it is brilliant and green and blue and the feathers of the sparrows are each visible. They tremble and flit and fluff, and I know when each bird will take off and leave me the instant before it does. I have been blessed with the knowledge of my death, that is, with the sharp and insatiable eyes of a visitor who hears the embarkation whistle on the quay for the last time.

Anna Gertrude sleeps beside me, and the bassinet still flakes its paint. She is so fat! She breathes quietly, I have to listen closely for the whisper of air moving between those sweet, fat lips. She will not remember me, she will not remember our lying here in the last of the summer's heat, exhausted still by the struggle to live, sleeping the afternoons away. She will not remember this time, when we were at peace. She will know me as a stone marker, a photograph, the slowly diminishing memories of her older sisters and brothers. Keep these diaries safe, Lydia, so that perhaps she might at least know one day what her mother thought about this life.

I want to keep this illness from your father, but I suppose I musn't. I would like to die quietly, without the disruption of grieving and worrying and nursing and confessing.

Quiet, simple, slip off. I do not want to say good-bye.

But he must be warned if I have the fever, there will be steps to take now. I wish you would come into the room, Lydia, right now, so that we could play checkers. Will you remember playing checkers with me? Remember that, it was fun. He must send you away. He must send you all away. I will be alone at the end, except for God, and He doesn't make sweet sounds of glee running after His sisters in the hallway. It will be quiet.

Remember this year, remember this wonderful year we've had together. When we returned from the fish camps, healthy and poor and free, there was nothing for us to do but *live*. Nowhere to go, nothing to buy, no one to see.

I am giggling now, but there is no one here to see. What silliness this state of affairs would have seemed to me ten years ago. Then there was always someone to see, someone to call on, some place to sing and laugh and whisper about the million trivialities that concerned us, my cousins and my friends. We read the newspapers for our names, we imagined death to be the exclusive possession of the poor and the old. Who could ever die in a new crinoline from Paris, who could die who danced a reel? All of us could disappear, every one, but with that knowledge lies insanity. We live as immortals, even though we pray for our souls and listen for the sounds of the afterlife from the altar. I don't know that I ever believed in my soul, not until lately.

We had spent all our money, of course. What little we had left. I'm afraid I am to blame for this, for shaming your father into this, but I have no regrets and I don't believe he has any either. Most of you children are too young to notice your poverty, or to think of it that way. To you there are merely fewer adults around the house to tie you up in proper dresses and scrub your faces and make you play proper games. There are no servants anymore, that is. Perhaps the world is bigger and more interesting now! The whole house is yours to roam. The shrubs are unclipped and wild, yours to hide beneath. We make supper together, you children chop the potatoes and the greens with great enthusiasm. Why did I never let you help with supper before? Perhaps because I never helped with supper either.

Do you remember when we walked to the river and ate our cold fish and raced sticks in the water? Your father took his leg off and hopped around after you children calling you little Comanche? He fell and he rolled around and little John Junior helped him up, so serious and concerned and such a little boy! It was cold and we gathered in our blankets, which were moth-holed, but I believe only I noticed. Some of them were the blankets we'd used at the fish camps last summer.

There was no more business for John, and I was glad of it. There was no longer any hope that we would be rescued, that there would be money coming to us by virtue of who we *were,* because we were the General and his society lady. The plague had made sure that every old connection was severed, every old relationship abandoned. Disease, such pervasive disease, puts things into its own order. It is hard to forget the fear, and it is hard not to forget that there were trains of the dead, but that you survived. How hard it was to forget the quick thrill of sighting a coffin and knowing that you weren't in it, that the dying had to end sometime, and that the unknown person in the coffin had died to bring the end, and freedom, just that small bit closer. Once you have thought such things, there is no forgetting and there is no forgiving. There is only the complete and terrible knowledge of your own greed for one more breath and one more day. No. Ten thousand more days, an infinite number of days. That is how many more we want. That is how many more I wanted.

But now I feel the corruption in my veins, my arms and my legs are heavy and drawn down to earth, and I do not want even a hundred more days. I am tired and happy. I was a girl like so many other girls, I was a young lady like my cousins and their friends and a hundred other young ladies, and then I was a wife to a general and a mother to eleven children, only that as far as I knew. And then I discovered that I was Anna Marie, and that I cared about the friend I had abandoned, Paschal, and that I mourned the dignity of the dead, and that I could be outraged, and that I could be courageous. Your father knows a kind of courage, a courage that exposes itself to sharp and flying things, that tests itself against the fear of violent death. But I have discovered courage in the abandonment of the past and in the embrace of a new life. I have walked away from a particular girl who also called herself Anna Marie, who would have lived and died ignorant of life's bounty only because she had assumed it would always be bountiful, that she was infinite, and that those for whom it wasn't bountiful lay accursed. I see no farther than the house now, perhaps the street, too, and within those bounds our lives are more complex and more interesting. I know the freckles on the back of your neck now, Lydia, when once I might not have known they were there at all. I know the rasp of John Junior's breath when he is hiding behind the curtains, and I know that John is superstitious about snakes. The vessel of our lives is small now, but life has filled it. I have no other way to describe it.

I would do nothing different now. That's not true. If I could wait to die until you were all grown, so that I could know what kind of men and women you will become, I would. I can only hope that in these pages you'll find what your mother wanted for you, and that was to be loved.

This will be the last that I write, I am quickly running out of energy, and so I suppose I must explain some last things.

I believe that Father Mike is dead. I know that John thinks he ran away, that he ran away from his responsibilities and from the mission that had begun and could not be ended, the mission to the poor and benighted and woebegotten who would never share in the prosperity of the city and would be allowed to die as so much raw material to be chopped and burnt and discarded. With our impoverishment the mission had become tough, there were no more rich friends with money to give to Father Mike's mission, and so he left, according to John. One day he was out there at St. Geneviève's supervising the last of the stone carving, the next day he was meeting with Rintrah in the house on Chartres, pointedly excluding John from the discussions, and then a few days later he was gone.

John was mightily disappointed, more so than I understand. We had given away our money in the expectation that the work would continue, that it would change something. Truthfully, I suspect we thought it would change *us*, and that we could not live without it. I could understand his frustration, and I felt it myself. But he was enraged like someone jilted, and then he became despondent. He sat in the living room chairs and brooded, occasionally calling out to me as I passed through the room, on my way to save one of the children from the tangle of weeds and the creeping ticks.

"He retreated, he is a deserter."

"That doesn't sound like Father Mike." I pretended to dust the mantel.

"He told me once, he told me." John yanked at the strap on his leg, pulling it tight until the skin around his wound turned death white. "He told me he was there to remind me of my obligation to God, to Him. He saved me from myself. And now where is he? Has he forgotten?"

I finished with the mantel and rubbed John's shoulder before heading out to the backyard, where you, Lydia, were rolling in the mud like a pig.

I thought Father Mike was dead even then, but I would never say anything to John about it. There was an absence and I could feel it, as if the city was lighter, less consequential, a thing beginning to float away unmoored. Sometimes I dreamt of Michel's heartbeat and I could hear it stop. I don't know when it happened, but I was sure it had happened. Michel had died. He could not have fled. John did not know my old friend quite as well as I did. There was nothing in Michel that would have allowed him to quit a fight. He was much like John in this regard.

Soon your father overcame his anger, forgot his disappointment. He took it out on Rintrah and refused to speak with him. There was no more sick ward for John to attend, no more dying people to depend on him. Rintrah's house became an empty shell of what it had been, full of life even if that life was always approaching its end. It had been light and clean, a good place to die among people who cared. Rintrah drew the curtains, kept only a few of his old henchmen around him, lived in the dark. He abandoned the fish camps and let his business deteriorate until all he had were a few captains on the wharf willing to do business with him, to let him move their goods through the underground. He appeared on our doorstep three times since the summer. I spoke with him the first time on our front porch. His words were mad, his eyes shined. He had something to tell John that he could not tell me, and I said that he could not possibly have any secrets from me who had known him since he was a boy, and he said that there were too many such secrets and that he was ashamed.

"Then speak to me," I said. We sat on hard wood stools that had been painted by mildew at their feet.

"It is man's business," he said.

"Pah."

"There is such a thing, Anna Marie."

"Vanity it is, in my experience. Men's *business*."

He rolled his hat in his thick hands. It was felt, and black, and had the shape of a pie left out in the rain.

"Do you miss it? The old times? We are the only two left."

"There are plenty left, Rintrah. Look around. Do you hear the children? There are ten now."

"Soon to be eleven," he said, smiling sadly.

"Yes. And then there's John."

"They are not mine. I do not belong to them, and they do not belong to me. It is different for me, Anna Marie. You did not answer the question, but I will. Yes, I miss those times, and I miss who we were."

Then, at that moment, I knew why I could be happy while the house around me moldered and gathered dust. The life in the house did not molder and gather dust, it grew. I could be happy because I did not miss who I had been. I did not miss the balls and the dresses and the amusements, but most of all I did not miss the girl. I did not know the girl anymore, I had forgotten what had interested her, I could not remember how she had dressed her hair.

She had become a stranger, that Anna Marie Hennen. She had been married, and she had given birth, and she had become unhappy and perhaps even mad, but that was not who she had become. She was a traitor to her class, to her *people,* and this filled her with excitement. She was her own creation, now, and if very few could see any beauty or peace in that creation, the better for her. I had become something, I was not merely created. No person had made me become this woman, and in my daydreams I imagined that John had been changed by *me,* and not the reverse. I had not been molded by my husband or anyone else. I had been changed by love, specifically the love of others, and most specifically the ability to love people I didn't know, and the will to truly know the people I loved without reservation whatever their sins. May you discover that love yourself, Lydia.

I did not miss Anna Marie Hennen, but I did miss my friends.

"What happened to Michel, Rintrah?"

The question surprised him and he dropped his hat. He fumbled it back into his lap and closed his eyes.

"I can't say. It is too complicated. Where is the General?"

"He's dead."

"The General?" Rintrah looked alarmed, as if the porch was about to collapse beneath us.

"No, Michel."

He looked at me for a long time, straight into my eyes. He was not embarrassed to look at me so closely, as he had been for so long. And I thought to myself, *When did Rintrah get such kind eyes?*

"I don't know where he is, and so I reckon anything is possible."

"Did he run off?"

"That is what they say."

"And what do *you* say?"

He sighed. He looked very tired and thin, especially around his mouth, which was drawn at the edges and wrinkled.

"I say nothing. I must leave if the General isn't returning."

"He'll be here sometime, don't you run off. What happened to Michel?"

He got to his feet and pulled that awful little hat down to his ears. He looked at me as if I might break at any moment, and that he would be very sad when it happened.

"I don't know what happened, not exactly. Not why it happened, specially. But I know he wouldn't ever run off. And you know it too."

"I do."

"Tell the General I need to speak to him. I need to explain something to him, something he thinks he understands but doesn't. Tell him to come visit at the house if he has a mind to."

"You know he won't."

"Ask him anyway."

Rintrah walked off, up Third Street toward St. Charles, and it was only then that I understood that he had walked all that way from his dark, cold house and I had never invited him in.

CHAPTER 24

Eli Griffin

To the poorhouse. I reckon that just after he wrote those words, he just got sick and lost his will. I know this: he never wrote another word that I know about, and certainly not anything as ridiculous as what Beauregard claimed was the man's last request, that his surviving children be split up and sent away with the scattered members of Hood's old Texas Brigade. Shit. But this is a matter I will take up later.

I have faithfully recorded the words of Anna Marie and General Hood here, I haven't left a word or a letter or a period out of any of

it. You will understand, then, why the end of
it made me miserable. The story was only beginning, for Christ's sake. Even I, a cracker-ass
grifter and ice attendant, who had only *just* acknowledged the presence of something other
than a business transaction between himself
and M., my beautiful and hardmouthed Irish
lass—even *I* could see that God had played
an awful trick on them, that they had found
some kind of secret about love just in time
for death. I am not a sentimental man, but it
couldn't end there. If it ended there, shit, why
should it have ever been begun? Why should
anyone begin, why should anyone try to love
anything, if all that's going to happen is that
you suffer, and suffer some more, and then
just when you've come to the end of that suffering and found some peace, off with your
goddamn head, off to the cemetery with you,
here's a tombstone. I was *angry*.

And because I was angry, the story did not
end there.

Because I was angry, I ginned up some courage for myself and went riding on down south,
into the distant swamps that bled finally into
the sea just past the last hummocks of land at
the bottom of the world. The old man at the
tax office said Lemerle had sold his property

in the city the year before and that he'd left only a brief note in the file: *Gone south.*

I lied to Rintrah. I told him I knew nothing more about Lemerle, that I still hadn't tracked him down. Rintrah absentmindedly tossed a fat orange in his right hand, up and down, nodding his head.

"You're either a hell of a lazy young man, an idiot, or a liar. I'll be kind and say you're an idiot. But you better not be an idiot much longer. Ain't many more days left for being an idiot. You got one day, in fact. After that, I'm going to think you running a game on me. You running a game?"

"No sir."

"Now I *know* you running a game on me, calling me sir. One day."

He put the orange back in its crate and tipped it up on a brick so the negro ladies in their bright tignons and the bearded white Creoles in their tall black hats could get a good look. Down the street, I could see one of Rintrah's men, a slim dandy in a sky-blue suit they called Dagger Don, watch me closely. He picked his long yellow nails with a short blade.

I began to walk off.

"So where you going today?"

"More of the same. Got one more day, right? Might get down on all fours and go sniffing out after him like a redbone."

"Go to Hell, Eli."

"We'll see."

I walked back toward the Shell Road where I could hire a horse, and prayed he wouldn't notice when I'd disappeared from the city.

When Lemerle said he'd gone south, this turned out to mean he'd gone on down into the flat and marshy Terrebonne Parish, back off a little bayou in an Indian camp. You could tell it was an Indian camp from the little perfect hills that ringed the clearing, some of them full of dead Indians, some of them full of broken pots and oyster shells. It was a strange place to make a home, most people avoided the old Indian settlements for fear of what kind of red man's houdou might be on it, haunting the place. I'd have thought an old Indian killer would have steered far clear, but this wasn't the case.

It was a long ride, and as I went the road became ever more narrow and straight, and the cottonwood and live oaks and cypresses ever more stunted and twisted in the hard salt wind that stung my eyes whenever the road turned due south in the direction of the ocean. I had time to think, I had the quiet for thinking. After a couple hours I'd got so far away from the city and its noise that my ears throbbed and hummed, making noise out of nothing. Like they might fall off and die if they didn't have something to hear. But down there in the parish, only the insects made any sort of noise, and then it was only a sort of hum, sometimes a trill. It took some time to get so I could hear the birds and the slap of a bream tail on the water, but finally I got my old country ears back, and I felt calm. Purposeful and certain. Strong. The city could never be my domain, I was weak on those streets and in the shadows of tall brick towers. But among the peepers and thrashers, the hot peaty smell of wet wood in my nose, I was a master.

I steeled myself for the mission, which had grown some since Hood had put it on me. In the saddlebag sat a copy of Hood's manuscript, which I would show to Lemerle. I would wait for his answer to Hood's question: *Have I cast off the Devil, am I a new man, truly?* But I had some questions of my own now. I would ask him about Paschal, the ghost who had begun to haunt me, and if I didn't like his answers—if he dared to *lie* to me—I would take his head back to Rintrah in the other saddlebag. I would ask him about Father Mike, too, and why the priest saved his life on that day when Hood himself had ridden down into this very country and hunted Lemerle like a coon. He knew more than Hood realized, I was certain. I wanted him to tell me what he knew about Father Mike. And then, maybe I'd kill him anyway on principle, for being unfit to live as a human.

I was very certain of myself and convinced of my power to whup ass. I was convinced I could kill, though I'd never done it. I should have known better.

When I saw the break in the weeds and vines off to the right, the dark spot right there in the middle of the trees dusted white with road dirt, I knew I'd found the place. There was a post at the break, a cypress post driven hard into the ground, and from it hung a man's black hat that had a faded band of woven honeysuckle circling it at the band, and an old gray crucifix woven from split cane leaves. At its base someone had left a small black doll in a torn calico dress, sitting up among a heap of dandelion heads. It was the kind of shrine a child might build. I thought, *They saw me coming*. I spurred my horse and tore into the brush and down the narrow path. I wanted to arrive in a clatter of hooves and shrieks. I wanted fear.

I felt foolish when I pulled up finally, a quarter mile down the path, in the middle of the clearing. Three colored and naked children played in front of a rambling barge-wood shack. They looked up for a second and then paid me no mind. I couldn't tell whether they'd seen me coming, so that my arrival was no surprise, or whether they thought that they generally had nothing to fear from white men come whipping down their lane, rifle slung, horse sweated and angry. It was the latter, I would learn.

When I asked the oldest to go find Monsieur Lemerle, he told me he was six and didn't know no Monseiur Lemerle, and then ignored me. He had wavy brown hair and looked nervous. He and his brothers batted around an old coon skull with long pieces of driftwood. I could see a storm rolling in off the Gulf, and had I been in the mood, I might have recorded the picturesque scene in my notebook: the white, roiling mountains of sky, the shiny and dark bodies of the negro children, the sweet yellow of dying cane in the clearing beyond.

The children had been city children, and

two still wore the scuffed and laced-up boots of a city child, but they behaved as if they had never lived anywhere else and as if they had never been so happy. The coon skull was just the greatest goddamn thing that had ever come into their lives, if the expressions on their faces told the story. They were free, dirty, and ran as a pack. The boy waved beetles under the noses of his sisters, and the girls slid frogs down his shirt. These were children Paschal might have seen. He might have even known them by name, something I would never bother to do. I regret that now.

I rapped on the front door with the cane Rintrah had given me. I could hear scrabbling inside the place, but no one came to the door. Around the left side, where someone had built an improvised kitchen half open to the elements, I saw something boiling in an iron pot. Steam drifted my way, but there was no one tending it. I'd eaten nothing since the night before. The steam carried with it the trace of potatoes, onions, sassafras, and the musk of some kind of beast, fish or fowl, possibly both. It began to boil over and so I walked over to take it off the rusty old stove, giving it a stir first. I dipped the ladle in, drained it against the side, and took a bite. Then a second. It was thin soup, but once I'd got it on my tongue I had to keep eating. Mullet, I think.

"Get your own fish."

The voice was low and crackling, and I didn't have to hear the hammer click to know I was in some trouble.

"Just tending it, friend. Meant no harm." I didn't turn around. Either he was going to shoot me or reveal himself, and neither one required that I turn around. I'd rather get shot in the back of the head, I've always thought.

"Who are you?"

I hadn't thought of how I would begin, and seeing as how he was the one with the gun on me, I wasn't going to scare him into cooperating with me, either. What was I supposed to say? Better to start simple when the hammer's cocked.

"My name is Eli Griffin, friend."

"Oh, then, well, I didn't know I had a friend named Eli Griffin."

"I'm from New Orleans."

"No, *I'm* from New Orleans, you're an *américain*. Upcountry, I reckon."

"We have a friend in common."

"Seeing as how I don't have any friends who are still alive, I'm going to call you a liar."

"I was sent here by John Bell Hood."

He had been scratching his finger against the butt of the pistol, but now he stopped. I knew this because as soon as I heard his voice and heard the gun cock I'd been able to hear the slightest flicker of the smallest gnat. Silence. I was standing right over the steaming pot of fish, and I thought my face would just slide off in a pool of nervous sweat. I heard the hammer click down.

"I wouldn't call him a friend."

"Acquaintance."

"Well, he's a little more than that, no? If he sent you here, you must have suspected that, mmm? I would have thought he'd have sent a man, more, mmm, *capable* to have done with me, but my luck is still holding. And shit, turn the hell around already."

I did, and there was Sebastien Lemerle just as Hood had described him. Shiny and black hair, but perhaps less of it than I'd imagined. Behind him, standing in the doorway to the rest of the house, I saw a tiny, sweet-faced colored woman in a tignon, frowning at me before flouncing back into the house.

Lemerle stood straight and lean and stared at me. He wore a pair of black trousers cut off at the knees and nothing else. He was brown like an Indian, sinewy and scarred. His chest had scars that looked like the work of a large animal. He glided past me to the pot, pistol raised again and cocked. He stirred it, tasted it, put it back on the stove and closed the damper, all the while keeping the pistol pointed dead level at my forehead. When he turned back around, he was smiling.

"And where's your weapon, anyway?"

I turned and nodded my head off toward my horse, which was happily grazing the brush and pulling out great mouthfuls of vetch, and at the old rifle in its holster swinging crazily and seeming a thousand miles away.

"That rifle over there? That's what you brought? I ain't a goddamn possum, Mr. Eli Griffin. This ain't hunting."

"Didn't come to hunt you." I tried to make my breath come slower, deeper. I heard ringing in my ears. My stomach was taking to sick. Even with the pistol at his side, hanging from his finger casual and loose like a jug of liquor, I knew this was a dangerous man.

"Well, that's a very good thing, since you're so awful bad at it. Don't ever leave your weapon, even if it is a big old rifle that ain't worth a damn when a man's got a pistol dropped on you. Shit, I could be covering you with a goddamn leather punch and you'd still be in trouble at the moment."

He looked at me thoughtfully, as if I were an amusing puzzle, a riddle he could have some fun solving.

"He didn't send you to kill me, did he?"

"No."

"Because if he had, he'd have sent the dwarf. Or the dwarf would have sent someone." He leaned back against the gunwale of a busted-up pirogue, good for nothing but stove kindling now.

"Rintrah."

"I know that demon's name."

Why did I smile right then? I think it was the idea of the Devil calling someone else a demon, like it was an insult. Hood's writing, and Rintrah's raging, had convinced me that the man Sebastien Lemerle was not human, and it had become a matter of faith with me that I would find him out in that swamp prancing about on goat's legs wielding Death's own scythe.

There is not anything colder than the barrel of a pistol pressed hard between the eyes. Nothing in the ice factory is that cold, not even the great pipes clad in ice. I should not have smiled. I went cross-eyed and stared at the long barrel, pitted here and there from the forging. I vowed to play this like poker from here on, to put on my grifter's face for the duration, assuming he didn't put me down right then.

"Is there something funny?"

"No, Mr. Lemerle."

"You smile when I say Rintrah King is a demon. Is he not?"

Testing me. Wanting to see if I was a man who could be frightened into disloyalty. Someone to despise.

"No, he's not."

"He's your friend."

"Not a friend. But not a demon either."

"I was hasty, then?"

I didn't answer, just shrugged my shoulders and looked off toward the stove, where the fish was still steaming, as if I didn't care what he did with that pistol. He lowered it again, and bent low before me, sweeping his free arm back behind him. A bow.

"My apologies, I was hasty. He's not a demon, just a criminal who poisons my people with his cheap liquor and takes life without respect, for whom killing is a business expense paid to brutal thugs."

I struggled mightily against the smile, and this time I won.

"I'm sorry, I thought that killing was *your* business, Mr. Lemerle."

"It was never business."

"And what was it?"

"It was what I am. There is a difference. It is also my art. And when you have lived a life knowing that God has cursed you with only one talent, and that you are less than nothing without it, and that this talent is repulsive and destructive and ensures your entrance to Hell, then you can laugh at me. But I suspect you do not have this problem."

He walked over to a seat carved from a cypress stump and motioned for me to come sit by him. At his feet, on the ground wet with leaf mold, as if I were a pilgrim come to his shrine for a blessing. I had no plan anymore. The plan I'd devised on the long ride had been naïve, vain, corrupted by anger. I should have abided by Hood's wishes, come into Lemerle's camp with the respect he'd intended for me to show, carrying the words from Hood with honesty. Instead, he'd smelled the conflict on me, the deception, and now I had sat in a clearing in Terrebonne Parish, far from the city, far from any settlement even, where a man with a pistol whose *art* was killing stared at me, still distrustful. I wished I'd at least told M. where I was going.

"Now. Why are you here?"

And so began the strangest day of my life.

I told him the truth, as well as I could, leaving out the fact that Hood had died. I don't know the reason. I reckon it was the old grifter's instinct, to always hold something back, that kept me from telling him the story of Hood's death. I wouldn't lie to him if asked, I just didn't want to volunteer it.

"He wrote a book, you say. And he wants me to read it?"

"Yes."

"What's it about?"

"Him, mostly. Also his family."

"Sounds like torture."

"You're in it too."

"Ah, the *whole* family of the great Hood. His bastard son too!"

"I've read the book, and I'm fair sure he doesn't think of you as a son."

"Don't be smart."

We were eating bowls of his fish stew, which had smelled better in the pot than it tasted. No spices. Lemerle was on his third bowl, and every once in a while he paused to ladle out some for the children who came up by ones and twos. They were beautiful young things, the boys and the girls, delicate curls drifting down the sides of their faces and across their backs. Some had light brown irises, some of them had green. The children each received their bowl with thanks in cupped hands, and walked off slowly not spilling a drop. The oldest's bowl contained a fish head and he seemed particularly grateful for it, lording it over the others while the fish stared up at him, white-eyed. They looked at me straight, unafraid, even the littlest, who was naked. Their skin was golden and shining in the heat.

"But, I reckon he decided he had something he had to say to you, that he had some responsibility to you," I said. "I don't know, most of the time I don't understand the man."

"Why would I want to read about that war again?"

I hadn't been clear. "It's not a war book."

That caught his attention. He wiped the face of his littlest girl, who was dressed in a cotton sack dress dyed blue and carried a small colored doll made from straw and tiny buttons.

"Then what is it?"

"It's about what happened since then."

"Since then."

"In New Orleans."

"Ahhh."

He shooed the children and put aside his stew. He had become grudgingly hospitable, even a little warm, since we'd begun our meal, but now that it was over he brought the pistol back to his lap.

"You had better explain. Quick now."

I told him that Hood had been writing about his life since the war, about him and Anna Marie and their children, their friends, his failures, and finally his happiness in the ruin of that godforsaken house on Third Street. He asked me why Hood would write such a thing, and I said I didn't know, but Hood assumed that Sebastien would understand, and I guessed that was why I'd been sent to see him.

"Who else does he write about?"

"His friends. People he knew."

"*Which* people?"

"Rintrah, General Early, General Beauregard, his business partners, Mr. Plessy."

"Don't be coy."

"You."

"Yes."

"Father Michel."

His face softened and he smiled, petting the revolver gently.

"How is Father Mike?"

He asked this question as if he'd known the man, as if he had fond feelings for him. And I suppose he did, since Father Mike had saved him from murder by Hood, but even then he seemed more than just passingly familiar with Father Mike. As if he'd known him before that day in the swamp when the two killers had been separated by the great priest bear, perhaps the only human alive who could have made either of them afraid. Had Hood known this, had he suspected that Sebastien and Father Mike were known to each other? He had not, I had read his pages too many times to doubt it.

Now there were two deaths I held back from Sebastien, and I reckoned that was two too many at that point.

"Father Mike is dead."

He took this calm and quiet. Then his eyes closed hard, and the blood drained from his temples. He pulled himself in tight, grasped his hands in front of him, in his lap, and bent over as if praying. When he sat back up again and opened his eyes, he looked around him as if he were seeing everything anew.

"Did they catch the killer? The murderer?"

"What makes you think he was murdered? I didn't say nothing about that."

He was a very fast man, though he always seemed to have barely moved. He had been sitting across from me, contained, and then he was standing in front of me with his fingers pinned around my neck. I tried to fight him off but I was soon swooning, the swamp began to darken before my eyes, and my arms became dull and heavy. I slumped to the ground, and when he finally released my neck the blood ran hot into my head. I thought my eyes would explode.

When I looked up he was sitting back on his stump, as if nothing had happened.

"We are at a crucial moment, Eli Griffin, and so you're going to have to make some important decisions. Are you going to go it straight and honest, or are you going to play with Sebastien until he tires and feeds you to the alligators? I am trying to be as reasonable as I can. But what you are talking about now is obviously beyond your understanding. You're either going to answer my questions straight, tell me what you know, cracker boy, or you're not going to live much longer. Remember my art."

I understood.

"So, did they find his murderer?"

"No. And I just want to explain, Mr. Lemerle, that I didn't . . ."

"Quiet now."

I was quiet.

"When?"

"The lottery. At the lottery, the big drawing last fall."

He nodded his head, as if murdering the big priest at the lottery had been one of just a few possibilities, as if he, Sebastien, had already worked out those possibilities. I was very scared then, and I became convinced I would die. Soon enough I took comfort from knowing that I would die soon, and from knowing who would do the killing. He was right, I didn't understand what we were talking about anymore, and I didn't understand the man in front of me. Had he planned the murder of the priest? I nearly ran for my rifle.

"Who does Hood think did the killing?"

"He thought Father Mike ran away. He didn't know that he's dead."

Sebastien looked at me queerly.

"Why would you know and not tell Hood? Why would Hood not know?"

I struggled to answer, but before I could

get a word out he crossed his arms and leaned back, frowning at me. The pistol remained in his lap, the fish stew in my bowl had developed a thick skin. I put it aside.

"I understand why Hood doesn't know," he said.

I watched him.

"Hood is dead, too, isn't he?"

I nodded.

"And you just found out about Father Mike."

I nodded again.

"Hood was not murdered."

I got my words back, the flush had gone down out of my face.

"He died of yellow jack not long ago. Him and his wife and his daughter."

"Which daughter?"

"Lydia."

"A beautiful girl. How tragic."

He seemed truly saddened by that news, and this made me angry. It gave me life.

"How would you know about Lydia, or any of the other Hoods anyhow?"

He leaned forward and I could smell the onion and mullet on his breath.

"General John Bell Hood has been my special subject of study for many, many years. Of course I know who his children are. I could draw them each for you. I could tell you what they like to eat, and when they go to sleep. I can tell you what time that house used to go dark and what time they fired the cookstove in the morning."

"You been studying him since the Indians, I guess."

"He writes about the Comanche? Devil! But you're a smart boy."

He looked into my eyes, his were brown flecked with black and gray. Looking to see if I was lying. Again he lowered the weapon, this time sticking it in his pocket. At that moment I heard the children again, playing over on the far side of the clearing. The woods were clear and sweet and deep and full of color. I didn't need to piss so bad anymore. I slid over to another stump braced by roots and sat down. He crouched on his haunches and poked at the wood in the stove. It was a long time before he spoke, so long I watched a brown spider lower itself from the overhang of his house to the ground and haul itself back up again.

His woman came out of the house and smiled sweetly at me, though I could see in her eyes the distaste sliding by. She called out in French, and the children came running. Narrow and sharp faces like Lemerle's. Was the silent and malevolent colored woman his wife?

He introduced the woman as Danielle. She said nothing, just backed up slowly and took a seat behind me, next to an old live oak. I could hear her clicking her tongue. I became comfortable there. It was nice out in the country, I'd forgotten what it was like. It was not much like the rocky hills of Middle Tennessee, but it was quiet and the sun filtered down through the green, and I was swaddled in the warmth of sweet air. Their house, I could see, rambled on into the woods beyond my vision, one room after another, some smashed together, others piled atop the others. Everything was angled, interrupted, and covered in tin. Vines slithered through windows and behind the tin, framing the house in the green and yellow. Hundreds of goosenecked and deformed gourds hung off the house. The vines looked strong, like I could climb them.

The first vine came around my neck quick, wrapped twice. She was very strong. The harder I pulled against the vine, the more it choked me. I watched Lemerle come around to assist her, and the two of them pulled me back until I was sitting on a small stool with my back against the old oak tree. I couldn't speak, I saw black spots everywhere. Soon they had me tied to the tree, harnessed by the neck, legs, and arms. The fissures and depressions in the trunk of the tree cut into my back. Danielle came around to the front and spit in my face, but Lemerle told her to apologize and wipe my face. He told her I was not his enemy. "Though," he said, turning to me, "you might think you are." She shrugged and wiped my face with the rough hem of her raw cotton skirt. I could feel each stitch scratching, I smelled sweat and perfume.

Lemerle sat back down across from me and smiled kindly.

"Don't worry, if you're being straight with me, I won't hurt you. Just a precaution. Can't have you rambling around the place while I'm trying to read this book of Hood's. You could get into all kind of trouble. Now where is it?"

I tried to talk but the pain in my throat was too great. Danielle loosened the vine just a little.

"With the horse," I said.

He whistled a strange high keening sound, and the two oldest children came running.

He spoke to them in English I couldn't understand, and then I watched them lope over to my horse who, traitorous git, whinnied in delight at their approach. The girl pulled the package of paper from the saddlebag and came running back to her father. The boy pulled the rifle from its holster and began to break it down, tossing the receiver one way, the barrel the other, pieces every which way into the underbrush.

Lemerle took the pile of paper and thanked the girl. He turned to me.

"This might take some time, I'm not learned."

I shrugged. Where else was I going to go? He laughed.

"You'll be well fed, don't fear."

There was something else I had to tell him. I wasn't sure if I should, but I decided that I ought to just carry out Hood's order like he'd said.

"Sebastien."

"Mmmm."

"Hood said you're to judge whether he's cast off the demon or not. Based on those pages."

He held the pages as if they were glass and might break. I thought he might cry.

"He remembered that, did he?"

And so began the strangest day and night of my life. Sebastien did not sleep. First he read by the light of day, and then by the light of the cookstove, and then by the light of the red, blue, yellow, and white candles Danielle placed around him in a circle, some shoved into the crooks of low-lying tree limbs, others ground into the dirt at his feet. And he might have been a god, or the statue of one, unmoving and intent on the thing in front of him. Only his hands moved. In the dark I couldn't see his eyes, only the flash of light against them. My mind wandered. I thought I saw lights far off in the woods. At times I wished they were the lights of Rintrah's men, come to find me, and sometimes I prayed they weren't. But they were just swamp lights, or possibly ghosts.

When Sebastien ate, I ate. After the stew, it was mostly hard pan bread and nuts, but I appreciated it all the same. I even thought that maybe Danielle had softened toward me. She brought me an extra crust in the middle of the night, and a cup of coffee that she held to my lips. It warmed me. Then she stood up and stared at me, cocking her head like a bird. She looked me up and down. She whispered something, but I couldn't hear it, I only saw her lips move. *What are you?* I thought she said. It was a good question to pose to a man trussed up like a Christmas pig in the stinking and gurgling south Louisiana swamp, far from anyone who loved him. A good question.

In the morning the children took turns riding my horse. They painted him with berry juice and hollered in French while racing up and down the clearing, and then down the hunting paths that ringed the homestead and, I could tell by the honk of their voices, led far into the wild country around. I had slept some, and when the morning came it seemed only moments had passed since Sebastien had first opened the manuscript. But when I was fully awake, I could see that he had finished it. It sat on the woodpile in front of the cookstove, neatly arranged and tied again. Sebastien offered me more coffee, but I had to piss so I said no. He got up, slowly as if in pain, or like an old man, and untied me. He helped me up and massaged my arms. When the feeling came back I nearly cried in pain. He helped me to his seat on the stump, in front of the warm stove, and then he paced, looking at me.

"Do you think you know who Paschal was?" he said.

I stretched my legs and began to scratch at them. I'd been feasted on by biting things all night. Whatever was going to happen needed to happen soon, I was too tired. I decided to answer his questions as best I could, no games, no grifting.

"He was a colored who had been their friend."

"That's true, what else?"

"Piano teacher."

"Yes."

"I don't know what else."

"Oh, now, that ain't true."

He was right, but I didn't know how to tell him what I thought I knew. But he already knew it.

"I'll help you," he said. "You came here by yourself. You came here with a rifle that you could have easily used to kill me from out there in the goddamn wood without riding up in here like a damned cavalryman and then poking around in my stew. You didn't want to kill me right away, you thought you would do it later. You wanted to talk to me first."

"Yes. But that was only because Hood had told me to bring you these pages and get your verdict on them, and I'm a man of my word."

"Oh shit. If that was true, you'd have walked

up nice and polite and delivered the message and the book and been on your way. No, *you* wanted to talk to me. That had nothing to do with Hood's request."

"That's true."

"Why?"

"It's a long story."

"You know more, or think you know more, than Hood did. You found out about Father Mike but Hood didn't, and you're wondering what else Hood didn't know. And I'm ready to bet this plantation and mansion right here, such as it is, that you're wondering about Paschal. Because this book right here," he said, tapping at it with his foot, edging it dangerously close to the fire, "describes the man like he was some sort of angel, not part of the dirty and sinful world like the rest of us. And that, if I'm guessing right, doesn't square with what you know about this life. There ain't no angels, for men like you and me that's well settled."

"I ain't like you."

"No. But we both seen the worst, mmm? Hood ruined your life like he did mine, didn't he?"

"Yes. But I don't hold it against him no more."

"The hell you don't. You always will. But

you might not act on it, mmm? You can learn to love the man you hate, that's true. That's what it means to be a man, *mon frère*, but you don't just up and change your mind about what you know of men. Men are beasts, they are not angels. Hood wanted that to be true. He wanted to believe there were angels he could protect and heal, who could then clear the books of his debt to God. Everything, *everything*, in that man's life was either something he owed or something someone else owed him. Of course you see this in what he writes. Even I see it, and I am not as learned a man as you."

"I reckon that is all true."

"Ahh, but in the end he knew it was only the Devil who could clear him, mmmm? Me."

"Yes."

"Not an angel. Not Paschal."

"Paschal is dead."

"Ahh, you're being a smart mouth."

"I'm sorry."

"Paschal was no angel."

"I agree."

"I think you require evidence."

"Maybe you're right."

"Okay, then, here it is. This is what you come for, anyway."

He shouted out in French toward the house, and after a while the oldest boy came to where we were sitting carrying the youngest, possibly three years old, maybe younger. When the taller boy left, the young one sat down in the dirt and began to chew oak bark and play with ants.

"This is Paschal."

"I don't believe in voudou. He ain't come back from the dead."

"No, of course not. That is just his name."

"Seems a bad joke to me. You killed the man."

"This one was born and got his name some time before I saw Paschal at that goddamn ball."

"A coincidence."

"No, that's not what I mean. He *was* named for Paschal, the man you knew and have read about. Named by me, for the benefit of Danielle."

I only nodded my head. I watched the boy close, looking for some sign. I stared at his fingers. Were they long and delicate? Was he beautiful?

"Does he look like me?"

"No."

"You already knew this."

"I guessed. I didn't know there was a child."

"There was, and as far as he knows I am his father. And I will remain his father. I love him like the rest."

"Paschal . . ."

"I don't want you to say it. Just look with your eyes. Don't say it."

We sat silently while the boy mumbled to himself, occasionally barking orders to the ants. His voice was pure, like a plucked guitar string.

"You can imagine, I was angry," he said. "But I love my wife. My *wife*. No matter what anyone else says, she is my wife before God."

"I understand."

"You don't, but you can imagine understanding, and that's a good quality. It is a kind quality. I do not have it."

He picked up Hood's pages and sat them in his lap, still too close to the fire for my comfort. He stroked the rough string and considered his next words.

"I would have left him alone, had he not been there."

"At the ball."

"Yes. Yes. I would have left him alone. Danielle had made me promise. Danielle, who had loved me when I was only a murdering wraith, a beast, who had given me children who I could love and who loved me also. Hood and I are not so much different, no? Is that not what Anna Marie did for the General? Mmmm? Yes, she did. That's what this book says." He thumped it.

"The difference is that we were always shunned, we had only ourselves and these children and that little house on Marais Street. Long ago I would have killed Danielle, too, and the children. I would not have hesitated. But I had been too long grateful to her, too much in love with those children. But she fell in love with Paschal. I know this is true. She loved me, and she loved him. And why not? I was the worst kind of man, I was shunned by my own people, I was a white man living among negroes, hated by many people. And Paschal was a loved man, a cultured man, a *negro* who was as white as I was and many times more interesting. Why wouldn't she fall for such a man, a man like her, one of her own, someone who understood things about being a negro I never would understand? My children would understand these things, and my grandchildren, but I could never understand it. I knew what it was like to be cast out, but it was never a permanent condition. I could change, I could reform, I could remake myself. Is that not what you *américains* do? Is that not the way? I was not born an outcast, but she was and so was Paschal, and so why wouldn't she fall in love with him?

"I found his letter. It doesn't matter what it said. Except I should say, he wasn't nearly the lover I would have imagined. He was very formal and yet very clumsy. Cold. I was angry. You can imagine. I was made for anger, bred for it. But there was also a child growing in her, whose she did not know. When she told me this I was so angry and so afraid I would do something terrible, I left and slept in Jackson Square. I had a job the next few days, and I stayed away. My quarry suffered for my anguish. He was a man who had beaten his wife to death and yet had not been tried in a court. I had been hired by her brother. I asked him, *What did she do?* and when he said he'd been drunk and didn't remember, I cut off his nose. I asked him again, and he said she had been a nagging, frigid cunt. I cut the rest of his ears off and laid them on the ground where he could see them. Finally, when he knew he'd be dead soon, he said, *She didn't love me,* and I slit his throat.

"When I returned home I was surprised to find Danielle still there, waiting for me. The children played in the little yard out back and on the furniture. The boys argued over the role of Lafitte in their pirate games. They had no idea that anything had happened. They were happy to see me. I played with them and allowed myself to be forced off the plank a dozen times before I went in to see Danielle. She was shaking, but I could see in her face she was ready for whatever would happen. And so, I decided, nothing would happen. I asked her if she loved Paschal, and she said yes. I asked her if she loved me, and she said yes. I told her that the child was mine and she agreed. Whatever had happened, the child was mine. I told her she must not see him again, and she agreed. She said she had not heard from him since she told him about the baby. I was not surprised. As far as I was concerned, he was gone forever and thank the Lord.

"How easy it would have been to kill him! That was my calling in life, that was my craft! If I had set out to kill the man, believe me, I would not have done it in front of a hundred witnesses with the help of drunk buffoons by such a clumsy means as hanging. Believe me, had I meant for him to die, he would have died quickly in an alley on a dark night and been found by the pigs the next morning. He would have disappeared from the earth without sign, unless the pigs left something of him behind. A bone and a mystery. That was how I killed.

"But then, the ball. I went as the guest of a man who thought he needed protection, a weak man who talked too much and yet feared the duel. I despised such men, but they are often rich, and this one paid well. It was his sister that Paschal danced across that ballroom floor, spinning and sliding and turning, so beautiful. He was a satyr. He was flesh and blood! This is what is so awfully amusing about Hood's little book here. He and his friends thought Paschal was somehow above such things, above the satisfaction of flesh, above the devouring of virgins. Danielle had thought that, though I'm not sure why, since she knew his unblemished flesh quite well, his cock. Hell, even *I* thought that, having seen him around the neighborhood, helping his cousin with their garden and bestowing his lovely and pure smile on all the old women. But at that ball, in the instant I saw his face leering behind the back of his partner, I knew what he was. He was a man of the flesh. Not the man Danielle spoke of in her sleep, not the man she had fallen in love with, not the man I knew she missed dreadfully. He'd broken her heart and I was trying to fix it, and here was this man harvesting more women as if they were all his. It was then that I told my client that the man with his sister was a nigger. And you know the rest, or most of it.

"I lied to Hood when he found me in the swamp. I had meant to kill Paschal in the most painful way possible. I tied that noose tight. I tied it so he would strangle to death, not die instantly. I am very sorry that branch broke and he survived, such as he did. And the rest of what I told Hood? That I admired him? It was a lie. Or, not a lie, because I have grown to admire him, but not the correct explanation. I was a jealous husband angered by the way I had been cuckolded, and how my wife had been trifled with by a prancing fop. Paschal had treated my wife as something that could be thrown away. It was too much to take. I attacked a man for the most ancient of reasons. Such a simple reason.

"But I killed him, up there in that attic, for better reasons, the same reasons I gave Hood, the reasons he reports here in this book. Those were not lies. I was responsible for the monstrous existence of Paschal, for his death in life. The job had to be finished. It was cruel otherwise, and I had learned to avoid unnecessary cruelty. *Unnecessary*. Cruelty has its place. Sometimes a man's nose needs to be cut off. So I suffocated him with his pillow, and I left a sign for Hood to find. I believe I wanted to die, then. I was tired of being Sebastien.

"I would have died, too, if not for the priest, Father Mike. He had no love for me, but he is a priest, and priests preach love and life and forgiveness. He is no hypocrite. And I know he heard Paschal's confessions as his priest. He admitted as much to me and Hood. Hood didn't write this, perhaps he didn't hear it the way I heard it. I'm still Catholic after all. Father Mike said, *Paschal has been reconciled through me to the Church*. It was the only explanation for Father Mike's presence there at what should have been my execution. Paschal had confessed, and Father Mike knew our history, and he would not allow his friend Hood to commit a mortal sin out of ignorance. What had happened to Paschal was not as simple as Hood thought. Hood might act differently if he knew the whole truth. I wonder why he didn't tell him the truth right then. Perhaps it hurt him to say it aloud, about his friend, that his friend was no angel. I do not know. Whatever the reason, I was already damned, and he would not let his friend be damned with me. And maybe that's what I thought I wanted: I wanted to bring Hood down with me, I wanted again to see the Hood of Texas, the Indian hunter, the murderer, and I wanted the two of us to go twisting down to Hell together. Father Mike saved him from that and, no small thing, gave me my own time to struggle with God. I do not know if I am damned, I'm not sure I even understand damnation, but I know that I love Danielle and the children selflessly, and I know that's what God wants, even if I do not know God. That must count, though it doesn't with your vicious little friend, Rintrah. After the ball I slept all over the city, sneaking into the house only once every few days, when the moon dimmed. He harassed Danielle and the children but he did not touch them, and for that I am grateful. I am also grateful for Hood, now that I know why Rintrah stopped looking for me. I have been dead these last two years! It should have been obvious.

"But now, I think, it is time for me to give it up. We have to return to the city now. You and me."

I had been mesmerized by his voice, so absorbed that I hadn't realized that Danielle had slipped out of the house and was standing behind me, crying silently.

"Why do we have to go back?" Did I like this man, the damned monster? I believe I did for a moment.

"Because I know what happened to your Father Mike, and I am in debt to him. I must see Rintrah."

"He will kill you."

"He won't when I make my proposal."

Danielle let out one long wail, and then gathered herself. She wiped her eyes and walked over to Sebastien. She gave him a hard kiss on the lips, picked up little Paschal, and went inside. He watched her go as if she were disappearing into a dark and unfathomable hole. She shut the door and we both watched it for a minute. It never opened again. I could hear the sound of the children inside, sniffling and whining and asking their mother questions. I heard her cooing and shushing. *Shhhhhhh, mon ami*. After another moment Sebastien shook his head and stood up with Hood's book in his hand.

"Why, Mr. Eli Griffin, why would Hood think anyone would be interested in reading this thing?" He let it flap over in his hand, and some of the pages wavered in the heat coming up out of the cookstove. *Of course he would burn it*, I thought.

"Dunno."

"He writes as if he was the first man to love a woman."

"Yes."

"But perhaps that is true. We are always the first men to fall in love, no? No one else knows how it feels, not like *we* do. And when you have lived most of your life hard and grim and merciless, when you finally fall in love it must, *must*, be unlike anything else on this earth, unlike anything anyone else knows. Otherwise love carries the despair of all that you have misunderstood in the world and all that you have failed to see. Too painful, it's much better to think that it is one of a kind."

CHAPTER 25

Anna Marie Hood

I do not know what I am supposed to say to a daughter who will soon be motherless. There is too much to tell you about this life, I cannot not begin. Remember when you were happy. Remember when we were happy, remember this last year. Remember what we had, and what we didn't need anymore. Love your brothers and sisters, they will need you. You are the oldest, you have responsibilities. Teach them to be lovely and kind and strong. You are, I know you are, Lydia. Teach them how you became that way. It is a great gift. And whatever happens, stay close to your brothers and sisters. Do not let them grow up and disappear to places unknown. Keep them close.

It is tiring writing such platitudes. I suppose it is impossible to try to write down advice for a child without stating the obvious so generally it couldn't possibly be useful. The urge itself, to prepare such advice, feels strange now. I face death, and a future in death, and it is difficult for me to turn my attention to the past, my past, and find anything instructive in it or even interesting anymore. I want to die well. I am prepared for this. I wonder if that's all that you really need to know, the greatest comfort I can present you: the knowledge that I was prepared to die and that I was not afraid. Everything that has happened to us of late, all that I've written in these pages, has prepared me for this moment. If you've read this far, you understand why I feel that my life hasn't been wasted, and that I've overcome regret.

Take care of your father. Go to church. Leave me fresh flowers. I think that's all I can say. I feel very sleepy. I hope someone comes in to look after Anna Gertrude, because I can barely hold this pen and my eyes feel heavy. She is asleep, twisted up in her sheets, her little mouth open and vibrating with her breath. The soft sheets, the pillow, I feel the exhaustion settling in, I only want to sleep.

Is my death sudden? Yes, I suppose. But it doesn't feel sudden. I have had a long life. God bless you. I believe in you, and in your father, and in your brothers and sisters. I believe in Rintrah, and Father Mike, and Paschal. I believe in the resurrection of the body. I believe in the communion of saints. I believe in life everlasting.

I wish John had . . .

CHAPTER 26

Eli Griffin

Good Lord, the man would not stop talking. I didn't give one good goddamn for his opinions on love, all I cared about was what he would do with that book in his hands. I frowned, and he saw me looking at the pages flapping above the cookstove.

"So, the book." He looked down at his hand, waved the pages from side to side. "What will I do with it?"

"The question is, What will *I* do with it, Lemerle? All you have to do is to answer Hood's question."

"Do you really think he cares about my answer now?"

"That wasn't the point. It's a matter of honor."

"Hmmm."

"I gave my word."

"Yes, your word. Hood was always very fond of the rules of honor, did he teach you those? They could be made to explain everything he did, and so he never did wrong. Do you realize that?"

"The book."

"Was he a changed man? Was he still marked by the Devil?"

"Just an answer, that's all I need."

He held up his hand to me, begging me to wait, and walked around the back of the house and out of sight. I heard him cursing and slapping, and then the jangle of loose tack. Soon he appeared astride a crotchety old mule. He held up the book so I could see it. Then he slipped it into his saddlebag.

"This is not the work of a man marked by the Devil. Just a common sinner like most of you. I myself am not a common sinner, so I know what I'm talking about. I see it more clearly."

I felt great relief. I felt tears welling up, but

blinked them away. I knew I would not die that day. I had no idea what would happen next, but I would not die. The first thing I thought was, *I will see M. again.* It was all the talk of love. I did not love her. I did not.

"Get your gear, Eli, and get your horse."

"I could use my rifle."

"You won't need it." He opened the flap on his saddlebag and inside I saw an array of knives and little pistols. He handed one of the pistols to me and I stuck it in my pocket. He put his hands on his knees and bent toward me, sizing me up.

"You will take me to Rintrah?"

"Not if you're going to use those knives on him."

"They are not for him."

"Who then?"

"They are for the man who killed your friend. The man who killed Father Mike. And, possibly, for the man who hired him."

"How do you know that the killer was hired?"

He waved his hand impatiently toward my horse. I went over and mounted, I looked vainly into the underbrush for the pieces of my rifle, but no luck. Soon we were on the path out to the trace together, his mule in the lead. My horse nipped at his mule and we trotted on at a good clip. When we reached the turn at the black hat and the doll, I asked the question again.

"What do you know, Sebastien?"

"Many things. What do you want to know?" He rode with the easy rhythm of a man accustomed to long distances on dusty tracks.

"About Father Mike."

"I know that *I* was hired to kill Father Mike."

He had taken the job, he said, and vowed to himself that he wouldn't do it. That way, he thought, he'd save Father Mike's life and then they would be square. He should have warned the priest, he said, but he was afraid of him and of Rintrah. He should have guessed they would hire someone else also, someone to make sure it was done. He should have protected the priest.

"Who hired you?"

He wouldn't say. It was for Rintrah to hear first, not me. "What I know keeps me alive, no?" He looked back at me and grinned, a mouthful of crooked and small teeth. Sharp. "And we have plans to make. You have to finish the command of the General, correct? Get the other book back from the General

Beauregard? That will not be easy, *mon frère*. He has devilish friends."

"I don't need your help."

"Yes you do."

I felt the late afternoon sun bearing down on the back of my neck. It had been more than a day since I'd left town. Rintrah would be looking for me, I was sure of it.

"And, anyway, I have some business to conduct on behalf of Michel, Father Mike."

I was so tired, I barely heard him. I grunted and tried to find a comfortable spot on the saddle. He looked back at me again.

"It's why I brought the knives. I've got a good use for them now, at the last."

We arrived in the city around midnight. Sebastien could disappear into the darkness, and sometimes I thought I'd lost him, but it was only the trick of light and shadow. Every once in a while he would reach into his bag and pull out a knife, hold it to the light, and look at it curiously, before finding a different hiding place for it. In his sock, in his belt, in the pocket of his coat, in a hidden pocket of his sleeve. As the night had worn on and the road became longer and the limbs of the live oaks flexed their clawing fingers toward us,

I had become very glad to be the companion of that murderer, that devil. His knives gave me confidence. At times, as my mind wandered, I imagined us a knight and his squire. A black knight, sure enough, but a knight girding himself for battle. Were we the two creations of Hood, as the General had said? It was impossible that I had anything in common with the man, and yet he was familiar to me, it did not feel strange to be riding with him.

When we entered the city by the River Road, I took note of every bend, every stray dog, every liquor shack, every scent: of flowers, standing water, coal smoke, melting sugar. At first I was only trying to scan the road for Rintrah's men, who I was sure would shanghai us if we weren't careful. I thought I saw them creeping behind every tree. They never appeared, and soon I realized I was *memorizing* everything I saw and smelled and heard and felt. It crossed my mind that I might not ever enter that city again, and that I might soon leave it. There are moments when you know in your gut that near everything would change, and that there would be no returning, and that night was one of them. The moon was clearer, St. Charles Avenue was wider and emptier, the lights in the top of St. Louis's were sharper.

Sebastien didn't seem to notice. He looked relaxed, and even more with every knife he stowed away. It was only when we turned up toward the Bayou St. John and then down through Treme that I noticed that he had begun to grip his reins so tightly his hands glowed white in the dark. He didn't look scared. He looked to be punishing himself, trying to hurt himself. His eyes were narrowed, his mouth drew tight. But it was just a moment. Soon we had ridden up to a small house with bright light shooting through the cracks in its tight shutters. I heard music, shouts. He dismounted and told me to wait. He was relaxed again.

When he emerged through the bright doorway of the colored saloon, he was accompanied by three negroes who he pulled aside around the corner of the house. The heavy leaves of a banana tree hid them from sight. Sebastien talked directly to the oldest, a tall bald man with a gray beard. He bowed his head as he spoke, and finally the old man put his cracked and powerful hand on his shoulder as if to reassure him. It was all a mystery to me, but it weren't my business and I didn't get in the middle of it. When they were done talking the old man and the two others—a short, dark, powerful man with his sleeves rolled up nearly to his shoulders, and a dandy in a green suit who carried a cane—went off into the dark in three separate directions. Sebastien stood there for a moment watching them, took a big breath, and then returned to his mule. We rode on over to Esplanade and then down toward the Quarter, toward Rintrah's house.

"You ain't going to ask me who they were?" he said, sounding tired.

"No. All I care about is getting to Rintrah's safe."

"You got more cares than that, young one. And if you even come close to completing Hood's strange little mission, you will have those men to thank."

"Doubt it."

He laughed.

We rode straight up to Rintrah's house. There were no lookouts on the corners, no sentinels at the tops of the house. The gate was wide open. We rode straight through the porte cochere and into the courtyard, where we dismounted and tied up. There were no lights in the windows, no sounds except for the sound of water dripping to the pavement from the palms.

I looked up at the room I knew to be Rintrah's bedroom and when I looked back down I'd lost Sebastien. He had evaporated, taken up in the dark. I peered into the dark beneath the loggia but I saw nothing. I walked up against the wall and nearly broke my nose on his chin.

He didn't speak. I saw his eyes for a second in the starlight, and they were sickeningly wide, moving fast, taking in everything. His body was still, and in his hands he grasped two knives, one short and one long. He moved down the covered walk along the edge of the courtyard and made no sound, touching nothing. He opened a window and it made no sound. It should have squeaked, it should have rattled, but it was silent. I am a brave man, I think, but I will tell you that he scared me. He seemed more animal than man, and I wasn't sure he recognized me until he climbed through the window and, looking back, nodded at me to climb through after him.

We were in one of Rintrah's storage rooms. This one contained gunpowder stolen from Federal armories and corn liquor made upcountry. He walked between the barrels and the crates as if he'd been there before and knew it blind. I cracked my shins twice and nearly cried out before I remembered the knives. *Holy Mother, pray I will get my ass out of here safe.* It was my first spontaneous Catholic prayer. A mighty strange place for it, but there it is. *Pray for us sinners now, and in the hour of our death in the room packed to the ceiling with liquor and killing powder. Amen.*

The next few minutes went quick, and I only remember little things flashing by in the dark. Lines of wall sconces snuffed out in the hallways. Broken bottles in the corners. On the wall next to the stairs leading up to the second floor, the word *L'Monstre* drawn in wax with a woman's hand. Everywhere the air reeked of overripe fruits and broken jars of pickled onions and of meat left out in the air. I opened my mouth to speak, to tell Sebastien I thought the place had been abandoned, that something bad had happened, but just then he looked back and frowned and I knew to keep my mouth shut. I palmed the pistol in my pocket and brought it out. We went up the stairs, past the old curio cabinets on the landing, and farther up to the floor where Rintrah,

Hood, and Father Mike had once kept the dying.

Down the hallway to the left, at the very end, there was a light that snuck under a door, and from behind that door I could hear a fiddle. It was the only door that was closed. The rest, half a dozen doors, were open and shaking in the breeze that rushed and groaned from the open windows in each of the empty rooms. The wind talked, I was certain, but I didn't understand. That's what I remember, I ain't trying to explain it.

I knew the rooms were empty because Sebastien cautiously surveyed each of them, stepping in ready for a fight, looking around at the perfectly clean and empty rooms, every one of them freshly swept and mopped. I smelled ammonia.

We came to the last door, and now I could hear the fiddle and the sound of a man singing the words to that old gospel tune, the one about the wayfaring stranger. The voice was strained, low and then cracking high. Sebastien looked back at me like he was going to ask a question, and I just nodded. *Yeah, that's Rintrah.*

The door came open quick and silent and then I lost track of Sebastien. There was one candle and it got knocked over and snuffed out. I stood near the door, not knowing what to do. I should have stepped in and gotten some licks in for Rintrah, but I couldn't see them real good and, anyway, I was scared of those knives. Rintrah cursed and laughed, and soon the struggling was over. He was dead.

He was not dead. He said, "Boyo, how about you light that candle right there, some of these others, if you're just going to sit there like you shat your pants. Get some light on this here thing."

A box of matches hit me square on the chest, and I got about lighting the tapers. When the lights had glowed up and the room was filled with the orange flicker, I could see that Sebastien was sitting on a liquor crate behind Rintrah, and had his knife casually placed against the side of Rintrah's neck. Rintrah sat on the floor. In his right hand he held his fiddle, which had come apart at the neck and was only held together by the strings. Off to the side, near the little door to the attic, I saw a mop and a bucket and smelled the ammonia again. This room had also been scrubbed clean of everything except Rintrah, the crate, and that fiddle.

I saw Sebastien whispering fast and hard

into Rintrah's ear, what, I don't know. It made Rintrah slump even farther to the floor, but it also seemed to cheer him, whatever it was. Finally Sebastien let him go.

I'd have thought that Rintrah's business would be with Sebastien, but he turned on me first.

"What the hell took you so damned long? I been waiting here for two days. Fuck, Griffin, you'd take a week to put your pants on if you had your druthers. This is life-and-goddamn-death business, boy, you should have been quicker about it. It's almost too late now."

I wanted to sit down, I was so road tired, but I reckoned I might have to be ready to run so I stayed swaying on my feet. I remembered the pistol in my hand and made a show of putting it in my belt. Rintrah snorted and turned to Sebastien.

"That one's empty, right?"

"Of course." Sebastien grinned at me and kept his big knife pointed at Rintrah. He stuck the short knife in his sock.

"I could still beat your ass with it, little man," I said. Angry and embarrassed.

"Ah, you could try, but we got other business here."

He turned to Sebastien.

"You got the floor."

Sebastien leaned forward, always with the tip of that knife waving in the general vicinity of Rintrah's neck. Rintrah sat on the floor to his left.

"Where your men?"

"Gone. Been losing business, I ain't been paying, and then they got sick of looking for you all the time. Thought I'd gone crazy, losing control. They can go to Hell, I don't care. But the women left, too, and I take that sore hard."

"When did this happen?"

"Ever since young Eli here went and got himself a horse and went riding down into the wilderness near two days ago."

I must have looked shocked and outraged, because Rintrah held up his hand to me, as if to calm me.

"Now, boy, you ain't hard to follow, and it weren't hard to figure where you were going. You ain't the only one who been to the Cabildo to find out where this one had gone off to. But I couldn't get a single damned man to take off after you."

He turned to Sebastien.

"They thought I was out of my mind, and also, you might be happy to know, they were right scared of you. You've got a reputation, I'm sure you know. You ain't a human as far as they're concerned. They drew the line, they said they weren't going nowhere, and that's when I told them to get the hell out. So they're gone now. And the women, they were just frightened of me, I reckon. Frightened of you, too, Lemerle, and angry that I'd sent a young man like Eli off to die. They left, though they might come back if I change my ways." He spit on the floor, got up, walked to the mop, and cleaned it up before sitting back down again.

Off to die. That was news to me. Before I could get up and pistol-whip the bastard, Sebastien spoke up.

"How did you know I would come, that I would come here? Why did you send the boy?"

"He didn't send me. I ain't a boy."

Rintrah ignored me, kept his attention on Sebastien.

"If I hadn't suffered this mutiny, you *wouldn't* have come here. You'd be catfish feed right now," Rintrah said.

"Why send the boy at all?"

"He didn't . . ." They wouldn't listen to me.

"I respected the wishes of the General, that he wanted you to read that thing of his, and you wouldn't have done it if you thought you were going to get strung up afterward. But Eli's harmless. You read it, right?"

I sat down on the floor, ready to keep being humiliated. Fuckers.

"Yes, I read it."

"I reckoned that afterward you might get it into your head to come settle up with me, especially when you realized that the only reason you were still alive was because Hood had lied for you. You would have seen that I was going to get you now, and that there wasn't anything to stop me."

"Except mutiny."

"Except that."

"Now what?" Sebastien let his knife swing between his fingers like a pendulum on a fancy clock.

"I guess you end this, right now." Rintrah opened his arms wide, like a bird cooling itself, exposing his chest and his neck to Sebastien's knives. "I got nothing. I can't kill you with this here fiddle. I depended on the love of money for my strength, which I bought off a dozen big and stupid men who knew how to shoot and fight. They liked my money. Now I got none of either, no money and no power. So . . ."

"So why would I kill you now?"

This question flustered Rintrah, broke his thinking up. His mouth was moving but he had nothing to say. Sebastien continued.

"You can't hunt me down anymore, so why waste my time? Enough. No more talk of killing each other. I didn't come here to settle up with you, as you say, Monsieur Rintrah. I came here for another purpose, and you must help."

"Hell I will."

Sebastien's eyes fired up.

"You would leave Eli Griffin to his task alone?"

"To hell with his task. I don't give one shit about it. Stupidest fucking thing I ever heard." He looked straight at me. "You ain't never gone to get that book from Beauregard, I know because I had men who heard him talking about it. Hell, he's looking for *you*. He already found your rooms up there at Levi's, he's already got in and took him some *other* book. And some pile of pages I now hear you been writing. Since when, while I'm thinking about it, did you care one bit about books? And now you got them spilling out of your pockets and your rooms and your saddlebags. Shit. You're hopeless, son. If I ever thought I'd take you on permanent in my crew, that's over. Guess you a scholar now."

My face went red, and I didn't know whether to kick Rintrah in the throat or go running for my rooms right then. I got to my feet and sat back down and got back up again. I think Rintrah took pity on me, sorry he'd said what he'd said.

"She's fine, Eli. M. wasn't there. She's a smart, smart girl. Don't know where she is now, she disappeared into the street when she saw 'em coming. She's good at that, you know, looking like everybody in a crowd. She can take care of herself, don't worry about that."

I sat back down. I was despondent. Beauregard had made off with Anna Marie's ledgers, the thing she wanted Lydia, and now, I suppose, her children, to see. Another thing I'd screwed bad. I'd never get that back and, worse, they now knew all that I knew. I shouldn't have written a damned thing down.

Sebastien was surprised and confounded for the first time I could recall.

"What are these books? What do they know now?"

Rintrah looked at me and jerked his head toward Sebastien. "How the hell should I know?" he said. "The boy never told me about these other documents."

Now I had to do the explaining to the man with the knife.

"There's nothing of use to them in there, except that they know that I was looking for you, and that I know that it was Father Mike who was killed at the lottery. They know, most of all, that we're gone to try to get that war book from Beauregard, and that it's what Hood wanted. Beauregard didn't know that before. Shit."

Rintrah went over to the mop, wrung it out, and began to mop distractedly. Sebastien watched him close, and pulled out his second knife, the small one, which I assumed he could throw.

It was quiet in the room for a few minutes, just the sound of Sebastien tapping his knee with the flat of the big knife and Rintrah dragging his mop across the floor, *shhhhh shhhhhh shhhhhh thump shhhhh.*

I reckoned it was over, that Beauregard would have taken the war book and hid it away. I could see no reason for us going on anymore, though Sebastien didn't seem at all put out by the news. He stood up, which made Rintrah flinch a little, but all he did was pace.

He paced from the crate to the window and back. Finally he stopped and addressed us like we were in his squad.

"I would have liked to have helped Mr. Griffin on his mission, but this might be difficult now. Difficult, but maybe not impossible. When did they go through his rooms?"

"This afternoon. I had a man watching Eli's home."

"For what?" I nearly shouted.

"It doesn't matter," Sebastien said. "This is good news. They have not had much time to make a plan. Maybe the book is still there. I would guess that the book is not what worries them the most right now."

"Oh, and what then?" Rintrah mumbled, swirling his mop in the bucket.

"They realize that you, Eli, are one of the few people who understand that Father Mike was murdered, and that you have gone to talk to the only person who knows who murdered him. They will be uncertain about me, they were likely confused when I never showed up to kill Father Mike myself."

"What the hell are you talking about, goddammit? You were in on that too? Good God." Rintrah had dropped his mop and looked ready to leap on Sebastien, the knives be damned. "Why do you kill the only people I give a damn about?"

"I didn't kill Father Mike, as Eli will tell you. I have a debt to Father Mike that now, now that I realize what has happened, must be paid in blood. I would not have killed him, but I will kill for him."

"What is that rot?"

Sebastien cinched up his belt and pulled his coat around him. "We have many reasons to go to the Beauregard house, and we must do it tonight. Now. Eli has his mission, and I have mine."

"I have none." Rintrah, stubborn, tears in his eyes.

"You have one too."

"What?"

"I think it will become apparent to you if all goes well. And dammit, Rintrah, you're the only man in New Orleans I was ever afraid of crossing, quit your whining like a woman. You've got interests here. Hood was your friend. He was not my friend. Father Mike was not my friend, either, but he was yours. And Paschal would have been outraged to see you like this."

"The hell you say. You got no right to talk about Paschal like you knew him."

"I did know him. Now get the hell up and let's get some real pistols. Do you still know how to get in a second story? You were a burglar once, no? Your money didn't appear out of nowhere. You can break in?"

"I can." Rintrah looked at me sideways, checking to see if I'd caught the mention of his previous occupation. I made a face at him.

"Then bring your ropes."

Sebastien walked out of the room and down the hallway. I followed behind Rintrah, who never stopped clenching his fists but marched on anyway.

We got into the house easy enough. At the back entrance, behind the courtyard, the gate had been left open. Inside, in the portico, two men lay bound, gagged, and tied to each other. One was unconscious, the other was starting to stir. They'd been gagged hard with twisted pieces of burlap. Blood ran down their heads and into their ears. Sebastien didn't barely look at them. Rintrah looked down and whistled appreciatively.

Later I would be on the roof, among the gables and dormers, slipping on the slate tiles. From there I would see three sets of bound and trussed men, the two men we'd seen on the way in, and a pair each at the two front entrances, all of them pulled into the shadows. These were big men, big white Creole men, and it was amusing to watch them roll around on the ground like potato bugs. They'd been tied up good. In fact, the whole house had been prepared for our arrival. Lights in the courtyard had been doused, the servants' quarters cleared out. In an empty cistern in the back corner of the courtyard lay two long pistols.

"This one is for you," Sebastien had said to Rintrah. Rintrah had looked at him in surprise, but nodded his head.

"And this one, for Mr. Eli Griffin," Sebastien said, handing me the other. "It's loaded this time."

"Well, thank you for that, mister."

"Don't shoot yourself."

"Go to Hell."

Later, from my perch on the roof, I saw three men in the distance, slipping in and out of the shadows on street corners surrounding the block. They stopped people walking down the street and told them to move on. White and black, man and woman. No one got past them, and no one challenged them either. Now I knew why we'd stopped to see the three negroes. One of the men, the old man, looked up at me and saluted.

It was Rintrah who had sent me up onto the roof as a lookout. I'd climbed the water-spouts in the corner, tied a rope around one of the chimneys, and thrown it back down to Rintrah and Sebastien on the ground. Sebastien climbed using every ledge and uneven brick and crack in the masonry to ascend, only rarely putting his weight on the rope. I had the pistol in my pants so I could hold on to the roof with both hands. Rintrah struggled with a long thin wire and tried to flip the inside latch on the window. Finally he got in and stuck his head back out to signal Sebastien up.

Sebastien had disappeared. I hadn't seen him go. Rintrah craned his neck up at me, or up at the moon, or some such, and hissed, "We're getting cocked up good on this one. Son of a bitch, he's going to have us killed, you watch. Lying bastard."

I didn't intend to watch. If it came to it, I reckoned I'd run across the roof and slide down one of the far waterspouts and out into the dark city before anyone could catch me. I was invincible up there on that roof, above everything, even the mist coming off the river.

The roof was dirty and the soot came off in my hands like chunks of earth, but even so I felt clean like a man whose got a second chance, like someone who's a new man. I would be leaving the city soon.

I sat up there like a cat for a long time. One hour by the bells. I kept looking for Rintrah, and listening for his whisper, but there was nothing.

I could see over to Rintrah's house, through the forest of lightning rods and vents and chimneys. During that hour I watched it, close. I imagined I could almost see the hearses moving in and out, the men pulling out the crates of liquor, the negroes climbing in to make their escape from the plague. I imagined that attic room where Paschal had lived his last days and died. I wondered if the bed was still there. There had been so much going on behind my back, out of my sight. Mystery on mystery, secret behind secret. It was too much, I wanted to be gone.

A fire broke out in Rintrah's courtyard. Not a big fire, but big enough to send up a column of dense black smoke. I remembered the horses, and nearly slid back down to the ground, but I didn't dare. There was too much at stake to leave Rintrah behind. Had I been thinking straight, nothing would have stopped me from getting back to Rintrah's house. But I was thinking like a man above everything, someone who'd got others to do his dirty work. I was half asleep. Fifteen minutes later I understood the mistake I'd made.

An ugly man with a yellow feather in his hat ran into the courtyard as if being chased by hellhounds. I recognized him instantly, though I'd never seen him with my own eyes. I saw Hood's eyes, in that box above the lottery, looking down on the floor as they dragged off the dead and as a man with a yellow feather in his hat hurried away from the scene. I saw him through Anna Marie's eyes, having his drink in the café, watching the old men whisper about him. *Hector, the negro killer.* I felt Anna Marie's hate then, just as real as my own.

He looked behind him, in front of him, below him, whipping around like a man battling unseen things, ghosts. He even looked up, and I don't know if he saw me or not. If he did, he didn't care. He should have looked again to the top of the garden wall before he tried to run for the back door of the house. There, crouching, appeared Sebastien Lemerle, his hands full of knives.

Sebastien leaped to the ground in front of Hector, cutting him off. Hector's ruined, pocked face glistened. He pulled a pistol out of his coat pocket and began to raise it. Sebastien calmly threw a knife ten feet and buried it in Hector's right shoulder. Hector groaned but did not scream. He tried to raise the pistol again, but when he did he dropped the weapon. He bent to retrieve it and as he did so Sebastien moved quickly behind him and bound him in his arms. From a distance it was an embrace as if between lovers. I could see Sebastien whispering in Hector's ear, and Hector shaking his head, *no, no, no, no*. He was crying, he was praying. Sebastien reached down and inserted his knife and ripped at the back of his leg roughly, hobbling it. This time Hector screamed the scream of hellfire, like he was burning up. Sebastien shushed him and patted his head, but the screaming would not stop. A lamp was lit on the second floor at the other end of the wing Rintrah had disappeared into nearly an hour before. I saw a figure in the window looking down.

Sebastien hobbled the man's other leg. Hector screamed like a beast tumbling over a cliff. He fell to his knees and Sebastien walked around to face him. He kneeled down and held Hector's chin in hand. He looked straight into the man's eyes, and then leaned forward as if to kiss him. When he pulled back, Hector had no nose. Sebastien spit something into the yucca plants that lined the courtyard. He stood up and Hector fell over, now screaming without sound. Sebastien walked over to the wall that he'd come over, reached up, and pulled down a smoldering thing he slung over his shoulder, sending black ashes lighter than air up toward me. He threw the thing down in front of Hector, and I recognized it as my saddlebag. *The fire. It was in the fire.* I nearly slipped from the roof, but held on to the near chimney. Sebastien crouched in front of Hector, who had swallowed some of his pain and had quit screaming. Sebastien asked him something, and Hector nodded. Sebastien stood up, looked around at the roofs until he saw me. He called up to me in a voice that was deep and full of gravel, a voice I didn't recognize. "I'm sorry," he said. Then he turned back to Hector.

The Hood book had been in that saddlebag.

Sebastien lifted Hector from the ground and made him kneel. He ran the knife across the top of his forehead, sending blood spilling down Hector's face, and prepared to peel the scalp back. Then the figure in the window called out.

"That's enough, Sebastien. Bring him in. I have a friend of yours up here who would like to say hello before he dies."

"I've got no friends, monsieur." Not startled at all.

"Bring him up here." Calm and cold.

Sebastien glanced quickly at me and then, probably realizing he was giving me away, looked up all the way at the sky and rolled his eyes dramatically, covering for me. He hauled Hector up under his shoulders and dragged him up the back steps and through the door, disappearing into the dark house.

In the courtyard my saddlebag still smoldered. *The book. The book.*

I took hold of the rope around the chimney and swung down and into the open window Rintrah had used. I walked through the room, which was a woman's dressing chamber, and into the thick carpeted hallway. I walked down toward the light, to my reckoning. I had failed. I pulled the pistol out and held it in front of me as if it could light my way.

They were in Beauregard's library. Through a crack in the door that led onto the hallway—there were three doors that opened into the room, which was at the heart of the house—I saw a thin, slight, black-eyed man dusting ash from his crisp-pressed sleeve before tossing the last sheets of a pile of paper into the fireplace. In his other hand he held a pearl-handled revolver pointed at Rintrah, who slumped in one of Beauregard's horsehair chairs, angry and humiliated. I recognized the paper the man tossed into the fire. It was the scrap paper I'd used to write my own words down. The last of Anna Marie's ledger books turned orange and green and blue in the fire. Rintrah watched it, his face sagged with sadness and horror.

I could see the door from the back hallway across the room, and as I watched it was flung open and Hector flopped into the room at the prissy man's feet. He was barely conscious, and he looked up at his master as if he wished to be put down.

"The blood on the rug will cost you, Sebastien!" the man called out. "And when I tell General Beauregard who perpetrated this atrocity, he will have your head."

He paused, listened.

"Who else is out there? Is the idiot Griffin out there? Are you listening, idiot Griffin?

Would you like to know why I have kept your little friend alive? This abomination, this freak? Hmmm?"

He kicked Rintrah in the stomach and I heard the *uumph* as the air went out of Rintrah. He slowly brought his eyes back to his attacker, looking up through his hooded eyelids.

"My name is Jean Dauphin, and this man tried to steal from me. Sebastien! Do you mourn the death of the priest, Father Michel? This is the man responsible. Listen to me, Sebastien. This is the man who bribed the blind boys at my lottery. My. Lottery. This is the man who got a priest, peace be upon him, to play his role in the swindle, the role that got him killed. This is the man, Sebastien, not me."

Then I saw it, for the first time. The lottery man, Monsieur Dauphin, who had the gall to try to enlist Hood in the lottery racket, who had turned Generals Beauregard and Early into his dancing puppets, this man of great wealth and resource was *scared*. His hand shook, his eyes swung from door to door to door, waiting for them to open again. Hector groveled at his feet and he did not notice.

"Should I have let them steal three hundred thousand dollars from me, Sebastien? Would that have been right? Is it my fault that this dwarf thought that there would be honor among the accursed, and that the blind boys would have loyalty to a half-man? They sold him out! They came and told me about the fix just as soon as he arranged it. He should have known better! Sebastien!"

I was pushing the door open then, ready to fire my pistol, when a set of big hands wrapped themselves around my neck and lifted me off the ground. Beauregard's big butler, the one who had chased me out the last time I was in the house. He smashed my head against the wall in the dark, and I saw bright lights on the inside of my eyelids. He laughed a big belly laugh and called out, "I've got that killer right here, he ain't nothing much, sir," he called out. "He look familiar."

"Good, good!" I could hear the sound of relief in Dauphin's voice.

I was tossed to the ground and I was preparing to be beaten when I heard a great gurgling, and then the butler fell on me. Something hot and wet ran over my chest where his head lay. A hand helped me up. I couldn't see. I leaned against the wall and felt Sebastien's dry hands against my cheek.

"More to do, *mon frère*. Come on."

He went through the door first, and I

followed. Dauphin tried to turn and fire but Sebastien was on him quick and took the pistol right out of his hand and whipped him with it. Dauphin sat down in Beauregard's chair with a thump, dazed. Sebastien turned the pistol on Dauphin and pulled a second from his pocket. This one he turned on Rintrah, who had leaped from his seat with a big smile on his face.

"Sit back down, little man."

"What is this?" Rintrah shouted, his face red and puffing.

"Sit. Down."

Rintrah sat. Sebastien turned to me.

"Put your pistol on the desk there, next to the dwarf's."

I'd forgotten I even had it. I was dazed, I was happy to give over control to someone else. I put the pistol on the desk.

"You *are* an idiot, Griffin," Rintrah muttered.

Now the only person in the room who was armed was Sebastien. He pushed the oily hanks of his long black hair behind his ear and considered all of us. He lingered on me.

"I thought we would be in time to save the books, but I miscalculated. I am sorry, Eli. And I wasn't able to track down Hector until it was too late. The fire burned very fast. I am sorry."

He turned to Hector.

"You killed a priest. You killed a priest who saved my life. He is owed, as I'm sure you understand."

Hector looked up at him with tired eyes. He was already dying, his skin had turned white and he was shivering. The carpet had turned red beneath him. He nodded his head and turned away from the apparition with the guns. Sebastien stepped over to him and fired one shot into his ear and Hector was still. I coughed up everything I'd eaten since the day before. There was too much blood, I had seen too much killing. It would never stop.

Sebastien had everything planned perfectly. I wonder now when he devised his plan. Was it after he left us scaling the house? Was it on our ride into town? Was it when Danielle kissed him before going inside their rambling little shack? Or had he been planning it much longer? He might have been making that plan, or something like it, since that day in Texas when he put the knife to his first Comanche. Whenever it happened, he accomplished something extraordinary that night: he stopped the bloody violent cascade of hate and violence that he and Hood had set in motion so many years ago. I remember what Hood wrote, I remembered it even clearer after it had been burned. He'd asked himself if the events of the last two years had been a result of the howl they'd let loose in that Comanche camp, whether the plague and the failures and the murders were the howl itself, which one of them would have to silence. I don't know about that, I don't know how God works. God is beyond my understanding, as the priests like to say. I know this: it was Sebastien and Sebastien alone who knew what his atonement would be and stood up to meet it.

He put down the little pistol of Dauphin's and emptied the other pistol, the big pistol, of all but one round. He tossed the other bullets around the room where they rolled up under couches and rested against dusty books. He did the same with the other guns. He closed his pistol again, checked to make sure the bullet was chambered properly, and cocked the hammer.

"Now," he said, looking at Dauphin, who had just come to his senses after his pistol-whipping. "You, Dauphin, you get up."

"You will be found if you kill me."

"Tell them how we know each other."

"I've never met . . ."

"Tell them!"

Dauphin let his head slump, defeated. He mumbled.

"I will not be held responsible for this."

"Speak." Sebastien said it quietly, almost tenderly, all the time with the pistol drawn on the old con man, the lottery commissioner.

"I hired you to kill Rintrah and Father Michel."

"Who else did you hire?"

"Hector, that man there."

"And who killed Father Michel?"

"Hector."

"And where was I?"

"I don't know."

"I was far, far away on a bayou, thinking I was done with killing. I was wrong about that, no?"

"Obviously."

"I am done with it now."

Dauphin looked elated and puzzled at the same time. Rintrah and I were still too scared of Sebastien to move.

Sebastien turned the pistol around and held it by the barrel. I held my breath.

"You invited me up here to say good-bye

to my friend before he died, so"—he turned to Rintrah—"good-bye. I am truly sorry about your friends, and I hope you will someday forgive me for what I did to your friend Paschal. I must atone for that, I hope I know how. Perhaps someday Mr. Eli Griffin will tell you the whole story of Paschal and me."

Rintrah grimaced and told him to go fuck himself, that he'd never forget him, and that he was a coward for letting Dauphin, the goddamn fop, do his killing for him. Sebastien nodded his head and turned back to Dauphin.

"So, here is the pistol, you may kill the man who would have taken your money if you'd given him the chance. Now you can finish the job. But consider this, my friend. I will be standing here, five feet from you, and if you do choose to use your one and only bullet on Rintrah, I will close those five feet and cut you from ear to ear. If Rintrah dies, you die. Very simple, yes?"

Silence in the room. No one moved.

"However, if you choose to turn your pistol on me, you will walk away."

More silence.

"To put it more simply, I want to trade for Rintrah's life, and I will not give you much of a choice. How much is it worth to you to kill a man who would have merely taken money from you? How much is your life worth? Now, here it is."

He handed the pistol to Dauphin, butt first, and took one step backward. He pulled a giant knife from his coat and stood there with it at the ready.

Dauphin looked confused at first, and held the pistol like it was a turtle that had just appeared in his hand. Slowly his fingers wrapped around the butt and he held it halfway up.

"I want to ask Rintrah a question."

"You may," Sebastien said, watching him close.

"Was it worth it, Rintrah? Was all that money worth it? Why would you do such a thing?"

Rintrah stood stock-still off to Dauphin's right.

"We did it for the Hoods. We'd made them poor when they should have been rich. And there's no shame in grifting a grifter, whatever you say."

Dauphin turned to me.

"And you? All this running around and exposing of secrets that should have been buried and left buried? Futile! Beauregard is away because he is arranging to have Hood's book on his war experiences published, and

everything else has been destroyed. Beauregard knows nothing about any of this, nor
will he ever know anything about it. While
you're here, he's sending Hood's children, the
orphans, to homes around the country. He's
splitting them up, they may never see each
other again. What do you think of that? I suppose you haven't thought of it. No, you're standing here. You had to keep asking questions.
How many people will die because of your
goddamn curiosity? Why did you persist?"

I was too tired and too sad to say anything
else right then.

"I did it for Hood, too."

He turned, finally, to Sebastien.

"And why would you come back here? Why
did you care about these people? You don't
care about anyone, you're a monster. Why
these people?"

Sebastien closed his eyes.

"Because Hood would have wanted it."

The bullet made a neat hole in Sebastien's
forehead and he fell back. I caught him before
he hit the floor and laid him down softly.

CHAPTER 27

John Bell Hood

I wish I had more time. I wish I had more time with her. I wish I had been good to her. I changed, we changed, the poorhouse was warm and full, full of children and talk and humility. But how will it be now, she is nearly out of her mind in the other room, and I can no longer talk to her. I change the sheets, I wipe the sweat from her brow. She holds my hand, my good hand, and that's all we have left.

It is a cursed fate. I am cursed. The Lord works in mysterious, brutal ways. How is it that we could come to know each other again, or perhaps even for the first time, truly, and yet have only a year to live with that knowledge and to be guided by it, bound by it. Was that all there was, was that all we get in this life? Brief happiness interrupting the woe and grief? It feels this way now. I must fight the bitterness, the hate. I feel it welling up in me, I want to strike out. I want to track down Father Mike and drag him back to this city to tell me what I am to make of *this,* my love and his friend, dying with eleven children in the house. Eleven children who I watch all day walking by her door, peeking in and running off. They are quiet and dutiful and scared. What, Father Mike, does your missal have to say about this? Coward, he has run off and I shall not forgive him. He promised me he would remind me of my obligation to God, but what of God's obligation to me? Has He none? I want Father Mike to answer that question for me.

I must reject the bitterness. I am scaring the children myself. I stomp from window to door, window to door, all day muttering to myself. I have thrown open the window so that Anna Marie might smell the jasmine and sweet olive, the old roses that have gone to rambling across the yard. When she holds my hand it is still soft, though also hot and dry now. I should put down this pen and lie beside her so that she will know she is not alone. I shall.

I left the lottery thinking we would have to move on, that I would have to pack up Anna Marie and the children and march on up to Kentucky where we could throw ourselves on the mercy of my family. Anna Marie's family had nearly disappeared. Her father was dead, her mother lived far away around the lake, her cousins had apparently disappeared. We would farm, I knew how to farm. I could make a crop of tobacco, or corn, we could raise hogs. I thought that Anna Marie would make a good farmwife. It amused me to imagine her learning to slop hogs and prime tobacco, I saw her in her Creole best tiptoeing around the hog pen and it made me laugh. But I knew that she would adapt and flourish. She was always less of the flower than I had at first thought, not so delicate as I had imagined. I had to learn this, and I had. I have made no money, what we've had I've borrowed from my family and some of my army colleagues, and ten years ago this would have shamed me. I suppose I should still be ashamed, but

I'm not. If it is for the benefit of Anna Marie and the eleven blessed children, I don't care what it is or what it says about me. It is an odd realization, to know that the right life is one lived without concern for worldly reputation or success, one that is subordinated to anything good. And my family, my family is good.

In quiet moments, when I am not so bitter, I wish Father Mike was here so that I could tell him this. I've learned humility, not the worldly kind but the kind that causes a man to pale before God. That is what happened to me when I walked out of that lottery building. I fell before God and gave Him my will. And He gave me peace.

The funeral was quick. I invited almost no one. I saw Eli in the trees but I would not acknowledge him. I had only known him when Anna Marie was alive, and now that she was gone everything was new and threatening. He was a stranger now, a stranger from another place. I was overcome, obviously.

I had sent the children away, and so they didn't see their mother laid to rest. All the children except Lydia. She had refused. She was tired, she said, and she worried about me, and when I put her on the carriage to her grandmother's with the other children she screamed and would not quit screaming until I lifted her back down and took her inside the house.

I had no words, no tongue for speech. There is a spot on the ground next to her for me. There were no eulogies at my insistence. I wanted the funeral to be quick, for every moment that she lay between resting places was a moment of agony for me, and I thought I might be swallowed up by the hole that had been opened up between the living and the dead by my wife, my friend. At her family's insistence, we gathered back at the house in the yard after the Mass and burial. I didn't speak to a soul, and soon they left me. I went inside and made camp stew for Lydia and we ate it on our laps in the living room, the dining room being too empty and dark.

Lydia had grown much in the last year, and even at twelve years old she had already developed laugh lines at the edges of her eyes. This last year she had learned to take care of the children and to clean and to hoe vegetables. She wore her hair up loosely like a working woman, and her arms had become brown and freckled. She was our daughter and our helper. She dusted, she cooked, she cleaned the young ones, and at slow moments of the day she stood out on the front porch, in full view of the passing menagerie: the men and their ladies strolling past us whispering and hiding their faces behind hats and fans, the silly Mussons up the street who spoke only in French when within our hearing and who gaped at us like we were caged things. She stood up in front of all of them and, hell, she looked *proud,* dauntless, as if daring any one of them to say anything to her. To any of us, for that matter. She flapped her apron out at the yard, flinging the crumbs and dust away and looking as if she were shooing the world off, too. She was tough, boy, and I believe she got that from her mother. She didn't care what people thought, as her mother hadn't, at least after a while. I myself have only recently learned to ignore the opinions of others, and now it is too late.

I hate these two words, I loathe them: *Lydia was.* She is in the next room, and we are both coming to the end. I've already begun to think of her as someone gone. I prefer to think of the past and not this terrible present. I cannot help my girl. You, whoever is reading this, must understand: I loved all of our children

ferociously, but Lydia was special. She had
been the first, the first perfect child born to
a father so entirely imperfect that he'd forgotten what a sinless being looked like. And there
she was, on her mother's breast, eyes closed
lightly, her cheeks pillowed, her nose gently
flaring with each soft breath. I will admit that
I fell in love with my daughter. She was part
of me, like a new limb. Something good. It
is all the more horrifying, then, that I spent
so many of her years occupied with my business, my reputation, my *own* life, as if I had
one separate from hers, while she was living
hers here in this house and wondering where
her father had gone. And now we are going
together, and she is down the hall and does
not recognize me anymore.

I have decided that I must give this to Eli.
He is the only one who will understand these
pages. He has suffered loss at my hand, and
now I am doing the same, and also at my own
hand. We are bound by that, I suppose. He
would have every reason to take these pages
and burn them as soon as I am gone, but I
think that he won't. He is a better man than
I was long ago, when I would have burned
them without hesitation. I shall ask him to
take these pages and make them known. The

other book, the book of infernal war, will have to be destroyed, of course. They are incompatible now, they do not share the same author. I am a different man. He will have to go see Beauregard. I must send for him now.

I suppose I should pay him something for this, some compensation, I cannot just load him with these burdens as if he is obliged to me. He will not want money, though he needs it as badly as we do. He is proud and stubborn and, most of all, averse to indenture. He will not want to owe me anything, and this is how I will get him to come, to take these burdens. I will tell him that he owes me. For what? For trying to take my life. Only *trying,* and barely. Still, he waylaid me like a common thief and put the knife to my throat, and I can use this. He owes me nothing for that, and if I had been in his position I would have finished the job and not shown mercy. But I will tell him that he must make amends, because he is proud and he will hate that he might be indebted to me.

Perhaps he would come of his own accord. Perhaps I am underestimating him. I have made this mistake many times. I lack faith, Lord. And anyway, what shall I give him as compensation? What indeed. I shall tell him a truth.

*　　*　　*

Though Eli has never told me, I know what happened to him back in Franklin. To him, and to his sister and her infant child, and to his sister's gallant but foolhardy beau, and to his father. Between letters to former commanders and colleagues, between the endless tracing of maps, I found time to investigate the mystery of one Eli Griffin, orphan.

He was a boy when our army marched up from Spring Hill, Tennessee, and toward Franklin, heading straight up the pike not knowing we were condemned men marching to our doom. Near what would become the battlefield we passed several small farms on either side of the pike. We had seen hundreds, perhaps thousands of such farms during the war, but these would be among the last. They were like so many of the rest, homesteads centered on small square houses and dotted with gray outbuildings spilling with half-starved chickens and hogs and rotting grain and old plows polished to gleaming. One of them was the Griffin homestead, though I don't know which. I can remember the farms, though, and thinking that I had come to defend them, when in fact I would destroy them.

I have great faith in my own power, do I not? *I would destroy them*. But I was no god, no destroyer of worlds, hurler of thunderbolts. I was just a man who, for the moment, other men would obey. We all destroyed the Griffin family, I was only the first among many.

Eli's mother had died years before. His sister, Becky, had become something like a mother to him. I know this from an old woman who has buried the dead, my men, in her own yard and given them numbers and obsessively walks the cemetery as if she were the keeper of Heaven and Hell, ticking off the numbers of the souls. I have forgotten her name. In her letter she told me she had sheltered Eli for a time, but that finally he had run off. She asked me rather plaintively if I had seen him, if he was ever coming home to Tennessee. I never wrote back, which was cruel.

He is a delicate boy, however he appears. At least, that is how I remember him. If you see him, or hear of him, please be kind. He has not been treated well by this life, General Hood.

Eli's sister died in childbirth, carrying the child of one of my officers. He was a young adjutant, I have gathered from the old woman. That was all she would tell me, and so I have no idea who he was, only that he died with the colors in his hand, flapping in the cannon smoke in an impossible charge on a frightful battlefield of my choosing. I wonder if he even knew he was to be a father. He wore my uniform, he had no doubt, as adjutant, handled messages from me to his commander. He had seen my handwriting, my name, on the orders that sent them charging off to die. Where there had been three souls, a mother and father and child, there were soon none. The sister died in childbirth, the old woman said, but she always thought it was heartbreak.

Soon afterward Eli's father disappeared. I wonder if he is dead too. Or one of the wanderers who live by the river bridges and meander from town to town, waiting out this life among the ruins of war. Such men were a common sight in the southern lands.

Eli became an orphan. I made orphans, that was my occupation. I confess it, and will confess it to Eli if he ever gets here. One of the thousands, I assume. If I pass on, if I get ill, too, there will be ten more orphans. It will have been my life's work! My tombstone shall read, *He stole their parents.* They do not tell you this at West Point. They teach you to form lines, to skirmish, to properly set the deflection and elevation on a cannon, to ride, to dig entrenchments, to properly supply a company.

They do not teach you that there will be others on the battlefield who have never studied such things and don't know they exist, that these people might have lived their lives quite happily never knowing what a cannon sounded like, or the buzz of a tumbling ball shot out the end of a rifle.

I know what Eli saw the next day. I watched the boys venture out onto the battlefield, slow and amazed, and I assume that Eli was one of them. It is always the boys who go where they shouldn't, who see what they later wish they hadn't. I was there the morning after the battle. I woke up to the smoke of smoldering barns and the queer drapery of a thin snow laid on the gouged and torn red earth. I saw it and I didn't think much of what I saw on that field, having seen it before. Now I see it through new eyes that have of late, so late, recognized suffering as the corrupt and permanent condition of man, something inescapable and best faced square on, for in suffering is life, and its denial is a kind of death.

Or perhaps these are the eyes of Eli Griffin. Suppose they are one and the same.

The ground was red not because of the clay, but because of the blood. It had run in rivers, as if it had been prophesied in Scripture, and perhaps it was. The dead lay on the field as if they'd fallen from a great height. Here they had clung to each other as they plummeted to earth, and they were piled limb upon limb. Over there they had struck out on their own and fallen atop themselves, split and twisted and frozen. Thousands of men lay there, having suffered every kind of grievous wound, most too horrible to conjure into memory, even more than a decade on. I shall see those faces again, I am sure: the men without jaws, without noses, with only half a head. I shall see the shattered bones and the swollen flesh. I am not afraid, I welcome my penance.

We were about to ride out, on the tracks of General Schofield's Union Army, on our way to our final destruction at Nashville. I must have known that it would be the end of us, but I refused to act accordingly. It was better to be destroyed than to be weak. I couldn't see the contradiction.

I paused there on my horse while my staff began to ride ahead, their heads shrouded against the cold and the lingering snow, my cowled and stooped monks. I am certain they thought me half out of my mind on laudanum when I stopped. I bent my head and swayed in the saddle, I'm certain

I looked drunk, but I was only momentarily consumed with pain. My leg burned, as it often did, and the only way I knew to make the pain pass was to disappear into it quietly, to keep still and suffer. I did not take laudanum, that is the honest to God truth, whatever the gossips said. Now I wish that I *had* taken the cure, if I had to suffer the rumors anyway. *Hood must have been out of his mind on the tincture, or he'd have never charged that town like that.* I wish I'd had that excuse.

I swayed in the saddle and closed my eyes, concentrating on the pain. Horses could always sense that pain and it frightened them. This time the horse fidgeted around in a half circle until, when I'd opened my eyes, I was looking straight into the eyes of a young blond boy, not one hundred feet off, who was staring at me. Or, rather, at the scene at the feet of my horse. There below me ran the entrenchment the Union had dug, against which my men had flung themselves. Now it had been filled with the butternut brown and the gray of the Confederate Army, an open grave, a human abattoir. I remember thinking, *Good, he is seeing our sacrifice, the evidence of our great courage.* Fool.

Now I realize what I saw in *his* eyes: he saw a devil on his black horse, mutilated and fire-eyed, possessed and under the command of Satan himself, towering over the spoils of five thousand souls. The other boys walked slowly across the battlefield, daring each other to look. One by one they broke away and ran into the town and disappeared without a word. But the blond boy, he would not move. I believe he was waiting for me to take him too. I nearly called out to him, but there was fear upon him and it gave me strength. But I know now that fear was only part of what I saw in that boy. Had I known to look for it, I would have seen hate and shock and the melancholy of knowing he could no longer be a child, now that he had seen what men could do to men. I rode off.

I want Eli's forgiveness. Who was that boy? I don't know, it could have been any boy, and thus I had decided that it was Eli. In Eli I can find forgiveness. I want to tell Eli that now, or if I had been the man then that I am now, I would have dismounted and held out my hand to him, that I would have taken him home to his father and to his sister, and that I would have protected them. I would have changed his fate, I would have provided for that boy, the only living thing on that field that morning. I would have done it, Eli, I would have done it.

He will see. I will send him to see my other creation, not an orphan but a killer. Sebastien. The killer and the orphan, the Janus face of my life's work. I have made peace with them separately, but now it is time for them to meet.

I am wasting time. My memory will not submit, it plays across fields I'd rather forget even as I struggle to remember when, precisely, I knew I had fallen back in love with my wife, when I became undeniably happy. It was not so long ago. It was only months ago. Or I suppose it's possible that I never fell out of love with her, I merely forgot about her. And now her memory recedes and I wish I would die and be free to catch up with her, wherever she's gone. I want to remember the great moments, the crucial moments, but the thing that keeps coming to my mind again and again and again is something of such little significance! It is a trifle, and yet it insists that I remember.

We had dismissed the last of the servants, and the children were, by and large, in their beds. Those who weren't pretended to be asleep, anyway, which was good enough. There was quiet. I sat in one of the parlor chairs and I could feel that pain coming on again, the pain in my leg that I had felt on the battlefield that snowy morning, the same pain of the saw and the knife even now, so many years after I'd lain upon that surgeon's table. I closed my eyes. I swayed in my seat. I saw explosions of red and yellow behind my eyelids and I bore down harder on them until I could trace the veins. I let my head rock back against the chair back and could feel every raised thread in the cushion scratch against me. I became painfully aware of everything, even the weight of the ashes blowing gently out of the fireplace on soft hot breezes slipping through a crack in the flue. And then I felt her hands on me, first at the top of my boot. She pulled it off, the boot on my real foot, and the sock too. I opened my eyes. She sat on her knees and massaged the bottom of my foot, the inside of my foot, the hard tendons and bones and ligaments, until I could feel coolness and calm that moved through me and scattered the pain in my other leg. She held my foot close to her, she leaned her head against my knee. I thought about it and told myself no. Then I silently cursed my cowardice and reached out with my hand and rested it on her head. I sifted the black and silky hair through my fingers. She closed her eyes. And there we sat until it was dark.

She didn't think I was drunk. She didn't think I was light-headed on laudanum. She wasn't afraid of me. She only knew that I was in pain, and that she could make it subside. She knew without my telling her. It seemed at that moment that she had always known me. No, that's not it. It seemed that she had always *loved* me. And instantly I thought, *I've always loved her.* I don't know by what magic this happens, but it seemed just then that between us, between lover and loved, there was something that had always existed, something sacrificial and nourishing and perfect. Love. That is to say, God. I knew God then and for the first time. Afterward He was everywhere, and especially with Anna Marie. In her I found rest, and through her I spoke to God.

I think that is all I ever needed to say. But now I must say this: Lord, save Lydia. Lord, have mercy on Lydia. Lord, take me instead.

I am tired.

CHAPTER 28

Eli Griffin

If you are reading this, you are obviously aware that Anna Marie's ledgers and my own scribblings survived the next two hours. You also might know that I was not able to get the war book back from Beauregard. As Hood's official literary executioner, exector, I'm not sure of the term, he got the thing published. It's called *Advance and Retreat,* which Beauregard had published the next year, in 1880, to benefit the Hood Memorial Fund. That's the outfit that prints up all them postcards with the photograph of the Hood Orphans—John Junior and the eight others—looking so sad and lonely in that dark and dusty room. God knows where they made that photograph, or when they made it. It sure has been a moneymaker for the fund, though, hasn't it? I'd bet a week of suppers and my left arm that you'd give up some cash money if you got one of those postcards, or saw one of those posters. You'd have to have a hard heart to turn your back on them. They're looking at you, and their parents are dead, and so are their oldest and youngest sisters, and they're alone, alone, alone! They don't tell you that Beauregard had them all split up in every direction, to Texas and Maryland and Kentucky and New York and all over the place. No, in the picture they're all there, together, waiting for you to help them. Oh, well, hell, ain't nothing to be done about that now.

But Hood's real book, the book he wanted me to get published? Well, here it is. Too late to change the story of John Bell Hood, but I kept my word. Hood has been remembered as the stubborn man, the willful man, the foolish man, the self-righteous man, the immodest man. The incompetent commander. The drug addict. The cripple. Nothing's going to change that now. I wonder, though, if that was ever what Hood wanted. I'm not sure he cared at the end about changing that reputation for all the rest of you. At the end I think he only cared about what his friends and his children thought, what they knew about him and Anna Marie. He succeeded at that, at least. But I often wonder what might have happened had we got ourselves up into the Beauregard mansion and found that damned book and taken it away for burning. I wonder how things might be different had this book been the one published, and not that one. I wonder whether anyone would have believed it. Do folks want their generals to be the kind of men who write about their families, their children, as if there was nothing else in the world? Do they want to remember their generals as flesh-and-blood sinners like the rest of us, capable of regret and of change? I don't think we want that from them. I think we want them to be gods in an American mythology, unchanging creatures who are purely what they seem to be, and different from the rest of us. Because if they aren't different, if they are like us, then what the hell are we capable of? These are the gods of war, able to bring destruction and stride across the fields of dead like they were walking through wheat fields, reaping their crop. They can't be like us, or we are more terrible than we think.

I woke the next morning to the sounds of the wharf rousing itself, the shouts of the jobbers and foremen, the smells of the sugarcane, the rumble of the great cotton press. M. lay beside me, so pretty and untroubled. The sun through the window cast shadows on her face, highlighted her cheeks and her eyes. She had said nothing to me when I arrived home, nothing about the blood on my clothes, nothing about the men who had ransacked the place and left it wrecked, nothing about the manuscripts that had been taken.

The night before, after the final shot, the three of us—me, Rintrah, and the man Dauphin—had sat quietly for a few minutes before getting up and going our separate ways. There had been nothing to say, no other thing to do. Well, there was one thing to do. Rintrah helped me.

We carried Sebastien's body across the Quarter and down the river to Levi's factory, to my home. On every street we turned we passed hunched, black-cloaked figures of men and women who turned their back on us. No one offered to help, no one shouted for the police. They only turned their heads and walked on, past the two men carrying the body that still dripped a thin, precise line of blood down the banquette, marking our trail.

Around the back of Levi's, surrounded by broken furniture and worn-out looms, stood a horse cart that looked in decent shape. We lifted Sebastien into it and covered him with an old oilcloth tarp. Rintrah said he'd send over a cart horse in the morning, and I thanked him. Those were the last words we ever exchanged.

Now I slipped out of bed, careful not to wake M., who the night before had held me for hours and whispered nonsense to me until I had calmed and fallen asleep. I looked out the window. The mist burned off the river, and in the receding fog I could see an old white horse hitched to the cart. One last thing to do.

The trip back down into Terrebonne Parish went faster than I remembered, probably because I never wanted to arrive at my destination. The bright white clouds, pure against the blue, whipped along the coast and made it seem that I was moving as fast as air. When I got to the turnoff, the hat and the doll were gone. I pulled up in the clearing outside the crazy-quilt shack, and suddenly knew with certainty what I would find. There were no voices and the stove was cold. I knocked on the door, but there was no answer. I pushed in.

They had cleared out. She hadn't waited. By the looks of it, she had started packing just as soon as we'd left. Not a sign of them remained. Everything to identify them had been taken.

The place had been swept, the windows dusted. Someday the shack would be discovered by fishermen, and they'd never guess who had lived there. The people who had built it had disappeared and would not be found.

I buried Sebastien at the very top of one of the old Indian mounds outside the clearing, underneath a great drooping willow. The ground was soft and I used an old rusted pot I found in the woods behind the cookstove. It took me a couple hours to dig the hole. I wanted it to be right. And all the time I was digging it, I kept wondering why I really gave a damn about this man, this killer. He was nothing like me, he was a Creole and a native son, he was a brutal and sadistic man. And yet I couldn't leave him alone. I had learned, I suppose, that there were some things that needed doing and you were to do them however you felt about it. And whatever else was true about the man, he had lived by that rule and, in the end, he had died by it. Hood would have wanted me to bury him.

When he was deep in the grave, buried with his knives, I went over to the side of the shack and yanked two boards from the siding and lashed them together as a cross. On the cross I wrote the words *Died for another man,* and stuck it deep in the earth at the head of the grave. I was afraid to write his name, afraid he would be disturbed if anyone ever knew who it was buried there in that Indian mound.

I meant to go back and erect a proper headstone one day, but I never did. I don't even think I could find that place now. It's only a very dim memory.

I got back to my rooms after M. had gone to sleep. On my table, which she had mended, there lay a large stack of paper covered in her clear but crabbed handwriting. On top there was a note: *I told you I could read, but I didn't tell you I could write, too. I was bored. Maybe I can sell these? Don't you dare take them, this here is my property. Love, M. P.S. They were hidden in the wall, and thank God.* How long had it taken her to copy Hood's book, and Anna Marie's diary, and my notes? She must have done it in less than a week. I watched her breathe and began to pack up what few things I had. I found my adventure bag and stuffed in my clothes, the pistol Sebastien had given me, and my knife and fork. I left the pages on the table and went to sleep.

*   *   *

We left the next morning.

"Oh, we're leaving, are we?" M. said, carefully wrapping the pages of the books in an old sheet and packing it in my adventure bag. "What makes you think I'm going with you?"

I just looked at her, and looked down from the window at the horse and cart. The old horse was happily chewing weeds at the base of the building.

"All right," she said. "But you don't touch this book right here. This here is mine. This is not your story, whatever you think."

"Can I add some pages?"

"That you may, boyo."

I hauled everything down to the cart and waited for her on the box with the reins in my hand. She came down a few minutes later in a simple blue cotton work dress and boots.

"Ah. And where are we going?" she asked.

We were headed uptown, toward the River Road and north.

"Home."

"Don't be cute."

"It's in Tennessee."

She slept. The journey took weeks, and by the end of it we were husband and wife, at least that's how we looked at it. And I've never been away from her again.

EPILOGUE

I was wrong about never returning to New Orleans. I went back once, two years later, in 1881, when Anna Marie's family finally decided to dig up their daughter and General Hood and move them out to the Hennen family plot in the Metairie Cemetery north of the city. I had been baptized a Catholic by then, and so I understood a little of the ceremony's gravity.

They had been buried in identical pine boxes, the coffins of the poor. These had rotted and become packed with dirt. Anna Marie's family was prepared, and had purchased two beautiful oak caskets, polished to a bright sheen. The priest said his prayers and the remains were transferred to the new caskets. I took a piece of Hood's old casket, just a sliver, to bring home.

The Hoods, of course, had become very famous in death. Or, I guess, it's truer to say that their living children had become famous. The Hood Orphans, those pitiable symbols of a nation ruined by war and disease, had broken hearts and opened purses across the nation. Nine children, the children of a beautiful society girl and her famous husband, all orphaned during one terrible summer month in 1879. The Hood Orphans were as well known as the president, and more well known than any congressman or governor or theater actor or opera singer. And as the parents of such extraordinary children, the Hoods now deserved special attention. They rolled to Metairie Cemetery in a glass-sided hearse followed by a long train of mourners. People on the street stopped and doffed their hats. At the cemetery, they were buried in tombs that had been carved in great detail and with great care, hard and solid and made of stone that would not wear and would never disappear.

I had already seen the Hoods buried once, back when only a few people could be bothered to attend, and so I wasn't terribly moved by the ceremony, though the priest did a fine job. I wasn't even there to be a mourner. I was there to deliver something.

John Junior was the only one of the orphans in attendance. He was the oldest, and I suppose he was the only one of them deemed old enough to participate. He looked awfully like his father. You could see he would become tall. At fourteen, he was already growing his beard. He stood perfectly erect, and when he smiled he tended to sneer. He was imperious and very sure of himself, even if he was terribly young.

After the funeral I approached him. I began to tell him about his father, and what he had done those last two years, and about the book that had been made out of what his father and mother had written. All the while he stared at me, unblinking. Finally he spoke while adjusting the sleeve on his new suit.

"Who are you?"

"My name is Eli Griffin, and I knew your father. He used to come and visit me at the ice factory."

"You made his ice. An ice maker. Well, sir, I'm certain that my father would not have given this mysterious book to one of the help. I do not believe there is such a book. There is one book, and it has been published by General

Beauregard, a great friend of my father's, and there is no other. Have you read it?"

"Yes, I have." A terrible, obsessive book, but I had read it.

"Ah, good, you can read. You never know. You read it, so you'll understand when I tell you that I think there is nothing more to say."

He was stubborn and confident, very much like his father, but stupid. I could see the stupidity in his dull eyes and his fussy suit.

"You are young, how can you know what else there might be to say?"

"I know plenty enough about my parents, I have no interest in reading the forgeries of his servants. But if, as you say, this book is rightfully mine, I will take it." But I had already begun to walk away.

I would wait for the next orphan to come of age, and the next, and the one after that, until I found the child who would listen to me and who would care for the book as M. and I have cared for it. The child who could understand what happened to the Hoods, and who would be moved to change their life upon reading about them.

It was a long wait, but so is life.

ACKNOWLEDGMENTS

WITH GRATITUDE

Thanks to my family, for the circumstances of my birth. That I was born in the South, surrounded by stories and storytellers, has to count for something. I remain grateful for those who have always kept windows of the past wide open to me. I am grateful to those, now gone, who have let me say that I cannot remember a time without stories and tales of lives before me.

Most of my people are gone, but included among the living are my brother, Marcus Sand-

ers, and his wife, Candy Allen, his daughter,
Nova, and her husband, Danny.

Jeff Kleinman, my agent, and Folio Literary
Management have served me well. I grow more
grateful over the years for Jeff in his roles as
agent, sometimes-editor, mentor, and friend.
In whatever role, I could not wish for more
in an agent than I've been given. My circle of
friends includes a lot of writers, and I know
few who can make that claim.

Likewise, I landed on equally solid ground
with Grand Central Publishing. These are pre-
carious times, yet the folks at Grand Central
have supported me at each and every turn.
My editor Deb Futter's support and encouragement fueled me through this process. I
can never thank her enough for her expectation that I deliver more and better work. Likewise, I would be amiss not to thank Dianne
Choie for holding down the fort on a day-to-
day basis.

To my publisher, Jamie Raab, goes my sin-
cerest heartfelt thanks. I also want to thank
David Young, chairman and CEO; Emi Batt-
aglia, associate publisher; Karen Torres, VP,
trade sales & field sales; Jennifer Romanello,
director of publicity; Elly Weisenberg, publicity manager; Martha Otis, SVP, advertising

and promotions; Bob Castillo, managing editor; Nicole Bond, associate director, foreign rights; Nancy Wiese, VP, subrights; and Bruce Paonessa, VP, director of sales.

With regard to the book, itself, we were lucky enough to have Anne Twomey, VP, creative director, back to design the magnificent cover. With her this time were Charles Brock at the Designworks Group; Stephen Gardner, who did the photography; James Montalbano, who rendered the title type; and Laura Wyss, who researched the photos.

Thanks too to Tom Whatley, production director; Harvey-Jane Kowal, SVP, executive managing editor; Ann Schwartz, copy chief; Huy Duong, associate copy chief; Giraud Lorber, associate production manager; Blanca Aulet, assistant art director; Flamur Tonuzi, executive art director; Oscar Stern, creative director, advertising & promotion; Janice Wilkins, promotion director; Brad Negbaur, creative director, advertising & promotion; and Christine Valentine, my copyeditor.

I cannot forget folks who have moved on but not out of my world completely: Amy Einhorn, Todd Doughty, Ivan Held, and Larry Kirshbaum.

The care, wisdom, and encouragement of

so many friends are not forgotten. I am forever grateful for Andrew Glasgow and Olivia and Justin Stelter, as I am for all those who hung in there when it all must have seemed like an unending bad play: Mary-Springs and Stephane Couteaud, Rick Warwick, Julian Bibb, Sherrie and Duncan Murrell, Monte Isom, Eric Jacobson, Caroline and George Ducas, Carol and Joel Tomlin, Charlene Corris, Ellen Pryor, Jay Jones, Angie, Gore, and Tamara Saviano, Riley May, Carroll Van West, Susan Whitaker, Beth and Peter Thevenot, Catherine Anderson, Hibah Qubain and Rob Hodge, Jim Duff, Tasha Alexander, John Bohlinger, Tim Young, Michael Balliet, Kelli and Bo Bills, Curt Jones, Doug Howard, the entire Vander Elst Clan—Lynn and Ghislain, Jenilee and Philippe, Nathalie and Tyler Stewart, and Marcelle Vander Elst—Bill McInness, Howie Sanders, Danny Anderson, Pete Donaldson, Lallie Wallace, William Pratt and Mrs. Ditto, Matt Futterman, Dave Pelton, Tommy Peters, Adam Goodheart, Kate and John Dyson, Deborah Warnick, Diana and Gary Fisketjon, Toby Standefer, Margie Thessin, Joe Cashia, Doug Brouder and all the great folks still at C.W.P.T., Bunny Price, Marianne and John Schroer, and the rest of the folks who allow me to work with them in preservation and for the community. Of course, any list should include the never-ending Heller Family: Kay and Rod, Patty and Hanes, Mary and Winder, and all the rest.

This book began when friends and I left a bachelor party in New Orleans, with Katrina on our heels. In the wake of the disaster, I found myself drawn back again and again to the city. When folks began to point fingers and talk about what had gone wrong in a place that has always seemed so right to me, I wanted to know how it had happened. We all knew about the Army Corp of Engineers, the inept and crooked politicians, the looters and all the rest—but, I wondered, did it really begin with Katrina?

I began to make my way back there again and again. I found myself wandering the streets of New Orleans and reading about the city's history. While this isn't a complete bibliography by any means, I was well served by the following:

The Grandissimes (novel), by George Washington Cable

Old Creole Days (short stories), by George Washington Cable

The Awakening (novel), by Kate Chopin

Inventing New Orleans: Writings of Lafcadio Hearn (short stories, journalism, etc., ed. by S. Frederick Starr)

New Orleans: The Place and the People (history), by Grace King

The French Quarter: An Informal History of the New Orleans Underworld, by Herbert Asbury

Fabulous New Orleans (memoir), by Lyle Saxon

Degas in New Orleans (cultural history), by Christopher Benfey

Degas and New Orleans (exhibition catalog, published by the New Orleans Museum of Art)

French Quarter Manual: An Architectural Guide to New Orleans Vieux Carre (a legendary work of architectural history, by the late, great Malcolm Heard)

Creole New Orleans: Race and Americanization (a collection of historical papers/chapters), ed. by Arnold R. Hirsch and Joseph Logsdon

Robert Hicks invites you to go to www.robert-hicks.com for more information about *A Separate Country* and *The Widow of the South*. You can also follow him on Twitter at http://twitter.com/robert_hicks.